"Do you mean to say that all these years the Church has been covering up the existence of a second Messiah?"

Maxwell felt the bedrock of his convictions shift beneath him. He grabbed at the table for support.

"But . . . if what you say is the truth . . . if this information were to leak out, Christianity and all that it stands for would be called into question. There would be chaos. Complete, utter chaos."

The Cardinal nodded. "I'm afraid so. But Robert, there is one more thing I have to tell you. The second shroud contains on its surface an image as well. It is the image of the second redeemer . . . a female image."

THE FINEST IN SUSPENSE!

THE URSA ULTIMATUM (2130, $3.95)
by Terry Baxter

In the dead of night, twelve nuclear warheads are smuggled north across the Mexican border to be detonated simultaneously in major cities throughout the U.S. And only a small-town desert lawman stands between a face-less Russian superspy and World War Three!

THE LAST ASSASSIN (1989, $3.95)
by Daniel Easterman

From New York City to the Middle East, the devastating flames of revolution and terrorism sweep across a world gone mad . . . as the most terrifying conspiracy in the history of mankind is born!

FLOWERS FROM BERLIN (2060, $4.50)
by Noel Hynd

With the Earth on the brink of World War Two, the Third Reich's deadliest professional killer is dispatched on the most heinous assignment of his murderous career: the assassination of Franklin Delano Roosevelt!

THE BIG NEEDLE (1921, $2.95)
by Ken Follett

All across Europe, innocent people are being terrorized, homes are destroyed, and dead bodies have become an unnervingly common sight. And the horrors will continue until the most powerful organization on Earth finds Chadwell Carstairs — and kills him!

DOMINATOR (2118, $3.95)
by James Follett

Two extraordinary men, each driven by dangerously ambiguous loyalties, play out the ultimate nuclear endgame miles above the helpless planet — aboard a hijacked space shuttle called DOMINATOR!

Available wherever paperbacks are sold, or order direct from the Publisher. Send cover price plus 50¢ per copy for mailing and handling to Zebra Books, Dept. 117, 475 Park Avenue South, New York, N.Y. 10016. Residents of New York, New Jersey and Pennsylvania must include sales tax. DO NOT SEND CASH.

THE LINZ TESTAMENT

LEWIS PERDUE

PINNACLE BOOKS
WINDSOR PUBLISHING CORP.

PINNACLE BOOKS

are published by

Windsor Publishing Corp.
475 Park Avenue South
New York, NY 10016

First Pinnacle Books printing: June, 1988

Printed in the United States of America

To William Lewis Perdue Jr.
1912–1985

PREFACE

This is a work of fiction based on fact. Hitler did set up an organization called the Sonderauftrag Linz whose purpose was to loot the finest public and private collections of Europe. He planned to exhibit the stolen art in a magnificent museum to be constructed in his hometown of Linz, Austria. Plans for Führermuseum were drawn up by an architect, but the structure was never built.

Hitler's liaison with the Sonderauftrag Linz was a man called Heinrich Heim, with whom I spoke in Munich in December of 1983. There is a close-knit community of Nazis still residing in Munich, a group that includes two of Hitler's former secretaries and his personal pilot. They meet with each other and console themselves on their losses.

Heim lives in an old World War II bomb shelter in the Schwabing section of the city, a few blocks from the Staatbiblioteque—the Bavarian equivalent of the Library of Congress. In addition to the meager royalties he collects from a book he wrote that discusses his spying on Hitler for Hermann Goering, Heim generates a small amount of revenue by answering requests for information that are sent to him from all over the world. Most of his research is conducted at the nearby Staatbiblioteque.

A friend of mine, Werner Meyer, the chief reporter for Munich's evening newspaper *Abend Zeitung,* introduced me to Heim one night just before Christmas. Snow, sleet, and freezing rain poured down on us that evening as we parked Werner's car in a dark unpaved lot and—accompanied by Werner's assistant, Johanna

7

Kerschner—made our way down a cluttered alley littered with paper and illuminated by a naked streetlight bulb.

Werner knocked at the metal blast shield that served as Heim's front door. I noticed that the other two windows set into the concrete wall of the structure were covered by blast shields also.

Heim came to the door and after some difficulty pushed back the protective barrier and welcomed us.

The phrase "stooped but unbowed" characterized Heim exactly. At first glance, he looked like a street derelict, dressed as he was in two overcoats and a layered succession of sweaters and shirts. But Heim's eyes still shone with a bright pale icy blue that could have served as a model for Hitler's viril Aryan superman.

He showed us into the room that he used to conduct his research, and once we were seated amid the prodigious clutter of papers, solicitously placed threadbare blankets over our knees lest we get cold. The bomb shelter was not heated.

Meyer began to talk with Heim as Johanna took notes and I—with a novice's grasp of the German language—listened. Heim and Werner spoke for a few minutes about their progress in trying to locate some of the original scores of the composer Wagner, which had disappeared during the war. It is Werner's passion.

The conversation then turned to the American, and his attempts to track down missing pieces of art. As part of my research for *The Linz Testament*, I put my talents as a former investigative reporter to work, not only in gathering material for the novel, but also in keeping my eyes open for some find that might serve as the basis for a good magazine article, or even a nonfiction book.

We talked only a few minutes before Heim began to speak fondly of Frederick Stahl, the painter—favored by Hitler and other Nazis—mentioned in this book. Heim quickly grew misty-eyed as he remembered Stahl and, I suppose, the old days. He spoke of the beauty of Stahl's work and of how Hitler treated the artist as if he were a brother, or perhaps a surrogate father.

By now, he had begun to include all of us in the room each time he used the word *unseren*—the German familiar form. I grew increasingly uncomfortable as he expanded his use of the word to refer to his Nazi comrades and even to the Führer himself. Heim, incidently, refused to refer to Hitler by name, as if he were afraid to take his name in vain. Instead, he referred to Hitler as "A.H.," pronounced in German, "Ah-hah."

After a time, the old Nazi produced a sheaf of papers and an envelope of small photographs. He showed the photographs to us. They were all small black and whites, about two inches on a side and each depicting a painting. All the paintings were Stahl's and all were inventoried on a sheet of paper Heim handed to me. The paintings, he said, had last been seen in Zurich before the fall of the Third Reich. He wouldn't say exactly when they had been seen or by whom.

He gave me one of the photographs and the inventory after I promised to look for the paintings and let him know—through Werner—if I had made any progress.

From Munich, I went to Zurich to learn if there were any remaining traces of the Stahl paintings. After checking into my hotel room, I made inquiries and obtained the names of several art galleries that had been in existence during the period of the paintings' disappearance.

I went to the oldest of the galleries and spoke with the owner. I showed him the picture Heim had given me and said that I represented a wealthy collector who was interested in acquiring the painting.

The man threw me out of his gallery.

He said he had nothing to do with the paintings of which I spoke and furthermore did not want anything to do with them or with the people who might be interested in them. I had a difficult time determining whether he was frightened or angry. Probably both. I was certainly frightened.

In the course of my investigative reporting, I had had my life threatened, but having left the business, I was now committed to staying healthy and hearty. Thus it was that I washed down a *rosti* with a liter of beer that night, went to bed, and took the train back to Munich the next morning. To this day I remain ignorant of where the Stahl paintings are, and what's more, I don't want to know.

There are many other things in this book that are true; for example, the stories of how escaping SS troops used looted art to buy their freedom. You can rest firm in the knowledge that many of the art works lost during the war are hanging on the walls of chateaus in the alps. Many more rest beneath the streets of Zurich.

There *was* an Emperor Henry IV who was kidnapped by the bishop of Köln, and of course, there was an Emperor Constantine. And the Catholic Church is still ambivalent about Veronica and her place in history, although she is very real to devout Roman Catholics.

It is also a matter of public record that Pope Pius XII turned a blind eye and a deaf ear to the atrocities of the Third Reich. As to the Pope's motives, one can only speculate, but certainly his silence at the time does seem at odds with his perceived role as a moral authority. His unwillingness to raise his voice in protest to Nazi policies is—and no doubt shall remain—a mystery.

Students of history, theology, geography, and political science will find many, many more things in this book that are true.

But in the end, the book as a whole is—after all—a work of fiction. At least, I believe it is.

Lewis Perdue
March 1985

PROLOGUE

Dawn spread like a bloody stain across the eastern sky. Beneath the stain a white-haired man threw himself desperately against waist-high drifts of snow, cutting a ragged ditch that snaked back across the frozen lake and pointed to the spot where he had emerged from the forest.

The man was more than halfway across the lake—Die Altaussersee—when suddenly he felt the need to stop, if only for a moment. They hadn't spotted him yet, he thought, as he crouched in the snow. More sinew than flesh, he had bright blue eyes that were set in a long, ascetic face, and in the dim light, shadows cut deeply into his craggy features, accenting a prominent chin that jutted over an exposed clerical collar.

That he had outdistanced them for this long, more than three hours now, was a testament to a long vigorous life. Except for his time in the seminary, he had skied and hiked these beloved hills almost every day of his sixty-two years. He had rowed his shell on the lake in the summer and skated it in the winter. He knew this little pocket of Austria better than anyone but God himself.

As he crouched there in the middle of the sleeping lake, only the ragged chuffing of his breath and the faint creaking of ice beneath his feet reached his ears. The ice was too thin for skating. But that was fine. Nobody skated these days anyhow. He strained his ears to hear the sounds of death, but there was nothing. His head drew quick jerky arcs in the morning twilight as he tried to spot them. Nothing moved, though, not in the forest behind him, not in the village to his right, not in the mountains that surrounded the lake. That worried him. Evil you could see was evil you could fight.

Father Werner Meyer's legs quivered now as he straightened up in the hip-deep snow and gulped greedily at the sharp morning air. Panic and fear ebbed and surge in his throat. He tried to will the exhaustion from his legs. But old flesh took its time. He felt like a nightmare dreamer, feet snared by sticky darkness, moving in slow motion as a locomotive bore down with all its smoky, fiery, mechanical clanging determination.

"Yea, though I walk through the valley of the shadow of death, Thou art with me," he prayed softly, his frozen breath punctuating each word.

He had covered a lot of ground these past few hours, running all the way from the *Salzbergwerk*—the salt mine—at Habersam Mountain. The relic had been shown to him in the abandoned mine. The SS guarding the entrance thought he was one of the clergy working with the Reich. They had let him see the shroud. He had actually held it, taken it from the silver chalice box in which it had lain for almost two thousand years. He still had difficulty accepting that the bolt of cloth he'd held in his hand had felled popes, toppled governments, made and broken empires for almost twenty centuries. Men had corrupted, murdered, lied, and stolen for it, he'd learned, all in the name of God. And for the last six years, it had been used to keep the Vatican silent on the excesses of Hitler's Reich. Father Werner Meyer intended to change all that.

A righteous anger rose in his chest and, as it had done so many times over the last month, cut through his fear and steadied his nerves. That someone could do this to his Church, in the name of his God! Father Meyer looked about him with steadied vision, details growing sharper. Yes, he thought; there they were coming down from the hills above Fischerndorf. He could see the feeble dots of their electric torches. From the looks of things, the size of the force had dwindled. Moments later, he heard the distant human static. . . .

At first, the Nazis had come to Altaussee in small numbers and with great secrecy. They had come privately, before the war, be-

12

fore Hitler annexed Austria under the guise of uniting the German people. Hitler had visited Altaussee, had hiked the trails in the hills above the town, and eaten at the inn's table with the townspeople. He had even bought a worthless piece of land on Habersam Mountain whose only merit was an abandoned salt mine that ran deep into the earth.

Then came the war and Nazis in great numbers. Townspeople were banished from the area around the old salt mine at Habersam Mountain. The SS built quarters there for more than two hundred fifty men, all restricted to their billets and forbidden to talk with outsiders. Supplies and replacements for the soldiers came through town in covered lorries. Dignitaries flew into the airfield at Bad Aussee and sped recklessly through town in long sleek autos with curtains to hide the identities of their occupants. Just before Christmas 1941, a rumor swept the village that Hitler himself had paid a secret visit to the mine.

The villagers were grateful that the SS kept to themselves. True, some of the shopkeepers occasionally complained that they could see the business that an additional 250 customers would bring. But mostly the residents of Altaussee were very grateful to be spared the excesses of an occupying force, contenting themselves with speculation about what the Nazis were doing with the old salt mine at Habersam Mountain. Curiosity led many to the very edge of the forbidden zone, but all they ever saw was a garrison occupying an alpine meadow, guarding the entrance to an unremarkable salt mine.

Some said it was a hideout for SS officials in case the war turned against the Reich. Others ventured that it was some secret underground laboratory manufacturing Hitler's promised secret weapon.

On the face of it, either guess was not preposterous. The cool alabaster white corridors of Altaussee's *Salzberwerk* were deep enough to be impervious to any known weapon. The mines were stable, not subject to cave-ins, and maintained a constant temperature and humidity that was not inimicable to human comfort. They were, in short, an ideal place to hide almost anything safely.

The *Salzbergwerk* at Habersam Mountain remained the only Nazi presence in the hills surrounding Altaussee until lorries and boxcars full of priceless art, statuary, rare books, manuscripts, and religious icons began arriving in 1945.

Meyer had learned that for the past six years Hitler had looted the greatest public and private art collections in the occupied countries to enrich the permanent collection of der Führermuseum, a magnificent structure to be constructed in the grimy industrial city of Linz, Austria, his boyhood home. Hitler, the frustrated artist, wanted to build the greatest art museum of all time so that his hometown would never forget him. But Allied bombers had interrupted the Führer's plans, and so he rushed his collection to the salt mines of the Salzammergut for protection against the almost daily raids.

Unlike the icy secretive units guarding the Habersam mine, the Wehrmacht units accompanying the art were frightened boys, thankful to be away from the thick of the fighting, yet acutely aware of their role as guardians of a fortune in stolen goods. They rushed about frantically, confiscating salt mines all over the countryside, storing much of the art in the mines near Bad Ischl and Bad Aussee, and especially in the large deep mines at Steinberg and Moosberg. Accompanying them were museum curators—many of them now prisoners of war—traveling in the back of boxcars and transport trucks over steep mountain roads lethal with winter to take up their assigned task of protecting the Führer's acquisitions.

The trucks thundered purposefully through town day and night, making the merchants happy. Father Meyer, occupied with his duties, had almost forgotten the unobtrusive SS unit at the small mine at Habersam Mountain. Then, suddenly, his church was overflowing with Wehrmacht parishioners. They confessed to him such tales of anguish and horror that Meyer found himself wondering if God could possibly find enough forgiveness to absolve them.

It was a teenager's insatiable curiosity about what might be hidden in Habersam Mountain that finally shattered Werner Meyer's world and set him running before a pack of SS. Two months after the art started to arrive, thirteen-year-old Franz Dietrich veered close to the Habersam mine one afternoon as he skied the trails above Altaussee. He was shot and killed. The SS sergeant who dumped Franz's body on the sidewalk in front of his home told his family that even younger boys had fought with the Resistance.

In the gloom of 4 A.M. the next morning Meyer opened his door to a young SS sergeant torn by Franz's death. The sergeant had witnessed the killing of the boy. It had been for sport, he told Meyer, two lieutenants taking target practice on a local.

As the sergeant begged for forgiveness, he revealed to Meyer the secret of what lay inside the salt mine, why the mine had been so closely guarded. Meyer might spend the rest of his life wishing he had never heard the boy's confession, but he had and now he was so enraged that he determined drastic action had to be taken.

Since the SS contingent was forbidden to enter the village, Meyer had the sergeant arrange for him to hold mass and hear confessions at the garrison.

The day of his arrival news of Allied advances had brought the young soldiers to the edge of panic. They prayed with the faith of desperate men. Losers. The Allies had entered Austria already, it was rumored, and grew closer every day. More than anything, the SS seemed terrified that they would be treated as they had treated others. It was a difficult fate to accept for men who, in six years of ruthless war, had all but forgotten the meaning of mercy.

The nervous troops spoke quietly with Meyer about slipping away in the dark. More than one asked him to bring civilian clothes to make the escape easier. None of them seemed to know what they were guarding. That secret seemed restricted to a select handful, among them the sergeant who had come to Meyer for absolution.

After holding mass and suffering through more ghastly confessions from a makeshift confessional, Meyer slipped away from the main barracks and accompanied the sergeant into the mine.

Meyer spoke with the sentries at the mouth of the mine and with those inside assigned to guard its contents. The great cavern had been turned into a fortress. All through its corridors were caches of arms, ammunition, explosives, and booby traps. They showed him how the entrance was mined, designed to produce a controlled cave-in to block access. They were willing to die inside the mine to prevent its contents from falling to the enemy, they told him, but behind their brave words Meyer read the doubt in their eyes.

Once past the entrance, and with the sergeant to vouch for him, Meyer was accepted without question, his requests for a tour of the mine readily granted. Meyer had struggled to control his anger and disgust, trying instead to act the role of co-conspirator—God's reasonable servant. He had assured the sentries inside that they were performing a reasonable and valuable task, but the deeper they walked into the mine, the higher the bile rose in his throat.

Meyer hadn't wanted to believe the sergeant's story, was convinced he must somehow be mistaken, but when the makeshift vault was opened and the shroud revealed to him, doubt gave way to awe. Hands shaking, the village priest actually held the shroud and examined the documentation that traced its origins back more than 1,800 years. After the cloth was returned to the vault, the sentry opened a separate compartment and displayed the pact between Hitler and the Pope. As he read the text of the papal concessions, Meyer felt a lifetime of devotion collapse in on itself, an implosion of his faith that unhinged his self-control and made him boil with anger.

The next instant he watched himself with detached amazement as his fist flew toward the smooth whiteness of the sentry's neck. For the rest of his life, Meyer would always remember how his arms seemed to be controlled that moment by a force beyond him. Again and again Meyer struck the sentry until he slumped to the floor, bloody and unconscious.

Without another thought, Meyer reached for the shroud.

"Stop," commanded a voice from behind him.

Meyer whirled. The young sergeant who had shown him all this stood facing him now, his service Luger leveled at Meyer's chest.

"Shoot me!" Meyer said defiantly. "I'm ready to die."

The sergeant shook his head. "No. You must leave."

Meyer's jaw dropped in amazement. "But the shroud . . . ?" He craned his head toward the vault, realizing as he did that the shroud's safe was closing of its own accord, actuated by the mechanical whirring within the wall. Meyer turned to reach for the cloth but the sergeant lunged forward, shouldering Meyer out of the way as the safe door closed.

"No!" Meyer gasped as he watched the door close. "I must have the—" The door closed with a solid thunk. Meyer rushed toward it and tugged desperately at the handle, but the sergeant pulled him away.

"There are security devices even within the safe," the sergeant explained. "It's booby-trapped; you could be killed or even destroy the shroud by trying to remove the box without neutralizing the switches and levers."

"But how . . . ?"

The sergeant pointed at the sentry lying unconscious on the floor. "He was one of the few here who was acquainted with the system. There's a diagram in a safe deposit box in Zurich," said the sergeant. "I know where the combination is, but I'm certain that others will empty the box before you could get to it."

They stood in the silence for a moment, the priest and the SS sergeant.

"You will have to tell them, father," the sergeant said finally. "You will have to tell the world what you saw."

"But I must have proof," Meyer protested.

Suddenly from the distance came voices, sounds to remind them that staying alive long enough to tell the world might be harder than making the world believe what Meyer had just seen.

"Quickly," the sergeant ordered. "You must leave."

Meyer looked at him, confused and uncertain.

"I will create a diversion—I'll shoot at you," said the sergeant. "But I will miss. I will tell them you ran deeper into the mine. Then I will trigger the charges that will seal the entrance to the mine. The shroud will be kept here safe."

The voices grew louder. They could make out three distinctly.

"You must leave. Tell the world, father. Tell the world."

Meyer nodded dumbly.

"Go," the sergeant said. "Quickly."

Standing now in the middle of the frozen lake, Meyer shook his head and tried to forget the subsequent explosion at the mouth of the mine that had painted abstract patterns of red, khaki, and flesh on the snow. He struggled to expunge images of the young sergeant and of the young boy whose death had started it all, Franz Dietrich. But the images would not go away. They hovered at the edge of his consciousness, gathering strength as the sounds of his pursuers grew louder.

Meyer pressed on, shoulders slumped as if weighted down by the memories of all the Franz Dietrichs this filthy war had produced. As he threw himself into drift after drift, his thoughts took a different turn and he found himself saying a silent guilty prayer. He prayed his son would escape Dietrich's fate and that God would forgive him for the weakness that had conceived him. He prayed also that God might overlook the pride he felt each day as he watched the boy develop.

It was a torture looking into the boy's eyes, listening to his son call him "father" and not being able to tell him how true that was. He wanted to tell him, but he knew it would be years before the boy could accept the reality that his real father was not the brave Oberleutnant who died valiantly fighting Polish barbarians, but a village priest who had truly loved his mother more than her husband ever had. He'd had no right to do what he'd done, but sometimes . . .

Meyer glanced to his right, eyes fixing for an instant on the inn by the lake that Gretchen now operated in her husband's absence. Its steep chalet roof reached up and caught the first of the morning sun. He thought again of the fantasy that played day after day in his thoughts, of renouncing his vows, marrying Gretchen, raising his son.

And again he reminded himself that he was married to the church—even if certain highly placed men had compromised it for a "higher purpose." No, there was no denying that his son was a sweet sin for which he truly needed forgiveness.

He turned away from the sight of Gretchen's inn—and the thought of their son—and toward the small stone cottage on the lake's southern shore, where Joseph Roten waited for him. Roten had connections to the Resistance. Together, they would get the secret to the Americans and through them to the rest of the world. He would do it, even if it killed him.

Richard Summers and Anatoli Czenek were halfway between Bad Aussee and Alt Aussee when their platoon heard the explosion. The dozen men, wearing the white winter coveralls of the Allied Expeditionary Force, stopped and leaned on their ski poles as the explosion's shock wave combed through the overhead fir boughs and sent fluffy white loafs of snow foomping down on their shoulders. Several of the platoon looked up at the softly falling

18

snow. Summers thought they looked like vaudeville comedians getting smacked with a whipped cream pie in the face. He stifled a laugh as the men sputtered and cursed.

Moments later, the radio crackled as the main force behind them called to see if anyone on the point team was still alive.

"Sorry to disappoint you," the radioman answered in an Oklahoma accent. "The action's ahead of us."

"Tell 'em sounds like the Nazis is blowin' hell outa stuff they don't want us tuh get," said Sticks, the point team's demolition expert.

Summers and Czenek looked anxiously at each other. They hoped that whatever was being destroyed wasn't art. Both of the men worked not for the Army but for the Art Looting Investigative Unit of the Office of Strategic Services.

Summers was a lean muscular young man with closely cropped blond hair and an energetic, powerful air that made people forget he was a bit shorter than average height. He had just graduated from UCLA some six months ago with a degree in art history when he got his draft notice. At the time, a warm but cramped office at OSS headquarters, in Washington, D.C., seemed the best bet. Like most young men, he had learned the hard way that appearances are frequently deceiving. Czenek was older, twenty-six, and had worked for the owner of an exclusive art gallery in Warsaw before the Germans rolled through Poland. He had come to the OSS by way of the Polish Resistance, the Dunkirk evacuation, and the American embassy in London.

Summers had worked with Czenek for four months now. They got along all right, Summers supposed, except for a streak of anti-Semitism that Czenek seemed unaware of. The Pole had a habit of prefacing some things with "You Jews . . ." As hard as Summers tried to convince himself that he was being too sensitive and that Czenek probably didn't mean it anyway, it still got under his skin enough to make Summers look forward to the day when one of them would be assigned to another unit.

But Czenek had at least been dependable so far. They had come north with Patton, and developed that peculiar bond between men who know they must depend on each other to stay alive. Besides staying in one piece, their first job was to identify and protect buildings and monuments of value and then try their best to keep the advancing Allied forces from bombing, destroying, defacing, or covering them with graffiti. That usually meant assignments with reconnaissance patrols and point teams whose casualty and capture rates were chillingly high.

Czenek liked to make jokes about what the Germans would do to Summers if they captured him. Czenek told concentration camp jokes the way Americans told Polish jokes. In response Summers tried to convince himself that all humor depended on whose ox was being gored. He usually failed, however, and ended up angry and ashamed to admit that he was frightened.

They did their jobs, though, arguing with platoon leaders and company commanders, saving some historical edifices, losing others. Later, when the OSS learned of Hitler's huge art caches, Summers and Czenek, along with every other OSS art expert with combat experience, were sent to the front lines to capture the art intact and prevent the Germans from doing something stupid. They had learned just how stupid the Germans could be two days before when a tiny, bald, owl-headed man was ushered into their encampment by members of the local resistance. The man had been a restoration expert with the Rijksmuseum in Amsterdam and had been pressed into service by the Nazis to look after the works they had stolen from his museum.

Excitedly, the little man told them how he had made his way from the salt mine near Bad Ischl where the Nazi colonel in charge of the art was planning to blow it up rather "than have it fall into the hands of the Jews." Tears streamed from the man's eyes as he told of explosive charges planted among priceless works by Titian, Rubens, Michelangelo, Leonardo, Van Dyck . . . the list was a roster of the world's greatest art.

The little man looked meek enough to be intimidated by shadows, yet when Summers and Czenek gave him a crash course in demolition he handled the explosives bravely and without hesitation. Yesterday, he had sneaked back to the mine, planted explosives in the entrance, and detonated them, effectively cutting off the colonel's men from their own explosive charges. The art was saved and the Nazis forced to flee.

As the Allied forces advanced, Nazis throughout the area had shed their uniforms and scattered into the hills, many of them carrying paintings and works of art that they hoped to use to barter for protection and transportation. The Allies had rounded up many of them and confiscated the art works, which ranged from small paintings taken from their frames and rolled into tubes, to antique coins, books, and tapestries.

It was a scene that was being repeated time and again all over Bavaria, southwest Austria, and the Tyrol of northern Italy. Summers and Czenek realized that no matter how hard they and the others like them tried, much of the looted art would be scattered across Europe and beyond as fugitive Nazis traded a Vermeer for some farmer's truck or an antique coin for silence and sanctuary in a basement. In all likelihood, many of the paintings would remain in a trunk, a closet, or on the wall of a cottage in some remote village, perhaps forgotten forever.

They had been headed for one such remote village—Altaussee—when they heard the massive explosion in the hills above. They waited quietly in the snow, listening for other explosions or for the telltale rumble of an avalanche it may have triggered. But as the last of the snow drifted from the trees, all they heard was the crackle of small-arms fire. And even that stopped after less than a minute. The radioman relayed the information to the main force while they waited.

Finally, after the snow had settled, the young second lieutenant from South Dakota who thought all this snow was a summertime romp waved them forward.

Summers listened to the shushing of the alpine skis and felt their tingling vibrations under his feet as he and Czenek moved effortlessly at the front of the column. As they crested a low rise and coasted downhill, Summers loosened the back of his field blouse to vent some of the heat.

During the next three hours they heard nothing more. The platoon skied along the deserted road, unmarked by human footprints or tire marks. The Germans were headed the other way, and the locals knew enough to stay indoors when they thought there might be gunfire. In house after house, Summers caught glimpses of half a face here, a pair of eyes there, as the inhabitants stared out through parted curtains or shuttered windows. The main force paused to knock on every door and search each attic, basement, and outbuilding, but the point team pressed on. Summers hoped that none of the eyes he saw were lined up behind a gunsight.

The platoon had scattered itself for safety when they entered Puchen, a section of modest cottages just east of Altaussee on the southern shore of the Altaussersee. The soldiers halted by a small bridge that cross the frozen stream they had been paralleling, and while the second lieutenant briefed his men on the tactics they would use entering Altaussee, Summer and Czenek shared a map covered with red circles, squares, and triangles. The circles were churches and cemeteries, the squares monuments, the triangles historic houses. The maps were prepared with the help of existing maps, old tourist brochures, and assistance from local resistance movements. Altaussee wasn't exactly a shrine to fine art—there were three circles, one square, no triangles.

"There, just ahead of us," Summers said as he pointed first at a circle on the map and then ahead of them about a hundred fifty yards at a modest chapel. It had no steeple. That was good. Steeples made good redoubts for snipers.

"Want to check it out?" Summers asked. Czenek shrugged. Summers folded the map and handed it over. "Well, let's look to see if it's worth saving from the CO. We haven't had an argument with him for two or three days now."

The CO had a thing for churches, having been sniped at from them too many times. Now his first tendency was to level any church he came to unless Summers or Czenek had checked it out first. Which frequently meant they had to move in advance of the point team, a practice they found increasingly unhealthy. Summers kept wondering why he gave a shit about somebody else's churches and kept coming up short for an answer. Still . . .

Summers leaned into his ski poles and headed for the fieldstone chapel. Czenek followed. The chapel sat in the middle of a flat plain near the edge of the Altaussersee. The village of Altaussee lay about half a mile to the left; to the right a modest hill blocked the view of the lake. The land surrounding the chapel wore a mantle of mature fir trees, their boughs swept of snow by the earlier explosion. Although dawn had begun to paint the tops of hills to the west of them, the trees offered a columned darkness.

Summers and Czenek made it almost to the fence surrounding the chapel when they heard the shots. First came the report of a single pistol shot from beyond the modest hill to the right of the chapel, then the burping of a machine gun from the same direction.

Before they could cover the twenty yards that separated them from the platoon, a whining rattle came from the direction of Altaussee, accompanied by the unmistakable sounds of shifting gears and churning tires. It was a column of jeeps, and coming from that direction they could only be painted with the Iron Cross.

"Bloody hell." It was Czenek's favorite English expression. Summers realized that if they made a run straight for their platoon they'd undoubtedly be overtaken by the jeeps . . . and if they headed into the woods they'd likely run into the source of the gunshots. Looking down the road, he saw the lead vehicle in the column slide around the curve some two hundred yards behind them.

"Come on," Summers said as he skied past the side of the chapel and into the darkness of the forest. They took long quick strides toward the lake, trying to put distance between themselves and the jeeps, skiing a dimly lit slalom among the trees, scarcely aware of the lower limbs of the trees slapping at their faces, or of the uneven ground as it rolled under their skis.

Gradually the trees surrendered to thick scrubby brush. Beyond, nothing but open spaces. A scruffy beard of winterworn reeds outlined the edge of the lake. They turned to the right, staying in the darkness of the forest, hoping to describe a wide clockwise path that would take them back to the platoon.

Now the land rose again, and they bent forward, climbing a modest rise they both recognized as the hill that had originally separated them from the gunfire. Summers felt his skis slipping badly. Czenek of course was having the same problem. For every two strides they took uphill they slid back one. They pushed on, though, and by the time they'd climbed half the rise the sounds of the jeeps had faded to a mumbling in the distance. Summers felt the sweat dripping down his neck, trickling along the trough between his shoulder blades. Both men were breathing hard as they stopped for a moment and leaned on their ski poles. To the left they heard distant voices, and although it was impossible to make out individual words, they could make out the ugly intonations of a lynch mob. Ragged machine gun bursts punctuated the voices.

The two men pressed on and quickly gained the top of the rise.

Down the hill, about two hundred yards to their right, they saw the little chapel, the snow in front of it churned by the column of jeeps. But it was the sight on the other side of the hill that neither man would ever forget—some fifty feet below them and a hundred yards to their left, a ragged group of a dozen or so German soldiers closed in on a lone civilian, apathetic figure desperately lunging past snowdrifts, falling, picking himself up, falling again. The mob made quick time using the deep path he'd already broken through the snow. Occasionally one of the soldiers would pause long enough to loose a volley of shots at the man. It seemed a miracle he hadn't already been hit. Stunned, Summers and Czenek watched as the civilian made his way past the reeds at the edge of the lake and into the brush, apparently heading for a small stone cottage at the edge of the treeline.

Czenek pulled out his field glasses, training them first on the civilian, then on the German soldiers, and finally back on the civilian.

"Jesus . . . it's a *priest,*" Czenek said.

Summers took the glasses. In the horizontal hourglass image he too could make out a clerical collar at the man's throat. The priest's face was a wide-eyed mask.

Summers handed the binoculars back to Czenek, and began to unshoulder his M-1 rifle. Czenek looked at his partner uncertainly. "If we open fire on them we're dead."

Summers continued to unshoulder his rifle, working the bolt to chamber a round. "Could be," he said as he skied over to a large fir at the edge of the wood.

Summers had shed his skis and pack and was rummaging through its contents when Czenek slid silently up to him.

"We're pretty well hidden here. We can each fire a shot and go for cover—"

A blast of machine gun fire drew their attention back to the lake below them.

"What good'll that do?" Czenek argued. "There's a dozen of them . . . with machine guns. Even if we get two of them . . . what good'll that do? Just get us killed along with him."

Summers shrugged. "The main force is less than a mile away. We have to do something."

24

More shots cracked up from the lake . Looking down, both men saw the priest fall and the German mob surge forward.

Summers stood up abruptly, pulling from his pack a single cylindrical object the size of a Coke bottle, a rifle-launched grenade. As he fitted the neck of the grenade over the muzzle of his M-1, he looked hard at Czenek. "You ready?" Summers asked. Not waiting for an answer, Summers turned and raised the M-1 to his shoulder. Below, less than a hundred yards separated the mob from the priest, who had somehow gotten to his feet and was again thrashing forward.

Summers sighted down the barrel, then raised the muzzle slightly to accommodate the effects of gravity over the distance. He had only one shot and had to make it accurate. He also knew the recoil was going to knock him on his ass and probably rearrange his right shoulder. As he aimed between the mob and the priest he heard Czenek release his ski bindings, unshoulder his own M-1, and drop his pack.

"Bloody hell, aim good," Czenek said as he knelt down in the snow. Summers thought he heard his partner mutter a prayer as he manipulated the bolt to chamber a round.

Joseph Roten strained against the handcuff that bound his left hand to the massive iron bedstead. He was an unremarkable man, with round soft shoulders, moist pale blue eyes, and a nearly chinless face beneath a receding hairline that made him look older than his thirty-eight years. He had a perpetual squint and blinked frequently as if the intensity of light threatened to blind him. It was worse than ever this morning. As he leaned toward the window, and caught a glimpse of his bruised and bloodied face in the mirror, he wondered what in hell had possessed him to get involved with the Resistance.

He was a talented man, had been treated with some respect by the Nazis because they valued his expertise in caring for their looted art treasures. He could just as easily have spent the rest of the war in relative comfort waiting for the Allies to arrive. Rumors had it they would be here in a matter of days. Already troops and officers had deserted, some taking precious works of art with them.

Roten stretched out now to the full limits of his arm span, the handcuff biting into the thin flesh of the inside of his wrist. The bed moved a fraction and sent a scraping vibration through the room. The little man froze. Had the Oberleutnant heard? He waited for the footsteps that would shake the floor of the cottage, waited for the door to the bedroom to explode open and slam against the wall. The Oberleutnant liked to hit people. Especially when they couldn't hit back.

But there was no sound from the other room. No angry footsteps, only the sighs of a gentle wind washing against the eaves. Maybe the Oberleutnant had left, deserted with the others. Maybe he'd had a seizure. Outside, Roten heard gunshots, shouts.

He stretched forward again and with his right hand cleared a ragged porthole through the frost that had glazed the windows of the tiny stone cottage. He peered through the hole, trying to catch a glimpse of Meyer's approach, hoping the priest had been diverted, that somehow he'd bypass the cottage and their meeting. It was crazy . . . why had he agreed to meet the priest? What could have been so damn important?

Daylight had now washed out the warm reds of dawn, and through the window Roten could almost see the shadows shrink. The harsh light reflecting off the snow began to hurt Roten's eyes . . . and then he heard Meyer's loud defiant voice. . . .

"The Lord is my shepherd, I shall not want; He maketh me to—" Father Werner Meyer sucked in sharply through clenched teeth as the pain seared down his arm from his shoulder, where the bullet had struck him. He felt the sticky warmth running down the inside of his clothes, the icepick stabs as the wind entered the passage through cloth and flesh.

" . . . He maketh me to lie down in green pastures, He restoreth my soul . . ." He felt his knees buckle again and pitched face first into the snow, which softened the harsh cries of the men behind him.

He was almost beyond caring. Please God, I'm not afraid of death, just let me die before they get to me. From some hidden reserve he found the strength to climb to unsteady feet . . . "Yea, though I walk through the valley of the shadow of death I will fear no evil, for Thou art with me . . ." He looked behind him; he could see the expressions on the faces behind him.

Suddenly Meyer stopped.

"I will fear no evil," he said out loud as he stood on shaky legs and turned around. "I will fear no evil," he shouted with a volume that surprised him. His words sounded across the lake as he began to walk toward the Germans.

For several moments they watched as the man they had pursued for hours took one suicidal step after another toward them. Then, first one man and then another raised his weapon and trained it squarely on the approaching figure.

"Christ almighty, what's that idiot doing?" Summers muttered as he watched the priest stop and suddenly start walking back toward the German soldiers. "Quick, open fire."

Summers and Czenek squeezed their triggers. Instants later Summers's grenade landed between the priest and his pursuers, closer to the mob than to the priest. From the top of their little rise they could see the explosion split the thin ice covering the lake and lift it in giant slabs that shed the men, throwing some to their faces, flinging others into the black olive-green waters beneath. Then, almost majestically, the slabs settled back like battered pieces of a jigsaw puzzle.

One of the Germans tossed to the edge of a slab hung half in the water as the ice surface healed itself, and Summers and Czenek watched as the man's waist was crushed between two unforgiving slabs of ice. His shrieks started low, guttural, swiftly climbed the scales, then suddenly stopped.

Summers and Czenek surveyed the scene below them. Meyer was struggling to his feet. So too were the four surviving Germans. Despite his wound Meyer was the first to his feet but he didn't run, just stood there, swaying on a slab of ice, staring at the four German soldiers.

"Go, man, move it, *move it,*" Summers said under his breath. The Germans now looked for the source of the blast, and Summers watched as one of them pointed directly at him.

He quickly worked the bolt of his M-1 to chamber another round, lined up the sights, and squeezed off a shot at the first German to pick up a weapon. The man sank slowly to his knees as if he had been drawn feet first into the ice. Beside him, he heard Czenek fire.

The shots seemed to galvanize Meyer. "I will fear no evil, for Thou art with me," he said gratefully. "Thou *art* with me." He picked his way carefully across the bobbing slabs of ice toward the cottage. He was God's messenger. Nothing would keep the secret of the second shroud now. God would protect him. God gave terrible burdens but never more than a man could handle as long as he had faith.

Indifferent to the shots behind him, Meyer pressed on with new strength. He saw the door ahead of him, knew that he would soon be safe and warm . . .

Czenek and Summers watched the remaining Germans fall, easy targets on the frozen lake with nowhere to hide. Meyer was almost out of sight now, approaching the front door of the cottage. Summers borrowed Czenek's binoculars and trained them on the priest as he knocked on the door. The door to the cottage opened, to reveal a tall figure wearing the unmistakable uniform of an SS officer. Summers watched the SS officer raise a Luger and aim it at the priest's chest. He saw the muzzle flash, saw Meyer collapse at the German's feet. The sound of the shot reached them seconds later.

"Bloody hell," Czenek muttered.

CHAPTER ONE

The mid-December storm rolled in off the Pacific, driving before it angry sheets of rain that pounded the waters of Marina del Rey and the decks of the boats huddled there against the fury of the Pacific Ocean. The wind made hungry slicing noises in the rigging of the marina's sailboats and breathed life to ambitious little harbor waves that slapped like applause against their hulls. It was nearly 8 A.M.

A hundred yards east of the marina's easternmost edge, commuters struggled to get to work. Streets and storm gutters designed for dry weather overflowed the curbs and ran across the sidewalks. At almost every intersection stalled cars rested like the carcasses of drowned animals, their soaked owners standing disconsolately nearby waiting for a tow truck or an ark. The few pedestrians out that early leaned into the gusts and wrestled the storm for possession of raincoats and umbrellas. The storm was winning.

It was not the sort of Southern California weather a pop songwriter would care to immortalize.

In the main cabin of the 44-foot sloop *Valkyrie,* Derek Steele tossed uneasily, as if the storm had infected his dreams. He twisted fitfully among his tangled sweat-soaked sheets and waited for the dream to come. It usually came to him on the soft padded feet of a half-sleep between waking and sleeping, between reality and fantasy. It was always the same and it always ended badly, just as it had in real life.

Steele turned over and buried his head in the pillow. He didn't want to relive the pain again, but as much as the dream hurt, it

29

was his only link with her and it was better he remember the pain than forget her.

The dream came.

As always, he saw their hotel room at the Eden au Lac in Zurich. It was the end of June. The French double doors had been thrown wide to admit the late afternoon air and the view of the lake and the mountains. Below the green hills, the lake shimmered like poured silver. Sailboats glided across the surface, their sails tinted a soft peach by the setting sun.

Stephanie had gone off by herself that day, all the way to Kreuzlingen, some forty-five miles northeast of Zurich. Kreuzlingen is Swiss and sits on one side of a narrow bosphorus that connects two alpine lakes: the relatively small Untersee to the west and the huge Bodensee to the east. On the other side of the bosphorus is Germany, and the city of Konstanz.

"It's purely business, darling," she told him before driving away in the Volkswagen they had hired at the airport in Zurich. "And you know how damned skittish collectors can be about strange faces."

Steele had smiled as he kissed her that morning. Not even the harshest judge could ever call Stephanie's large liquid brown eyes and full lips strange, nor, for that matter, her open, straightforward manner that inspired confidence and trust. He loved her so much it sounded trite to his own ears every time he tired to tell her. But words were rarely necessary.

Steele turned in his bunk and wrapped the sheets even tighter around his legs as he felt the concern that had swelled in his chest that June morning as she drove away to the north. He didn't like her boss sending her off alone to deal with wealthy men who had acquired their fortunes—and their art collections—in ways hard to trace.

But when he protested she always countered that it was a great honor for the gallery owner to send her instead of going himself. And she had already done it well on more than a dozen European trips since leaving UCLA with a Ph.D. in art history five years before. Since then she had negotiated multimillion dollar deals and located priceless works of art, some of which had been believed lost or destroyed during World War II. She had negotiated the sales and made the gallery and herself outrageous amounts of money.

In fact, she had made more money on one sale during her final quarter as a student than Steele had made in two years as an assistant professor of philosophy. He had never decided whether the outrageous part was the menial salaries UCLA paid its faculty, or Stephanie's commissions for just a few days' work.

But it didn't matter, at least not to their relationship. Somehow they transcended ordinary things. The money wasn't his and hers but theirs, and it didn't matter as long as there was enough. And there was.

Unconsciously Steele's right hand fumbled through the sheets and touched the wedding ring he still wore on his left hand. Six years. Six years ago she had walked into his philosophy class—he'd taught logic that quarter—and for the first and only time, he fell in love with one of his students.

Theirs was a marriage of infinite variety: the ethereal art history expert and the down-to-earth former policeman who taught philosophy. Everyone liked to wink at the way they met. All except UCLA's administrators, who usually acted like people congenitally lacking a sense of joy. They frowned. And the deeper they frowned, the deeper Steele and Stephanie laughed. Their parties were a clash of cultures: SWAT team commanders and art gallery owners, beefy squad commanders who thought Dada was the second word uttered by an infant, and disheveled art critics who had never before met a cop unless they had been arrested during a demonstration in the Sixties.

It was everything but boring.

These images and more invaded his thoughts that June day as he waited anxiously for her return. He rented a sailboat and sailed down as far as Zollikon. He ate a desultory lunch, missing her face at the other side of the table. He savagely beat the hotel's tennis pro in straight sets. He pulled on his running shoes and ran. But every time he returned to the room she still had not returned. He grew aware—as he did whenever they were separated for any length of time—of the huge void that she filled in his life.

Finally, exhausted but still concerned, he had thrown his running shoes and socks into a corner of the bathroom, and was stripped to his shorts when she came in.

Steele moaned in his sleep now, for this was where the dream began to run faster and faster. He wanted to catch sight of her, to hold her, to look at her once again, but like a piece of film out of control the dream raced by. She came into the room, exhilarated by the afternoon.

"I did it! He's agreed to sell me everything!" she said breathlessly. "But that's not the half of it. I've got one helluva surprise for the art world."

He didn't care about the art world or what might surprise it. Having her back was the only thing that mattered and he told her so. They embraced and then she broke away.

"Why don't you take your shower first, then I'll come in and attack you." Her words sped up and raced by as she kissed him on the lips and stood back and looked at him laciviously. "Youlooksoluscious!" She turned back toward the bedroom. The dream accelerated. Derek Steele watched himself in the dream turn slowly toward the shower. No! He wanted to shout. Don't let her go. Don't let her out of your sight. But the dream slammed downhill out of his control, a nightmare luge racing to the end.

"Ihavetomakeonephonecall." He heard her voice racing along with the dream.

"I'lltellyouallaboutitwhenyou'redonewithyourshower."

But when he was done with his shower she was gone.

Derek Steele woke up to realize he was crying.

He cursed as he slammed his fist into the pillow. He felt like sucker for not waking himself, but somewhere in the back of his mind he always clung to the hope that the dream would turn out differently and he'd wake up beside her again and they'd make love like they had that morning in Zurich five months ago.

He lay there for a moment, emotionally sucker-punched, breathing heavily into his knotted-up pillow, tasting the saltiness of his sorrow. Then slowly he turned, unwinding the sheets that had wrapped themselves around his legs. He tore them away from his sweaty body and lay on top, listening to the rain thudding against the deck above him. It was a sad soothing sound and he let it wash over him as he thought about Stephanie and ran over in his mind what he could have overlooked.

The room had been undisturbed. He remembered his bewilderment when he walked out of the bathroom, his hair in wet disarray, the towel wrapped around his waist. Puzzled, but convinced she had gone downstairs for a moment to pick up the surprise she had mentioned, Steele dressed and then sat on the foot of the bed and half-watched a television program about a Swiss air show.

He watched the door expectantly for nearly forty-five minutes before he was sure something was wrong. He called the front desk. They had no word from her. He ran down the steps to the front lobby. He checked the hotel's restaurants and shops, and finally the rented Volkswagen. It rested in the same spot the valet had put it when Stephanie had turned it over to him. The engine was still warm from her trip to Kreuzlingen.

Old reflexes returned to the former homicide detective. Steele searched the Volkswagen, the room. He took notes.

He questioned the front desk, the bellhops, and the thin balding man who parked the Volkswagen. The telephone call she had made while he was in the shower was apparently a local one. The front desk had no record of it.

Two hours later, there were no clues and no Stephanie. That's when Derek Steele called the police.

The Zurich police were unimpressed that Steele had once been a policeman, and more than a little annoyed that he had already interviewed all the logical people.

Later, they sat in the comfortable chairs in the room overlooking the lake and discussed the case.

"There is no sign of foul play, Herr Steele," the ranking officer had reminded him. "Perhaps there has been a misunderstanding?"

It took Steele a moment to grasp the man's meaning. Had they had an argument that caused Stephanie to disappear? Steele controlled his frustration. Back when he was a cop he had reached similar conclusions and said similar words to men and women whose spouses had taken sudden leave. He could hear his own voice as the official continued. "Perhaps there was something she was upset about and that you were unaware of?" he said. "It happens. Perhaps in a few hours . . ." He shrugged. "In any event, without any indication of foul play there is nothing we can do. There is no law against running away."

Steele wanted to tell the policeman about their love, about how Stephanie would never do such a thing. But the words of others who had told him similar things in his own years on the force came to his ear.

The police left as discreetly as they had come. But he still received dour frowns from the front desk every time he passed—his punishment, no doubt, for performing such a tasteless act as summoning common policemen to the lobby of such a fine establishment.

Steele got no sleep that night. He paced the room, pausing each time to gaze at the lake as if it had something it could tell him about Stephanie. But through it all the pulsing void inside of him grew. Never had he ever felt so alone. Horrible visions from his police days replayed themselves over and over.

He was exhausted and nearly ready for sleep the next morning when the breakfast he ordered arrived with a newspaper. He intended to eat and then catch a few hours sleep before continuing his investigation. But he got no father than the bottom of the first page. A headline on the right-hand side leaped out at him and chased the fatigue from his thoughts:

Kreuzlingen Estate Burns
Owner Suffers Heart Attack

He read the story. Just hours after Stephanie had concluded her negotiations with the estate's owner it had been destroyed by a massive fire. According to the story, the contents of the estate—including its priceless paintings—had been consumed by the flames. The owner, the story continued, had suffered a crippling heart attack and serious burns trying to save his collection.

With the newspaper on the seat beside him, Steele had pushed the rented Volkswagen to its mechanical limits during his crazed drive to Kreuzlingen. But all he found there was another frustrating dead end.

Local police and fire officials insisted there was no sign of arson or other foul play. Faulty wiring in the centuries-old structure had been the cause, they said. And the American should realize that the gentleman was advanced in age. Heart attacks are common among such men, they pointed out.

He fared no better at the hospital. The estate owner was unconscious and had been so since being brought to the hospital. And even had he been conscious, the doctors had no intention of letting him be interrogated.

The man died three days later with his secrets and—Steele was convinced—Stephanie's fate unrevealed.

Steele shook his head, trying to clear away the memory. He listened as the December rain drummed steadily on the *Valkyrie*'s deck. He pushed himself to his feet and stumbled into the head. As he urinated he caught a glimpse of himself in the mirror above the sink. He didn't particularly like what he saw. In the nearly six months since Stephanie had disappeared, deep plum-colored bruises had smudged themselves beneath both eyes. A layer of fat had crept around his waist for the first time in his life. Although the 185 pounds still looked taut and firm on his six-foot frame, Steele knew that unless he started exercising again, he'd start to look sloppy in another six months. Worse than that, the old wounds might start acting up. The doctors said they did that sometimes. But, somehow, it just didn't seem important anymore. So what?

Steele spat as he pumped the marine toilet empty and leaned over to examine himself more closely in the mirror. All his life he had appeared younger than his age. The other police officers called him The Kid. The last time a bartender had asked him for proof of his age had been just a month after he had gotten out of the hospital. He was twenty-nine years old then and recovering from the slugs that had torn through his chest and back and kidneys, but he still looked like a kid. Twenty-nine years old and the department had put him on permanent disability. The doctors had told him he probably wouldn't walk normally the rest of his life. But a year later he was fitter than the best recruit turned out by the academy. Unfortunately, bureaucratic rules were inviolable. They wouldn't give him his old job back.

But even in the worst of those days, alone, in pain, lost without the police life—even with all that he still looked like a kid. Then the years all seemed to catch up with him at once when Stephanie disappeared. Now every one of his thirty-seven years seemed tattooed in the lines of his face.

Steele went back to the *Valkyrie*'s galley and pulled open the refrigerator. He stood there for a long sleepy moment staring intently at the refrigerator's contents without seeing them. What he saw instead was the way he had spent the rest of the summer. He stayed on in Zurich, arriving back in Los Angeles just in time to start teaching fall classes. But despite more than two more months of investigating he had little more to show for his time than an outrageous hotel bill at the Eden au Lac, a proficiency in speaking German, a close friendship with a number of Swiss law enforcement officers, and a working friendship with an American attached to the U.S. consulate in Zurich.

The American, a Midwesterner named Gerry Anderson, had proved invaluable in leading Steele through the diplomatic and bureaucratic jungles that surrounded an American making unofficial and therefore irregular inquiries about his missing wife in a foreign country. Anderson also turned out to be a regular, if somewhat unchallenging, tennis partner.

At first, Steele had been put off by Anderson's solicitous manner, thinking perhaps the man was gay or maybe a consulate baby-sitter assigned to make sure the former cop didn't do anything rash. But over the course of the summer Steele realized that Anderson was just another lonely American, unmarried and more than a little homesick for the Illinois farm country where he had grown up and gone to college.

Through Anderson's help Steele got permission to look over the ruins of the Kreuzlingen estate before the cleanup crews moved in. For three weeks he sifted through the ashes and rubble, growing more convinced by the day that the local police had been right.

But at the end of every day something about the ruins had still nagged at him. Finally, the day before the bulldozers were ready to clean up the blackened mess, it came to him: the estate's owner had been a wealthy German art collector with one of the most precious collections in Switzerland. Yet there were no picture frames in the ashes, no glass, no charred bits of pictures or frames, no evidence of hanging wires or brackets. Fire, Steele knew from investigating arson homicides, rarely consumed everything. But at the Kreuzlingen estate there were none of the bits and pieces—a corner of a frame here, a scrap of hanging wire there. It was as if all the art had been removed from the estate before it burned.

The local authorities discounted Steele's newfound proof that the fire must have been arson and refused to halt the bulldozers and their cleanup operation. Their patience had run thin and their sympathy for the bereaved American no longer restrained their annoyance. They told him they were sure all of his questions would be answered and would he please stop second-guessing them and poking his nose into matters that didn't concern him.

There was nothing else he could do. He watched the bulldozers raze the only clues he had to Stephanie's disappearance, paid his bills, told Anderson good-bye, and then came home to teach his classes. . . .

Steele dumped the cold grounds from the coffeemaker basket and poured beans in to the grinder. His classes were going poorly. Before Zurich he had been highly praised for his classroom work, by his students and by other faculty members. He never missed classes, always prepared fresh, interesting materials, never delivered boring lectures.

Zurich had changed that. This year he was delivering half-hearted lectures using last year's notes . . . when he managed to make it to class at all. Claude Tewles, the department head who had originally hired him eight years before, had taken to asking him if he had a drinking problem.

But it was worse than a drinking problem. It was the wondering. The wondering had made him old. If he only knew if she was dead or alive he could get on with his life.

Steele slid the basket with new grounds into the coffeemaker, poured in a pot of water and turned the machine on. He stood there, blankly staring at the machine. Finally the coffeemaker's burps and gurgles cut through his reverie and he turned his attention to the gray and white storm lashing by just beyond the portholes. One minute he could see the boat in the slip next to his and the next only a wash of static like a bad black-and-white TV image.

He stared at the storm several minutes, then turned to the table where the binder containing his lecture materials had lain untouched since his last class. He approached the binder as one approaches a deformed child who ought to be loved but who inspires only disgust, sat down in front of the lesson plans, and opened the thick loose-leaf binder. He glanced cursorily at one page and then another before he realized he didn't care about them any more this morning than he had any other morning since he returned from Zurich.

He continued dumbly to thumb through the yellow-ruled pages covered with clippings, scrawled notes, and citations. He had planned to talk about Kant's categorical imperatives this morning. But he had no energy left for Kant or for the students who seemed to tear at his mind, wanting to strip it bare of knowledge. He had no patience to face them.

The coffee maker popped and gurgled its last drops and hissed a cloud of vapor that condensed on the portholes. Weary after a night's half-sleep, Steele slammed the lecture notes closed, shoved himself away from the table, and went to the telephone hanging by the galley. He punched in the number of the philosophy department. The phone buzzed in his ear.

"Philosophy, Mrs. Mills speaking," he heard the departmental secretary answer. Dorothy Mills was a delightful woman in her forties with long elegant features and graceful movements.

"Good morning, Dorothy," Steele replied in his cheeriest voice. "Is David around?"

"Good morning, Derek," Dorothy replied, her concern apparent even over the telephone. "How are you this morning?"

"Oh . . . not bad, not bad, all things considered."

"That's good. I believe Professor Marshall is in his office. I'll ring him for you."

But instead of the dull clicking of the antique GTE telephone switching Steele heard only silence. She had put him on hold. Cradling the receiver between his shoulder and chin, Steele leaned over to pour a cup of the fresh coffee into the chipped and beloved mug his first squad car partner had given him for a birthday gift. On one side it had his name and rank, sergeant at the time, and on the other a cartoon of two buzzards sitting on a desolate tree limb. The caption under the cartoon read: "Patience, hell! I'm going out and kill something." Another time, another life, Steele thought as the memory almost coaxed a smile from him.

The telephone began to ring as Steele sipped from the cup. He swallowed quickly as he prepared to ask David Marshall to take yet another class for him. He tried to think of what excuse to use this time.

"Derek?" It was Claude Tewles's voice Steele heard, not that of Associate Professor David Marshall. Steele felt his mood plummet through the deck.

"Ah, yes, Claude, this is Derek Steele."

"Sorry for intercepting your call but I happened to be walking past Dorothy's desk when you phoned."

An awkward silence hung over the phone as Steele tried to think of a reply. When he didn't his department head continued.

"I don't suppose you were calling young Marshall to ask him to take another of your classes, were you?" Tewles said, his voice heavy with accusation.

"Well, I . . . I haven't felt—"

"I thought so," Tewles interrupted, his voice growing angrier. "Derek, I've talked to you about this before and it can't continue."

"I know that, but—"

"No more buts, Derek. Either you get in here this morning and teach your class and the rest of them for this quarter or I'm going to have to consider terminating you."

Steele listened numbly, mostly feeling guilty for disappointing the man who had offered him a career after the force had retired him.

"I've never seen you like this before," Tewles said more calmly. "You've always been the fighter, the instigator, the trouble-maker—even when you were taking my classes at Cornell. But I've never seen you just give up like this. When the doctors said you'd never fully recover from the shooting you didn't give up, and you didn't give up when the force refused to take you off disability.

"I *watched* you attack the books after that final disability hearing, Derek. You always did have a good mind for philosophy—I saw that in you as an undergraduate—but the way you went after that doctorate was astounding. You took your rage, harnessed it, and transformed yourself into a first-rate scholar. That's why I offered you the teaching position. You're a scholar with experience out in the real world. That's a rare and valuable thing and I don't want to have to suspend you. But you've got to get hold of yourself!"

"It's different now," Steele protested. "I'm not the same man any more."

"Damn right you're not!" Tewles exclaimed. "You're turning your rage in on yourself instead of channeling it into your work."

"If I just knew about Stephanie . . ."

"Damn it man, she's dead. You've got to accept that and move on. Because if you don't there'll be two murders. Even if you haven't noticed, it's clear to the rest of us that you're right now among the walking dead."

Steele had no answer. Tewles was right.

"The bank called yesterday. They asked me as your employer whether or not you're planning to sell the house, or what. You're six mortgage payments behind."

Steele vaguely remembered the envelopes. He had ignored them, along with the rest of the mail that was still being forwarded to his office at the philosophy department. He had never gotten around to notifying the post office that he had returned from Switzerland.

He had intended to pay all the bills, especially the mortgage, for as long as it took to sell the house. He had to sell it; his professor's salary just couldn't cover both the mortgage and boat payments. He had lain for hours in the boat, staring out at the harbor, visualizing the visits to real estate brokers. But he had never gone through with it because he knew if he did he'd have to face the house and what it held.

The house was haunted with the evidence of the years he and Stephanie had spent together. And to sell the house was to admit that those years were over. But he had to do something. The unoccupied house had become a target for vandals. There had been three incidents so far . . .

"Yes," Steele's voice cracked. "I'm trying to sell it now . . . I . . . I'll call them. Claude . . ."

"Yes?"

"I'm sorry they called you. I'm sorry you had to get caught up in my problems. I"—Steele felt the sloop sway. A good sailor knows all the motions and sounds of his craft, knows the ways it moves in the wind and waves, recognizes the movements that could only come from other human beings. Someone, he was sure, had just stepped lightly aboard the *Valkyrie*.

"Can I call you right back, Claude?"

"No, Derek. I want you to get things straightened out now. I want to—"

Knuckles rapped politely at the companionway hatch.

"Claude, there's someone at the door, I have to—"

The polite rap turned into a more urgent tattoo.

"Look, Claude, can't you hang on for a minute?"

"No, goddamnit. I'm not going to let you run away anymore. You hang up on me and you're damn well fired."

The knocking grew louder. Steele set down the receiver and turned toward the stern of the boat. He made his way toward the companionway, the main entrance to the boat, stopped at the navigator's station to pull a Smith & Wesson .357 Magnum from a drawer. He didn't get many visitors, especially at 8 A.M. in the middle of a December rainstorm. He'd be prepared; they wouldn't get him as easily as they had Stephanie. He slipped the revolver into the deep right-hand pocket of his robe, pulled the sash cord tighter round his wait.

A rapid pounding sounded against the companionway hatch.

"All right, all right" he yelled as he climbed the steps of the companionway.

He reached the top of the steps, grabbed the hatch handle, and pulled it back a crack. Waves of icy wind howled through the crack, carrying with it a sneeze of rain. Outside, huddled under the protective awning that covered the cockpit, Steele saw a wrinkled old man whose time-eroded face was a solid mass of gullies set with two brilliant blue eyes. They looked at each other solemnly.

The wind whipped the man's thinning white hair about his head and tugged at the buttons of a camel's-hair coat spotted dark with the rain. The old man was tall and gaunt as a cadaver. Behind him stood a massive fellow in a chauffeur's uniform stolidly holding an umbrella. In his other hand he held a stubby machine pistol. He held the gun casually by its handgrip, the barrel pointing at the deck, at no one in particular.

Steele felt his mouth go suddenly dry. He froze for an instant as his eyes took in the old man and the chauffeur. His thoughts of Stephanie, Claude Tewles, and Kant's categorical imperatives vanished in a surge of fear. Right now, surviving was all that counted.

With his body mostly hidden from them by the companionway hatch, Steele held their gaze and slowly reached for the Magnum.

Trying to keep his movements as unobtrusive as possible, he pulled the Smith & Wesson out of his robe pocket and held it out of sight at his side ready to shoot through the wood of the boards. The .357 would easily go through the boards, the chauffeur, and the transom of the *Valkyrie* and still have enough power to kill.

"Mr. Steele?" The old man's voice was cultured, soothing, unthreatening.

"Yes?" Who the hell would show up on his boat with a machine gun. Someone he had arrested? Steele tried unsuccessfully to match the old man or his chauffeur with a face from a bust, from a courtroom. But revenge had a longer memory than a street cop. And people didn't always do their own dirty work.

"I'm Myron Davidson," the man said, extending a long bony hand with a pencil-thin wrist behind it. "May I come in? It's rather inhospitable out here." He saw Steele looking intently at his chauffeur.

"This is my chauffeur and bodyguard, Eric." Eric nodded toward Steele, gave a little half-bow which looked comical performed by such a huge man. "My life has . . . been threatened on a number of occasions," Davidson said. "Eric is here to make sure *I* come to no harm, not to harm you."

Unconvinced, Steele glanced suspiciously from Davidson to Eric and back again. "I'm not used to seeing machine guns this early in the morning."

An annoyed look passed briefly across Davidson's face, replaced immediately by a grimace.

"Could I *trouble* you for a bit of shelter?" Davidson persisted. "The sort of proposition I have for you should not be discussed in a doorway."

"Only if your man Eric gets off my boat with that portable cannon."

Davidson turned and nodded to the chauffeur. "Go wait in the car. It's unlikely they're prepared to launch an attack from the water."

Eric looked angrily at Steele and worriedly at his employer.

"Go on," Davidson insisted. "Mr. Steele here isn't going to hurt me." The chauffeur, still dubious, slipped the machine pistol into a holster inside his coat and climbed onto the dock. He stood

42

there for a moment, and with the hand that had held the gun, reached inside his coat and pulled out a portable walkie-talkie.

"Please take this, Mr. Davidson. I'll listen on the radio in the limo. Call me if you need me." He leaned over to hand the radio to the old man, then disappeared in the direction of the limousine. Steele watched him climb the steep incline the gangplank made when the tide was out, then stand for a moment on the land looking back at them. Davidson waved, and Eric, who still looked larger than life across the distance, opened the limo door, got in, and firmly closed it.

Steele's eyes lingered on the limo, hesitant to return to the gaunt old man. He listened to the beat of the rain on the cockpit awning, felt himself growing angry, and tried to fight the emotion. Fear to anger. It happened to every street cop ten thousand times in a career. The fear of a life-threatening situation turned into an emotional hangover of anger as the body tried to figure out what to do with all the adrenaline. Steele had learned early to recognize it, to deal with it so he wouldn't take it out on other people.

He took a deep breath, held it and let it out slowly, then another. He closed his eyes and thought of sailing. The whole process took less than half a minute, and when he heard Davidson's voice, he was calm again.

"Mr. Steele?" Davidson's aristocratic voice was now faintly plaintive. "I'm not as young as I once was and would appreciate a warm place to sit for a minute or two."

Steele hesitated, and then: "Okay." Steele replaced the Smith & Wesson in his robe pocket and began to remove the polished teak companionway hatch.

He placed the last of the hatch boards below and offered his hand to Davidson. The old man accepted the assistance gratefully, placing his arthritic fingers into Steele's young, powerful grip. Together they slowly navigated the half dozen steps down into the main cabin, Steele watching as pain knotted the man's face with every step.

After helping Davidson to a seat beside the table, Steele turned toward the galley. The sight of the phone still lying off the hook reminded him that he had left Claude Tewles on the line.

"Claude?" he said bringing the handset to his ear. "Claude?"

"Derek?" It was Dorothy Mills again. "Professor Tewles had

43

to leave for an appointment. He told me . . . he said I should tell you that . . . Oh, I get so mad when he makes me do his dirty work. He said if you didn't teach class today he'd fire you.''

In the embarrassed silence that followed, Steele closed his eyes, tried to think. He was behind with the mortgage. Even as disgracefully low as it was, he needed his UCLA salary to hang on to everything else. He opened his eyes and glanced at his watch. He was due in the classroom in half an hour. In the rain he'd be hard pressed to make it if he left immediately. He glanced over at Davidson.

''I'm sorry, Derek,'' Dorothy Mills's voice broke the silence. ''I really am.''

''Don't apologize, Dorothy,'' Steele said. ''I'm the one who should be apologizing. I'll try to make it.''

They rang off.

''I'm afraid I have very little time,'' Steele said as he stood back and looked down at the elegant, wrinkled old man. ''I have to get dressed and teach a class.'' Steele looked at his notes on the table next to Davidson. The old man's eyes lingered on the notebook for a moment, then returned to Steele.

''But—''

''Talk to me while I get dressed,'' Steele said, moving toward his cabin. ''I'll leave the door open so I can hear you.'' But before Steele could reach the door of his cabin he heard a dry scrabbling behind him, felt thin gnarled fingers grip the backs of his arms.

''Mr. Steele, I have come a long way to see you,'' Davidson said. ''Don't brush me off like this.'' Steele turned and looked at the man. The pain caused by his rapid movement was apparent on his face. Davidson's voice had grown shrill, desperate, as if the exertion had exhausted his last reserve of self-control.

''You *must* give it to me,'' Davidson said, his thin twisted hands and fingers held up in a sort of supplication. ''*Please* give it to me. I've come prepared to compensate you handsomely.''

Steele backed up, surprised by Davidson's outburst.

''Here,'' Davidson said, reaching into one pocket of his camel's-hair coat and drawing out a banded stack of currency that he thrust at Steele. They were American one-thousand-dollar bills. No wonder the man traveled with an armed chauffeur.

44

In Steele's experience the only people he had ever seen with stacks of thousand-dollar bills were Colombian cocaine dealers.

"Go ahead," Davidson said, shaking the stack of bills at him. "It's honest money from good people . . . and there's more." To prove his point Davidson reached into his other pocket and pulled out a matching stack. He moved closer, shoved one stack of bills into Steele's robe pocket on top of the Smith & Wesson. "Take it. All you have to do is give it to me and the rest is yours too."

Steele slowly withdrew the stack of bills from his pocket and looked at it. There were at least fifty bills there. He looked at Davidson, and tucked the money back into his robe pocket. Along with the other stack, Davidson had walked onto his boat with at least a hundred grand in cash. The answer to his financial problems had just walked into his life. He could quit his job and go back to Zurich and search for Stephanie. Suddenly Steele wanted very badly to give this crazy old man what he wanted. Only he had no idea what that was.

"Mr. Davidson," Steele began slowly, "just what is it that you want from me?"

"Please don't play tiring games with an old man like me," Davidson said. "I know she must have gotten it from him."

"She?"

"Your wife."

"My wife? What about her? What are you talking about?" Steele's voice rose. "What the hell about my wife? Where is she?" He grabbed Davidson and lifted the frail man off his feet and shook him like ventriloquist's dummy. "Where *is* she? Tell me or I'll take you apart piece by fucking piece—"

"Stop, please," Davidson yelled in pain as Steele shook him. "Stop, I . . . we . . . we tried to stop them . . . please, Mr. Steele, stop . . ."

Steele put him down on the settee. God, what was *happening* to him? His head hurt. He put his face in his hands and rubbed away at the pain. The insanity of all this was causing him to lose his bearings. He looked down at the frail old man he had begun to abuse. He had to get control of his life again.

Davidson looked up warily at Steele and ran his fingers through his hair, as much to assure himself that his head was in one piece as to straighten his hair.

"I know what you're thinking," Steele said. "I'm sorry, but I thought you were—"

"There's no need to apologize. This thing has made men insane for centuries." Davidson said this in an oddly calm way. It was as if both men, having acted out, could now deal reasonably with each other.

"The important thing for you to remember, Mr. Steele, is that we are prepared to pay you a lot of money for the painting."

"I don't know about any painting," Steele said, "and I don't care that much about money. I'd rather have Stephanie back—"

"Of course you would, and if you cooperate with us I believe we may be able to locate her."

"She's still *alive?*"

"I didn't say that. I said we'd help you try to locate her. We don't know what those madmen might have done to her. But I do suspect she's still alive, since she knows what was on the back of the picture, and they don't . . ."

"Picture?" Steele took his coffee and sat down at the table across from Davidson. "I don't understand. What's a picture got to do with all this? And who the hell are you?"

"I told you. Myron Davidson, I—"

"No, I mean who are you with? Who sent you? How do you know about Stephanie?" Steele's hand shook a little as he lifted his mug to his lips. Coffee sloshed on the table. He took a sip and set the mug down in the spill. "Why would—?"

"Why is always the hardest to understand," Davidson said. "We can understand the hows and the wheres and the whos, but the whys provide jobs for philosophers and priests."

Steele just looked at him, waited.

The old man seemed to consider a moment, then slipped one thin hand inside his coat, drew out a small black-and-white snapshot, and passed it across the table, careful to avoid the spilled coffee. Reluctantly, Steele picked up the photo and looked at it.

The photograph was of an alpine meadow, with mountains rising above a broad grassy open area ringed by conifers. Davidson searched Steele's face for signs of recognition, found none.

"So?" Steele said as he passed the photograph back.

"The painting is oil on wood, about six inches high and five inches wide," Davidson said. "It was painted between 1936 and

46

1938 by Frederick Stahl, a German painter. Stahl painted it in warm tones, much like the Italian Renaissance masters whose style he tried to emulate." Davidson paused, looked expectantly at Steele.

"So?" Steele said again. "What's the point of all this? What's it got to do with Stephanie?"

"The point is, do you recognize the painting?"

Steele shook his head. "Should I?"

Davidson studied Steele's face. Finally he sighed and nodded his head like a man who has just made a momentous decision. "Mr. Steele, I don't know exactly why, but I believe you. I don't think you've ever seen the picture. But yes, you should have. I have every reason to believe that your wife had it in her possession when she left Kreuzlingen.

"I did it! He's agreed to sell me everything!" Steele's head spun. There is was, the clue that had hovered just beyond the edge of his consciousness for six months, the known but overlooked missing piece. *"That's not the half of it! I've got one helluva surprise for the art world,"* she'd said.

What could she have found? Something important enough to be kidnapped . . . killed . . . ?

"Why don't you take your shower first. Then I'll come in and attack you." Derek found himself swept back into his nightmare, watching the dream gather speed, watching Stephanie move away from him . . . *"Ihavetomakeonephonecall . . ."*

A picture. She could have brought back a picture. The one Davidson was after. Five by six inches. It could have fit in her purse. Or the Eden au Lac's safe deposit boxes. She was a nut about using the boxes for valuables, even cameras and passports.

"I'lltellyouallaboutitwhenyou'redonewithyourshower—"

"Mr. Steele? Mr. Steele, are you all right?"

The room at the Eden au Lac faded away and once again Steele was looking across the table at the old man with the timeworn face.

"You turned almost white there for a moment," Davidson said. "It looked like you had some kind of attack."

"Just nerves." He set the mug down. "These last few months have been tough and your visit this morning just sort of shot my nerves the rest of the way to hell."

"I'm sorry," Davidson said. "I know this is a strain but it's necessary to find out what happened to your wife."

"Tell me more about the picture," Steele said.

"You're still sure you know nothing of this picture?" He held the photo up again. "Or its whereabouts?"

Steele shook his head. "No," he lied, "I don't have a clue."

Davidson looked at him, then went on.

"Stahl, the artist, was a favorite of the SS. Hitler, they say, loved the man and his work. In fact when Stahl died in 1940 Hitler wrote the epitaph that rests over Stahl's grave, wrote and delivered the eulogy himself."

Steele took another look at the photograph. "Why the fascination? This Stahl doesn't seem to be that much of an artist."

Davidson smiled. "There are many who share your feelings, Mr. Steele. The Führer, though, wasn't one of them. Hitler, you may know, wanted more than anything else in the world to be an artist, a painter. He was turned away from the best art academies and spent years in near poverty trying to peddle his works among the patrons of cafes and bistros in Vienna."

Davidson got up, took off his camel's-hair coat, and folded it carefully on the seat. Steele toyed with his coffee mug, spinning it in half turns as he watched his strange morning visitor.

"The world might well have never suffered through its bloodiest epoch so far in history," Davidson said after he was seated again, "if someone had just let little Adolf into art school."

"That's fairly well known," Steele said, impatience in his voice. "What does it have to do with Stephanie and this . . . Stahl painting?"

"Patience. I haven't come all this way to waste your time. That period in Hitler's life had two specific consequences for you, and your wife.

"First, it drew his sympathy to another struggling Aryan artist—Stahl—and it made him determined to prove his artistic merit to the world, by whatever means it took. He saw in Stahl someone like himself—a struggling artist of skill but no particular genius."

"Are you saying Hitler was a good artist?"

"He was a competent craftsman who probably could have made a good career today as a commercial or graphic artist. But another Rembrandt? Hardly. And neither was Stahl. Hitler adopted Stahl, introduced him to Nazi society. They were pleased that not all of the artists in Germany were Jews or exiles . . .

"The second consequence for you of Hitler's failed art career," Davidson continued, "concerns his passion for building the world's largest and finest museum. The Führermuseum, as it was to be called, would be built in his hometown of Linz, Austria. To fill this museum's collection Hitler created a special task force in the SS called the Sonderauftrag Linz, whose job it was to make sure the best art, antiques, statuary, relics, icons, coins—whatever— were taken from public and private collections in occupied countries. The art came from all over Europe by the boxcarload to Munich to a central collecting point. Later in the war the art was moved out of Munich to old castles and salt mines where it would be safe from Allied bombardment."

Davidson paused and leaned toward Steele. "The estate near Kreuzlingen that your wife visited was filled with pieces of art that had disappeared into the Nazi art machine. Most of it made its way across the border from Germany with SS officers who used the art to buy silence, food, lodging, and transportation away from the Allied tribunals."

"Jesus!" Stephanie had never mentioned any of it to him, the danger. Maybe she didn't know about the looted art, maybe she'd gone there to buy the legitimate collection, *had* bought the legitimate collection. If she had . . . Steele didn't believe in Nazis stalking the world, but he did believe that millions of dollars worth of art could make murder seem inconsequential. "You think Stephanie . . . ?"

"I'm almost sure your wife learned the secrets of the estate at Kreuzlingen," Davidson said. "And I'm even more certain that she left that day with a painting by Stahl, the one in the photograph."

"But with all of the priceless masters there, what's the significance of a mediocre painting by a second-rate Nazi?"

Davidson's voice speeded up. "I was just getting to that. Sometime before the invasion of Poland, Stahl visited Hitler at Berchtesgaden and the two went for a long ride into the hills. Nobody knows exactly where they went. But when they returned, Stahl had the sketches from which he painted this picture." Davidson tapped the photo with a well-manicured fingernail. "The painting was supposedly hung in Hitler's private quarters at a top secret military installation in Austria. Probably located near the scene depicted in the painting."

Steele reached over and picked up the snapshot again. He studied it more carefully this time. "What's that in the corner over here?" He leaned across the table and pointed to the corner of the photo.

"We believe that's the entrance to an old salt mine," Davidson said. "It's not significant. Austria and Bavaria are riddled with them. *Salzberg* means 'salt town,' you know."

"What's the name of the picture?"

"The Home of the Lady Our Redeemer," Davidson said.

"Strange. I'd expect to see saints and halos and maybe the Virgin Mary—that's who the name refers to, isn't it? The Lady Redeemer?"

"Remember a moment ago," Davidson began cautiously, "I told you they looted more than just art? That they also took antiques, reliquaries, religious objects? Well, very early in Hitler's searches for art and valuable objects his agents managed to obtain by bribery and coercion—and murder—a religious object of great value, valuable enough for Hitler to actually use it against the Catholic Church . . . to all but silence its leadership . . . the Pope himself . . . on the Nazi treatment of the Jews. Before you say nonsense, remember how little comment on the subject came from the Vatican during those years. Some have directly attacked the Vatican for this, calling it a scandal . . ."

Steele looked at Davidson, shaking his head. "Yes, I've heard that. But how . . . I mean, what could have *that* kind of influence . . . ?"

"Something, Mr. Steele, that would undermine one of the Church's strongest foundations . . . That's what Hitler and Stahl went to see that day they took their ride." Davidson's voice was rising. "Somewhere in that painting"—he tapped the photograph agitatedly—"is the key to finding it, and I believe your wife knows what the key is—"

"But what's the painting a key *to?*"

"Knowing that would be very unhealthy for you," Davidson said. "There are men who have devoted their lives to making sure the world never finds out."

Steele was not satisfied. "But if my wife's involved . . . if there's still a chance to find her, I've got to know everything." He looked at Davidson suspiciously. "What's your role in all this, Davidson? Why is it so important you get to the painting first?"

The old man chose his words carefully. "Those men I just mentioned—the ones who will stop at nothing to preserve the secret. I was once one of them. I was a fool. It took many years before I realized that it was not the Church they were trying to protect, but themselves."

Steele got up. "I may know where the painting is. Then again, I may not. But you'll never find out unless I know more . . . a lot more."

While they measured each other, a nondescript rented sedan glided slowly into the parking lot at the end of the pier and nosed into a space some twenty yards west of Davidson's limousine. A cinder-block building containing public restrooms sheltered the sedan and its occupants from Eric, who had been watching the *Valkyrie* intently.

Unseen by Eric, two men dressed in yellow rain slickers got out of the rear of the car. Two others, similarly dressed, stayed in the front with a clear view of the *Valkyrie*.

"It's your life," Davidson told Steele again.

"It's my life, yes. So . . . ?"

Davidson nodded, was about to go on, when hell started to break loose. First the telephone rang. Its buzz cut through the tense silence of the *Valkyrie*'s cabin and startled both men. Steele reached over and grabbed the telephone from the receiver. "Yes?"

"Derek? This is Claude Tewles."

The voice pulled Steele back to his mundane reality. He looked at the brass clock on the cabin wall. His philosophy class should have started seventeen minutes ago.

"Derek? I hoped you wouldn't answer. Then at least I could assume you were on your way here, that maybe you'd hit on a legitimate delay."

"Claude, I—"

"Forget it. I hate to do this, but as of right now you've been suspended. I want your office cleaned out by the end of the day and I want that huge box of your personal mail out of our storeroom. We're not a goddamned post office box for your conven-

51

ience. If it's not out of here this afternoon I will personally go down there and throw the stuff away." The line went dead before he could answer.

Steele was still looking at the dead instrument in his hand when the portable radio crackled in Davidson's pocket. The old man fumbled to get it out. "Hello, Eric?" Panic was in his voice. "Eric, are you there?"

There was no answer.

Steele heard the running feet first. He turned and looked out the porthole. Through the tangled sheets of rain he saw a man in a yellow storm slicker close the door to Davidson's limousine. The man turned and spoke to a second man, also in a yellow slicker, who had walked around from the rear of the car. The second man leaned over to look through the window of the door for a moment and nodded. The two men exchanged words, then started toward Steele's dock.

"Were you expecting someone?" Steele asked without looking at Davidson. He pointed toward the limo. The two figures in yellow slickers were making their way quickly down the dock, looking neither left nor right but directly toward the *Valkyrie.*

"Eric?" Davidson called into the walkie-talkie, his frail voice cracking. Only static. He stared at the instrument in his hand as if it had personally betrayed him.

Steele drew the .357 Magnum from his robe pocket, felt it slide past the wad of thousand-dollar bills Davidson had forced on him earlier. He thought briefly about handing them back to the old man, but the footsteps sounding on the dock seemed more serious business.

"I think you'd better sit this one out a minute, Davidson," Steele said. "Go into the forward cabin, and keep quiet."

Davidson seemed to shrink as Steele led him quickly forward and eased him down onto a bunk.

Steele spotted his khaki trousers hanging on the hook behind the cabin door. The realization that he was naked under his bathrobe did nothing for his confidence. Quickly, he laid the Smith & Wesson on the bed and reached for his pants, hearing above him the sound of one man and then another stepping aboard the *Valkyrie.* He had just snapped the catch on his trousers and pulled the zipper shut when the inch-thick teak companionway boards above his head exploded inward, torn by a silenced machine gun into a maelstrom of long twisted splinter.

"Back in the corner!" Steele shouted, grabbing the Smith & Wesson and throwing himself against Davidson. He heard the old man groan in pain as they tumbled into the corner of the cabin, just forward of the head. Instants later, Steele watched in awe as the teak door and bulkhead wall on the other side of the cabin erupted with tiny brown geysers, spraying the area with a deadly pattern of slugs. He felt Davidson shaking. But what he noticed most as he lay there with his cheek mashed against the forward wall of the head was the dull thudding vibration of slugs as they embedded themselves in the wood less than an inch from his head. Luck had tossed them at least one miracle: without silencers to rob them of their muzzle velocity, the slugs would have sliced right through both walls of the head, killing them both.

As suddenly as it had started, the firing stopped. Wind whistled through the bullet holes and Davidson started to move.

"Be still," Steele whispered. They lay there some time, listening for a sound that was not part of the storm overhead. Eventually it came, the faintest of scraping noises, the sound of street grit grinding between a hard-sole shoe and the *Valkyrie*'s deck. The sound grew louder until it was directly overhead.

Whirling onto his back, Steele fired twice through the ceiling. In the confined space the pistol sounded like a cannon. Though his ears were ringing, Steele heard a surprised grunt of pain. Moments later, there was a heavy thud followed immediately by a metallic sound of a gun skittering across the deck.

"Quickly now," Steele urged as he helped Davidson to his feet. The badly arthritic old man choked off a cry of pain. He followed Steele uncertainly as he guided them through the galley and into the main cabin.

"You'd better crawl under that table," Steele said, pointing to the massive teak slab that afforded the cabin's only protection. Painfully, Davidson did as he was told.

As soon as Davidson was safely under the table, Steele spun and made for the after cabin. There was a hatch there that would afford him a clear shot at anyone on deck.

He had barely started toward the after cabin when the roof once again exploded inward with another burst of automatic weapon fire. Steele fell to the floor and crouched in the darkened passage-way. Inches above him a fire extinguisher bracketed to the bulk-head exploded like a hand grenade and blanketed him with foam. He wiped at his face to clear his eyes but the torrents of rain pouring through the rents in the deck quickly washed it away.

Slugs continued to slam through the deck as above him Steele saw what he thought was the figure of a man. He sighted along the barrel of his Smith & Wesson and began to squeeze, when suddenly he heard a muffled cry of pain from Davidson. Steele glanced under the table. The old man's arthritis was so bad that he had been unable to draw his right leg completely behind the heavy teak slab. A dark red stain was visible on his trousers.

Steele fired upward and then clambered over to Davidson's side. Behind him, an answering burst of slugs stitched a tight crosshatch in the foam beneath the fire extinguisher. Steele raised the leaf of the teak table and gently shifted Davidson's leg until it was entirely shielded.

"How are you?" Steele asked.

"I've had more pain in my life," Davidson answered.

"Don't worry," Steele said. "We'll get you out of this and to a hospital soon." Steele started to crawl out from under the table when a furious blast of slugs shredded the carpeting less than an inch from his face.

"Goddamnit!" Steele shouted, "that's enough!" He rolled out from under the table and fired three quick shots. One of the bullets evidently found its mark . . . a long shriek of pain cut through the roaring of the storm. Hearing it, Steele allowed himself a grim smile. Most people who had seen that expression in the past thought it meant satisfaction. It did, partly, but it was also a way to mask the frustration Steele felt at having been forced to kill.

Wearily, Steele pushed himself up on one elbow. He craned his neck and looked at Davidson. The old man's pants leg was now soaked with blood.

"Mr. Steele—"

"*Quiet,*" Steele said. Getting to his feet, he cautiously mounted the steps to the companionway. In one swift movement he cleared away the debris and, with a single shot remaining in his gun, stepped warily out onto the deck. Directly in front of him lay a dead man, two blood-red eyes staring up from a yellow rainsuit.

54

On the bow of the boat, thirty feet away, lay another corpse, also in a yellow slicker. Steele heard the slam of a car door and pivoted around to spot two more rain-suited figures running from a dark sedan parked next to the rest rooms.

Feeling the knot in his gut ratchet tighter, Steele barreled down the companionway into the main cabin and bent over Davidson.

"We've got to get out of here. There's more coming." Davidson took hold of Steele's hand and allowed the younger man to pull him out from under the table.

"But .. how?" Davidson stuttered. "I can't swim . . . there's only one way off the dock?"

"My tender," Steele said. "A small skiff with an outboard." Making their way onto the deck, Steele guided the limping Davidson to the dock finger that ran alongside the *Valkyrie*. There, nuzzled into the space between the finger and the *Valkyrie*'s stern section, was a small white fiberglass skiff. For the first time since the shooting started, Steele felt some hope.

He ignored the shouts behind him, fell to his knees, and pulled the skiff closer to the dock.

So engrossed was he in his task that he did not hear the muted reports of silenced weapons.

When, a few moments later, he turned toward Davidson to hurry him along, Steele froze at the sight of the old man's throat—or rather what was left of it. Automatic weapons fire had replaced the protruding Adam's apple and its shroud of loose wrinkled skin with a gaping red hole.

Davidson's face wore a puzzled expression. His lips moved, but no sound came from them, just a raspy liquid sound as blood and air spewed from the ragged hole where his larynx had once been. And then, slowly, almost nonchalantly, he closed his eyes and pitched forward onto the dock.

"There! Next to the old man!" A volley of gunfire followed the shouts. Steele looked over just in time to see a line of slugs cratering their way along the dock toward him. There was no time to think. Reflexively he dived into the dark cold waters of the harbor.

CHAPTER TWO

The pain knifed through his knees as he bent down to examine the body. I'm too old to be still doing this, Anatoli Czenek told himself as first his knees, then his back, then the old shoulder injury Beria's men had inflicted during their questioning flared up to remind him of six decades of physical abuse. Sixty years old and still wading through rainstorms looking at corpses. But he was careful to keep his opinions and his pains from his younger colleague. There were those at Polish State Security who believed that sixty years was too old for a man to remain in the field. And the younger men were the most vocal. Kick the old geezers upstairs to a desk and open up the field to new blood.

But he had survived Beria's torture, outlasted the repeated Soviet purges of the Polish government, and outlived most of his detractors. He would survive those who wanted to bring him back to Warsaw and chain him to a desk. He had to. Czenek was honest enough with himself to know that he wouldn't last five minutes as a communist if he had to be trapped behind the same desk, inside the same office the rest of his life. Field men were given extraordinary privileges to travel, and exorbitant freedom to make their own decisions. He needed that. Czenek knew he'd remain a loyal Polish communist only as long as he had the ready opportunity to defect to the West. It was this constant option that held his allegiance. If he thought that option was in jeopardy, he'd waste no time calling the secret phone numbers he had carefully held over the years, landing in a safe house outside London, or maybe in the Virginia countryside, within forty-eight hours.

Czenek knelt on the deck of the *Valkyrie* and examined the body of his fellow agent, Roger Skrentny—a good soldier who followed orders, a nice kid who should've been back home sitting in front of a fire holding hands with the girl he'd married the year before. Czenek shook his head. Such a waste.

"One of the shots went right straight up his groin," Czenek commented in disgust. The younger agent who accompanied him didn't reply. Instead he scanned the water for signs of Steele.

"He can't stay down forever," the younger agent said. "But the damn storm's so loud, he could come up for air anywhere and we wouldn't know it."

"The water temperature's extremely cold," Czenek reminded. "Ten minutes, maybe fifteen and he'll be unconscious. He'll die of hypothermia. All we have to do is make sure he doesn't get out of the water."

The younger agent looked at him skeptically.

"And he probably knows that," Czenek continued.

"So?" the younger agent said.

Czenek looked at the man. Twenty-seven years old, single, gung-ho, a product of Soviet schooling and Soviet indoctrination. Regulations and doctrine hammered in, humanity and humor slashed out. Inwardly Czenek sighed. There were more and more ambitious automatons like him entering the service every year. They were depressing and worthy of contempt. Apparatchik clones. The state was all, and the sad thing, Czenek thought, was that poor suckers like this one believed it and were all the more dangerous for it. The kid would probably file formal charges of antistate activity if he knew Czenek carried a Bible with him on every mission, read it secretly each night, was carrying one in his inside suit pocket at this very moment. Czenek wondered what the kid would be like after thirty-three more years of skulking around stormy docks littered with corpses.

"Get his body," Czenek said pointing at the yellow-wrapped heap on the bow of the boat. That agent had been a mean, evil-tempered subhuman with no redeeming virtues. Czenek felt a twinge of guilt for delighting in the man's death.

"But . . ." The young agent pointed wordlessly at the water.

"Let him swim a bit," Czenek said, half hoping they'd never find the man. They had come for Davidson and they had gotten

Davidson. This professor was just a complication, unless there was something special about him that Warsaw had not briefed them on. Reluctantly, Czenek told himself that they had better get the professor after all. Leaving him alive would be a mark against him, and that would be perhaps all the ammunition it would take for his detractors in Warsaw to fix it so that he wound up chained to a scarred desk with uneven legs and cigarette burns.

"Get your comrade," Czenek told the agent again. "That's an order. We'll place them in the automobile. It's on higher ground and affords us a better look at the harbor. Czenek's eyes swept over the "G" basin at Marina del Rey. The basin was one of six that led off the main channel of this, the largest man-made small craft harbor in the world. The steep poured-concrete seawalls describing the perimeter of the basin drew a rectangle some 600 yards long and 100 yards wide with one narrow end opening onto the main channel and the other closed like a box. The hundreds of sailboats moored in the basin looked like a strange winter forest of pencil-thin trees swaying with the storm's fury.

Docked almost at the box end of the basin, the *Valkyrie*'s mast swayed in unison with the others.

"The tide is out," Czenek said. "The top of the seawall is a good ten feet above the waterline and there's a fence on top of that. The man has to come out on one of the docks if he is to get out of the water at all. He can't swim very far because of the cold.

"Come, we'll put the bodies in the automobile, and then split up and walk each side of the basin area. If the cold water hasn't already taken the professor, he's ours."

Czenek struggled with young Skrentny's body, his fingers cheated of a grip by the rain-slickened plastic of the foul-weather gear. With more than a little satisfaction, he heard the younger agent struggling up on the bow with the other dead agent. Czenek pushed himself harder, managing to slip his hands under Skrentny's armpits and pull him to a sitting position on the cockpit seat. Then, kneeling in front of the body like a supplicant, Czenek let it slump forward over his shoulders.

The pain in his knees staggered him as he stood up with the agent's body across his shoulders. He managed to climb down from the boat and step confidently onto the dock, hiding the pain provoked by the extra weight.

"Do you need some help?" Czenek asked the younger agent, who still had failed to get a grip on the corpse.

"No thank you, Comrade," the younger man replied, surprise on his face, resentment in his voice. Czenek smiled. Such small victories made life bearable. And kept wolf pups like that one off guard.

"Very well," Czenek said evenly. "I will meet you at the automobile." He turned and started up the dock.

As the agent in charge of the operation, Czenek would have to arrange for the disposition of the bodies. He would have liked to take Skrentny's body back for a proper funeral mass but . . . that was a direct route either to an American prison cell, or to a less comfortable one in Poland.

When he reached the rear of their rented Chrysler, Czenek shoved his free hand in the pocket of the foul weather gear, pulled out the keys, and fumbled until he found the correct one. Pain seared through his back as he leaned over and dropped Skrentny's body in the trunk. He removed the agent's sidearm and all of his fake identification. The clothes would offer no clues, having been purchased off the rack from American stores. Pausing, Czenek considered removing the Bible from his pocket and reading an appropriate passage. He thought better of it. The professor was still out there perhaps—alive.

Steele shook uncontrollably as he clung to a concrete piling under the pier. Through the narrow slits between the boats, he had watched the two men carry the bodies of their comrades back up the dock. The tide was too far out for him to be able to see up to the parking lot. The nearest seawall loomed like a giant cliff.

He could see across the basin a little better. The men had split up. The shorter one who walked as if his feet hurt had chosen to patrol the far side of the basin, watching intently for some sign of movement around the docks. The other man, Steele surmised, was somewhere out of sight on this side, doing the same thing.

Fighting drowsiness, Steele weighed his chances of swimming further. He knew it was no use. He had only been able to make it three docks down toward the main channel, diving deep to cross

59

the spaces between piers, pausing to catch his breath in the relative seclusion of the boats.

Now the cold had permeated the deepest parts of his body, driving out even the heat generated by exercise. It was all he could do to cling to the piling and he knew that he either had to climb out and face his assailants or die in the water.

Steele had heard stories about hypothermia, how pleasurable it felt to slip into unconsciousness. It was so comfortable that those who were later revived showed anger toward their rescuers for returning them to the world. He closed his eyes and felt the tension vanish. . . .

The water was warm and Stephanie was at the wheel. They had the large genoa up, and through the slim space between the sail's foot and the deck they could see the island of Salt Cay sliding past on the horizon. Steele took a glance at the compass and the chart draped over his knees. The island of Jost Van Dyke lay ahead in the distance. He leaned his face into the sun and thought of the fresh lobsters and pina coladas at Foxies. He closed his eyes and let the sun's rays bleed through his eyelids. He felt Stephanie's hand in his hair and . . .

Suddenly salt water was choking him. His eyes clouded with muck. He had let go of the pilings! He was sinking. His arms seemed frozen and his legs felt like stiff lifeless appendages, but the told his legs to kick and they obeyed. His head broke the surface and he breathed greedily, trying not to make noise, though it was hard to hear anything above the storm. Steele treaded water for a moment and looked about him, brought back to life by the near drowning. To his right, a rope arced down from the dock and then back up again out of sight. Steele kicked desperately and stretched out for the lowest point of the arc. The tips of his fingers brushed the rope but failed to catch it. Again Steele went under, but this time when his legs propelled him to the surface his hands found the rope easily. He pulled himself upward on the rope and as he did found it was a slack mooring line between the dock and a small powerboat.

Steele continued pulling until his hands grasped the cleat the rope was made fast to. He remained there for a moment, looking around him. The awkward flying bridges and superstructure of a powerboat blocked his view of the near dock. Across the way, the man who limped was just a speck heading away from him.

Steele leveraged himself against the mooring line with one leg and threw the other over the edge of the dock. Straining until the muscles in his shoulders screamed, he heaved against the rope and pulled desperately at the cleat. For one long moment, his body seemed frozen in space, spreadeagled and perfectly taut, and then the next instant he was supine on the dock with the rain pounding at his face. He turned his head and gulped greedily at the sharp wet air, coughing softly.

Slowly, he propped himself up on his elbows and struggled into a sitting position. To his left, on the other side of the basin, the man who limped continued his march away from him.

Steele felt his knees go slack as he rose cautiously to his feet. He waited for the numbness to fade, then moved slowly toward the main part of the pier. Reflexively, his right hand fumbled in the pocket of his robe for his revolver, but all his fingers closed around was a thick wad of thousand-dollar bills. He put the thought of the money and the gun out of his mind and continued ahead.

When he had climbed onto the dock, a large power boat had hidden Steele from view. But now as he made his way up to the bow of the boat and reached the main dock, he could clearly see the fence at the top of the seawall and the buildings beyond it. And just as clearly as he could see, others could see him. Move.

Breaking into a run, Steele made his way rapidly up the dock toward the steep ramp that led to the land. He looked for the other man. What had happened to him? Where was he hiding? As Steele neared the ramp, he paused by the bowsprit of a large ketch and scanned the top of the seawall. No sign of anyone in a yellow rain slicker.

Had the man seen him? Was he up there, just out of sight, waiting for him to walk up the ramp? Steele knew only that he had to move; he had to go up that ramp no matter what was waiting for him. To stay on the dock was to die. He took a long shuddering breath, then started up the ramp's steep incline.

Steele was almost at the top of the ramp when he caught a glimpse of yellow out of the corner of his left eye. He fell quickly to the ramp and lay on his stomach. Options. What were his options? To go up the ramp was to face the man with the gun, to go back down was to face certain death by exposure. He began to crawl upward.

Just short of the top Steele raised his head and saw that the man was standing at the fence along the seawall, looking down at something. At any moment he expected the man to turn around and spot him. How long would the man occupy himself with whatever it was he saw in the water? Steele knew he had to move and move *now.* Summoning the last reserves of his strength he pushed himself up to his feet and burst forward.

Anatoli Czenek felt the water soaking into his boots as he trudged along the top of the seawall, swapping his gaze between the land and the basin below. The American was either dead by now, or an exceptional physical specimen. Czenek stopped and half turned toward the other side. He had violated his own rules by not keeping his agent on the other side in sight at all times. But he was not himself today. Skrentny's death had upset him, and all this running about in foul weather had made his left foot ache badly. He had broken the ankle years ago outside the Austrian village of Alt Aussee, as he and the American, Summers, rushed downhill to a tiny cottage.

It had happened so quickly, the Germans on the lake, Summers's lucky shot with the grenade, the priest at the cottage, the SS officer who shot him. Summers got his bindings on first and started to ski downhill. Czenek hurried to follow. But the American was a better skier and was barreling downhill faster than Czenek should have dared.

But he was young then, and more foolish than many men his age, so he tried to catch up with Summers.

It was the scream that unsettled him. He had almost caught up with Summers when a shriek from the direction of the cottage assaulted his ears with such shocking animal intensity that Czenek lost his concentration and fell. As he lay there holding his shattered foot, Czenek heard the scream again and again, the pitch climbing almost beyond the range of human hearing. He turned his head toward the direction of the cottage but couldn't keep his eyes focused on it. Everything was spinning. The screams continued until they were punctuated by a single gunshot. Czenek crawled the remaining twenty-five yards to the cottage, and the sight he found there was grisly enough still to visit him in his nightmares. Czenek shook his head slowly and wondered how many more years the image would haunt him. He wanted to have an end to it, but yet saw something inevitable in the succession of events that had brought him to this rainswept Los Angeles dock.

Testing the tender ankle gingerly, Czenek started walking back toward the end of the basin when he saw the American stumble awkwardly through the chain-link gate on the other side and bolt for the cars. Nervously, Czenek looked to see where the young agent had stationed himself. To the left of the odd-looking restaurant adjacent to the parking lot, he spotted the familiar yellow slicker.

For some reason, though, the agent failed to pursue the American. Czenek wondered if the professor had somehow managed to injure the man. Czenek ran painfully toward the end of the basin, pulling out his gun as he did.

It was then that it registered. As suddenly as he had begun to run, Czenek stopped and looked back at the agent. He squinted his eyes to make sure, then relaxed.

Replacing his sidearm in its holster, he resumed his walk, slowly.

Steele felt his breath rasping in his chest as he raced toward the cars. He passed the killers' black sedan, then the public rest rooms. He felt his bare feet slapping against the asphalt, and for one instant thought that it was a good sign that feeling had returned to them.

The storm blew at his back. He breezed past his own car—its keys were somewhere aboard the *Valkyrie*—and made for the limousine. No matter what they did to Eric the Hulk, the keys were probably still there, he hoped.

Splashing through an ankle-deep puddle of water, Steele crossed a narrow gutter and cut through a line of anemic shrubbery to the limousine. The sound of his desperate breathing came to him over the storm as he leaned against the hood of the limo, urging his knees not to collapse.

He raised his head to look behind him. Across the basin, the man with the limp ran for a moment, then slowed. The other agent still stood against the fence some forty to fifty yards away.

With a deep breath of decision, Steele pushed away from the hood, stood up shakily, and walked to the driver's door and opened it. The rich warm coppery smells of blood wafted out.

As a rookie, Steele had worked traffic detail and seen mangled bodies, their limbs twisted away, their torsos ripped open, their exposed internal organs. As a homicide detective he had seen the perverted things human beings intentionally did to others. But never had he seen anything as hideous as the sight that greeted him when he opened the driver's door of the limousine.

Davidson's bodyguard sat spreadeagled in the middle of the front seat, his hands and legs bound with a rope that led to doorposts and other parts of the car. The man was completely naked and had been slit expertly from the top of his pubic hair to the breast-bone. His intestines spilled from the slit and coiled on the leather-upholstered seats.

At the sound of the door opening, the butchered body groaned. Eric was still alive. His face, colored slate gray, turned toward him. The eyes opened and after several long seconds filled with sad recognition. The mouth opened, but closed again wordlessly as if the exertion had been too much for him. The eyes closed and the huge man's head lolled back on his shoulders.

Steele felt his skin tingle and tasted the sour acid of fear and nausea. His mouth worked rapidly, like a fish out of water. Finally he willed his eyes away from the horror and with a supreme effort convinced his legs to move. He backed up a step, turned to run and found himself staring at a young man with a silenced machine gun and a victorious smile.

"We've been waiting for you," the young man said in heavily accented English. He looked toward the front seat of the limo. "Eric and I have been waiting for you."

The man wore jeans, a windbreaker over a V-necked sweater, and running shoes. The clothing was soaked and plastered to his skin. His short hair was also soaked and plastered to his skull. He appeared to be in his late twenties, with the sort of lean, angular muscularity associated with a long distance runner. A crazy glint showed in his eyes as if the light were reflecting off something fractured behind them.

Steele backed away from the young man, unable to respond. He felt the cold metal of the limousine pressing against his back as he leaned against it, hoping the icy calm and old instincts that had saved him so many times as a policeman would not fail him this morning. Steele looked desperately around him, his eyes searching for help, for a weapon, for an exit.

The rattling of the machine gun's bolt drew his attention back to the man who stood professionally in front of him, out of Steele's effective reach yet close enough to make running hopeless. "Don't try to escape," the man said as if he'd read Steele's thoughts. "You and I need to have a talk."

Keep him talking, Steele thought, as he measured the odds. The longer he could keep the man talking, the better the chances were that he'd make a mistake.

"A talk like you had with . . . Eric," Steele said, trying not to look at the grim butchery in the front seat.

"If necessary," the man said. Still holding the machine gun steady, the young man plunged his free hand into the pocket of his trousers and withdrew a slingblade knife. With a flick of his wrist the blade made a solid click as it sprang open and locked into place. The young man's eyes shone in the dim gray morning light as he searched Steele's face for signs of fear. The light was brighter now as the storm slacked off.

"Eric wasn't afraid of me either," the young man said evenly. "He didn't want to cooperate." He glanced quickly at the knife and then back at Steele. "I had to . . . convince him." The man pronounced it "conwince" and for an instant Steele almost surrendered to an insane urge to break out laughing. He was half a step removed from hysteria.

Consciously, Steele forced himself to focus on the man, on his words, to divorce his thoughts from the sight of the butchered man, from the cold, from the danger.

"I don't think you'll need to use that," Steele said, pointing at the knife.

"Keep your hands to your side," the man snapped. And then, with a flourish, he folded the knife and stowed it back in the pocket from which it had come. "We'll see if you need that sort of convincing or not in just a minute. Now get inside—in the back."

The thought of getting inside the car with its warm sweet smell of death set Steele's stomach churning harder.

"You must be very good with that knife," Steele said.

"I once wanted to be a doctor," the young man said. "I got very good grades at the university. Then the state showed me how my skills could be put to better use. My university classes taught me how to cut without killing." He glanced quickly toward the slaughtered chauffeur. "And state security taught me how to use it to get answers. You'd be surprised how quickly a person answers your questions when you've shown him his insides, held the pieces in your hands. Even then the strongest sometimes resist. But when they watch you slice the exposed intestines, burn them, wash them with acid, no one can resist. Yes, even with today's mind-altering drugs, it's possible to get false answers. But with my method? I always get the information I need.

"Of course, it takes great skill. Even most surgeons can't cut up a man like that and have him live for more than a couple of hours. Unless I feel generous, this man," he nodded toward Davidson's bodyguard, "will live to see tomorrow. It will seem like a dozen lifetimes to him." He paused for a practiced effect. "Or to you. Now get in to the back of the limousine and stop trying to stall me. I'm a professional and I will not allow you to delay, hoping for a mistake I will not make."

The man moved around toward the rear of the car to cover Steele as he opened the limo's rear door. The warm nauseating smell billowed out.

"If you will look inside, you will see two handcuffs, one fastened to the handhold over the door on the other side and another attached to the front seat brackets. Take your seat and I'll show you how to put them on."

Steele sat down on the blood-soaked upholstery.

"Look on the other side," the man said as he moved closer to keep Steele covered. "You'll see that the free end of each handcuff is open. I want you to attach the upper handcuff to your left wrist, and the lower one to your left ankle." Steele realized that the young man enjoyed his surgical skills and would carve him open regardless of how much he cooperated. "Move it!" the young man barked.

Eric chose that moment to groan. It was a long low complaint of exquisite pain from deep inside his tortured body that grew in pitch and intensity until it expanded and blocked out every thought of Steele's head save that of escape. Steele flew at the door on the opposite side, preferring a bullet to slow death by dissection. The door wouldn't open. Steele smashed frantically at the door, then at the window, cracking it with his fist.

Behind Steele, a burst from the machinegun put a stop to Eric's unholy screaming. Steele recoiled as a yellowish-white blob of the guard's brain smeared the side of his head and splattered against the window. The discrete gunshots flashed white in his mind and connected with the fatigue and the cold. He froze. Then—after a few moments—he heard the killer's voice.

"Put on the cuffs," the man said. His voice was all threat. Steele was trying to calculate how quickly he'd die of the gunshots if he lunged at the killer when he caught a glimpse of a blur so swift that it seemed to segue into the gray morning rain.

An arm appeared from behind the killer and jerked his head backward. Reflexively, the man pulled the trigger on the silenced machine gun. Steele rolled onto the floor of the limo as slugs pounded into the closed door behind him, tracking up into the roof.

Steele looked up and saw the aspiring surgeon's face grow wide with surprise, then pain. Finally the man closed his eyes and his facial muscles went slack.

Struggling up to a sitting position, Steele watched as the young man's body was tossed aside. Through the open door, Steele saw two rain-splattered legs clad in gray slacks, and above them a navy-blue windbreaker. His savior's face was not visible. Steele watched as one of the arms of the windbreaker pulled along folding woodsman's knife from the young man's back. The other hand pulled a cloth handkerchief from the rear pocket of the pants and wiped the blood from the blade. The hands folded the blade, then placed it in a pocket of the windbreaker. A moment later, the man leaned down.

"Steele?" came the voice. "Steele, are you all right?"

Steele looked up into Gerry Anderson's clean-shaven face, and for one insane moment all he could think about was what a lousy backhand the man had shown in Zurich.

CHAPTER THREE

Huge cottonball snowflakes sailed along on the gentle wind that blew through the darkened streets of Zurich. Streetlights reflecting among the snowflakes gave the city the soft, even lighting of a studio portrait photograph.

In the midst of the portrait, maintenance crews clanked discreetly, clearing snow with the methodical zeal the Swiss seem to bring to everything. One of the plows made its third pass of the evening in front of the Schweizerhof Hotel, sweeping close to the curb and dumping snow on the sidewalk. The doorman scurried to fetch his shovel to clear a path for hotel guests who might choose to arrive by taxi or limousine, but few did. Since it was located directly across from Zurich's main train station, the Schweizerhof usually catered to first class train passengers desiring the hotel's convenience.

The lobby was nearly empty save for a couple of elderly women registering at the desk and a group of chain-smoking businessmen who sat around a small cocktail table in the corner sipping *Glühwein* and talking in conspiratorial whispers. David Simon sat next to the front window in such a manner that he could keep the front door, the desk, and the rest of the lobby in his vision without appearing to do so.

Simon's navy pinstriped suit, hand-sewn Italian loafers, and soft-leather attaché case marked him as yet another affluent commercial traveler on whom the hotel's profitability depended. He was a trim, muscular man in his forties with gunmetal gray hair cut short enough to make him appear respectable—respectable enough not to draw attention from the police.

Simon rested his copy of the *Zuricher Zeitung* in his lap and gazed through the window at a group of travelers as they trudged from the station across the *Bahnhofplatz,* looking like a fatigued arctic expedition one step away from having to cook and eat one of their own to survive. He recognized none of them, not from this distance at least.

He glanced at his watch. It was 6:37, early yet. El-Nouty had said between 6:30 and 7:00. You never knew with that man. He could be waiting for you half an hour early or arrive two hours later. It was all part of his method, and this method was why no one had ever caught him.

Simon raised his hand and the lobby porter moved quickly.

"Another cognac, Mein Herr?" the porter asked when he stopped next to Simon's chair. Simon shook his head.

"Armagnac," Simon answered as he leaned back in the chair and pretended interest in his newspaper.

The porter brought the Armagnac a few moments later and Simon nearly forgot the tension between his temples as he sipped the sharp fragrant drink, letting the aroma climb up the back of his throat into his nose. He closed his eyes for just a moment.

When he opened them again, the porter had returned.

"Sorry to disturb you sir, but this just arrived." The porter held a polished silver dish with a sealed envelope sitting perfectly in the middle. "The gentleman who brought it said you'd want to read it immediately."

"Thank you." Simon smiled warmly as he fumbled in his pocket and withdrew a five franc note. The porter accepted the note, thanked Simon, and withdrew to his station between the elevators and the front desk.

Simon looked at the heavy rag-bond envelope for along time without opening it. He didn't want to open it; he only wanted out of the insanity. For nearly three decades now, he had convinced some of the world's most unsavory people that he was actually Palestinian. His dark skin and facial features had made that part easy. It was the plastic surgery to re-create the foreskin that had been painful.

But it had worked. And for the better part of those three decades, he felt it had been worth it. Now he was no longer so sure.

Fortifying himself with another sip of Armagnac, Simon pulled a Swiss Army knife from his pocket and used the large blade to slit the envelope open.

Inside was a train ticket to Vienna. Simon sighed as he folded the knife and shoved it back in his pocket. El-Nouty and his method.

As Simon brought the Armagnac to his lips for another sip, he froze. He took another quick look at the ticket. The train to Vienna left in five minutes. Swallowing the rest of the Armagnac with a single gulp, Simon got up immediately from his chair and, dressed only in his suit, walked quickly into the snow.

The locomotive had just eased forward to take the slack out of the couplings when Simon arrived at the track. As the noisy chain reaction worked its way back to the rear of the train, Simon threw open a door on the rear coach and boarded. He made his way to his assigned compartment in the first class section and took a seat by the window.

The train gathered speed as it left the station and pulled into the forest of rails in the switching yard.

A few minutes later there was a knock at the compartment door. Simon parted the curtains and faced a man in a conductor's uniform. Simon reached for his ticket and the man slid the compartment door open.

"You won't need that," the conductor said quietly. "Not right now."

Simon smiled. The method, he thought, always El-Nouty's method.

The train slid smoothly to a stop as Simon and the conductor approached the exit. Behind him, Simon heard the loudspeaker announce an unavoidable delay due to a switch that had frozen and jammed.

"Such a convenient problem," Simon said to the man as they stepped from the train. The man nodded but showed no expression.

The train had stopped in a vast railyard filled with boxcars and tankers and flatbeds strapped with covered cargo, all waiting to be shuttled onto sidings nestled next to warehouses and manufacturing facilities surrounding the vast conglomeration of tracks.

Simon followed the man around rail cars, under couplings, and across myriad tracks until finally they arrived at a windowless building with concrete walls and metal roll-up doors spaced evenly to conveniently accommodate a string of boxcar doors.

They climbed a short ladder to one of the doors. The conductor rapped on the metal with his fist, creating a sound like chains rattling in an oil drum. Simon didn't like the noise.

He heard the whine of an electric motor at the top of the door and watched as the door rolled upward three or four feet and stopped. He bent low to enter, and as he did, turned to see if his guide was also coming.

What he saw was the conductor heading back toward the Vienna-bound express that waited patiently in the distance.

The door began to close as soon as Simon had entered the shadowy darkness of the warehouse. The overhead lights were extinguished, but a pale blue light from two glass-fronted offices on a mezzanine level painted eerie shadows in the nearly empty space. A lonely stack of boxes, half covered with a plastic tarp, were all that occupied an area half the size of a football field. Simon looked nervously about him.

Voices drifted down from the partially opened door of one of the offices. A drowsy female voice told someone she had no more to say, that she had told them everything. There was a despondency in her voice that spoke louder than the actual words.

The door to that office eventually opened wider, spilling a new shaft of light into the hungry darkness. Moments later, El-Nouty's powerful frame filled the doorway.

"Simon" El-Nouty called down, filling the darkness with deep resonant tones. "Are you down there?" He spoke in Arabic.

"Of course," Simon replied in Arabic. "You know I can never resist one of your invitations."

"Well then, please honor my humble quarters with your presence," El-Nouty responded.

Simon climbed the stairs and walked along a narrow railed platform that ran in front of the two offices. Both had large glass windows to allow their occupants to overlook and supervise the activity on the warehouse floor. As he walked toward El-Nouty,

Simon noted that the first office, the one from which El-Nouty had just stepped, was occupied by two well-dressed men and one extremely attractive woman who sat in a chair with her wrists handcuffed in front of her. She still insisted she had told them everything. They had given her the drugs, she said; they should know that she couldn't lie under their influence.

Simon stared at her, his heart torn by the desperation in her voice. She was a striking woman with along face and high cheekbones. Her hair was swept back from her face and tied at her neck. Her eyes were puffy, either from the drugs or lack of sleep. She began to cry. Simon wanted to turn around and walk away from this whole filthy affair. Instead he extended his hand to greet El-Nouty.

"It's been too long," El-Nouty said as he bent his six-foot, seven-inch frame down to make it easier for the two to exchange formal hugs.

"Far too long," Simon agreed as he followed El-Nouty into the second office. It was a standard industrial quarter in most respects: about eight feet square, institutional green walls, a desk, two chairs, a telephone, and last year's calendar on the wall. What made the room exceptional was the art. Simon's mouth dropped as he looked at one masterpiece after another. There was a Titian propped against the end of the chipped gray metal desk. Against the back wall he caught sight of something that appeared to be a Vermeer sitting on top of a packing crate. Simon stared about him, and from every angle priceless art stared back.

When Simon finally wrestled his attention away from the art, he found El-Nouty standing behind the desk with a smile on his face. He was an elegant man, El-Nouty. Tonight, despite the informality of the setting, he wore a silver-gray double-breasted suit with a striking silk foulard. A full-length coat of some sort of fur—Simon had a hard time telling mink from ermine—hung from the tall Libyan's shoulders like a cape. There were few men in the world who could avoid looking foppish dressed like that, but for El-Nouty the elegant clothes and manner served a vital function: they disguised not only his extreme hatred but also his animal muscularity.

Only by looking into El-Nouty's eyes could one truly sense the depth of his hate, the savage intensity that drove him, unless of course one knew how he had acquired the prosthesis that substituted for his right hand. Nearly four decades ago, two British soldiers had had a bit of fun with a small Bedouin child. They had threatened to cut off the young boy's penis but had settled finally on slicing off his frail hand. The loss of that hand provided the inspiration that eventually changed Mustafa Salem El-Nouty from a malnourished Bedouin youth into one of the world's most dangerous men.

"The art is quite striking," El-Nouty said in his understated manner. "We stumbled across it in our search for a smaller, less beautiful, but incalculably more valuable painting." He paused, as an actor does, for effect. "We didn't find what we were looking for so we took what we found. Stunning works. Wouldn't you agree?"

Simon hesitated. "Decadent Western art," he replied finally, trying to sound disgusted. "If it pleases you, my brother, I will take joy in your happiness. But I simply find it to be the scrawlings of infidels."

In spite of the cold of the unheated warehouse, Simon felt the sweat trickle down his back as El-Nouty dissected him with a look. Finally El-Nouty's face softened into a full smile.

"Now how did I know you would say that?" El-Nouty asked, friendly and sinister at the same time. "It's always comforting to know that the true believers of this world will always remain consistent while the wayward like myself continue to struggle with their demons." He paused. "You're a comfort, do you know that, Simon? A real comfort to me."

Before Simon could answer, El-Nouty dropped the smile and sat in the chair behind the desk. He winced visibly as he settled into the chair.

"The wounds never heal quite as quickly as they did in our youth, do they, my friend?" El-Nouty said, answering Simon's curious look. "In London, three years ago I met a man whom I should have killed." He looked up at the ceiling as if the image of that meeting were painted there. "Instead, he nearly killed me. It was an American named Nathaniel Worthington." Simon was aware of El-Nouty's close scrutiny as he spoke the name.

"The name means nothing to me, my brother," Simon lied. "Should it?"

El-Nouty stared at him for a long time. Then: "No. Worthington is my affair. He has blackened my face, and I must have revenge before I can rest. Many of his bullets found their mark, enough to kill me had not Allah been at my side. I lost a kidney and I must live with a constant pain in my back. I tell you, my brother, that the pain never stops." El-Nouty's voice rose. "But I am glad! Glad for the pain! And do you know why?"

Simon shook his head respectfully.

"Because when I hurt, I remember this Worthington, and since the pain never stops, I will never forget him . . . until he is dead. Then, my brother, then I believe the pain will stop."

Simon had stood awkwardly by the door during El-Nouty's angry soliloquy. For the first time, the tall Arab seemed to sense his visitor's discomfort.

"Forgive me for my lapse in graciousness," El-Nouty said. "Make yourself comfortable." He waved the black kid leather glove that covered his prosthesis at the office's other chair. Simon pulled it to the front of the desk and sat down.

El-Nouty made a show of looking around the room at the art.

"I find much of it impressive," he said finally. "But then, I do not take my ideology so seriously as you."

"I wasn't aware of an ideology," Simon said. El-Nouty smiled broadly.

"Ah, the moral superiority of the true believer," El-Nouty said smiling broadly at Simon. "I envy you. Do you know that?" Simon shook his head. "To be so comforted by the strength of convictions as you are."

Strength of convictions? El-Nouty scoffed inwardly. It was more like insanity. Simon was smarter than the rest, but he was still insane. Insane just like the mad Islamic bombers in Beirut willing to strap themselves with dynamite and walk into a store crowded with Christians and blow themselves up. Straight to Allah. They believed they were God's soldiers and would go straight to heaven for doing His work. Insanity.

They were mostly all Shiite Muslims and they revered the Ayatollah Khomeini as they did Muhammed himself. The only reasons were his reasons; the only methods his methods. If the Ayatollah said they must die to overthrow moderate Islamic countries so he could install pure Islamic rule, then they threw themselves against the enemy, confident in their belief that they would go straight to heaven.

There was no arguing with fanatics, no reasoning, for they were driven by motives they themselves did not understand. And there was no protecting yourself against people willing to die for a cause. The truck bombs that had blown away American marines and embassy personnel in Beirut stood as irrefutable proof of that. All you had to do was convince one of these fanatics that it was God's will and they would do it. No questions.

Simon asked a few questions every now and then. That made him different. That and the fact that he was still alive.

"Lech Walesa is in Vienna," El-Nouty said, abruptly changing the subject. Simon looked at him blankly.

"The Polish Solidarity leader," El-Nouty said, taking Simon's blank stare for nonrecognition.

"Yes," Simon said, trying to keep the impatience from his voice. "I know who he is. But it was my understanding that he wasn't allowed to leave the country."

"So the Polish government has decreed."

"Then . . . how did—"

"Religion is a tremendous force in Poland," El-Nouty began. "As much a force in many circumstances as Islam is to . . . our . . . peoples. In Poland, people are faithful to their country. The Catholic Church, the Roman Catholic Church, smuggled him out of Poland."

"So?" Simon replied.

"So, he's meeting with Cardinal Neils Braun, the archbishop who heads the Catholic Church's Secretariat for NonBelievers. The meeting can only mean trouble for the Polish government, which sees the Church as the biggest stumbling block to a perfect communist state."

"That's been the Russians' attitude for a long time," Simon said. "But I still don't understand what this has to do with me . . . with us."

El-Nouty's sigh filled the tiny office. He slowly shook his head. "You and your precious Palestine. Look," El-Nouty leaned on the desk. "I keep telling you, you must cultivate a more global outlook. Events that affect Palestine can take place almost anywhere in the world . . . , and they involve more than direct armed struggle. Killing the cardinal and his Polish friend, for exmaple, is going to help the cause of your people immeasurably."

"But why?"

"You ask a lot of questions," El-Nouty said. "Sometimes I think you . . ." He broke off. "The KGB has its sources. They say that Lech Walesa and the cardinal will make an agreement that calls for the Church to support Solidarity with money, with an underground railroad . . . in short, to finance Solidarity's resistance to the Polish government.

"This puts the Church into what amounts to a state of war with Poland and, through it, Russia. The Church has been terribly careful to make sure all of its efforts have been well hidden. The Pope knows that neither the Poles nor the Russians would tolerate his intervention if they could prove it. Removing the cardinal and Walesa serves two purposes: first, it deprives their constituencies of leadership, and second, the presence of the two together in Vienna—dead in the streets—would be proof of the Church's covert war on the Polish government. That proof would give the Polish government the excuse it needs to crush the Church there and it would give Russian leaders an opportunity to tighten the screws on the Church in other countries they control. Proof of the conspiracy will prevent a world outcry."

Simon shook his head. "That has little to do with me and my people," he told El-Nouty. "You know I care little for infidels, be they Russian or American. Besides, the Russians are waging war against Muslim peoples. Why should I help them?"

"Look beyond your own borders, Simon," El-Nouty said patiently, a determined teacher to a worthy but slow pupil. "Unless we are strong enough to fight them directly, we have to use the power of the Russians and Americans to our own ends, cooperate with them when it is advantageous for us to do so."

"But you have a much different outlook than I," Simon argued. "You have worked for both the Americans and the Russians. I choose to work with neither."

El-Nouty smiled broadly and shook his head. "We've had this discussion many times before, my stalwart brother. But this time I have two good reasons for you to help me."

"The first?"

"The Church is a great threat to the Russians, particularly in

Poland," El-Nouty began. "They are expending huge amounts of their resources to suppress the Church there, resources that could be put to better use in the Palestinian war against Israel. Killing Braun blunts the church's efforts against communism all over the world, especially Poland. Killing Walesa with him neutralizes the Solidarity movement. The next result of both is to ease demands on the Soviet Union's resources, resources it can then devote to other causes."

Simon looked at El-Nouty thoughtfully. "But how can we be sure that such resources would be forthcoming? What assurances do we have?"

El-Nouty sat up in his chair. "My Russian contacts have promised me that as soon as our task is accomplished we will get all the help we need."

"And the second reason," Simon said, trying to sound as bored as possible.

El-Nouty flashed a triumphant look. "The second reason is by far the best. Though it may seem too much to hope for, I believe Braun's death will give us the information we need to destroy the infidel religions."

"How so?"

"Since the last world war, rumors have circulated in intelligence circles about some religious artifact or icon . . . something . . . that Hitler used to assure Pope Pius XII's silence on Nazi atrocities. There were even some references to this artifact in the interrogation records of several captured SS members who claim to have served at a secret installation in the mountains of southwest Austria.

"Unfortunately, none of the interrogators present realized the importance of these statements, and by the time the transcripts got to someone who recognized their significance, the SS officers were already dead."

El-Nouty turned. From his seat, Simon had to crane his head uncomfortably upward to meet the Arab's gaze. "Interrogation techniques back then," El-Nouty continued, "were not as sophisticated nor as temperate as today." He nodded toward the wall separating them from the handcuffed woman and her two captors. "Back then, she wouldn't have lasted a week. But we learn from past mistakes. This woman's been here for nearly six months and she's still relatively healthy. She'll be here a bit longer, I expect . . . until we decide she has nothing left to tell us.''

"What was this mysterious artifact you just spoke of?'' Simon asked, perhaps too eagerly. El-Nouty looked at him sharply.

"That's not your concern at the moment,'' El-Nouty said. "As always, I will give you only the information you need to know, enough for you to perform your job well, but just enough.'' He saw the disappointed look on Simon's face. "You must remember the lessons we learned together at the Colonel's training camp. What you know can be dangerous to you as well as to me. But I will tell you this: despite the value of all the art collected here''—he looked around the room—"I would exchange it in a minute for a certain painting still missing from the collection. I want you to be looking for it as we go about our task.

"Hitler had a favorite artist of his paint a picture of the secret installation,'' El-Nouty continued. "The picture is called, *The Home of the Lady Our Redeemer,* and it's about this big.'' He indicated with his fingers a rectangle about half the size of a sheet of typing paper. "It's painted in oils on wood, and in the hands of someone who knows the Austrian hills and can match the scene in the painting with the actual spot, it is priceless. It can lead us to the artifact that Hitler used to silence Pope Pius XII. And once we have the artifact in our hands, we can force the leaders of the infidel religions to do our bidding.''

Simon looked puzzled. "But I still don't understand how Braun's death would help us gain information about this 'artifact,' as you call it.''

"Braun is head of an organization that has devoted a large share of its resources to locating the painting and the artifact of which I speak. His organization is headquartered in a heavily guarded mountaintop chalet near Innsbruck, Austria. We've tried many times to penetrate it, but each time have failed. I am confident that in the chaos that will follow Braun's death, the security there will be disorganized enough for us to mount a successful attack on the chalet and obtain from Braun's files the information we need to recover the artifact.''

Simon nodded slowly, trying to absorb the immensity of the Libyan's words.

"Then you're with me?'' El-Nouty asked.

"Yes," Simon agreed, "of course I am. I have been from the beginning. I just like to see you worry a little."

A dark look flashed across El-Nouty's face, burning brightly as it passed his eyes. An instant later, he smiled broadly and laughed.

"A real camel trader. I don't see how anyone could ever doubt that you're the genuine article. No one but a born Arab can connive like you. You'd be a rich man by now if you'd only followed your hallowed father's wishes and become a merchant."

"Perhaps," Simon said, "but he died in the Palestinian camps, along with the rest of my family."

"I know," El-Nouty said sympathetically, "and I admire you for forsaking wealth for justice."

"It's only as it should be," Simon replied with conviction. "I will never rest as long as their deaths remain unavenged. And that won't happen until my people are secure."

El-Nouty nodded his head in assent, then stood up and walked over to a file cabinet in the corner of the office. From the top drawer he withdrew a piece of paper that looked to be a map out on the table in front of him.

"This is Vienna," El-Nouty said to Simon. "This," he said pointing to a spot on the map, "is where we will kill Walesa and Braun."

Brilliant moonlight burned shadows into the snow. In the distance streetlights ringed the hills above Salzburg like a necklace of glowing white pearls. On the platform facing track number four, passengers awaiting the train from Zurich wrapped their coats tightly about them as a sharp crystalline wind slashed at them and sent wastepaper scurrying around their ankles in miniature whirlwinds. They stomped frozen feet and squinted into the blackness beyond the station lights at the glaring eyes of the locomotive as it slowly negotiated the switches and controls in the railyard leading into Salzburg station. They stepped back as the train from Zurich pulled gracefully to a halt.

Even as the brakes hissed clouds of steam, doors began to open all along the train, framing anxious passengers in a hurry to debark. Among them was David Simon, who a few minutes earlier had carefully checked the schedule and noted the ten-minute stop in Salzburg. He stopped from the moving train and made straight for the bank of telephone booths inside the station. Hands shaking, Simon pulled out a handful of coins he'd gotten from the train's night porter and laid them on the narrow wooden shelf beneath the phone. He picked up the receiver and dialed the country code for Israel, the city code for Tel Aviv, and six more digits.

The receiver buzzed in his ear twice and was replaced by a high-pitched tone from a computer. "Four, four, seven, one, three," he spoke into the mouthpiece. The computer tone stopped, replaced by the complicated voice-identification device that recognized his agent-identity code—44713—recorded his voice, and compared it to the voiceprints on file to verify his identity. Once this was established, the computer would make the necessary connections, relays, and forwards to connect him with his case officer, no matter where the man might be. Other circuits in the computer instantly began tracing the origin of the call.

Simon checked his watch. Two minutes had passed. He looked through the glass of the telephone booth's doors at the thin flock of travelers as they wearily made their way from the train. The telephone clicked loudly and he scrambled to plug more coins in before the connection was broken. Come on, he urged silently. El-Nouty had arranged for him to be met in Vienna. If Simon failed to get off the train there, people could lose their lives. People more important than him.

The receiver began to click rapidly in his ear and then rang. On the second ring, Simon heard a sleepy male voice.

"Gold here," the voice answered.

Simon looked at his watch. It had taken less than three minutes for the computer to connect him with Adam Gold, Simon's superior officer and a colonel in the Mossad, the Israeli intelligence service.

"David Simon here, sir."

"Don't you ever sleep, David" Gold said, his voice suddenly clear of sleep. "Where are you? What time is it there?"

"About four in the morning. At the train station in Salzburg," Simon replied. "And I've got to get back on the Vienna train in seven minutes, sir, so if it's all right with you, I'd like to relay some information."

"Of course, the recorder is running," Gold said quickly. "Go ahead."

"El-Nouty is back in action." Simon paused as he heard the sharp intake of breath on the other end of the line. "I met with him just nine hours ago in Zurich. Cardinal Neils Braun and Lech Walesa are meeting in Vienna. El-Nouty intends to assassinate them."

"How the hell . . . No one's supposed to know about that meeting, much less a psychopath like El-Nouty. Who's he working for this time?"

"The KGB and their Polish counterparts," Simon answered. He looked at his watch. Six minutes remained. "You knew about this, sir?"

"We have a very active office in Vienna, as you may know, but that's not important. How do they plan to do it?"

"Tomorrow afternoon," Simon began hurriedly. "Walesa has been staying at the Palace of the Archbishops next to Saint Stephen's Cathedral in the center of the old town—"

"Yes, yes, I know it," Gold interjected. "The place is a fortress. The KGB's tried to remove Braun before. He's president of the Vatican's Secretariat for Non-Believers, which makes him the point man for dealing with the communist countries. How does the KGB think El-Nouty will be able to succeed where they've failed? Braun rides in an armored Mercedes; the Vienna police guard him like a national treasure."

"El-Nouty wants me to help him direct a suicide squad of fanatics from the Islamic Jihad."

"Oh Christ!"

Another minute had passed. Five minutes left.

"El-Nouty said he hand-picked them from the Syrian and Iranian training camps. They're the best and they're all convinced they'll go straight into the arms of Allah for their martyrdom. He said he wants me to help him coordinate the attack."

"Which is?"

"Rocket-propelled grenades to rip open the armored Mercedes, machine guns and fragmentation grenades to finish them off."

"Your role?"

"Attack coordination, then helping El-Nouty make sure none of them survive the attack."

81

"You mean Braun and Walesa?"

"Them and any of the surviving members of the Jihad team."

"Where will you be?"

"Across the street with silenced rifles."

Four minutes left.

"Where will the attack take place?"

"El-Nouty showed me the general area on a map—the northern section of the city—but I still don't have the specifics. Knowing El-Nouty, I won't be given the information until the last possible moment."

"Well, follow through," Gold said. "We'll handle things on our end."

"If you tell the cardinal to alter his plans, my cover will be blown."

"Yes," Gold said flatly.

"Adam?"

"Something else?"

"Yes. In Zurich, on the outskirts along the main train tracks leading south, there's a warehouse full of art treasures and a woman El-Nouty is holding hostage."

As he watched the minute hand sweep around the dial of his watch, Simon relayed the information he had gathered on the art, the missing painting, the woman hostage.

"The only reason she's still alive," Simon said, "is because there's a whole bureaucracy involved . . . the Russians, Poles, and El-Nouty. Nobody wants to step on anybody else's toes by really damaging her. But I don't think that's going to last. A Polish agent is on his way there now, and after he's through, El-Nouty says the woman's dog meat whether she talks or not."

Behind him Simon heard the punctually Swiss train groan and clank as the locomotive began to move forward and take up the slack in its couplings.

"I have to go," he said quickly. "Promise me you'll do something about the girl and the art."

"I don't have enough people to search every warehouse in Zurich, David. There are casualties in every war. We have to accept—"

Simon watched the train slowly gather speed.

"Promise me right now, Adam, or I'll warn El-Nouty off and

you'll never catch him. I'm tired of innocent bystanders getting hurt. I'll start seeing to it that some guilty bystanders get taken out next time."

There was silence on the telephone as the train gathered more speed.

"Find the girl, Adam!"

Simon slammed the receiver down on its cradle and sprinted for the train.

In the apartment in Tel Aviv, Adam Gold flinched as Simon's angry hang-up echoed over the long distance lines. Gold cursed at himself. The man was right. That was the problem. Most intelligence men lose their consciences gradually as the years progress. The years of killing, betraying, and surviving gradually build walls around the finer moral sensibilities. But not Simon. With him, it was just the opposite. Years as a field agent seemed to sharpen his abilities to prick the consciences of the people around him. It had not made him popular with the other agents, who, like Gold, would just as soon not be reminded of what others frequently thought of their line of work.

Gold sighed and turned on the gooseneck reading light next to his bed. He got up and pulled a Stewart plaid flannel robe over his pajamas.

Gold was a patient, perpetually tired man with none of the ramrod stiffness usually associated with colonels in a country's intelligence apparatus. But behind his keenly intelligent eyes, which shone brightly now as they watered under the glare of the lamp's bright light, was a ruthlessness and a fury that overrode his basic decency whenever the security of Israel was in doubt.

He pushed a white button on his telephone twice and then made his way down the darkened hallway of the Spartan quarters that the Mossad maintained for its bachelor agents and visitors. Gold's apartment was one of six on the seventeenth floor of a high rise overlooking the Mediterranean. Two of the apartments were unoccupied at the time and two others contained the personal effects of agents who had been killed. As he passed their doors, Gold wished the service would send around the crews to collect the items. There was something ghostly about their continued presence there.

At the end of the hallway, Gold paused before the door of the sixth, and largest, apartment on the floor. His keen ears heard the steady sonorous breathing of sound sleep. Reluctant to break the silence, Gold stood there for a long moment and thought about the man he was about to awaken.

Gold had first met Nat Worthington only three years ago, although he had heard of the outstanding young American many times from colleagues who had worked with him or who had graduated from the lethal hand-to-hand training sessions he'd conducted for new Mossad agents.

A peculiar young man, Gold thought, as he stood there listening to the breathing. New England blue blood—Nathaniel Everett Lowell Worthington IV was his full name—yet he had chosen to enter the navy and fight in Vietnam when he could just as easily have sat the war out in graduate school. And Worthington had chosen the elite Sea-Air-Land (SEAL) unit of the Navy, a highly trained commando force that made the Green Berets look like a troop of Campfire Girls.

After the war, a restless Worthington signed on with the CIA and found himself once again on the killing end of life. But his unorthodox methods and his steady string of successes made him few friends in an intelligence agency known more for its bureaucracy than its efficiency. He quickly made lethal enemies. Things came to a head in Amsterdam, when an assassin dispatched by Worthington's case officer came up behind him in a public toilet and shoved a knife into his back.

Worthington survived, and retired to nurse his injuries. But the CIA soon needed his unorthodox abilities and methods. They had lost agent after agent trying to kill Mustafa Salem El-Nouty. The Libyan, who enjoyed a personal relationship with Colonel Muammar al-Qaddafi and benefited by his unrestricted support, had grown into a major terrorist, sometimes working with the CIA, sometimes with the KGB, other times hiring himself out to anyone who could command his fee.

The CIA finally convinced Worthington to take on the assignment to kill El-Nouty. What they didn't tell him was that, as soon as El-Nouty was dead, he was slated to become their next target.

Worthington got El-Nouty. The Libyan had gone down in machine gun fire on the steps of the Libyan embassy in London. He had been pulled into the embassy and had not been seen since. And for the better part of two years, most intelligence services assumed he was dead. Worthington meanwhile managed to get wind of his department's plans to kill him and turned to the Mossad for help.

Gold remembered the battered Nat Worthington who turned up in his office more than two years ago. He had shown up with his wife, a Russian defector. Gold arranged for their resettlement to a remote section of New Zealand. There, they had lived a pastoral life for more than two years. Then, just last December, they received a note, a Christmas card of all things, from El-Nouty. El-Nouty had tortured a Mossad agent to death for the address.

That had been nearly a year ago now. Nat and his wife had come to Tel Aviv both for safety and so that Nat could finish the job he had started. They could have no peace until El-Nouty was buried.

It had been a long wait. Nat had used the time to consume refresher training courses available to him at the Mossad centers. His wife, Tania, had started taking ballet classes again. They had all tried to settle into something resembling normalcy. But in a market, on the street, watching a motion picture, like a nagging pain that can be endured but not ignored, El-Nouty was never far from their thoughts.

But now, Gold thought, as he rapped politely on the door, it looked as if David Simon's call might bring the long wait to an end.

"Nat?" Gold called.

Nat's half-whispered name spoke to him across the darkness. He opened his eyes and felt his heart still pounding from the nightmare, the same nightmare that had haunted him for the past few months. Always it was the same, images of him skiing down a long hill, anxious to get home, anxious to see Tania, and then . . . El-Nouty's face looming up in front of him, his eyes burning with hatred, his full lips curled in a triumphant sneer. He looked past El-Nouty to where his cottage had been—the same cottage where Tania had promised she'd be waiting for him—but there was no cottage, nothing left standing. All that remained were charred ruins, smoke-blackened bits of odds and ends still smoldering in the snow.

Nat swallowed and felt his tongue drag across the dry roof of his mouth. Tania stirred in her sleep and nuzzled her face against his chest. He heard the light rapping again. Gently, he disengaged himself from Tania and arranged her head on a pillow. She frowned in her sleep but failed to awaken.

Worthing went to the door in his pajamas. He opened the door and stepped into the hallway, pulling the door shut behind him.

"What's up?" he asked Gold.

"El-Nouty's back in the open."

Worthington felt his heart remember its nightmare pace.

"Where?"

"Zurich. Vienna next. I just took the call."

While they stood there silently weighing the implications, a slice of light appeared at the base of the door leading into the common living room shared by all the apartments. Moments later the door opened, spilling light into the hallway. Gold stole a quick look Worthington and guessed that the man hadn't slept well.

"Colonel?" The long shadow of Gold's attaché climbed the shaft of light from the living room. "I heard the buzzer. What can I do to help?"

Gold turned and walked toward the door. Worthington followed.

"Breakfast please, Abraham," Gold replied. "Another of those outrageous breakfasts our American colleague here likes so much." Gold turned his head and smiled at Nat.

"Yes, sir," Abraham responded. "And for Mrs. Worthington?"

"No thank you," Worthington replied. "We'll let her sleep for a while."

The aide nodded and walked quickly away. In moments, they heard the clash of pans in the kitchen. They followed the sounds without speaking. In the kitchen, they found a pot of fresh coffee waiting. Before going to bed each night, Abraham always filled up the machine with water and freshly ground coffee. The coffee-maker's switch could be tripped from his bedside so coffee would be instantly available in emergencies such as this one.

Gold and Worthington carried steaming mugs into the dining area and stood looking at the blackness that still painted the world. Worthing looked over and noticed that Gold was drinking from his favorite mug, a heavy china affair with a cartoon of Mickey Mouse painted on it.

"Let me tell you about El-Nouty," said Gold as he sat down at the table. Worthington sat down opposite him and listened intently as Gold relayed the contents of David Simon's early morning telephone call.

"The waiting is over," Gold said finally. "Thanks to David Simon."

"Have I met him?" Worthington asked, as he took both their coffee mugs to the kitchen to refill them. "The name doesn't seem to ring a bell."

"I'm surprised," Gold said, taking a sip from his mug. "He's one of our most experienced agents." Gold stared blankly over Worthington's head for an instant. "Of course, that may be why you never met him . . . too busy with projects in the field to come in for training. As with you, life—and death—have been the best teachers."

Worthington nodded. "Tell me about him. I assume I'll be working with him."

Gold nodded slowly as if to thoughts not yet expressed. He opened his mouth to speak, closed it with a wordless sigh, and stared down at the mug where Mickey danced a happy little jig. "I tried to bring him in from the field," Gold said. "He's been out there a long time, and field work is mostly a young man's job." He looked at Worthington for confirmation. Nat nodded.

"But he didn't want to come in," Gold continued. "He said the revenge of his family was all he had to live for."

"The revenge of his family?"

"David Simon's family were farmers," Gold began in a once-upon-a-time voice that said he had told the story before. "They lived on a farm outside Tiberias near the border with Jordan. They were dark-skinned Jews and sometimes suffered from not so subtle forms of discrimination when people assumed they were Arab . . . Palestinians. Despite this, young David was an exceptionally bright and talented student. He absorbed all his teachers threw at him and more. Besides the Hebrew and English taught at the school, the boy taught himself to speak German, French, and—I believe because of his appearance—Arabic. He—"

Gold paused as the door from the kitchen swung open. "I

thought you'd like some hot bread while you're waiting," Abraham said as he set a basket of rolls on the table along with a small tray of butter and preserves.

Nat plucked a roll from the basket, smeared it with butter, and asked Gold to continue.

"Yes, well . . ." Gold looked upward as if the script were written somewhere on the wall above Nat's head. "He . . . he was a fantastic student, and because of his appearance, he had a certain sympathy for Palestinians, an empathy resulting from the treatment he and his family sometimes got from other Jews. It was because of this that he made many Palestinian friends.

"There is a certain element within the Palestinian community that prizes hate. It wants no goodwill between Arabs and Jews. One afternoon after school, while David was visiting one of his Palestinian friends, terrorists slaughtered his family. They had all been horribly mutilated . . . horribly." Gold shuddered, pushing away the plate Abraham had just placed in front of him.

"At the same time, another band of terrorists came looking for David. The Palestinian family hid him in a small root cellar underneath the floor of their house. Ironically the family had also hidden relatives there before when Israeli security forces came looking for illegal aliens.

"Anyway," Gold continued, his voice winding down like a music box, "The family concealed him and wouldn't tell the terrorists where he was. The terrorists machine-gunned them all, even the two-year-old, and left. They did it with Uzis to make it look like a Jewish extremist attack.

"Simon disappeared after that. His teachers, neighbors, other who had known him assumed he had been killed or had run off." Gold's appetite seemed to return. He set his plate back in front of him and began to eat. "He turned up four months later in a Palestinian refugee camp in southern Lebanon. He was looking for the killers of his parents, and his friends. One of our agents in the camp spotted him in the latrine area. Young Simon, unlike most Arabs, had been circumcised. Our agent in the camp sent him to us. The young boy had grown quickly into a man.

"He looked and talked like a Palestinian, but he was a Jew. We couldn't pass up an opportunity like that, especially thirty years ago. So we brought him out with the promise that we'd teach him how to kill and how to locate people worth killing. He agreed.

"He went through some rather painful plastic surgery to have a new foreskin created. We sent him through our training and produced one of the most effective killing machines in the Mossad. Then we sent him back to the camp to make contact with the terrorist groups themselves. He was quickly accepted."

"He's been a double agent for thirty years?" Worthington's voice was incredulous.

Gold nodded. "Three decades of pretending to be a terrorist. That's why I want to bring him in. But he won't come. He won't come." He stared sadly down at his hands. "He won't come in."

Worthington was afraid Gold was about to cry, when the kitchen door saved them. Abraham came bursting through with a fresh pot of coffee.

After they had refilled their cups, Gold spoke, his voice settled and calm once more.

"Make no mistake about it, if El-Nouty succeeds, it'll set off the most vicious round of religious repression and persecution ever seen in the communist world," Gold said. "It'll be Egyptians and Jews . . . Romans and Christians all over again."

Nat ate slowly and looked at him.

"But why do you care so much?" Nat asked, "about the Catholic Church?"

"A lot of reasons," Gold replied. "Because if they can persecute Catholics they can also persecute Jews. But mostly because this isn't a question of religion, but one of politics. This is a political move by the Vatican, and whatever the Poles and Soviets do will be a political move to protect their own turf. But the end result of a success by the Soviets will be suffering and death for anyone who practices religion. And, of course, should the Catholic Church be neutralized as a force for freedom in the countries the Soviets now control, the Russians will have more resources to devote to making trouble in my front yard."

He ate a bit of his bread and washed it down with coffee. "Religion and politics make for a deadly combination where everything suffers—the spiritual as well as the secular. It's a lethal alliance to be sure. You Americans are right to be so careful to keep the two separated. Religion? Of course, for the soul. Politics?

89

Naturally, for the body. But together they spell disaster for body and soul. Of course, there are those in the Israeli government who'd try to bust me down to latrine duty for saying that.'' He tired to muster a smile to make it all sound like a joke, but wound up instead looking like a man with gas.

Enough had been said to occupy a month of thought. They finished breakfast in silence, gazing out the window as the sun tried to spread light over the world. Neither had much faith in its success.

CHAPTER FOUR

The single-story motel squeezed itself into a narrow slab of earth between the patched asphalt of the Pacific Coast Highway and a gullied embankment that sloped steeply down to a fringe of beach. A "Vacancy" sign burned vaguely into the deepening evening, appealing in vain to customers who had mostly taken their travel to Interstate 5, some five miles inland, and their business to the newer chain motels that hugged the interchanges.

The bored desk clerk who had checked in Steele, Anderson, and the rest of the party an hour before sat impassively, watching through bulletproof glass as cars straggled past, their headlights burning small temporary holes in the fabric of darkness. If this night's business was typical, he'd check in a lost traveler who took the wrong exit off I-5, and followed the road too far west and maybe a marine from nearby Camp Pendleton with his girl friend or somebody's wife. Which was all fine with him. After all, he had only four rooms to rent out.

The motel looked like the sort of place local people expected to close or fall into the ocean any day. It seemed to have a steady parade of owners and desk clerks, none of whom ever stayed long enough to get to know anyone locally on a personal level. None of them realized it had had only one owner since the U.S. National Security Agency had bought it in 1963.

The clerk had given Anderson the key to a suite of rooms in the back of the motel facing the ocean. On a calm summer day, the rooms out back had a view of the Pacific from San Onofre to Oceanside, its waves dotted with surfers, fishermen, and sailboats.

But tonight, the remnants of the storm tore at the motel, forcing little sighs and whistles under the door and through cracks around the windows. The curtains Anderson had drawn to keep out the wind swayed gently with each gust.

"Damn it," Steele barked at Anderson, "you had no right. No right at all."

It had been three hours of madness. Over and over the scene played itself just behind Steele's eyes: the inside of the limousine, Davidson's bodyguard moaning in pain on the front seat, the killer's head being jerked backward, the muscles of his face going slack, and then the image of the blood being wiped from the glistening woodsman's knife.

Steele recognized Anderson. But before words could be spoken, hands hustled him out of the limo and into a waiting sedan. Wet, shaking with cold, Steele shivered in the back seat of the sedan as it careened out of the parking lot, Anderson's partner, Gordon Highgate, at the wheel, Anderson beside him.

Highgate drove the sedan south out of Marina del Rey. They stopped at a shopping center near Long Beach where Highgate went inside and emerged half an hour later with a set of dry clothes, a paper sack filled with toiletries, and most importantly, hot coffee. Steele's hands were shaking so badly that Anderson had to hold the coffee for him, feeding him sips as if to a small child who hasn't yet learned to hold a cup.

The car had been silent as Highgate steered it expertly south, staying off the clogged freeways. Steele drank the coffee and dressed himself in the dry clothes, jealously guarding his blood-soaked robe with the thousand dollar bills in the pocket.

For the first forty-five minutes, Steele was content to be alive, dry, and warming up. But as his body warmed, his gratitude turned to suspicion and, finally, anger as Anderson explained that he and Highgate both worked for the National Security Agency.

"That was no accident bumping into you in Zurich," Steele said. He stared silently at Anderson as the auto's tires hissed over the wet streets. "You've been following me ever since I returned from Zurich."

Anderson nodded. "Since the day you walked into the consulate."

"You were using me as bait . . . hoping someone would show

up," Steele said. "Hoping you'd catch the people who came to my boat today."

Anderson nodded again.

"Damnit, man," Steele fumed. "What gives you the right to play God with my life?"

"It's not a question of having a right." Steele heard Anderson's voice behind him now in the motel room. "We've gone over all that. I wish you'd get past your anger so we could discuss things."

"There's nothing to discuss," Steele snapped as he turned from the window to face Anderson, who sat on the foot of the bed. Highgate stood impassively by the door as Steele regarded the doors and windows openly, sizing up his chances of escape. Anderson saw him.

"Don't even think of leaving," Anderson told him. "The building's locked up like a safe. Steel doors, bulletproof windows, filtered air. The door's got an electronic lock on it. Nobody gets out without the desk clerk throwing the right switches in the front office, and he doesn't do that until I give him the code.

"Nobody gets out. Nobody gets in," Anderson said. "We use this place mainly for debriefing defectors who come to Southern California to spy on the aerospace and high-tech industries and decide they like it better here than in Gorky or Gdansk."

Anderson shifted in his seat. "There's really no reason we can't talk about all this . . . about cooperating . . ."

Shaking his head, Steele walked over to face Anderson. "You're really something. You lock me up in what amounts to a jail cell and you expect me to sit around and have a chat?" He shook his head and turned away. "Other people may work like that, Mister Anderson, but not this one. I have nothing to discuss with you, not anymore."

"But we can be a great deal of help to you," Anderson persisted. "You need us to find your wife." Anderson looked at him expectantly.

"You could have told me in Zurich," Steele growled. "We could have worked together then."

"We've been over all this before," Anderson interrupted patiently. "We didn't know then what we know now."

"You could have told me what you knew."

"I couldn't . . ."

"You could have," Steele said angrily. "By every moral principle, you *should* have."

"Yes," Anderson admitted reluctantly, "I should have told you then. I wish I could have, but you wouldn't have believed me. The facts were so strange—they still are, you know—that what we could have told you would have seemed insane. You just wouldn't have believed us."

"What makes you think I will now?" Steele challenged.

Anderson stared off into the middle distances of his thoughts. Finally he sighed.

"There was the matter of security," Anderson said, almost to himself. "I had to have approval, clearance. This was . . . is . . . a classified matter. It takes time to get all the necessary approvals."

"The goddamned fire was no secret." Steele flared up "Stephanie's absence was no secret! Just what was so goddamned fucking classified about things?"

"There's no reason to get blasphemous," Anderson said quietly. "It doesn't help us solve anything."

Steele stared at Anderson incredulously and shook his head.

"Listen, I know you're angry," Anderson began. "You have every right to be. And upset too. But the best way to locate her is for you and me to work together."

Steel shook his head violently.

"We could have done that in Zurich," Steele said as he crossed the room and poured coffee into a plastic cup. He drank a sip. "We could have worked together there, but not anymore. I trusted you then and I was wrong. You don't get a second chance."

"I saved your life," Anderson said. "Doesn't that count for anything?"

"You used me as *bait*. You invaded my privacy, tapped my telephone, followed me everywhere, watched my boat so they could be there to catch them when they arrived . . . whoever *they* are. You seemed to have done such a trustworthy job that just about everybody is dead, almost including me. And for that I should trust you?" Steele shook his head and took another sip of the coffee.

Anderson got up and crossed the room to the coffee table. He reached for a plastic cup and then changed his mind. He tossed the cup on the table and then sagged wearily into a pseudo-Scandinavian chair next to the table. He wiped his face with the palm of his hand and leaned back.

He said: "We didn't put you in danger. Telling you earlier would have been an alarmist thing to do. We had no proof that anyone would ever come after you."

"But they did and I had no warning, no warning at all," Steele said, refusing to be mollified.

"Maybe I should have just let the man cut you open like he did Davidson's chauffeur," Anderson countered.

"Maybe you should have," Steele said quickly. "Because I'm going to be no damn use to you."

Anderson shook his head.

"What will it take?" Anderson said.

"For what?"

Anderson closed his eyes for an instant and grimaced. He took a deep breath and explained audibly.

"What would it take to get you to work with us?" Anderson asked.

Steele shook his head ruefully as he carried his coffee over to the foot of the bed nearest Anderson and sat down facing him.

"You don't understand," Steele said. "I don't trust you. I don't work with anybody I don't trust."

"Mr. Steele, I admire your principles," Anderson said. "But the world can't afford them. We've gotten ourselves involved in something that may affect the stability of the Western world and you just may hold the key. But you want to sit on your cherished principles while the rest of the world goes to hell!"

Steele rolled his eyes as he pushed up from the bed and walked over to the coffee table.

"You're a maniac," Steele said. "You and your friend Gordon there." He filled his plastic cup with coffee. "This isn't the first time I've heard people talk like this.

"Oh we can't afford principles now," Steele mimicked Anderson's voice. "The criminals and crazies have got control. Extraordinary times call for extraordinary people.

"I've heard it all before," Steele said. "In the squad room, on the streets, at muster. I've even thought about it seriously. I've even been tempted to act outside the law in order to enforce what

I thought was justice, but that would have made me a criminal, not a cop. And I believe strongly you can be one or the other, but never both. You're a cop of sorts, Anderson. Maybe you ought to start behaving like one."

Anderson's face reflected the worldwise smile of a whore enduring a Salvation Army lecture.

"Ordinarily, I'd agree with you," Anderson countered. "But the facts in this situation are unique. It's such a strange story that I have trouble believing it."

"Why don't you try out some of the facts on me for starters," Steele said. "Let me see if I can give you a new perspective on things."

"I can't tell you unless you agree not to reveal anything you hear," Anderson said.

"No, you *know* I'm not going to agree to that," Steele said, exasperated. "So why don't you lay down your book of regulations and your threats and your secret classifications for a while and tell me something I might believe?"

A sudden blast of rain slammed against the wall of the motel room and rattled like buckshot. The men fell silent, listening to the fury outside.

"I can tell you the truth," Anderson said finally, "but you may have a hard time believing it." Steele searched the man's wide, open face, looking for signs of deception. If the SOB's lying, Steele thought, he's a damned good actor.

"I'll settle for the truth," Steele said after a pause.

Anderson's head bobbed in grateful acknowledgment. He looked at his feet and chewed on his lower lip. Suddenly Steele saw, not the evil manipulator of moments before, but a thoughtful, professorial man gathering his thoughts.

"My unit of the NSA is assigned to tracking assassins," Anderson said. "We go after the master craftsmen of the business."

"You're the people that got Carlos?"

Anderson nodded. "Of course several other killers have used Carlos's name to claim kills since then, but they all lack the finesse he had." Steele heard a faint regret in Anderson's voice, a mourning for the passing of a worthy adversary.

"Several months ago, we got word that an assassin we thought had been killed was back in action," Anderson continued. "A

Libyan named Mustafa Salem El-Nouty. A powerful and cunning man. Qaddafi treats him like a brother. The Russians use him. So did the United States at one time. Mostly he works for whoever can come up with the outrageous sums he demands. There are plenty of takers."

"You said you thought he was dead?"

Anderson uncrossed his legs and recrossed them. He nodded. "Back in 1980, one of the CIA's best agents—their only really good agent, actually—had a gunfight with El-Nouty in London. El-Nouty was hit several times. He collapsed on the steps of the Libyan embassy and was pulled inside. The CIA's man then disappeared."

"Why?"

"Why did the CIA's man vanish?"

Steele nodded.

"Because he'd made some top-level enemies at the Company who wanted him killed. They tried and failed once. And he got word they would try again as soon as he'd finished his assignment to sanction El-Nouty. So he took off for parts unknown.

"Anyway," Anderson continued, warming to his task, "El-Nouty has now returned to the scene, as fit and dangerous as ever . . . maybe a little slower, but smarter."

"What's he got to do with Stephanie's disappearence?" Steele asked.

"I don't know, really," Anderson said, his voice heavy with regret. "We just know he's somehow connected with some cock-eyed KGB operation involving looted Nazi art and some kind of religious artifact. Our information is sketchy, mostly what we could piece together from intercepted cables and taped telephone conversation. Our sources tell us that the KGB hired El-Nouty to help them and the Polish State Security—those are the guys who almost got you this morning—locate some paintings looted by the Nazi in World War II. Apparently, one of the paintings is supposed to be the key to finding some object that he Nazis used to blackmail the Vatican during the war."

Steele's frown softened. "A painting?" He shifted uncomfortably as he remembered Davidson's words shortly before he was killed.

"Tell me more."

97

"We don't know that much about it," Anderson replied. "It was apparently painted by some obscure artist named Stahl . . . but that's not important. What is important is the fact that there is a secret section within the Curia at the Vatican that has been searching for this religious relic for centuries. We know this because the KGB has their telephones tapped, and we've got the KGB's phones tapped. We know the Curia works through a group called the International Ecumenical Council. We don't know much about them because they have no phones of their own and they only communicate face-to-face at a lodge high in the mountains above Innsbruck, Austria, in a place so inaccessible nobody has yet succeeded in bugging it."

"The Vatican has been a top priority for the KGB ever since John Paul II was elected Pope," volunteered Gordon Highgate. Steele turned and looked at him, still standing by the door, ramrod straight and devoid of expression like a guard at Buckingham Palace. "The Russians want to find a way to neutralize the Vatican's anti-communist influence, particularly in Poland and Latin America. They figure whatever worked for Hitler might work for them." Highgate looked to Anderson. Anderson nodded.

"Until the KGB learned of the secret Vatican task force," Anderson resumed, "they, and everybody else, assumed all of the talk about the blackmail of Pius XII was just one more of the outrageous rumors connected with the Third Reich. I certainly did until I listened to the tapes, looked at the cables. And even though we've only got the faintest notion of what's going on, we know there's something there."

Steele jammed both hands in the pockets of the new pants Anderson had bought for him and leaned against the wall next to the window. "How did Stephanie get caught up in all this?"

"We've been following Davidson—the man who visited you on board your boat—for nearly a week now," Anderson said, "since we'd heard his name mentioned in one of the KGB tapes. He is—was—apparently a wealthy Austrian art collector and had once been a member of the Ecumenical Council. He had tried to buy the art collection in Kreuzlingen that the KGB thinks includes the painting they're after. The KGB, through their Polish counterparts, got to Davidson . . . and you, before we did." Anderson's voice was apologetic.

"Like many wealthy collectors, Davidson used a gallery to negotiate the purchase so as not to drive up the price, which would have happened if the collector's identity were known."

"Jesus," Steele said softly. "The Summers Gallery. Stephanie bought that collection for Davidson, the one at Kreuzlingen."

Anderson nodded sympathetically.

"Does . . . is there anything in your information about where she might be?" Steele asked. Anderson shook his head.

"No," the agent said. "But we hope she's still in Switzerland, and possibly still alive."

Steele nodded faintly to himself. He pushed away from the wall, pulled a corner of the curtains aside, and stared out into the murky storm. The storm's fury mirrored his innermost thoughts. He had to cooperate with them, he decided. There was simply no other alternative. He'd never find her by himself. But he would have to be careful to use without being used. The NSA had a reputation for ruthlessness that a Borgia would be proud of.

"All right," Steele said as he turned away from the window. "I'll work with you."

Anderson smiled. "I thought you'd eventually see the wisdom."

"I have a few conditions, though," Steele said. "I work independently. We share information. I don't want you following me. If the Russians get on to you, I don't want them on my tail too."

Anderson tried to look unperturbed. "If that's the way you want it," he said. "I'd hoped we'd work a bit more closely."

Steele shook his head. "No way."

They locked eyes for along moment, each trying to see past the meaning of what they had told each other.

"What's the religious relic?" Steele asked finally. "What's so devastating it can be used to blackmail the Pope?"

Anderson hesitated. He looked at Highgate, at the ceiling, and finally back at Steele.

"You're not going to believe me," he said finally.

"You've already overused that line today," Steele replied.

The agent nodded. "I don't know what it is exactly." His words seemed to lurch from his mouth as if the thoughts behind them were rutted like a stretch of bad road. "But it's supposed to be irrefutable evidence of a second Messiah . . . a woman."

CHAPTER FIVE

The pain was excruciating. It felt as if someone had rammed a flaming sword up both legs from ankle to hip, skewering his Achilles tendon and hamstring. He wanted to scream.

Instead, he straightened up, took a deep breath, and bent over again, this time placing both palms flat and firmly on the floor. Down, up, down again. Palms flat fifty times. Then the pushups. Seventy-five. Sit-ups, one hundred within two minutes.

David Simon was drenched with sweat when he finished despite the open window admitting the sharp December breezes into his suite at the Ambassador Hotel. He walked over to the window and looked down at the heart of the ancient city of Vienna, the low stone and cobbled buildings dwarfed by the towering spires of Saint Stephen's Church, which rose nearly fifty stories into the sky. Simon stood there, heat rising off his body, and listened to the soft sounds of a city awakening to a snowy morning. It was nearly eight o'clock and the winter sky had the deep violet-black hues that presage dawn. Down below in the streets, pedestrians shuffled softly through the snow. There were no sounds of automobiles from the window, since it faced the central city's network of pedestrian streets. Only the faint scraping of a jet across the sky overhead reminded him that this was the twentieth century, not the nineteenth or even earlier.

It wouldn't really matter, he thought, turning away from the window and heading for the bathroom. Every age has its assassins. He supposed he would have been killing people back then, too.

But the thought failed to depress him this morning—as it had every other morning since he had killed his first human being thirty years ago. This day would be different.

The nightmare had spared him last night, for the first time in thirty years. The nightmare was always a variation of the same theme. He had been assigned to kill an enemy agent, and he succeeded. Only when he turned the body over, he found the face of his mother instead of his enemy. But that dream had failed to disrupt last night's sleep.

He felt young this morning, something he hadn't experienced since he had strangled the Al Fatah assassin as the man had slept on his bedroll in the Negev thirty years ago.

No, he thought as he peeled off his gym shorts, this day would be different.

He slid the glass doors open and leaned in to turned on the water in the shower. As the steam filled the enclosure, he looked at himself in the mirror and finally felt worthy of gazing into this own eyes without shame.

He was a legend among the very few people in the Mossad who knew about him. He was the adolescent who had avenged the brutal deaths of his family and friends.

It was true, most of it. But what he had never told anyone, not even Adam Gold, was that one of the killers involved with the massacre—the one responsible for planning it—had eluded him. Simon tested the shower water with the palm of his hand and then stepped in and closed the glass door.

It wasn't as if he didn't know who the surviving killer was. It wasn't even as if he hadn't had a chance to kill the man. He had had many such opportunities over the past three decades. No, he remembered, as he lathered his hard muscular body, it was because he had been ordered by the Mossad to work with the man. The man was Mustafa Salem El-Nouty.

But today was different. Adam Gold had told him to kill El-Nouty. He would kill El-Nouty and then he would accept Gold's offer to come in out of the cold. Thirty years of seething anger could come to an end. He would have no more nightmares.

Vienna had come to life now, Simon thought, as he leaned his elbows on the stone railing of the observation platform in Saint

Stephen's south tower. The wind at this elevation, nearly four hundred feet, was sharp and cold and penetrating. Simon pulled the neck of his parka tighter. He stood at the north side of the tower and took in the narrow tangle of medieval streets directly below. From the distance, they seemed like an archeologist's reconstruction of an ancient village. Simon lifted his gaze slowly, sweeping along a vista that stretched out to form a monochromatic winter tableau. Through the middle of it all, the Danube slashed across like a dirty brown sash. This morning is was not at all blue.

From the pocket of his parka, Simon pulled the map of Vienna El-Nouty had given him and fought with the breezes as he struggled to unfold it and align it with the terrain that stretched out before his feet. When he finally succeeded, he paid particular attention to the bridges over the Danube. He looked at the map and then at the land and back to the map.

The first of the triple spans he saw to the northeast was the Reichsbrücke. Then his eye followed the river north, past the Brigittenauer Brücke in Bau to the Nordbahnbrücke. Near it, he spotted first the spindly minaret and finally the domed mosque of the Islamic Center.

Simon looked around him—he was still the only person on the platform this early on a cold snowy morning—and when he was satisfied he was alone, pulled a compact pair of binoculars from the deep cargo pocket of his parka. He brought the glasses to his eyes and focused them on the mosque. It had been finished in 1979, paid for mostly by Saudi money donated by Faisal Ben Abdul Aziz. It was a place of worship, a place of study. Its library was one of the finest Islamic collections in the world.

For a moment, Simon was a youth again, fascinated by Islam. His fascination had sufficiently overcome his feelings of guilt to purchase a Koran. He had read the pages over the over, comparing them with teachings from the Torah. The similarities in the teachings awed him more than the differences.

The discovery had led him to read the Christian New Testament, and the Mormon book, and later the holy books of the Hindus and Buddhists. They all seemed the same at their foundations. Only the trappings, the embellishments made by generations of clergy and church officials, seemed to differentiate one from another. It was as if God, having given different peoples different languages, had given them different ways of worshiping. But regardless of whether a house was a *château* in France or a *haus* in Germany or a *casa* in Mexico, it was still the same sort of structure that served the same human purposes. Yahweh, Allah—God was God no matter what men called him.

He had really begun to believe that until one day a group of fanatics who felt they were instruments of Allah's will killed everyone who meant anything to him.

And suddenly he was a young man crouched in the icy Syrian hills, scanning mosques and minarets through a pair of binoculars, warmed only by his hatred for the people and their god who had massacred his family. Below, the imam of the mosque had hidden two of the killers. But Allah wouldn't be able to help them this day.

Life had been simpler then. Just him against the god who had wronged him. Motivations were simple, revenge and success or failure easily measured: kill or be killed. It had grown so different. Invasions of Lebanon, global politics, local politics, internal violence by Ashkenazim against Shepardim, Orthodox against Reformed. There was no unity in the people and no longer a consensus in his own mind.

Simon dragged his attention back across the better part of three decades, and cached the binoculars back in his parka pocket. Slowly he leaned farther out of the stone balustrade and strained to look down into the courtyard of the Palace of the Archbishops. From the tower, it looked just like any other set of snowy rooftops. From the ground, though, it looked just like the papal apartments that faced the square of Saint Peter's in Rome. He knew that from his walk past it this morning.

And from the information fed to him by El-Nouty's man the day before, Simon knew the highest-ranking resident of the palace, Cardinal Neils Braun, wanted to live in the real papal apartments, not an imitation. But so did every other cardinal, he thought.

The Palace of the Archbishops also housed the Vatican's Secretariat for Non-Believers—the Catholic Church's cutting edge for its anti-communist activities. A decade ago, back when people still tried to fool themselves into believing the Soviet Union could be trusted, the secretariat's focus had been on rapprochement, accommodation, negotiation.

But the Russian invasion of Poland, Czechoslavakia, and Afghanistan had shown the world, and the Vatican, that Russians viewed treaties in the same manner that Hitler had: to be used when useful and discarded when convenient.

Braun had been the right man to give the secretariat a new hard line on communism. In the mid-1950s, he had fought with the Hungarian Resistance and had now succeeded in turning the Secretariat for Non-Believers into something just short of an institution for armed resistance against communism. That was one reason he had been placed squarely in El-Nouty's cross hairs.

Braun was also the chairman of a group that called itself the International Ecumenical Council. Composed of twelve members representing Judaism, Islam, and Catholic and Protestant Christianity, the Council had dedicated itself to promoting cooperation among the world's religions.

That too had marked Braun as a target for the religious fanatics of the world, fanatics like the Islamic Jihad who, Simon knew, were at this moment staking out their tactical positions. The Jihad truly frightened him. For decades, Simon had rubbed elbows with the PLO and its members, and their motivations had always been understandable: they wanted a homeland.

But the Jihad? They were beyond understanding. They represented the blackest side of religion, people who gave their unquestioning obedience to their religious leader: the Ayatollah Khomeini. That unquestioning obedience had turned his followers around the world into buttons waiting to be pressed. Mothers loyal to the Jihad were proud to send their twelve-year-old boys out to die for Allah, and the widows of Jihad members who died in suicide missions against the infidels were eager to drive dynamite trucks against the enemies of Islam so they too could sit on the right hand of Allah.

Simon shivered more from his thoughts than from the weather as he turned his attention to the Nordbahnbrücke. This was a high, steel-girdered bridge that carried rail tracks north across the Danube. Simon squinted into the binoculars as his eyes followed the river north to the huge spans of the Floridsdorferbrücke, the auto bridge that Braun and Walesa would soon take. Simon spotted the yellow telephone company van parked just north of the bridge along the shoulder of the Hubertusdamm a little less than a thousand meters northwest of the Islamic Center. El-Nouty's men had stolen the van from the National Post Telephone Telegraph (PTT) just before sunrise. By the time it was reported stolen to the police, the assassins would be dead or gone. And so would Braun.

If El-Nouty was right—and he was rarely wrong—Braun and Walesa would cross the Floridsdorferbrücke in less than an hour, on the way to a meeting at the Islamic Center with a coalition of Islamic leaders concerned with the Soviet Union's continued occupation of an Islamic country—Afghanistan—and its apparent goals of widening its influence in the Islamic world.

From Braun the Islamic leaders were supposed to learn firsthand the lessons of the Polish Solidarity's rebirth. Braun and Walesa had no inkling that one member of the Islamic contingent they were about to meet had already leaked the precise time and nature of their meeting to their Jihad comrades.

Simon steadied his elbows on the stone railing as he fine-focused the binoculars on the PTT van. Through the glare of the windshield, Simon could make out the shadows of two men. He knew there would be two more in the back. Where was the other squad? Simon scanned the north bank of the Danube between the Islamic Center and the bridge. There, in a shadow just beyond the railroad bridge, he spotted the trailer truck parked on the Arbeiterstrandbad just north of where it intersected the Hubertusdamm. A single man lounged behind the wheel. Three more like him would be in the trailer, checking their rocket-propelled grenades and machine guns.

But where was El-Nouty? Simon wondered, as he dissected the landscape with the binoculars. El-Nouty prided himself on rubbing elbows with his troops. He was always there before the fighting started.

The tension in his gut ratcheted a notch tighter. El-Nouty was nowhere to be seen.

Then from directly below, the sounds of voices. Simon looked down and watched as a Mercedes stretch limousine pulled up in front of the Palace of Archbishops. Simon felt his heart catch and then stumble forward.

Quickly, he pulled the portable radio El-Nouty's man had given him out of his parka pocket, and—taking another quick look about the platform to make sure it was deserted—pressed the transmit button and spoke quietly into the mouthpiece:

"The delivery truck has arrived."

Simon felt his palms sweating inside his fur-lined gloves as he waited for the reply.

"We are ready to accept delivery," came the reply.

Hurriedly Simon stuffed the radio back into his pocket and pressed the call button for the elevator. The doors opened immediately.

According to El-Nouty's information, Cardinal Braun was a creature of habit. His limo always pulled up precisely fifteen minutes before he needed it. That quarter of an hour was all the time Simon needed to leave the observation tower, get into his rented Ford Escort, and meet El-Nouty near the Nordbahnbrücke. From a position in the steel girders of the railroad bridge, he and El-Nouty would have a perfect vantage point from which to pick off any survivors of the attack.

Simon almost wore the rented Ford's battery down before the cold engine started. It coughed and sputtered a fog of blue smoke as he backed out of the parking space and pulled onto the Rotensturmstrasse heading toward the Danube Canal. As he made his way around light traffic in the old town, he cursed at his sweating palms. He crossed at the Marianbrücke, and had to pull over to the curb as an entourage of policemen on motorcycles made their way over the narrow bridge. He turned in his seat to watch them as they slowed to a stop behind him in front of Number Two Rotensturmstrasse—the Palace of the Archbishops.

Simon checked the dashboard clock and pressed his foot down on the accelerator, pushing the Ford up to fifty kilometers per hour, fast for streets constructed with horses in mind.

What would be waiting for him there? He wondered. A battalion of Austrian army commandos probably, descending on the assassins with a vengeance, shooting at anyone who looked even remotely connected with the attempt on the cardinal's life—which under the circumstances included him.

But there was no thought of not showing up. El-Nouty was his to kill. He had waited too long for the moment.

The traffic along the Praterstrasse was slow rounding the North Vienna train station, but the Ford was making good time. He would make it to the rendezvous with El-Nouty before Braun and Walesa ever left the Palace.

Simon went over in his mind how he would kill El-Nouty. He would arrive and exchange greetings with the Libyan for the last time. He would smile and mouth the Arab brotherhood platitudes for the last time. Then, when El-Nouty handed him the sniper's rifle, he would swing the muzzle into position, sight in on the PTT truck in the distance, turned toward El-Nouty, compliment him on his wonderful choice of weapons, and then shoot him.

With any luck, he'd be half way to the airport by the time the Austrian commandos commenced to chop the Islamic Jihad's finest to pieces.

He allowed himself a rare smile as he crossed the Danube via the Reichsbrücke. He passed the Vienna International Center, and stopped in a line of traffic waiting to turn left into the center's grounds.

Traffic moved quickly, and he was nearly at the light for his turn when it happened.

The door on the passenger side flew open for an instant, and suddenly El-Nouty was sitting beside him in the little Ford.

"I regret startling you like this, my brother," El-Nouty said, with a gracious smile. "But we must alter our plans."

Simon stared at him wide-eyed for a long moment.

"I . . . you . . . What's happened? Have you called it off?" The blast of an angry horn sounded behind them.

"Why would I do a thing like that?" El-Nouty responded, surprise in his voice. The horn behind them blared again. Simon flipped his middle finger at the driver behind him and floored the Ford's accelerator. The balky little car lurched across oncoming traffic and into the grounds of the International Center.

"Drive on past the center and through the park," El-Nouty ordered in a flat emotionless voice. Simon nodded dully, trying to keep his nerves under control. He thought for a moment of the 9 mm H&K automatic in the waist band holster. But by the time he unzipped his parka and reached for the weapon, El-Nouty would be at his throat. It wasn't supposed to happen like this, he thought, as he drove past the International Center's soaring office towers that aspired to be great and succeeded only in looking like four tall office towers anywhere else in the world.

The road curved around to the left, delineating the gounds of the International Center. They reached the park entrance just off the Hubertusdamm, made a tight circle near the ice-skating rink, and entered the park's main gate.

At least they were heading in the correct direction. El-Nouty must have stashed the rifles at the site beforehand. The sudden appearance at the traffic light, the abrupt change in plans—they were all in El-Nouty's character, Simon told himself, all part of his bizarre method.

El-Nouty's silence were heavily on his nerves, but Simon knew that almost any question he asked now would be the wrong one. So he drove in silence, along a snow-covered lane striped with the snaking treads of the cars before them. Along either side of the lane, deciduous trees shivered naked in the morning breeze, their bare branches looking like someone had taken each tree and up-ended it, leaving the roots to reach into the gray winter sky.

"Head for the tower," El-Nouty said, and pointed at a slender spire that lay to their left, beyond the trees. Simon nodded obediently.

"Why so silent, my brother?" El-Nouty asked. "You're always so full of questions."

Simon shrugged. "I've been trying to heed your advice. For years you've said I ask too many questions, that I shouldn't know. I thought my silence would please you."

El-Nouty made a murmuring sound that Simon couldn't interpret, and fell silent again. They passed only one other car, a park maintenance vehicle, and finally pulled to a halt about fifty meters from the Donauturm. The 827-foot-high needle had a restaurant and cafe at the top that revolved to give a panoramic view of Vienna and its environs. Simon had visited the tower in 1964, the year it had opened, and found the experience both vertiginous and disorienting.

Following El-Nouty's instructions, Simon pulled the car into a space and let the engine idle while the heater struggled against the chill December wind.

"They should put better heaters in these things," El-Nouty said, "if they expect to sell them in these climates." He looked straight ahead, his face impassive.

"Why are we stopping here, Mustafa?" Simon asked. "What's going on?"

El-Nouty didn't answer immediately, but turned his back to the car door to face Simon directly. He looked distinctly uncomfortable in the cramped quarters. El-Nouty was a very tall man and the Ford Escort was a very small car.

"Did I ever tell you how my hand hurts sometimes?" El-Nouty said, waving the black glove on his right hand. "It's not there anymore, but it still hurts. The doctors call it phantom pain. It comes and goes." El-Nouty's gaze was intense. Simon saw the eyes shift, saw flashes of madness behind them.

"I hated the pain most of my life," El-Nouty continued. "It used to wake me up as a child. It interfered with my thoughts as a schoolboy. But I've learned to love the pain. It keeps me alive.

"You see, my brother," El-Nouty's voice grew confessional, "the phantoms visit when my life is in danger. Some people have arthritic joints that ache when the weather's about to change. The hand I no longer have aches when there are jackals about. And the pain I have endured the past few days has been almost unbearable."

Simon felt his insides constrict. He felt the panic clawing up from his belly like a wild caged animal. He fought to remain calm. El-Nouty was fast and strong and deadly and could kill him a dozen times in the instant it would take Simon to get his gun. The thought of opening the door and running flew through his mind but he stifled it. El-Nouty must not get away again, not from the Mossad, but mostly not from him.

"I don't understand," Simon replied finally.

"You will in a moment," El-Nouty replied enigmatically as he turned away from Simon and opened the door. "Follow me." When Simon hesitated, El-Nouty reached over and turned the ignition off. "Come on."

Without bothering to take the keys, Simon opened the door and walked with El-Nouty into the base of the tower.

As the elevator rocketed them upward, the acceleration set his stomach churning. El-Nouty had pressed the button for the observation platform. Forty-five seconds later, the doors parted and they emerged 558 feet above the ground. El-Nouty let Simon walk slightly ahead

109

"Remarkable view from here, don't you think?" El-Nouty said lightly, more a statement than a question. Again, Simon could only nod; he didn't trust his voice.

"Come on around this way," El-Nouty ordered. "I want to show you why we've come here."

They walked clockwise around the platform. Several elderly couples seemed to have propped themselves against the guard rail as they stared downward. A small group of schoolchildren listened half attentively as their teacher, an attractive blonde woman, explained the sights below. Simon caught a boy of seven or eight staring at him. Simon smiled at him. The boy turned around quickly, embarrassed.

A lukewarm relief thawed some of Simon's fear. He was safe for a while. It was not El-Nouty's method to kill where there were people who could identify him. They reached the side of the platform facing the Danube and the old city. The south spire of Saint Stephen's pointed skyward like a rocket ship.

"Take a look down there," El-Nouty said, pointing down at the Danube, his finger describing the area of the Floridsdorferbrücke. "Use your glasses. What do you see?"

Simon unzipped his parka, as if getting comfortable, and then took his binoculars from the one of its pockets.

"Where?" Simon asked. When El-Nouty's gaze had rested on the scene below them, Simon pulled his parka open to make it easier to get to his pistol.

"Down there," El-Nouty said, irritated at having to repeat himself.

Leaning forward, Simon placed his binoculars against the window glass to eliminate the interior reflections. He got an acute sense of déjà vu as he once again focused in on the two squads of Islamic Jihad members, this time from the opposite direction.

"A PTT van by the Floridsdorferbrücke," Simon replied.

"And closer to us?"

"A transport truck," Simon answered, wondering where this was all leading.

"Anything more?"

Simon moved the binoculars about. The streets of Vienna moved past the high-powered binoculars' gaze like microfilm moving too fast through the display machine.

Finally: "A railroad work train coming across the Nordbahn-brücke," Simon said as he watched the boxcar-like vehicle slowly making its way along the tracks. "A single-train car, self-powered."

"A work crew," El-Nouty said. "That's interesting. Anything more?"

"I don't understand." Simon said testily. "What am I supposed to be looking for?"

"I'm not entirely sure," El-Nouty said. "Let's keep looking."

Suddenly an unmarked brown van pulled up next to the PTT van. At the same time, the railroad work car stopped just beyond the Hubertusdamm. Simon watched with dismay as the work car doors opened and spilled out at least a dozen armed men dressed in winter camouflage whites. They scrambled down the embankment and ran for the transport truck.

"Now that is most interesting," El-Nouty said matter-of-factly, as if it were not at all interesting. Simon looked up and saw the tall Libyan train his own binoculars on the scene.

Simon returned his gaze to the drama on the river bank. A sudden firestorm erupted as the commandos reached the transport truck. A split second later, more commandos, identically dressed, spilled from the brown van and swarmed over the yellow PTT truck.

It was a surreal silent film. Simon could see the muzzle flashes from the commandos' machine guns, and he could see their targets jerk and splatter as the slugs ripped through flesh and metal alike. El-Nouty knew. He knew and yet he let his men go through with it.

One commando fell to his knees as a Jihad member managed to get off a burst from his Russian-made Kalashnikov machine gun, its distinctive banana-shaped ammunition clip visible over the distance. The Jihad killer was quickly picked up and danced about by a cross-stitching of machine-gun fire. Simon watched, fascinated, as the man's body swiftly transformed itself into a twisted mass of bloody pulp and sinew.

The commandos withdrew almost simultaneously, and suddenly both the transport truck and the PTT van erupted in flames.

"I believe that's the final act," El-Nouty said, as he placed his hand on Simon's shoulder. "Come. Let's take the elevator up and have something to eat at the restaurant."

Simon tried to swallow, but his tongue dragged across the roof of his mouth.

"What . . ." He hesitated. "What could have gone wrong?" Simon forced himself to look into El-Nouty's eyes.

El-Nouty stared at him for a long moment, like a snake sizing up his prey.

"Loose talk," El-Nouty said finally. "They are proud men, these members of the Jihad, but they don't understand the need for security. They don't understand that there are ears about just waiting to hear what they have to say." El-Nouty guided Simon toward the elevator that would take them upward to the restaurant. "It is hard to understand the need for silence when you have already accepted your own death. It's unfortunate."

"But what about Braun and Walesa?" Simon asked, trying to keep the relief in his heart from flooding into his voice. "We have to stop them. The KGB will be angry."

El-Nouty looked at Simon thoughtfully.

"Perhaps," he said as the elevator doors opened to swallow them. Simon stepped inside first. "But it would not be the first time they were angry with me. Or the last. I have other ways to accomplish their tasks in my own way."

The door to the elevator slid closed and the car shot upward.

"Besides," El-Nouty said, as the elevator came to a halt at the top, "that's my problem to worry about. I'm sure you have your own?"

The cafe was circular with a dim center core composed of restrooms, cash register, souvenir shop, a bank of telephones, and a kitchen. The core was decorated in a medieval style, with suits of armor, swords, battleaxes, and wall hangings of valiant crusaders riding into battle against the hordes of Mohammed. But what was most interesting about the interior was the strip of tables that ran around the core's perimeter like the brim of a hat. The brim moved, giving diners a constantly changing view of the countryside. It also gave some of them seasickness.

The maitre d' seated them in the nearly empty dining section, giving them a clear view of the massacre scene on the banks of the Danube. Police and fire vehicles had surrounded the scene. From

112

the distance, they looked like suckling piglets all struggling to get close enough to feed.

Simon looked at the menu without seeing any of it. His mind raced madly. El-Nouty knew. His story about the phantom pain in his missing hand aside, he had suspected something. He had not been sure enough of himself to call off the operation entirely, but just enough to keep himself at a distance. What did he know? Whom did he suspect? Had there been a leak at Mossad HQ in Tel Aviv? He dismissed the thought. More likely the leak came from within the Austrian government, which had been briefed by Adam Gold. The Austrians depended a great deal on good relations with OPEC, and someone had probably tipped off an oil minister or two, many of whom were indebted to El-Nouty. He had to tell Gold.

"Would you mind if I washed up a bit before we eat?" Simon asked deferentially.

El-Nouty shook his head. "Go ahead. I'll just sit here and watch the efficient Viennese cleanup the mess their commandos have made."

Simon walked as casually as possible up three steps and into the core of the cafe, past the suits of armor with their tarnished swords, past the bank of telephones, and into the men's room.

He made a show of washing his hands incase El-Nouty decided to follow him. He finished, threw the paper towel in the trash receptacle, then waited for several long moments, expecting El-Nouty to come in any second to check on him. But he remained alone.

He felt his heart pounding as he opened the door to the men's room and stepped back into the short hallway that led back to the restaurant lobby. There was still no sign of El-Nouty. Perhaps he was too preoccupied with watching the fire engines and police cars scrape his soldiers off the pavement. But he had to hurry. El-Nouty would quickly notice his absence and come looking for him.

He was alone in the corridor now. The dark wooden paneling and old medieval swords and furnishings seemed to close in on him. Simon felt his hands shake gently as he fumbled in his pocket for the right coins. He quickly checked the local directory for directions on how to connect with an international line, then reached up and plugged a 50-schilling coin into the telephone. The coin slipped from his fingers and rattled loudly as it bounced off the shelf below the telephone and clattered onto the marble floor.

Simon took a deep breath, held it for a moment, then exhaled. He replaced the telephone on its cradle, bent over, and picked up the coin.

The second time, he managed to insert the coin in the telephone without incident. He dialed the area code for Tel Aviv followed by Adam Gold's number. The phone rang once, twice. Simon looked at his watch. He had been gone from the table for nearly five minutes now. With his free right hand, he gingerly touched the H&K automatic in its holster. Maybe, he thought, maybe he should just go back in and shoot El-Nouty now. There were few witnesses to worry about. He could get to the Israeli embassy before the manhunt could begin. From there he would disappear. Yes, he thought, if he couldn't get Gold soon, he'd do that.

The telephone was answered on the sixth ring.

"Yes?" said the voice in the earpiece. Simon recognized Abraham's gentle voice.

"David here," Simon said. "I must speak with Adam immediately."

"One moment please."

Simon tapped his fingers silently on the shelf beneath the telephone. He knew his conversation had been taped and would now be compared with voiceprints.

"David, what is it?" The concern in Nat Worthington's voice carried clearly over the thousands of miles that separated them. "Adam's not here right now. What can I do?"

"It's total mess," Simon told him. "El-Nouty suspected the trap. Said his damned phantom hand told him to stay out of it. We're in the tower cafe in the Danube park watching the Viennese clean up the aftermath."

"I assume you both got away cleanly?" Worthington asked.

"Yes."

"Does El-Nouty suspect you?"

"No," Simon told him. "He laid it all on the Jihad members. Said they probably got to bragging to the wrong ears."

Around the corner from the telephones, El-Nouty stood with his hands clasped behind his back, pretending to look at a tapestry portraying Christian knights heroically slaughtering Islamic savages. He saw a certain synchroneity in the scene. Wasn't he, after all, a great and powerful knight taking vengeance on his natural enemies? The thought gave him comfort.

"The question is, should I shoot him now, here in the restaurant?" Simon asked in a low urgent voice. He looked toward the end of the corridor and saw nothing. "I wouldn't have any trouble getting to the embassy."

El-Nouty looked about him. The maitre d' was engaged in an animated conversation with the only waiter on duty and both were out of sight in a little service alcove with the flatware and coffee urn. With half an ear, he continued to listen to Simon as he reached over and silently pried a tarnished broadsword from the empty grasp of a knight's chain-mail glove.

He hefted the sword in his left hand. It felt right, like an extension of his arm.

"You've got to get the girl out of there," Simon urged. "She's a key to something big, very big."

El-Nouty said softly, "David?"

Simon whirled to face, his hand going for the pistol at his waist. El-Nouty shoved the point of the sword under Simon's breastbone with such force that the blade sliced cleanly through the spinal column and imbedded itself in the dark wooden paneling of the wall.

Simon felt the breath leave his body for the last time. There was no pain, no agony, just a profound sadness as he realized El-Nouty's method had won out again.

The receiver dropped from Simon's hand and clattered against the side of the booth. El-Nouty let go of the sword, but it remained firmly planted in the wall. Simon's lifeless body slid down the blade until the handgrips of the hilt pressed themselves into the front of his shirt. He hung there from the end of the sword, blood dripping darkly onto the floor.

El-Nouty picked up the telephone receiver. "Worthington, is that you?"

There was shocked silence on the line.

"You'd better get a rabbi over here fast if you want to give this man a proper burial."

"El-Nouty, you bastard."

"You've said that before, Nat. How is the farm?"

"You bastard."

"You're lacking in your usual creativity today, Nat," El-Nouty said. "A pity you didn't come here yourself rather than trust Simon to do your errands. It might have made for more excitement."

El-Nouty had to lean over Simon's body to replace the handset on the cradle. He smiled broadly as he walked to the elevator and punched the button for the bottom floor. His missing hand no longer hurt.

CHAPTER SIX

Stephanie lay on the sagging canvas cot and stared at the shadows that draped themselves weakly around the ceiling. The small lamp on the desk still burned, shedding too little light to see clearly by and too much to make sleeping easy. It had burned for as long as they had kept her here, and they had kept her here since the kidnapping. Not only had the light erased day and night from her memory, but the loss of her watch also left her unable to count the minutes and hours. There were no windows to see daylight and dark, no clocks to measure time by. The men even took off their wristwatches before coming in to interrogate her, lest she catch a glimpse. They had also fitted a curtain over the office's large window overlooking the warehouse floor, so that the comings and goings would yield no clues.

Time no longer had meaning. Instead of discrete minutes, hours, days, weeks, time had become elastic, stretching into an endless day that had begun the day the two men walked into the hotel room in Zurich and threatened to kill Derek if she didn't come with them quietly.

How long ago had that been? Right after the kidnapping, they had kept her up with no rest for what seemed like days. She knew several days must have passed because they kept rotating the interrogators.

Then came the men with the drugs. Russians. The drugs they gave her turned time into a crazy taffy dream of half-remembered sleep. She could have spent an hour or a month in that drugged state. There was no way to tell the difference.

But she knew time had passed. The warehouse offices had been air conditioned when they had first brought her here. Now the heat was on. Beyond that it could be October or March. She had one other indication that made her think it might be closer to December or January: her tan lines had almost completely faded. The triangles left by her bikini had nearly disappeared. They usually did by Christmas.

She twisted uneasily under the coarse scratchy blanket. The chain that bound her right wrist to the wall fixture rattled against itself as she turned on her side facing away from the light. The chain was just long enough for her to use the chamber pot at the foot of the cot or to reach the pitcher of water on the table at the cot's head. It wasn't long enough for her to reach the desk in the middle of the office, or the switch of the light that sat on it. There was nothing else in the room worth reaching, for there was nothing else in the room.

The chain, though, was long enough to get entangled in while sleeping. She shifted now, trying to arrange the anemic pillow to support her head. There seemed to be no good positions, just some that were worse then others. The blanket rubbed and prickled at her bare arms and legs. She reached down with her unmanacled hand and tried to pull down over her knees the large man's T-shirt they had brought her to use as a nightgown. Long forgotten was the feel of the silk peignoir she had worn for Derek.

As she lay there, she closed her eyes and tried to remember Derek's face. Already her mind's portrait of him had started to fade like color photograph left out in the sun. Time had washed away the details. She had cried about it the first time she realized his image was fading from her memory. But then an odd thing happened. As quickly as the image of Derek's face faded, her vision of his eyes grew more vivid. Now she could see in his eyes the tiniest details of color and structure, but only the vaguest outlines of his face. It was as if an artist had sketched out a face on his canvas but had painted only the eyes.

The eyes were enough, though. As she lay there thinking about him, she realized they had always been enough, for they truly mirrored the man behind them.

She had learned to watch Derek's eyes as others watch the sky to predict the weather. His eyes had as many moods: they were deep blue when he was lost in thought, gray when he had worked himself to the dropping point, turquoise when he was sad or melancholy, and a deep, almost pure green after they made love.

They had been a brilliant blue that first day in class. She remembered how they dazzled her that day as he strode back and forth in front of the classroom. He lectured with an energetic style that carried him from one side of the classroom to the other, always on the move, never static. He rarely referred to his notes, yet his performance had been cogent, continuous, more a compelling solioquy than a classroom lecture. She couldn't remember what he looked like that day, but she remembered that his eyes seemed to be speaking to her only.

And although her mind couldn't remember the topic of that first day's lecture, her heart recalled the passion with which he delivered it. He was the advocate, the counsel for the defense of his topic. Where others could make the discussion of ethics dry and lifeless, he put modern flesh on the dry rattling bones and dressed it with contemporary dilemmas taken from real life. His enthusiasm gave Socrates and Montaigne and Disraeli a personal meaning to each of his students and made them significant to the ways modern problems could be understood.

She had been taken with how different he was from other faculty members, most of whom seemed to look at teaching as yet another form of mass production. The others seemed bored to distraction and interested only in cramming a premeasured quantity of the same information into each head as it passed by them on the academic assembly line.

Steele's passion and enthusiasm made him seem younger than his colleagues. He was still capable of indignation, she thought, something time seems to leach from most people. And because his enthusiasm and his indignation made him seem younger, it made him more approachable to his students, many of whom turned to him for advice and counsel.

Some of the female members of his classes tried to turn approaches for advice and counsel into direct advances for much more. Stephanie learned that first day that she was not the only woman in the class who was taken with Derek Steele's eyes and manner. And she learned quickly, as did the rest of them, that his passion quickly turned to caution where women were concerned. He did not go out with his students.

At least, he hadn't until Stephanie came along.

She romanced him with endless hours of discussion over countless cups of coffee. Whenever students gathered after class to pursue a topic, she was always there, but never in the background and never as a seductress. If anything, she found herself at odds with him more times than not. She consistently argued with him, and unlike the other students, who hung on his every word, she refused to indulge his ego during those occasional moments when he became too taken with himself.

As Steele later told her, she had a "built-in bullshit detector." She seduced him with her earthy reality and absolute refusal to indulge him.

Her sense of reality and intolerance of the phony and superficial came naturally after spending three years as a fashion coordinator for Scandals, a women's boutique on Beverly Hills' Rodeo Drive. Whereas the rest of the world delved occasionally into the superficial and phony, Rodeo Drive had turned those qualities into major growth industries.

Her job at Scandals had been a profitable and, ultimately, educational way for her to apply her innate sense of color, design, and proportion. As an undergraduate at UCLA, she had spent her time helping to dress women with a great deal of money and no taste—a description that fit ninety percent of the people in the motion picture industry and three out of every four women walking about the sidewalks of Beverly Hills.

There, she polished her manner of dealing directly with the wealthy—as an equal, not as a serf. She found the wealthy, most of them, weary of being catered to. And though she offended some, she quickly developed a devote clientele who came to her because she told them the truth. When they looked awful in the latest fashion from the ragbins, she told them so.

One of her devoted customers was Estelle Summers, an overweight matron married to Richard Summers, owner of a Melrose Avenue art gallery. Stephanie often found herself invited to openings at the gallery, and very quickly, her artistic gifts and experience in dealing with the wealthy brought her a job offer. Less than a year after graduating from UCLA, Stephanie had earned more than $100,000 in commissions, becoming in the process Summers's chief negotiator. It was Summers who had suggested that she go back to UCLA to get her Ph.D. in art history.

She took her first course from Steele during the third and final year of her studies. It was just a lark—something to fill out her course load. The second course in philosophy she took because she had fallen in love with Steele. And she knew Steele had fallen in love with her . . . she had seen it in his eyes.

The memories came flooding back to her now, filling her with a sense of loss that very nearly equaled the pain she had experienced the past four months at the hands of her captors. It was as if her mind, deprived of other stimulation, had taken to amusing itself with replays from its own archives, replays that might have been pleasurable had they not been so incomplete.

She tried to remember his voice or the feel of his hands against her breasts, but he had disappeared, all but his eyes. She felt the tears swelling in her own eyes. She wanted him so. She wondered if he had forgotten what she looked like, too.

No, she consoled herself. He had pictures to freshen the image, to replenish the faded colors. He knew better what she looked like than she did. She hadn't seen a mirror since they had brought her here. Not being able to attend to her physical appearance bothered her for only a short time. Then her fear of not living long enough to ever see Derek extinguished the remains of her vanity.

Stephanie sobbed softly in the artificial twilight of the desk lamp, playing back the images of her captivity. She heard muffled voices beyond the wall, but didn't listen. She had tired at first to listen, but found she only frustrated herself by almost—but not quite ever—understanding what they said. The few times she had understood them, the words frightened and confused her.

She heard a new voice now, one she had never heard before. And while she couldn't understand the words, she thought they carried a tone of kindness.

"I got here as soon as possible," Anatoli Czenek was telling the blocky KGB agent as they stood on the wooden walkway that lead from the warehouse floor to the two mezzanine level offices. Their breaths hung in the chill air like balloons over characters in a cartoon strip. Czenek had arrived in Zurich by a direct flight from Mexico City less than an hour before.

"I understand you had a close call in Los Angeles," the agent said.

Czenek nodded. "I've had closer in my lifetime, but—yes, it was close, too close."

It was closer than Czenek wanted to admit to the other agent . . . or to himself. As soon as he saw the men descending on the limousine, he began to walk slowly away from the waterfront. His walk took him to a busy suburban shopping center with a bank of public telephones outside a large food market. He had been tempted to walk in and browse the aisles.

That was what he liked best about America—its supermarkets. In Poland, there were rationing and shortages. Here there were sixteen kinds of olives—he had counted them once in a store in New York. And bread, aisles and aisles of bread of every shape and description. Americans were such children. They argued with the store manager when the shelves had temporarily run out of their favorite kind of English muffins. The shelves would be bulging with a dozen other brands of muffins, but they had to have a particular brand. A Polish shopper could go a lifetime without ever having seen an English muffin. They were more concerned about getting the last loaf of whatever bread might have come in that day.

But he had resisted a stroll among the olives and muffins and called a taxi instead. The taxi took him to the airport where he bought a one-way ticket to Mexico City. There was no trouble. The passport he was using was a virgin one. He knew there would be no one looking for it.

"Look, I'm anxious to get things wrapped up here," the blocky KGB agent was telling Czenek. "She's tied things up in here for close to six months now." With a tilt of his head, he indicated the office where Stephanie tossed on the cot.

"I understand," Czenek said soothingly. "And your assistance is appreciated. Good work such as yours brings itself to the attention of the right people."

"That's all well and good," the agent said with a thin smile, "but I'm supposed to be running a legitimate shipping firm here. A few more weeks of inactivity and people are going to start asking themselves how I'm surviving. Then they'll start looking into things and wham"—he smacked one fist into the palm of the other hand—"the whole operation will be blown."

"Yes, I see. But I am new to this end of the operation," Czenek said. "I was only given the task of eliminating a related party."

"I understand you let the woman's husband escape," the KGB agent said pointedly.

"Unfortunately, that is so," Czenek replied. "But since the KGB had not been kind enough to inform me of the participation of his wife in this . . . operation, I had no orders to capture, interrogate, or kill him. Perhaps it was a mistake in paperwork, Comrade?"

"Perhaps."

The two men stood silently regarding each other.

Finally Czenek spoke: "Assuming I finish my examination of the woman in the next day or so, how do you plan to . . . dispose of her?"

The agent in charge of the warehouse smiled. He pointed to a row of oil drums huddling in the near darkness beside one of the warehouse doors.

"We fill one of the drums about half full of cement," the agent said, "shove the pieces firmly into it, and then fill the rest of the drum with cement and weld the lit shut. that way it's guaranteed to stay at the bottom of the lake."

Czenek grimly nodded his approval. "You are very thorough, Comrade. Now, shall we speak with the woman?"

The agent in charge nodded, withdrew a key, and unlocked the padlock to Stephanie's cell. He removed the lock and stood to one side.

The scrapes and clunks of the padlock being manipulated shocked Stephanie from her half-sleep. The chain to her wrist rattled as she sat up on the cot and pulled the blanket to her breasts. She felt her heart thrashing, her fingertips tingling with fear as the door opened briskly. Bright lights outside on the landing silhouetted a man of medium height wearing a long greatcoat. He removed his hat as he entered the room.

Stephanie sat up straighter, her back to the wall, and squinted at the man's dark backlit figure. For some reason, he didn't frighten her as the others did. He had a slight stoop, and moved slowly, as if his feet hurt him.

Her feelings were reinforced when he flipped the switch on the wall by the door, illuminating the fluorescent lights overhead. Her freehand flew to shade her eyes from the sudden bright light.

"Good morning, Mrs. Steele," the man said almost apologetically. "I'm sorry to have to disturb your sleep, but I must ask you some questions."

Stephanie watched the man as he crossed the room and pulled the chair out from the desk. He looked at it uncertainly for a moment, then moved away from it and perched himself on the corner of the desk nearest to her. She watched as the agent in charge of the warehouse—she knew him well enough now to know that was his function—stood at the door and observed. In all the time she had been there, the man had never come into the room, but instead stood outside leering at her, as if he didn't trust his self-control at any closer distance.

As her eyes quickly adjusted to the light, she examined the man who had entered. He had a gentle, nonthreatening manner and a face that looked as if it wanted good reason to smile. He held his left hand folded in his right, as some people who carry a pair of gloves do once they've taken them off indoors.

She tried to guess his age, but had a difficult time. The skin of his face and neck was creased and leathery, but it didn't sag under his chin or along his neck. He looked like one of those outdoorsy types whose exposed skin turns to beef jerky early in life and never changes again.

Anatoli Czenek felt a sharp-cornered emptiness in his chest as he looked at Stephanie Steele. Even with the lines from the pillow crossing her cheeks, and her hair tangled from sleep and lack of care, she looked like his Katarina had forty years ago. The watch she had given him declaring her love for him suddenly felt heavy and warm in his pocket.

They both had the same large dark eyes, high cheekbones, and reddish chestnut hair. He looked quickly away from her eyes. Damn! He cursed to himself. This would be difficult. But he would do his job because he must. He would look deeply into her eyes and pretend they were Katarina's in the midst of one of her Alzheimer's rages, when she was a different woman, a woman he had grown to hate because she had displaced the Katarina he loved so much.

Yes, he thought, that was the only way he could do the job he had to do. She would be the woman who took his Katarina away, and he would do his job.

"This shouldn't take long," Czenek heard himself saying, "and won't be too unpleasant if I have your cooperation."

"Does it matter if I cooperate or not?" Stephanie replied. "You'll do what you want, just like the others." Her words sounded harsh to her own ears. "I resisted them at first, but they took what they wanted, raped my mind with their drugs and electricity. Now there's nothing left, nothing left to tell."

Czenek stared at her, trying to organize his thoughts.

He only did his job because people told him to. He tired to remember that, because failing to do so would mean asking questions for which there were no easy answers; it would mean admitting the last forty years had been a mistake. Still, this woman troubled him. He wanted to believe he was different, wanted to believe there were depths to which he would not sink. Yet in a flash he remembered the almost endless procession of atrocities he had inflicted on others in the service of his country.

We're all capable of inflicting great cruelties and violence on each other, he rationalized. Most people in his position would not have the restraint he had exercised. Yes, we are all capable of great cruelties to others, but few people are given the opportunities and encouragement to inflict such cruelties as part of a daily routine. He did not doubt for a moment that he had been kinder than others in his place would have been.

Why, then, did this woman's words trouble him so? What was it she had said: that he was no different from the others . . .

"Perhaps you are right," Czenek said finally. "Perhaps I am no different from the others. But I still have a job to do, and you are the focus of it right now."

"I'm not afraid to die," Stephanie told him. And it was true. She was no longer afraid to die. She would regret it though, because it would mean never seeing Derek again.

"There are worse things than dying," he told her.

"I know," Stephanie replied.

Czenek stood up and walked toward her.

CHAPTER SEVEN

By the time Steele pulled his Volvo to a halt in the driveway of his house in Playa del Rey, the storm clouds had parted sufficiently to catch the last rays of the setting sun. Steele watched as the tiny orb struggled feebly to separate gray sea from gray sky. Gripping the Volvo's wheel tightly, he thought of all the times he and Stephanie had stood side by side, arms around each other, enjoying this view: it had been all the reason they needed to buy the house.

It was a little white two-bedroom bungalow that had been constructed in the late 1930s in a California beach interpretation of art deco. Its original owners had built it as a vacation home and had positioned it at the very edge of a steep bluff that rose more than seventy feet above the beach at its base. On a clear day, Santa Catalina Island seemed to wait just at the end of the driveway. The agent had wanted too much money for it, but they had bought it anyway. It had still been more reasonable than less desirable homes in the trendy sections of Marina del Rey just a couple of miles north.

Steele turned off the ignition of the Volvo and sat immobile for several minutes, listening to the complaints of the blustery wind as it swept up off the ocean, still angry from the storm. Reluctantly, he turned away from the view of the Pacific and looked at the house, their house . . . his house now. The sunset had stained the white stucco a nicotine yellow. Long deep shadows from the tall lithe cedars they had planted in front crawled across the lawn and up the sides of the house. One of the panes in the living room's bay window caught a bright moment of the sun and focused it on his eyes. The scowl on his face intensified as he squinted through the reflection.

The last two days had been insane and he didn't know whether he should be angry or frightened. He had slept the night at the NSA's motel, fighting nightmares and bizarre dreams through a thin exhausting sleep.

The next day, Anderson renewed his efforts to enlist Steele's closer cooperation. Steele remained adamant. He had agreed to share his information with Anderson, but not to work under his supervision. And he had refused the agent's offers of protection, partly because he feared a repeat of the morning's close call, but mostly because he sensed that the offer of protection came more from anderson's desire to keep tabs on him rather than from any concern for his safety.

Steele found himself particularly irritated at the liberties Anderson and his cohorts had taken. Anderson's cleanup crew had arrived at the dock just moments after they had hustled him out of the limousine and raced away from the scene of the killings. The crew had stripped his boat, taken it out to sea, and scuttled it. The items stripped from the boat, Anderson informed him, had been deposited in Steele's garage.

Steele knew that such measures would save him from answering difficult questions. Still, he was miffed that Anderson's people had obviously been able to go through all his belongings on the boat in search of the painting. He wondered if Anderson's men might have had some involvement with the two burglaries that had occurred at his house while he had been living on the boat. Obviously, it had been someone looking for the painting.

He allowed himself an ironic smile as he got out of the car, walked over to the garage door, and opened it. The painting wasn't here and never had been. Before this morning, he hadn't even been aware of its existence, much less where it might be. But he knew now, and he knew it was safe. He didn't intend to let Anderson or anybody else get their hands on it.

Steele surveyed the piles of sailing gear and personal belongings Anderson's people had stacked on the garage floor. It looked like a nautical flea market. His eyes scanned the piles for a moment and came to rest on a small leather-bound volume the size of a thin volume of an encyclopedia. It was the ship's log Stephanie had give him for Christmas three years before. He bent down and picked it up. Drops of rain had raised dark splatters on the cover. A snapshot fell out when he opened the log's cover. He caught it as it cartwheeled to the floor.

He closed the book slowly and stared at the photo in the half darkness. It was a picture of him and Stephanie taken just before the Zurich trip. Doug Denoff, who had been the best man at their wedding, had snapped the shot just as Stephanie had doused him with the hose while they swabbed the *Valkyrie*'s deck following a long weekend sail to Catalina.

Steele felt the hollow void in his chest grow wider as he gazed at the picture. Stephanie had a quiet beauty that didn't advertise itself: it was just simply there, a subtle foreshadowing of the deep beauty that lay beneath the skin. He thought of that day now, how it had been one of those ordinary occasions whose remarkable nature remained undetected until much later. It had been the last time they had gone sailing together. He wished now that he had realized then how special that sail really was.

He looked at the snapshot for another moment and slid it into his windbreaker. For a second he thought he was going to cry, then suddenly he shut the *Valkyrie*'s log and tossed it back on the piles of boat gear. The *Valkyrie* was gone too. He had sailed to Hawaii and back on the *Valkyrie*, had ridden out a Pacific hurricane near Los Cabos, had spent many of his memorable times with Stephanie on the *Valkyrie*. The craft was so intertwined with Stephanie that it seemed almost fitting they were both gone, taken from him by insane men who would stop at nothing in their quest to possess a missing painting by a mediocre Nazi painter.

Steele patted the snapshot in his pocket, turned away from the piles of boat gear, and headed for the door that led from the garage into the kitchen. He thought of Anderson, Davidson, the killers on the dock. They all wanted the painting he had, wanted it badly, and that alone was reason enough for him to keep it away from them . . . for now. It was his only leverage. Stephanie's fate, and his, too, for that matter, were intertwined with the painting. He'd let somebody have it only when he was sure he'd get Stephanie back.

If she's still alive.

She has to be, Steele thought. She has to be.

Steele pushed his way past the door and into the dark kitchen. He closed the door behind him and stood in the deepening darkness for a moment. The heavy staleness of a house shut tight filled his nostrils. A feeble light that filtered in from the dying sunset dusted the edges of the cabinets and counters and reflected weakly off the appliances. He looked at the Cuisinart Stephanie had given him for his birthday the year they were married. He had enjoyed cooking, then . . . for the both of them. Since Stephanie's disappearance, he had taken to eating cold cuts and TV dinners.

Without turning on the light, he made his way from the kitchen, through the dining room, and into the living room. Stephanie's touch was everywhere. There was nowhere he could look that was free from something she had done, some article she had given him, or he her. He closed his eyes for a moment and felt his face wrinkling itself up to cry. His eyes tingled for an instant and then he opened them and wiped at his face with his hand as if he could rub away the sadness. He sniffed once and then walked to the bay window. The spider plant Stephanie had hung there had turned brown from lack of care. He was about to turn away from the window to get the watering can when he saw it. A light-colored Toyota parked on the other side of the street, four houses down.

Keeping his eye on the Toyota and the man who sat behind the wheel, Steele slowly backed into the protective darkness of the living room. The car was familiar. He closed his eyes and tried to place it. In traffic. Definitely in traffic on the drive home from the marina. But somewhere else. Where?

He opened his eyes and stared at the car. He could see only the faintest outlines of the driver's head and shoulders. Then it hit him: he had seen the car parked in the lot at the motel Anderson had taken him to. Anderson had had him shadowed.

It made sense, Steele thought. He would have done the same thing had he been in Anderson's place. It was faintly comforting to know the surveillance was there for now. It might come in handy if he had unexpected visitors. But, he realized, he had to get rid of them for a couple of hours while he retrieved the painting. And he had to lose them without appearing to do so on purpose. He didn't want to make Anderson so suspicious that he would pull him in and question him thoroughly . . . an act Steele knew would mean drug-assisted interrogation. He was safe from that and would retain his freedom as long as Anderson believed Steele didn't know the location of the painting.

It was easy enough to lose a tail, to disappear. But most of the ways he had used before as a cop all looked suspicious. He had to lose the tail naturally. That left out wild auto chases and last minute dashes into elevators. Steele stared into space for several long moments. He thought of slipping away from a basketball game at the Forum—according to the car radio the Lakers were playing somebody tonight. No—too uncertain, and his absence would be easy to notice. Movie theaters and concerts all had the same problems.

He sat on the foot of the bed and stared aimlessly around the room. He rejected staging some sort of emergency blackout at a department store—so he could slip out with the crowds in the dark—as too complicated. It had to be in character. He began listing places he normally went, and places he could be expected to go in his current circumstances.

He sat nearly motionless for the greater part of an hour before a broad smile finally spread across his face.

The University Research Library at UCLA is a massive seven-story monolith set at the northern end of the campus. It was jammed with students when Derek Steele arrived. The students, some of whom recognized and greeted him, scurried purposefully among the brightly lit book stacks, looking like gold miners frantically scratching for mother lodes of information.

Holding his briefcase in his left hand, Steele stepped off the elevator at the fifth level. The briefcase was heavy with the tools, and he paused to swap it to his right hand. He walked over to the plan of the fifth floor and studied it earnestly. He looked at the catalog numbers he had scratched on a yellow pad, then back at the plan again.

Soon, he heard the whirring sounds of the other elevator approaching. It stopped at the fifth floor. Steele still pretended interest in the floor plan as he furtively watched the elevator doors part and disgorge the man from the light Toyota.

He was a tall, thin man in his mid-twenties, well over six feet, with muddy blond hair. He wore thick eyeglasses that magnified his eyes and gave him a surprised expression. He was dressed casually in running shoes, jeans, and a windbreaker over a crew-neck sweater. They all looked newly purchased for the occasion.

The man walked two paces from the elevator and stopped. Steele returned his eyes to the floor plan, glanced at the paper in his hand one last time, and then turned away and walked toward the art history section.

The man had followed him closely but professionally from Playa del Rey to the UCLA campus, and from the parking structure to the library. Steele had been careful to strengthen the pretense, going from one drawer in the card catalog to another, searching for topics in art history, Nazi Germany, Stahl. He was also careful to leave markers in a couple of the drawers so his tail would get a good idea what he was after. He wanted the man to think he was acting like a normal academic, hitting the books before taking action.

In the next hour and a half, Steele pulled books from the shelves, marked them with slips of paper, and carried them down to the photocopy machines on the second floor to duplicate several pages. He filled page after page of his yellow pad with notes, all of which he left in plain view. The stack of photocopied pages grew as did the pile of books on the carrel. He carried his briefcase with him each time, and made a show of pulling out a container full of nickles and dimes for the copy machines. He gave the impression of a serious scholar who carried the little necessities of his profession in the battered leather briefcase.

Over the next hour, Steele carefully built this illusion, leaving his research only long enough to locate some other document. His notes were there, his windbreaker hung over the back of the chair. He wanted Anderson's tail to get used to Steele leaving for varying lengths of time, carrying his briefcase and a stack of books.

It worked. The tail followed Steele down to the Xerox room three times and over to the snack bar at the North Campus Union building once. There he watched Steele drink a cup of coffee and eat a stale doughnut before returning to the stacks. After that, the man sat at a nearby carrel with a book he pretended to read. He was convinced Steele would not leave without the substantial pile of research that had accumulated.

When the tail stopped following him down to the Xerox room,

Steele gradually began to increase the length of time he stayed away.

The words in the book swam beneath Steele's eyes now as he sat at the carrel and tried to time the moment correctly. If it didn't work, Anderson would pull him in and they'd go over him with everything they had. The drugs would make him talk and the NSA crowd would get the painting, and with it the leverage he needed to get Stephanie back.

If she's still alive.

"Damn," Steele muttered under his breath. He wiped at his face and rubbed his closed eyes. The doubts, the fears, the sadness. They ran swiftly like flood waters, just beneath the surface of his thoughts, washing away at the foundations of his resolve. She had to be alive, Steele thought. If she wasn't, he had to be a fool to do anything but turn over the painting to Anderson and his crew.

He opened his eyes and looked at his wristwatch. It was 9:17. The library would be closing in a little less than two hours. He had to get moving; the work had to be finished by the time the library closed.

The tail barely raised his head when Steele got up and walked toward the elevator with his briefcase in one hand and a thick volume marked with a dozen pieces of paper in the other. From the corner of his eye, Steele saw the man look up briefly, and then return his glance to the book spread out on the carrel in front of him.

Steele got out of the elevator on the first floor, and after ditching the book in a return bin, walked out the front of the library and swiftly down the front steps. He made directly for the Northern Campus Union and drew another Styrofoam cupful of coffee. He sat at a table and scanned the door of the union for five full minutes. There was no sign of the tail.

Casually, Steele stood up, picked up his briefcase, and carrying the half-full cup of coffee, left the bright warmth of the North Campus Union and headed south along the broad concrete sidewalk decorated with animated groups of students talking excitedly about papers due, loves lost, parent problems, and other things more metaphysical.

Steele felt old tonight. The world was no longer a place for him to make over. That was for the young.

He stepped quickly now, trying not to appear urgent as he made his way among the twisted shadows of trees, their wintertime skeletons projected on the widewalk by streetlights.

The crowds of students thinned as he approached the main quadrangle of the campus. He resisted the temptation to turn around to see if the tail had finally caught up with him, and turned instead to his left, walking down a short ramp into the basement level of Haines Hall. The door yielded to his push, and Steele walked confidently into the hallway.

The philosophy department was located one floor above. If the tail put in a sudden appearance, Steele would make for his office, pretend to search for some book or file, then return to his carrel at the library.

But despite his fallback plan, Steele felt his hands grow cold from more than just the temperature.

He passed the elevator and then the stairs, and walked toward the unlit end of the corridor.

He stood at that end for several moments, buried in shadow, staring at a plain wooden door with a plain doorknob and a deadbolt lock. He tried his office key in the locks. It didn't work. He hadn't thought it would. The storeroom was seldom used and only Dorothy Mills and Claude Tewles had a key. That was why he had brought along the briefcase filled with the lockpicks and tools he hadn't used since his days with the LAPD.

He set the briefcase down on the floor and snapped open the hasps. Fumbling around in the dimness, Steele pulled out a set of lockpicks that folded into a handle like a pocket knife. It had been years since he had last used the lockpicks, so he set the work on the easiest lock—the one in the doorknob—first.

His rusty fingers manipulated the tumblers clumsily at first, but after a few minutes began to remember their old reflexes. In the old days he'd have picked a lock like this one in seconds. The lock and knob rattled as he worked in the dimness. Finally it yielded with a satisfying clack.

Steele paused a moment before setting to work on the dead bolt. He reached up with his right hand to sweep a strand of hair off his forehead. His fingers came back wet with perspiration, and abruptly he was aware of perspiration on his upper lip and the cold, damp spots under his arms.

After taking a deep breath, Steele drew his face close to the deadbolt and studied it. He leaned down and pulled a small pen-light flashlight from his briefcase. The extra light enabled him to get a look at the markings and the construction. The deadbolt was of reasonably cheap design, its only purpose to block entry to a room that contained old books, obsolete equipment, extra chairs, complete sets of Claude Tewles's *National Geographic* dating to 1946, Derek Steele's forwarded mail and newspapers that were too voluminous to stack on his desk, and a painting of inestimable worth.

As he pondered the attack on the deadbolt, voices drifted down the stairs. Steele turned out the flashlight and froze. The voices grew louder, a man's and woman's. Moments later, he heard the light clack of a woman's heels and then the softer, heavier tread of a man's feet as the couple started toward the basement. Hurriedly, Steele gathered his tools and briefcase and made his way into the farthest shadow under the stairs.

The couple's words grew more distinct as they neared the bottom. Her roommate was tired of leaving so they could use her apartment. Why didn't he move out of the fraternity house and get his own apartment? All they needed was a quiet, dark, comfortable place, he said, maybe there was an office open in the building. Steele thought he recognized the male voice as that of one of his students. The couple reached the bottom of the stairs and continued their discussion. She thought the idea of furtive sex in offices that had accidentally been left unlocked was degrading and unromantic. The male voice, which had sounded so much like a man's at first, gradually degenerated into an adolescent whine. Steele definitely recognized the male voice now. He had heard the same whine many times before. He identified it as belonging to a below-average student of his who was headed for academic suspension.

The couple continued their bartering at the foot of the stairs.

Go away, Steele thought, as he looked at the luminous dial on his watch. Time was creeping fast. It was already past 10 P.M. Anderson's man wouldn't wait forever.

And still they bickered and bargained the future for a few minutes of passion. From what Steele could tell, she was getting the best of the bargain. She was even sliping in references to marriage. In his fever, the boy was agreeing to things he would later try unsuccessfully to deny. His concessions made her more agreeable to his suggestions.

"Over here," Steele heard him say. "There's a storage room under the stairs that they sometimes leave open. There's even a couch inside."

Steele's insides went cold. There was no way they could avoid seeing him.

"You seem to know a lot about it." Her words were frostbitten around the edges. "Do you bring your dates here often?"

The boy stammered. "No . . . no I—It's just—the storeroom belongs to the philosophy department. I helped them carry some things down here once, that's all. I've never brought anyone here before, honest."

There was a long silence. Finally, Steele heard her laugh. Beneath the girlish giggle was the carbon steel sound of victory.

And before Steele had time to think more about it, the couple stepped into the deep shadows beneath the stairs and were quickly face-to-face with him. The boy had one hand around her waist and another slipped inside her blouse.

She gave a quick high cry of surprise and jumped back as she covered her mouth. The boy's face looked like a motion picture running full ahead fast: fear, embarrassment, recognition, and back to fear. Both their faces white and drained of blood reflected the dim light like twin moons.

No one said anything for what seemed like eons. Steele's insides churned. On the one hand, he was a member of the faculty and had the rank and authority. As a member of the philosophy department, he also had a valid reason to be there in the storeroom. On the other hand, he hadn't wanted to be discovered and had skulked there in the darkness listening to their very private conversation.

"Professor—" The boy spoke first, but the words seemed to stick in his throat.

"Good evening," Steele said awkwardly. The words were inane but they were all he could think to say.

Suddenly the boy began to speak furiously, making excuses that compounded his embarrassment rather than easing it. His companion's cooler feline instincts prevailed. She told him quietly to shut up and pulled him back toward the lighted portion of the corridor.

"Good evening professor," she said politely, "It was . . . interesting bumping into you."

As their footsteps faded in to the distance of the far end of the corridor and finally disappeared, Steele wondered if the boy had any idea just how far over his head he had gotten.

When he heard the door close at the end of the corridor, Steele left his briefcase in the deepest part of the shadows and set to work on the deadbolt. Despite its complexity, it yielded to his ministrations in little more than a minute.

He replaced the lockpicks in the briefcase and opened the door. There was movement in the darkness, frantic scurrying. The light from the corridor failed to penetrate the gloom. Steele reached inside the door for the light switch, but it threw no light when he flicked it. The bulb had apparently burned out. That was going to make Claude angry. On occasion he liked to get away from things by coming down here, sitting on the old sofa, and eating sandwiches constructed of unusual fillings and materials. Pulling his flashlight from his windbreaker pocket, Steele stepped through the threshold of the room. He heard a pattering, a series of scratchings, and a constant rustling.

He turned on the flashlight. The first image the light revealed was remarkable chaos. Someone had scrambled the contents of the room. Furniture was overturned, the contents of shelves swept onto the floor. Over it all was strewn a layer of paper. Someone had opened every piece of his mail that Dorothy Mills had so carefully stored here for him.

His heart suddenly grew so heavy that he felt as if it would rip itself from him chest. They must have found the painting. It should have been part of the large packet of materials the Eden au Lac Hotel had forwarded to him . . . the contents of their hotel safe deposit box that he had forgotten to empty on checking out. His leverage was gone, and with it, his hope for getting Stephanie back.

Steele idly swept the room with the flashlight's beam as he stood there in stunned silence. A moment later the light revealed a scene so horrible that even the worst moments of his police carreer had left him unprepared.

Claude Tewles slumped in the far corner of the room, a single red bullet hole puckering the middle of his forehead like a third eye. On his shoulder a large brown rat was burying its snout in Claude's neck. The rat turned toward Steele and stared arrogantly back, blinking eyes that shone red in the flashlight's glare.

Steele stood there for along moment, completely paralyzed. As he watched in horror, another rat emerged from the cuff of Claude's trouser, his snout glistening with blood. Steele leaned down to pick up something to throw at the rats when something warm and furry launched itself across the side of his face.

He lost his breath in an involuntary gasp, swatting the dark furry thing in a blind panic. A second later, Steele heard it thump against the far wall. With shaking hands, he trained his flashlight on the area, catching a glimpse of the rat as it lay stunned. It revived quickly and scurried away.

Steele fought the hysteria that rose in his chest and clutched at his neck like an unseen hand. Frantically, he swept the flashlight's beam about the room until he found what he wanted. Trying to ignore the wet biting sounds made by the rats in the darkness, Steele made his way to the near corner of the storeroom and grabbed a wooden-handled broom.

In a frenzy of anger and frustration bordering on tears, he swung the broom at the rats, clubbing them away from Claude's body. The claustrophobic windowless room grew thick with panicked pattering and scratching and a steady high-pitched chorus of indistinguishable screeches. Steele continued to sweep at the area around Claude's body long after the last of the rodents had fled into the hallway.

He dropped the broom and knelt down beside Tewles, reaching out his right hand and gingerly touching Claude's shoulder with the backs of his fingers. The body was still substantially above room temperature. He hadn't been dead long. Steele stood up and played the light around Claude's body. He hand't been beaten by his assailants. The only damage other than the large-caliber wound in his forehead had been done by the rats.

Unconsciously, Steele backed his way toward the door to the hallway. The sounds of shallow, panicked breathing filled his head, and he had to look around him before he realized the sounds were his own.

Stepping from the storeroom with its sweet sickly smells of blood and death, Steele stood motionless in the darkness, his back pressed against the cool concrete wall. He willed his knees not to collapse as he struggled to organize his thoughts.

The chain of events came gradually. Someone had learned of his mail being stored there. Who? Not Anderson's people, he thought; they would have mentioned it to him. There would have been no reason to have him followed. They'd have the painting by now. It had to have been the same people who attacked his boat. But how? How had they learned? Steele thought for a moment, and the conversations he had had that morning with both Claude and Dorothy Mills came back to him. They had both mentioned the mail and the storeroom. Someone must have tapped his telephone and learned where his mail had been stored. They had broken into the room just as he had. Claude had probably decided to make good on his threat to remove all the mail and had disturbed them in the act of going through it all. And they had killed him for that.

Steele felt the nausea only instants before the vomit filled his throat. He bent over and retched violently. He heaved until nothing more emerged, then wiped at his mouth and lurched over to his briefcase.

Somehow, he managed to get the briefcase closed and make his way to the men's room on the second floor without being seen. He plugged a sink with a wad of paper towels and ran it full of cold water. Repeatedly he immersed his face. The cold wet shock gradually soaked the nausea away, and he stood there, eyes closed, trying to breathe normally while his heart experimented with a slower pounding.

Gradually, rational thoughts crept back into his mind. He had to call the police and report Claude's murder. He had to call someone before the rats returned. There was no question of getting involved now, he thought, as he turned toward the door and left the men's room. Before this, there had been a compelling reason to avoid entanglements with the law. A lengthy investigation of the murders at the boat would have cast suspicion on him, delaying his search for the painting and for Stephanie.

But the painting was gone now, he thought, as he unsteadily made his way toward the philosophy department offices. The painting was gone, and with it, his only leverage. He had to turn things over to people better equipped to investigate. He leaned on the wall beside the departmental office door and fumbled for his keys. At least they'd believe him now, he thought, as he searched for the right key. There would be nothing of the skeptical chiding he had received in Zurich.

Steele unlocked the door, pushed in open, and turned on the light switch in the outer reception area. The fluorescnet lights flickered for a moment before casting their bluish illumination over Dorothy Mills's battered wooden desk and the scarred wooden chairs that lined the wall opposite it.

He turned quickly to the right and made his way down a short dark hallway to his office. He unlocked the door and made his way into the standard closet-sized quarters allotted to faculty members. The bureaucracy in Murphy Hall comforted themselves with thick carpeting and executive trappings, but those who did the actual business of the university settled for war surplus furnishings wedged into claustrophobic corners. His eyes fell on a sampler behind his gray metal desk. Stephanie had made it for him.

Those who can, do.
Those who can't, teach.
And those who can't teach become administrators.

The words were an expression of his own thoughts, and as such, had made him very unpopular with the UCLA administration. Truth was always painful.

Steele settled himself behind his desk and picked up the telephone to call the police, when an envelope with his name on it caught his attention. It bore Dorothy Mills's handwriting and had been taped to the shade of his desk lamp to catch his eye.

He replaced the phone on its cradle and peeled the envelope from the lampshade.

"Claude has been quite angry with you," the note began. "I realize how shocked you've been with Stephanie's disappearance. And I know you've really not been yourself. Neither has Claude. I was afraid he might do something precipitious with your mail,

139

so this morning after we talked I went down to the storeroom and sorted out any letters or parcels that seemed important. I've stored them in my filing cabinet, in the bottom drawer, at the very back. The key to the cabinet is enclosed.''

The note was signed ''D.''

Steele eagerly grabbed the key from the envelope. He got up so quickly that his chair tumbled over backward and clattered to the floor. With thoughts of Claude Tewles momentarily forgotten, Steele rushed to Dorothy Mills's desk. The two-drawer metal filing cabinet rested behind it.

The screams began as he sat down in Dorothy's chair and bent over to insert the key in the filing cabinet lock.

First a female voice. It began as a high scream of surprise and quickly deepened to thick shrieks of terror. Then the male voice. More a shout than a scream. And then the female voice again, quivering now, climbing higher, each note a step closer to hysteria.

Steele recognized the voices from minutes before. The couple had returned, desperate, he assumed, for a place to consummate their bargain. He had not relocked the door, and they had quickly found Claude Tewles's body.

The girl continued to scream. The volume seemed to be growing louder, either through sheer lung power, or because they were coming up the stairs.

Steele jammed the key into the lock. He had to hurry. The philosophy department office was the first one at the top of the stairs. They'd see the light and want to use the telephone to call the police; he'd never get back to the library in time. Everything still hinged on Anderson's tail suspecting nothing.

The cabinet opened easily. Steele slid the bottom drawer out and immediately spotted the pile of mail and parcels Dorothy had promised.

He grabbed it.

Oblivious to the screams, Steele sorted frantically through the mail. His hands quickly found what they were looking for: a parcel the size of a shirt box wrapped in brown paper with the Eden au Lac's return address. The wrapping yielded easily to Steele's determined fingers. He discarded the hardboard protector and bubbled plastic foam and found himself looking at a painting of an alpine meadow. "The Home of the Lady Our Redeemer" was printed on the back of the frame. He rewrapped the painting in its protective coverings, took it and the rest of the mail back to his office, then tucked the whole lot into his briefcase and headed for the door.

As he stepped into the corridor, Steele heard footsteps on the stairway and the sounds of the boy trying to comfort the girl whose steel-reinforced composure had finally shattered. Steele tucked the briefcase under his arm and ran from the building.

CHAPTER EIGHT

The Nockspitze is a ragged splinter of granite rising some eight thousand feet above sea level in the Austrian Tyrol southwest of Innsbruck. It's an inhospitable mountain: cold, steep, bereft of trees, and inaccessible to all but birds, skilled rock climbers, and those fortunate enough to ride in the private cable gondola that travels to the massive chalet perched just below the mountain's summit.

The chalet had originally been built as a guest house in 1921 by an Austrian innkeeper who had hoped to lure skiers up from the slopes. It had twenty-five guest rooms, all with their own baths and fireplaces, and a dining room situated in a soaring A-frame wing that cantilevered out over the precipitous cliffsides.

By the very isolation that made the inn attractive also served as a barrier to its success. Transporting guests to the inn required a lengthy trip up winding switchback roads from Innsbruck to the tiny cable car station at the mountain's base. In those days, unpaved roads made automobile travel impossible, so the journey had to be made by horse-drawn vehicle. In wet, frozen or snowy weather, the trip was either impossible or so arduous as to be completely unattractive to prospective guests. The inn went bankrupt in 1924 when the gondola cable snapped, killing five people.

Two years later, a wealthy Italian industrialist bought the inn to use as a private retreat and conference center for his business, and upon his death seven years later willed it to the Catholic Church.

Behind the windowpanes of what had once been the inn's dining room, Cardinal Neils Braun, archbishop of Vienna and head of the Pope's Secretariat for Non-Believers, stood at military parade rest, his back straight, feet apart, hands clasped at the small of his back. He wore a heavy alpine sweater, twill slacks, and light hiking boots. His scarlet robes hung in the closet of his room, where they always stayed when he came here. He ran a hand through his thick shock of salt and pepper hair as he gazed absently through the frost-glazed windows down at the tiny human specks gliding along the ski slopes below him.

Braun was a tall, sturdy man with a handsome chiseled face and a body tempered by a lifetime of cross country skiing and rock climbing. He had the phenomenal wiry strength found only in successful rock climbers who prefer not to use ropes, pitons, or other mechanical devices. He would turn fifty on Christmas day and he intended to spend the time alone, skiing in the nearby hills, or tackling a new face of rock. He looked across the valley and in the distance tired to pick out a mountain face he had not yet climbed.

From the front of the chalet, he could see the Olympic slalom runs of the Axamer Lizum where Jean Claude Killy made history in 1968. He squinted now as the afternoon sun edged its way from behind a cloud and burned deep shadows into the painfully white landscape. Overhead, the clouds hurried swiftly across the sky like tall ships under full sail. They were the remnants of a storm that had dumped nearly half a foot of snow in the Austrian Tyrol the night before.

In the valley below, his eyes followed the dark serpentine meanderings of the Inn River as it flowed between snow-covered banks. It hadn't yet frozen completely, much to the dismay of the skaters. His eyes followed the river now, as it ran past the hieroglyphic shapes of the airport's runways and smack into the heart of Innsbruck. As his gaze finally came to rest on the snow-frosted roofs of the city's Gothic architecture, he thought of the man he was about to meet, Robert Maxwell.

Maxwell's face and low, mellifluous voice were not familiar to the millions of Americans who watched the evangelical television programs on Sunday mornings. His name was even less familiar to millions more who either supported or feared the peculiar

American mixture of God, patriotism, and anticommunism that the television evangelists dished out with endless variation.

But the television evangelists themselves were familiar with Maxwell. Some disliked him, some revered him, but they all respected him. Indeed, all but the most solitary and jingoistic of the evangelists owed all, or a great part of their success, to Maxwell's efforts, support, or expertise.

Ordained in the Presbyterian Church in Charlottesville, Virginia, Maxwell gained skill as an organizer and negotiator that quickly earned him the respect of his elders, who elevated him to regional and national administrative bodies. His ability to reconcile seemingly impossible differences between intransigent parties made him a valuable spokesman for either side, and it was not long before he found himself enmeshed in the struggle between traditional, conservative church bodies, and the more energetic and innovative clergymen who looked for alternative methods— primarily television—to reach the souls of their flocks. The bitter disputes erupted more and more frequently and the divisions deepened. Traditional pastors complained that television evangelism was stealing their congregations away, that the medium itself was somehow tainted. The more conservative among them felt television was the devil's work. The evangelists, though, were of the opinion that preaching the word was the most important consideration, that all else was secondary. The only reason Jesus didn't use television, they argued, was that it hadn't been invented yet.

Maxwell's work behind the closed doors of local presbyteries and national boardrooms won him widespread respect among both factions. He succeeded where others had failed: by realizing that churches, despite pious protests from their leaders, are primarily political, not spiritual, organizations, bureaucracies whose paper pushers wear clerical collars. Experience had taught him that one bureaucracy is much like another, regardless of whether it is a governmental agency that procures fighter aircraft, a corporation that cranks out automobiles, or a church that dispenses spiritual solace to its members.

Maxwell knew that all bureaucracies become indistinguishable from each other once the desire of the bureaucracy members to acquire security for themselves outweighs the importance of their original task. That the original task might have a spiritual component made little difference.

As it turned out, hidden agendas and unstated priorities were what made it so easy for Maxwell to resolve disputes. What had to be done with churches, Maxwell quickly grasped, was the same as with governments or businesses: locate the individuals in power, determine their interests, then dig beneath the obvious to find where each of the personalities had invested his own tremendous ego. Maxwell knew that as long as he could feed the egos, keep the inflated sense of self-worth alive, a compromise could be reached. At bottom, all these individuals wanted was an assurance that their personal fiefdoms would remain secure.

Thus his greatest accomplishment in interfaith ecumenical work was the peace he brought to the pulpits. Without his work, the television pastors would have been reviled by the local clergy, and the electronic clergy would likely have responded in kind. Both would have been losers. And losers among the church bureaucracy, whether they be on television or the local green, meant losers among the faithful. Thanks to Maxwell, both thrived.

Maxwell's efforts earned him an appointment to the American Ecumenical Mission, the United States affiliate of the International Ecumenical Council. The council, chaired now by Cardinal Neils Braun, was composed of twelve members representing the major—and sometimes warring—factions of the world's religions.

To the world's press, to the members of the ecumenical missions in each country, and to the few others who might be aware of them, the International Ecumenical Council's ostensible mission was to discuss ways to decrease friction among the various religions, to devise ways to fight repression by secular governments. The members took no votes, kept no minutes of their meetings, wrote no manifestos, and sent no ultimatums to either governments or churches. Their decisions were free-form, achieved by consensus, and influenced only the upper church hierarchies. To the world at large, the impact of the ecumenical council seemed small. Only the twelve members themselves knew the primary reason for the council's existence.

Neils Braun turned now from the window overlooking the ski slopes and looked across the vast room that served as the conference room for the International Ecumenical Council. Large enough

145

to feed one hundred people at a time, it had only a single oblong oaken table nearly twenty feet long resting beneath the soaring A-frame roof with its huge rough-hewn timbers. At the far end of the room, embers glowed and cracked in a huge natural stone fireplace.

Besides the table, which Braun and the other eleven original members of the council had hewn by hand to symbolize the fellowship of faith, there were twelve chairs arranged symmetrically around its perimeter. There was no other furniture in the room. Braun liked it that way. The simplicity reminded the twelve people who assembled there six times a year of their singular mission.

The knock at the door at the far end of the hall came at precisely 3 P.M. Braun pushed back the cuff of his sweater, glanced at his wafer-thin watch, and noted with approval the caller's punctuality.

"Come in!" Braun called. His voice boomed in the silence.

Robert Maxwell opened the door and pushed his way briskly into the room. He stood in the entrance for a moment, blinking at the snow-reflected light pouring in through the windows. He was a man of average height, with medium-length brown hair parted on the side, brown eyes, and ruddy round cheeks that looked as if they would run to serious fat in another decade. In keeping with the rules that no clerical garb was to be worn in the council's meeting place, Maxwell wore gray wool slacks, penny loafers, and a navy crew-necked sweater over a gray turtleneck. A slight pudge spilled over his beltline.

"Good afternoon," Maxwell said. He looked around the room, eyes cataloging the ascending A-frame roof, the stone fireplace, the handmade table and chairs, and the obvious lack of anything else. Finally, he made his way toward Braun. The hard leather heels of his shoes clopped sharply on the highly polished wooden floor.

Braun met him in the middle of the room.

"It's good of you to come," Braun said when they were face to face. The Cardinal extended his hand. Maxwell shook it firmly.

"You were kind to extend the invitation," Maxwell replied.

The two men examined each other for a long moment, with only the popping of knots in the fireplace to break the silence.

"Shall we sit?" Braun asked. He motioned with his hand toward one end of the oblong table. Maxwell nodded and took the indicated chair. Braun seated himself at the opposite end. They were silent, sizing each other up.

"I'm thankful your life was spared," Maxwell said finally. "I read the accounts in the newspapers. I understand you were just moments away from the ambush."

Braun nodded. "Yes," he said leaning forward. "Apparently there was some sort of leak from the inside. If not for that . . ." Braun left the possibilities to hang in the air above them.

"Do you know who was behind it?" Maxwell asked.

"The Russians," Braun answered quickly. "They tried to disguise their hand by using a group from the Islamic Jihad, but reports . . . intelligence reports are conclusive that the Soviets were behind it all." He paused for effect. "You see, Lech Walesa was in the car with me." Braun saw Maxwell's eyebrows arch in surprise. "The Russians wanted to make an example of us both. To embarrass the Church and the Solidarity movement."

"But they failed," Maxwell said flatly.

Braun nodded. "Thanks to some help from the Mossad. They were the ones who picked up the leak from among the conspirators."

"The Israelis?" Maxwell said.

"Does that surprise you?" Braun asked. "The ecumenical nature of our organization runs deeper than just church politics. Like it or not, churches are political animals. But most church officials simply fail to see the situation as such, or wish to deny it."

"I suppose that was the reason I was singled out for this invitation," Maxwell said, more as a statement than a question.

Braun nodded quickly. "It is this same shortsightedness that has caused churches over the past two centuries to abrogate their social responsibilities. And what has been the result? Chaos, revolution, unstable governments, a moral vacuum at every level of every government." Braun shifted in his chair and crossed his legs.

"Churches bring stability to governments because they bring stability to the governed. Although his ultimate predictions were incorrect, Karl Marx made many perceptive observations concerning the world around him, including the maxim that religion is the opiate of the people.

"The manner in which he phrased his observation reflects his bias against religion," Braun continued, "but his basic observation is sound. People are more easily governed when their lives are strongly influenced by religion. They are more stable in their beliefs. Religion binds people together, gives them a common ground on which to work with each other. They are less likely to make precipitous, flighty decisions and more likely to yield to the direction of civil authority.

"Of course, history is ready with its exceptions to give lie to any rule," Braun said. "But as a whole, strong churches are the contemporary world leaders' best ally in the struggle to keep the social fabric from unraveling. And keeping the social fabric strong and sound is the best way to resist Russian attempts to exploit chaos and unrest. Churches are also the best, and sometimes the only, form of resistance to communist rule once it has taken over a government.

"But churches are effective at these roles only if they cooperate," Braun went on. "We have to fight our theological and doctrinal battles in private, and resist the temptation to turn the hearts of our congregations against other faiths. That's where your success and talent at quiet negotiation among the faiths have made such a contribution. You realize, as we do, that the collapse of religious authority and guidance in today's chaotic world would bring about widespread political instability and create the perfect climate for a communist takeover.

"We—the council and the ecumenical missions around the world—are trying to help churches of every faith meet this new challenge.

"It is unfortunate that our endeavors have provoked such extreme reactions from secular governments, particularly the Soviet government. The Russians tired to kill John Paul II for his strong role in helping the Polish people resist communism. They have tired to kill me many times. As head of the Secretariat for Non-Believers, I am the most visible symbol of my Church's resistance to the communist doctrine of atheism. Hardly a month passes that some Western intelligence service doesn't pass along to me information on one plot or another."

"They are afraid," Braun's voice grew louder. "Make no mistake about that. They will strike at us whenever they can. I learned just this morning that Polish State Security has killed a former member of this council." He paused. "We were like brothers once,

Davidson and I. Then he resisted, started working at cross purposes . . .'' Braun's voice suddenly trailed off. For a moment he seemed to be somewhere else.

Maxwell opened his mouth to speak, but thought better of it. There was nothing more he could offer. The two men sat in silence for several seconds, each with his own thoughts. They might have remained that way indefinitely had there not been a tapping at the door.

Braun's sadness lifted. "I took the liberty of having tea prepared,'' he said as he stood up quickly and walked to the door. Maxwell turned in his seat and watched as the archbishop of Vienna took a silver tray from someone who stood in the shadows. Braun thanked the person and returned with the tray, which he then put down in the middle of the table. Maxwell looked at him curiously. He wasn't accustomed to seeing cardinals engaged in the menial work of carrying trays.

"Only members of the council are allowed in this room,'' Braun said by way of explanation. "We have a small staff, but this room is strictly off limits. Please help yourself.'' He indicated the tray with its silver tea urn and pitchers of hot water and milk. The tray also contained two bone china cups and saucers, two small biscuit plates, linen napkins, and an array of tea sandwiches, biscuits, and condiments.

"High tea is a custom I picked up while a student at Oxford,'' Braun explained as he took one of the plates and decorated it with as assortment of food. "It seems to me such a civilized way to provide some rest and contemplation for long working days.''

Maxwell murmured his agreement as he got up and approached the silver service. He stood to Braun's right and prepared a cup of tea with lemon.

"You said only members of the council were allowed in this room,'' Maxwell began cautiously after they had settled themselves back into their chairs.

Braun studied Maxwell's face for several long moments before responding.

"That's true,'' Braun said. "And that's why I've invited you here.''

Maxwell took a sip of his tea and waited.

"We're not just a group of do-gooders who sit around and talk about lofty ideals," said Braun. "We are an organization that takes action. True, we are a small group, but we are people of considerable influence, both within our church organizations and our respective governments. We are owed favors. So we rely on individuals with direct access to power, to people, to large sources of money, to repay those favors. Individually, every member of the council has proven himself capable of using his influence and contacts to advance the goals of the council.

"You are just that sort of person and we need you badly. We have recently lost two members and their loss will be felt, both in our hearts and in the strength we will need in the coming days. None of us on the council could have guessed that we would be faced as we are now with the gravest threat to our religious institutions."

Maxwell wasn't sure how to interpret Braun's statement, but nodded anyway.

"You obviously know something of the International Ecumenical Council through your work with the ecumenical missions in the United States," Braun continued. "What you don't know is that your picture of the ecumenical council's work is incomplete," Braun leaned forward with his elbows on the table. "Our true work is, of necessity, hidden from the view of all but the twelve members who sit at this table."

Braun waved his right hand in the air as if to erase the subtle expression of surprise from Maxwell's face. "Oh, we do aim to decrease tension among the faithful and to fight government repression. That much is true; you haven't been laboring under a misperception all these years. But all that good work done by ecumenical missions all over the world is merely a base—resources, funding, eyes and ears, people, manpower—to help us with our most important task."

Braun took a sip of tea, his burly hands nearly concealing the tiny cup. He stared over the rim of the cup at Maxwell, who sat still as a mannequin, betraying nothing of his inner thoughts. He's good, Braun thought, the perfect poker player. Braun quietly eased his teacup back into the saucer.

"Have you any thoughts or comments on anything I've said so far?" Braun asked him.

Thoughts seemed to shift like floes of ice behind Maxwell's eyes as he framed his reply. He was known for his orderly thoughts and carefully phrased speech . . . and for never tipping his hand.

"I understand and agree with everything you've said so far," Maxwell began. "You are obviously familiar with my career and my own positions on the issues you've touched on—otherwise you would never have invited me." Maxwell paused. Braun tilted his head and urged him to continue.

"If I have interpreted your offer correctly, I have been elected by the ecumenical council to fill a vacant chair?" Braun nodded "But you've also informed me that the council has a hidden agenda. I'd like to know more about the hidden agenda before I commit myself."

"Fair enough," Braun said with a slow nod. He rose from his seat and refilled his cup. "I'd have second thoughts about you if you hadn't requested that information."

The cardinal took a sip from the cup, set it down at his end of the table, but didn't sit down. "It's a difficult story," Braun began. "Complicated." He walked to the windows where he had been standing when Maxwell first entered, and looked down for a moment. The brilliance of the day had started to fade with the winter sunset.

When Braun spoke again, his voice seemed to echo in the council's meeting hall. "You've heard, of course, of the Shroud of Turin?" Braun turned around to face Maxwell.

Maxwell nodded. "Of course. Who hasn't. Reportedly the burial shroud of Jesus Christ. It's a long roll of linen with the image of a crucified man on it. All of the wounds and marks, all of the physical characteristics of the man are consistent with the accounts of Christ's death. I remember there was quite a controversy over whether to recognize it as a true relic." Maxwell paused for a moment, seeming to search his memory for other relevant details.

"A team of scientists examined the shroud in the late 1970s to determine once and for all whether it was a fake." Maxwell continued. "As well as I can remember, they were forty to fifty experts drawn from many different countries and faiths, including several nonbelievers."

Braun smiled faintly as he listened to Maxwell's recital. The cardinal felt assurbd he had chosen well this time.

"The results of their test, I believe, were also controversial."

Braun walked slowly back to the table and sat down.

"The history of the shroud is obscure," Braun said as he settled back in his chair. "It was apparently discovered during one of the last crusades, but where and by whom no one can say. We only know its last six hundred thirty years of history and what the scientists tell us about it. The Shroud of Turin, as you mentioned, is a linen cloth, fourteen feet long and three and a half feet wide. The threads were hand spun and the fabric hand woven in a three-to-one herringbone twill." Braun's voice sounded like that of a museum tour guide who had taken thousands of visitors past the exhibits without losing his interest in any of them.

"On the fabric are two faint straw-colored images, one of the front and the other of the back of a nude man who was apparently scourged and crucified, with the hands crossed over the pelvis. The images appear head to head, as though a body had been laid on its back at one end of the fabric and the remainder of the fabric drawn over to cover the front.

"The cloth has many burn holes and scorches, although none are located in any area of the man's image. There are also large water stains.

"The shroud is kept in the Cathedral of Saint John in Turin, Italy, and the archbishop-cardinal of Turin holds the key to one of the three locks of the reliquary in which it is stored. The representative of the kind has the second key. The canon of the cathedral and custodian of the shroud have the third key. All three keys are required to get at the shroud itself.

"Over the years, there has been much speculation as to how the image was formed, with skeptics saying it's a clever forgery and believers calling it a miracle.

"In 1978 a team of scientists received permission to make an intensive study of the shroud, using the most sophisticated equipment to perform physical, biological, chemical, and microscopic tests. The purpose was to explain once and for all the origin of the image and settle the controversy.

"After four years of study, the scientists—whose religious beliefs ran the gamut from atheists and agnostics to faithful Jews and Christians—agreed there was no clear-cut answer. Computer scientists, physicists, chemists, blood chemistry experts, fiber experts—all agreed there was no evidence to prove that the image on the shroud was or was not that of Jesus Christ.

"But significantly," Braun went on, "they were also unable to determine how the image of the man was made. They found conclusive evidence it had not been painted on, woven in, made with a heated instrument, formed by application of chemicals, or made by any other method known today or two thousand years ago. All they could speculate was that the image was made by some short but intense burst of energy, an energy that couldn't be explained, an energy that couldn't be duplicated in the laboratory.

"They did know that thousands of burial shrouds exist from Christian and Coptic burials, and that this was the only shroud ever discovered that contained the image of a human being."

Braun paused to take a sip of tea. He used his napkin to dab at the light perspiration that had formed on his upper lip, then continued.

"That is a synopsis of the scientific report on the Shroud of Turin, at least, the public version. And as with the ecumenical council, what the public knows is true as far as it goes. But there is more, and that's where the council comes in." Braun leaned back in his chair, his voice slower now as if his recitation had tired him. "As you are probably aware, the Vatican has never taken a position on the holiness or authenticity of the Shroud of Turin. If you gathered together every fragment of the True Cross that the Vatican has blessed, you'd fill up a lumberyard. Yet the Vatican refuses to bless the Shroud of Turin. Why?" Braun's question was purely rhetorical. "Because they're afraid to, that's why. Because they know there is a second shroud out there . . . in better condition, with an impeccable lineage attested to by the most unimpeachable of sources. And if they bless the Shroud of Turin, with its obscure history, they fear that one day they will be called upon to do the same with the second shroud."

Maxwell looked confused. "But I don't understand. Are you saying a second shroud has been found that has been verified as belonging to Christ? If that is the case, why isn't it made public, why isn't it—"

Braun cut in. "No, you misunderstand me. This second shroud, the one that remains a secret, did not belong to the first Messiah at all. Rather, it belonged to the second."

Maxwell sat stunned.

"Second . . . but how .. how could . . ." He struggled to gather his thoughts. "Do you mean to say that all these years the Church has been covering up the existence of a second Messiah? What would be the motive for such duplicity? Why would the Church let the faithful remain ignorant of a second redeemer?"

Braun considered a moment before replying. "This second Messiah—redeemer, if you will—was . . . how shall I put it . . . 'eliminated,' snuffed out, not by the enemies of the Church, but by the Church itself."

Maxwell felt the bedrock of his convictions shift beneath him. He grabbed at the table for support.

"But . . . if what you say is the truth .. if this information were to leak out, Christianity and all that it stands for would be called into question. There would be chaos. Complete, utter chaos."

Braun nodded. "I'm afraid so. But Robert, there is one more thing I have to tell you. The second shroud contains on its surface an image as well. It is the image of the second redeemer . . . a *female* image."

Maxwell gasped.

CHAPTER NINE

Derek Steele lay on his back, staring blankly through the darkness at the ceiling. As usual, the sheets were coiled around him, twisted and knotted like rope, and the blanket lay in a heap at the foot of the bed. Again he swiped at his face to clear away the perspiration that beaded on his forehead and upper lip. He wiped his hand on the sheet and turned, trying to get comfortable enough to sleep.

But sleep would not come. In his dream he saw rats crawling over Claude Tewles, tearing off pieces of flesh, and then the image took the form of Myron Davidson and he saw Davidson on board the *Valkyrie* clutching at a throat that was no longer there . . .

Steele turned again and lay on his side. He closed his eyes, but every time he did, he saw the faces of death. He had gotten to sleep once that night, right after returning home with the painting. But the sleep had been shattered by a nightmare.

In the nightmare, he was sleeping. Then someone threw on a light. Steele opened his eyes and found himself lying in the philosophy department's ground floor storage room. Claude Tewles hovered over him.

"Get up, you lazy bastard!" Claude shouted at him. His face was red and bloated with anger. The veins stood out along the sides of his neck like thick ropes. "Get up and teach class!"

Claude's words grew so loud he couldn't understand them and the light on the ceiling seemed to grow brighter and brighter. He close d his eyes against the light, but it seemed to burn through his eyelids.

Then pain exploded through his chest and sides and for an instant he was back on the street. The coke dealer was ready with his Uzi. The first burst of slugs caught Steele's partner full in the face. The second burst slammed into Steele's chest and twisted him around, hammering into his side and back as he turned.

Darkness had been quick in coming then, but in the nightmare there was only the light.

Steele opened his eyes against the light and saw his partner's face on Claude's body.

"You asshole, you should have warned me," his partner snarled. "It should have been you; you should be dead, not me."

Steele tried to stand up; he wanted to explain. But his legs wouldn't move, nor his arms or mouth. He was paralyzed.

"You're a disgusting mess!" The face suddenly changed to Myron Davidson's, but the accusing voice was still his partner's. Steele felt the tears of frustration streaming down his cheeks; he could explain, he wanted to explain, but the words wouldn't come and finally Stephanie's face replaced Davidson's and the voice was hers.

"You let them take me," she said. "You let them take me away. Some cop you are!"

Then Steele felt himself split in two. One part floated to the ceiling and looked down on the second. He saw himself slumped in the corner with a bullet hole in his forehead and rats chewing gaping bloody holes in his body. Then he felt the grinding, searing pain, and the pressure of the clawed feet scratching at his eyes and the warm naked tails sliding across his belly and his groin. He awoke screaming.

Steele opened his eyes now and gazed at the luminous green display of the clock next to his bed. It was nearly 3 A.M. He'd had the nightmare nearly three hours before and still its vivid horror had not diminished. Sleep was clearly impossible.

He sat up on the edge of the bed and caught sight of his dim reflection in the mirror of Stephanie's dressing table. The carved wooden jewelry box he had bought for her during their voyage in the British Virgin Islands anchored one end of the dresser; a collection of bottles, nail polish, and other cluttery containers that seem to gather around women sat on the other end. They all seemed to accuse him of negligence.

He shifted slowly, then got to his feet. The bedsprings complained loudly as he got up, reminding him that Stephanie had wanted the springs replaced to lessen the noise they created when they made love. Something twisted in his heart as he remembered the times they had lain together in the bed, their bodies cleaving to each other, arm in arm, breath against breath. Would it ever be again?

At the bedroom window, Steele leaned against the sill and stared out at the street. The rain clouds had cleared, leaving the stars to burn tiny bright holes in the sky. Across the street, the Toyota had been replaced by a dark American-looking sedan with two men in it. He felt a momentary irritation at the surveillance, but quickly dismissed it.

Anderson was just doing his job. There was no reason to get mad at a man for that, he had finally decided. Steele had begun to think in the last three miserable hours that perhaps Anderson was right. Maybe the National Security Agency should control the operation entirely. He was probably better off taking orders from Anderson than he was operating alone. Having once been a cop was not sufficient to deal with this situation.

Fully awake now, he turned to his bed, reached under it, and withdrew the painting. He set the package on the bed and unwrapped it. He held it loosely in his hands in the darkness for several moments and then leaned over to switch on the lamp next to the bed. He examined the painting once again.

It was just as Davidson had described it. A painting of an alpine meadow, done in the warm yellow tones of the florentine masters. There was a prominent rock face at the right side of the picture, and what looked like the entrance to a mine in the distance almost at the left border. The picture itself contained no clues that he could find.

It was mounted in a plain black wooden frame and sealed with brown paper.

He turned the frame over and gazed at the oval sticker affixed to one corner of the sealing paper. "Joseph Roten and Sons, Fine Frames for Fine Art," the label read, "11 Augustinergasse, Zurich."

He stared at the label for several minutes. The name of the shop that had framed the picture was the only clue he had. Why, he wondered, had it been framed in Zurich and not somewhere in

Germany? He looked at the sticker again. There was a notation of some sort but the ink was too faded to decipher it. He held it closer to the light. The notation was illegible, but by holding the frame at the right angle to the light, he could make out a date. May 19, 1937. And a series of numbers: 16–16. Before the invasion of Poland, before the holocaust atrocities, while Hitler was still a respectable European leader and his people were free to travel without being hampered by battles or hostile borders. They had come to Zurich with the painting. And what else, he wondered?

He looked at the painting again and let his thoughts wander. Zurich was famous for its banks and for its stability. It was also infamous in his own mind as the place from which Stephanie had disappeared. The Nazis too were famous for their hoarding of gold and other valuables. Was it unreasonable to speculate that they had come to Zurich before the war to open accounts and to set up banking ties? Perhaps Hitler or Stahl or some other Nazi just happened to bring the painting along with him on such a trip and just happened to drop it by Herr Roten's framing shop.

Steele thought about it longer. If there was anything worth praising about the Nazis, it was their methodical nature. With them, hardly anything occurred by chance. The odds of the painting "just happening" to be along were slim.

He nodded to himself, picked up the telephone, dialed the operator, and asked for international directory assistance. He wanted to know if Joseph Roten, or one of the sons, was still in business in Zurich.

The phone rang twice before Steele replaced the receiver on the cradle. Anderson—or somebody else—had probably tapped the telephone. There was no telling who might be listening in on the line. The call could be made from a pay phone at the airport just as well.

Quickly, Steele pulled on a pair of corduroy slacks and a sweater. He emptied the briefcase of the tools he had carried earlier and placed in it both the painting and the damp piles of thousand-dollar bills Davidson had given him. On top of the bills, he threw the notes from his library research of the previous night.

He walked over to Stephanie's jewelry box and lifted out the top tray. From the bottom, he scooped up his passport and a healthy wad of Swiss francs he had brought back from Zurich. Absently, he opened the passport and gazed at the visas stamped in the back. Switzerland, England, Holland—every major country in western Europe and most of the minor ones, plus stamps from the little islands in the Caribbean that he and Stephanie had visited. He thought fleetingly of those halcyon days cruising the Caribbean, then abruptly snapped the passport shut and began packing.

Ten minutes later he watched the two men in the black sedan come to attention as he walked briskly from the house and tossed the bags into the Volvo's trunk. He climbed into the driver's seat and started the engine. Putting the Volvo into gear, Steele turned around carefully, drove slowly down the street, and stopped next to the black sedan. He rolled down his window and motioned for the men to do the same.

"Tell your boss I'm going to Amsterdam," Steele said, and with an airy salute rolled up the window and drove off.

An hour later, he smiled to himself as he hung up the telephone and turned toward the outrageously expensive snack bar in the cavernous hall of the International Terminal at Los Angeles International Airport. Joseph Roten and his sons were still in business, with a new generation of sons. The old man was still alive, they had told him, retired. Steele had mentioned the painting and artist by name, but neither seemed to evoke any recognition from the present Joseph Roten. He promised to mention it to his father, who—he was sure—would want to talk to the American gentleman about it.

I'm sure he will, Steele thought, as he walked into the nearly deserted snackbar and poured himself a cup of coffee, but I wonder what other people would like to talk about it as well.

As he settled himself behind a plastic laminated table to pass time before his flight, Steele felt burgeoning hope. For the first time, he believed there was a chance to find Stephanie.

Cardinal Neils Braun suppressed an ironic smile as he watched Maxwell's facial expressions run the gamut from disbelief to dismay. The stolid ecumenical negotiator's renowned self-control had abandoned him.

"But how could anything like this be *proved?*" Maxwell demanded. "We're talking about something that's nearly seventeen hundred years old . . . wars, the Crusades, the disruptions . . . how can you prove something of this import beyond even a reasonable doubt?"

Braun smiled. "You are a person who prides himself on his faith."

"Yes, but we're not talking about faith here," Maxwell countered. "We're talking about irrefutable proof of the existence of a woman's resurrection . . . we're talking about proof—proof so convincing that it would tear apart the institutions of the Western world."

Maxwell's eyes held the cardinal's gaze for a long moment.

"Then allow me to explain," Braun offered.

"Please," Maxwell replied.

"The history is intwined with the proof, so let me start at the beginning, with Saint Veronica, back in the fourth century A.D."

"But I thought that was myth," Maxwell responded. "All of the talk about Saint Veronica's Veil and such. There's nothing written concerning her, no independent historical accounts to verify that she ever existed."

Braun's smile deepened. "There's a good reason for that," he said. "And it's by design. Let me begin at the start—"

"I'm sorry for the interruption," Maxwell said.

Braun nodded.

"There most definitely *was* a Veronica," Braun continued. "She was born in 310 A.D. in a small village some one hundred miles from Smyrna, into a family of merchants, apparently as the illegitimate offspring of the merchant's eldest daughter. The circumstances surrounding the birth are not clear. The family tried to keep the birth of the illegitimate daughter a secret, and succeeded for more than thirteen years. The girl was never alllowed outside of the fairly comfortable family residence, and never brought in contact with any of the household workers. The obvious explanation for the secrecy was to avoid the shame of the unmarried birth. But from a diary kept by the girl's mother, we know the real reason had to do with paranormal occurrences that had taken place as early as the middle of the gestation period.

"The girl's mother, apparently, had begun a series of prophecies during her pregnancy, all of which dealt with mundane work-aday life situations, and some of which involved her father's business. All of the prophecies came true.

"Then after the birth of Veronica, people who bathed or held the infant were given fleeting powers of prophecy. The fact that Veronica was not put to death for being not only illegitimate but also possessed by demons is an indication that the family may have known more about Veronica's birth than they dared to put into writing."

"More?" Maxwell asked. "Such as?"

"Perhaps they had some message or indication of the baby girls' divine origins." He looked hesitantly at Maxwell. "But that's just speculation. I'd like to stick here with what can be proven." Maxwell nodded.

"Superstitions then, even more than now, were powerful insti-gators of violence. To be possessed by demons was to die quickly at the hands of one's superstitious neighbors. So, to make sure the word didn't spread about their daughter, and thus endanger her and the rest of the family, they raised the baby in total isolation.

"But locks and barriers were no match for the developing Ver-onica. At the age of thirteen, the girl appeared at her father's side at a trade negotiation. The incident was confirmed by the accounts of nearly a dozen men. According to those accounts, she mesmer-ized them, speaking as an adult and somehow finding the words to preach to them. They were stunned and captivated by her. Her terrified father rushed her away, fearing for his life, his business . . . for the lives of his daughter and the rest of the family. But the violent actions he expected never materialized. In fact, just the opposite happened. Afterwards, the men who had been present reported feeling totally serene and at peace. They were fond of Veronica and demanded to see her again and again. Soon she became a fixture in the village and began to develop a following. Then she started healing people."

"You actually *believe* this?" Maxwell asked incredulously.

Braun nodded. "I have no choice. The Documentation is too overwhelming not to . . . as you will see. Consider Valerius Daia . . . her first miracle, for example. Pressed into the service of the Roman army in 285 A.D., Daia's legion was sent to Mesopotamia by Emperor Diocletian in 295. A year later, Narses of Persia routed the Roman legions and their leader Galerious. The military records—the Roman empire really began the military paperwork that continued to plague the common soldier—were plain in the case of Valerius Daia. His right leg had been maimed and was paralyzed, rendering him unfit for further military service.

"The trail picks up again in the small village near Smyrna where Veronica lived. Under a general order from the emperor, the village diverted small portion of the taxes it had to pay to Rome into a fund that provided small stipends for honorably wounded soldiers of the empire. It was the first simple attempt at veterans' benefits. At any rate, Valerius Daia's name first appeared on these village rolls in 297 A.D. Then in 323 A.D., there is an unusual entry in the village records calling for a cessation of those payments due to 'extraordinary circumstances resulting in the healing of the palsied leg' of Valerius Daia."

Braun paused to let his words sink in. He fixed Maxwell's eyes with his own and leaned forward. "She touched his leg, you see. She touched his leg and he was healed. We have an account of the miracle as recorded by the village scribe, but we also have military and financial records to corroborate the event."

The room had grown cold, and for the first time since Braun had begun his extraordinary soliloquy, Maxwell noticed that the room had also grown dim. In the west, the sun appeared low on the horizon. Maxwell shivered.

"But all these records . . . how could they be preserved for more than sixteen hundred years?"

"There is a building on the grounds of the Vatican whose basement contains forty miles of shelves filled with books, parchments, stone tablets, dossiers, and manuscripts of the most remarkable significance. Here, for example, the church has stored court records of sorcery trials, the letters of Joan of Arc, the original handwritten records of the trial of Galileo, a petition from seventy-five lords of England pleading for the annulment of Henry VIII's marriage, documents concerning the Crusades, details of the scandalous lives led by the nuns of Monza, reports of prophecy fulfilled and prophecy yet to come. Millions of items of the most secret nature are guarded here in L'Archivo Segreto Vaticano—the Secret Archives of the Vatican," Braun said. "The records that irrefutably confirm the resurrection of Veronica are stored here."

He paused as if his thoughts pained him too much to translate into words. "And until Emperor Henrich IV sacked Rome in 1084, Veronica's shroud also rested in L'Archivo."

He looked silently at the veins on the backs of his hands for a long moment, as if seeing there a reenactment of the battle that had set the shroud loose on the world.

"But let me finish my story." Braun glanced at his watch. "And quickly, too, since the other members of the council will start arriving soon."

Maxwell nodded eagerly.

"When the reports of Veronica's miracles and teachings reached Rome," Braun continued, "they were regarded as extremely serious by both Pope Sylvester I and Emperor Constantine. To you and the Protestant branches of Christianity, the Reformation period was the most unsettled in our history. But there have been greater ones, ones more threatening to the survival of the Church. Think of what Constantine and Sylvester I must have thought when they learned of Veronica. There they were: Constantine, the first Roman emperor to grant Christianity the official protection of the empire; Sylvester, the first pope to rule legitimately in the eyes of civil authority after nearly three hundred years of persecution.

"By all rights, this should have been a glorious era for the Church," Braun said, "but it was anything but that. As part of an official, *protected* religion, members of the church started to lose the bonds of mutual dependance they had needed for survival. It had been easy to stifle heresy and maintain spiritual unity when the faithful had to depend on other church members for survival from roving bands of Roman legionnaires bent on eradicating them. Unity was survival. But the Church, once officially sanctioned by Constantine, quickly lost that coherence. Encouraged by its connections to official Rome, the Church quickly developed the bureaucracy that the Vatican is now so famous for. And as the bureaucracy gained a life of its own, it found itself frequently in conflict. The Church quickly transformed itself from a religious movement founded around a charismatic leader into a bureaucratic institution with the inevitable political intrigue and a collective instinct for the survival of the organization and its components, even if the survival were at the expense of the Church's spiritual foundations.

"This development sparked major debate within the Church, and in reaction, hundreds of congregations threatened to leave the Pope's fold. In addition, there were a dozen major spiritual splinter groups—chief among them the Gnostic movement—that had begun to challenge the basic tenets of the Church.

"Constantine recognized the advantages of ruling with the blessings of a spiritual leader," Braun continued, "and Sylvester certainly knew how hard it would be to rule as an outlaw from civil authority. So when they heard of this young girl in a distant village who performed miracles and preached to her elders, they knew they had to act quickly to avert yet another challenge to their authority.

"Emissaries from Rome, representing both Constantine and Sylvester, journeyed to visit this remarkable girl," said Braun. "When they got there, they found the situation even more serious than they had initially heard. Veronica, even though only fifteen by this time, had become the focus of a splinter religion that had captivated her native village and had started to spread to the countryside." Braun pushed his chair back and got to his feet. The room had grown almost completely dark. The hard leather of his shoes tapped sharply on the bare wooden floor as he walked to the door and flipped a switch next to it. Dim light flooded into the room and turned the windows and their vast view of the Alps into mirrors that reflected the stark simplicity of the room and its occupants.

Braun continued as he walked back to his seat. "The visitors from Rome knew they had to act quickly before Veronica's cult grew large enough to become a real threat. The Church was already being torn apart by these spiritual splinter groups whose beliefs were based on interpretations of scripture. They shuddered to think of the power and attraction of a group organized around someone with the power and charisma that Veronica exercised. The parallels that could be drawn between her and Jesus Christ were not lost on them."

Braun reseated himself. "Besides," he said, resting his elbows on the table, "she was female. None of the Apostles were women. Women have always been adjuncts, secondary worshipers in every church. Christianity had borrowed from Judaism and institutionalized the doctrine of male dominance in its new religion, rationalizing the authority to do so on spiritual grounds . . . Our *Father* who art in heaven. God was plainly a man, as was his son. To admit now that the Church had been wrong on this would open the Pope to criticism on other matters.

"Plainly, quick, decisive action was called for," Braun continued. "But the emissaries from Rome had no time to send a messenger to Constantine or Sylvester, so they made a historic decision. They invited Veronica, her family, and the entire village—a hundred fifty or so people—to visit the emperor. Veronica's family, and most of the villagers, were awed and delighted to follow the orders of the distinguished visitors. And further, the emissaries carried the seals and papers from Rome that gave them authority to direct the commander of Rome's forces to make sure that those who were not delighted to visit Rome did so anyway.

"Roman army units escorted Veronica and her followers to the port city of Tyre where they were put on ships bound for Rome. They reached the Holy City after a routine journey."

Braun paused to take a sip of his tea.

"The oldest volume in L'Archivo Sergreto Vaticano is a thick ledger filled with the fine handwriting of a scribe of Constantine's court, recording the interviews with the villagers as they were first welcomed, then questioned, by Constantine and Sylvester about Veronica and her life. They were questioned one at a time, their remarks recorded and compared to the testimony of those who had preceded them. Constantine and Sylvester saved the interview with Veronica for last, and when they had finished, reviewed the transcripts of the interviews and found them in agreement. I have a copy of the interviews for you to read . . . translated into English from the original Latin."

Maxwell nodded.

"And then what happened?"

"They were killed."

Maxwell's jaw dropped.

"All of them? All of the villagers?"

Braun nodded solemnly. "All of them. The scribe, one hundred fifty villagers, and Veronica."

"They were buried," Braun continued, his voice wavering.

165

"And a week later, when the shrouded bodies were inspected in the cave that served as a mass tomb, one of the shrouds was empty. It contained the image of a fifteen-year-old girl."

Braun slowly got up from his chair and walked to Maxwell's side. He put his hand on the younger man's shoulder and looked down at him. "We are the guardians of this secret," Braun told him. "We must make sure the world never learns the secret of Veronica. It would tear our institutions apart and in the end open the door for the enemies of the Faith. It would create only misery and death."

Maxwell looked up at him.

"Will you keep this secret?" Braun asked. "Will you devote your life to protecting the Faith against the secret's harm?"

Maxwell nodded. He had no idea that his simple nod had saved his life. Some secrets, after all, are kept at any cost.

CHAPTER TEN

Halfway between Washington, D.C., and Baltimore, on one thousand acres of rolling fields and forest, sits a sprawling complex of twenty buildings surrounded by triple cyclone fences ten feet high. The fences are topped with concertina wire whose razorblade edges have been designed with one purpose in mind: the flaying of human flesh. One of the fences is electrified. Security forces, heavily armed and accompanied by attack dogs, patrol the two strips of no-man's land traced by the three barriers.

In the daytime, more than fifty thousand people jam the twenty buildings protected by the three strands of cyclone fence. They work in the complex's offices, buy stamps at its post office, get their hair cut at its barber shop, purchase cold medicine in its drugstore, take classes at its college, and watch programs broadcast by its television station, which is powered by the complex's own electrical generating plant.

The visitor traveling along the Baltimore-Washington Parkway who happens to take the Fort Meade exit, and who happens to take a wrong turn after entering the army base, might happen to find himself looking through the meshwork of fences at a mammoth central building faced with green chipped stone. This is the Xanadu of spying, the Taj Mahal of eavesdropping, the colossus of intelligence gathering: the headquarters building of the National Security Agency.

In this one building is more usable office space than in the CIA's Langley Headquarters and the U.S. Capitol combined. In its basement is the world's largest concentration of computers, filled with so much sophisticated hardware that it is measured in acres. The last public leak put the concentration at more than eleven acres—enough to handle the computing needs of every business, large and small, in the United States.

But the business of these computers is not business. It is spying. Some of the brute force of all this computing power is used by cryptologists to break coded material. Some is used to translate messages intercepted in a foreign language into English. But by far the lion's share of the massive computer complex is used to analyze signals and conversations picked up by the NSA's gigantic system of signal intercepts.

Like a giant combine harvesting the kernels from a field of grain, the NSA scans billions and billions of messages that travel the world's airwaves every second: spy satellites comb the earth below for telemetry signals from Soviet missile launches; airborne spy planes snare conversations between MiG fighter pilots and their ground control; even the car telephone calls made by Kremlin officials as they travel to work somehow find themselves caught in the NSA's broad net.

But more than just the conversations of America's enemies fall within the NSA's area of concern, for the agency's job is also to determine who among the citizens of the United States is an enemy previously unidentified. To this end, the NSA's antennae intercept telephone calls, cable messages, and telexes made by ordinary individuals.

An internal NSA investigation would later reveal that Derek Steele's telephone call to Joseph Roten originated from a GTE pay telephone on the mezzanine level of the international Terminal at the Los Angeles International Airport. The signal quality of the telephone transmission was graded as severely degraded and substandard, similar to that originating from the crude telecommunications systems found in the Third World. NSA analysts, however, had grown accustomed to poor-quality conversations originating from the California areas whose telephone service was provided by GTE.

Steele's call was switched over to long distance ground lines leading to COMSAT's Jamesburg, California, earth station. All of the satellites' available circuits were occupied at the time, so the COMSAT switching computer connected the call to transcontinental land lines, where it eventually found an unoccupied circuit at TAT 6 (Transatlantic Cable 6) in Green Hill, Rhode Island. From here it made the 3,400 mile trip to the coast of France, emerging near Deauville, where its care fell into the hands of the French PTT—Poste Téléphone et Télégraphe. From the coast, the call was beamed via microwave to a switching center east of Paris. There the PTT computer passed the call via the primary land trunk cable to Switzerland's PTT computer, which then routed it to Zurich. At Zurich a series of computer switches finally located Joseph Roten's telephone and caused it to ring.

During this intricate process, Steele only half listened to the minute or so of clicks, clacks, thunks and echoes in the telephone's earpiece. He was thinking more about what he would say to Roten than about the static on the line.

The conversation seemed innocuous by any standards. Steele wanted to speak to the old man, who was out. What did it concern, the old man's son asked. A painting by a man named Stahl they had framed decades ago, a picture of an Austrian meadow called "The Home of the Lady Our Redeemer." The son was not familiar with it, but he would check with his father, and in any event, the old man would welcome a visit by Herr Steele.

Besides Steele and Joseph Roten's son, the conversation had significance for other sets of ears . . .

At Fort Meade, Maryland, the telephone number, mention of Stahl's name, and title of the painting all connected with alerts programmed into the eleven acres of computers. Since the phone number and two names were tagged with priority alert status, the first computer that had analyzed the taped conversation alerted a second computer known as Lodestone. Just as some humans are more equal than others, so it is with Lodestone.

Built by Cray Research of Mendota Heights, Minnesota, Lodestone is a five-ton supercomputer so powerful that it can process the equivalent of twenty-five hundreds books per second, each of them containing about three hundred pages. When pressed into service as a number cruncher, Lodestone can perform 150 to 200 million calculations per second. It is NSA's star. And so it was that Derek Steele's telephone call was sent to Lodestone.

Lodestone analyzed the short telephone call, then checked on the identity of the person entering the intercept keys: the telephone number, Stahl's name, and the name of the painting. The computer noted that the originator was an agent code-named Byzantium and that any messages relating to the intercept key were to be classified Top Secret Umbra. The message was for the eyes of Byzantium only. Less than three minutes after Steele had hung up, a coded message was on its way to NSA agent Byzantium, who at that time was on his way to the Los Angeles International Airport.

At a cramped but nonetheless efficient set of new prefabricated office buildings east of Paris, a PTT computer absorbed all of the information beamed to it from TAT 6. The computer was smaller, slower, and in human terms, dumber than Lodestone. But it only had to handle the traffic for some two thousand telephone calls at any given time, and that was well within the capacity of the Olivetti mainframe computer that was assigned to the task. Several PTT technicians strolled around, caressing the computer, watching its lights, tending its needs—human acolytes before their god.

In a room next to the computer sat a man in a business suit who worked for the SDECE—the French secret service. The man was one of three who manned the room twenty-four hours a day, waiting for the computer to recognize any of the code words and intercept keys they had entered into the PTT computer. The PTT was never particularly happy about having to devote some of the computer's memory and computing ability to the dirty business of spying. And the SDECE men assigned to the boring task of sitting in the adjacent room waiting for something to happen manifested little enthusiasm either. But since the SDECE and the PTT were both owned by the same government, neither had any choice, and the people from the two different agencies did their best to stay out of the way of the other.

The SDECE agent in the next room on this night was named Tom Dupree, and he had gotten his job with the agency as a result of his enthusiasm for the French Socialist party, which had finally won the government. Wary of the new batch of Socialists and Communists of dubious security value, the SDECE had placed people like Dupree in jobs where they could do the least amount of damage should they turn out to be spies for the Soviet Union, as Dupree was.

So it was that just after Dupree had settled down with his twelfth cup of *café au lait* and the crossword puzzle from *Le Monde,* the PTT manager in charge knocked timidly at his door to inform him that the Olivette computer had printed something out in a code that he didn't understand.

Languorously, Dupree followed the PTT manager into the main computer room to accept the message. What he found snapped him immediately to attention. The intercepts his KGB control office had instructed him to program into the computer six months before had borne fruit. Trying to control the shaking in his hands, Dupree took the message back to his office. The message was in book code. Like all codes based on published books, it was decipherable only to the person who knew which book had been used, and he was that only person.

By the time he got back to his little office, his fear had transformed itself mostly into exhilaration. After a lifetime as a common trade unionist, he would now be able to truly serve the cause of communism. He folded the paper carefully and put it into his pocket. He couldn't wait to get home and pull the book from its shelf and start translating the code. He smiled when he thought of his clever irony in using Adam Smith's *The Wealth of Nations* to encode his messages.

Less than ten minutes after Joseph Roten's son gave him the message from the American, the old man shut himself away in his office and placed a long distance telephone call to Munich, West Germany. Roten's call sounded in the dim corridor of the Jesuit-residenz, located in an old stone baroque building that faced the Sparkassenstrasse in the old quarter of Munich.

The old quarter's hodgepodge of medieval, Renaissance, and baroque buildings crowd shoulder to shoulder, eaves-to-eaves with each other around the narrow winding cobblestone streets and alleys. The old quarter is barely fifteen hundred meters across, yet more than a dozen churches crowd themselves in among the beer halls, private residences, and government buildings. The most prominent of the churches is the Dom und Pfarrkirche Unserer Lieben Frau—The Cathedral and Parish Church of our Lady—known locally as the Frauenkirche. Founded in 1271 as a chapel dedicated to the Virgin Mary, the Frauenkirche has become the trademark and symbol of old Munich. The church's twin towers, which are topped with curious cupolas that resemble skullcaps worn by Roman Catholic clergy, have appeared in more tourist brochures and snapshots than any other Munich landmark save the famous glockenspiel.

But besides serving as a postcard landmark, the Frauenkirche serves as a cathedral and major place of worship for Munich's faithful. Its status as both cathedral and parish church warrant a greater than ordinary staff, many of whom live at the Jesuitresidenz.

The telephone rang twice before being answered by the residenz's most junior novice. He answered politely and requested that the caller please be patient while he summoned Father Meyer.

Meyer was a strange man, the young novice priest thought, as he walked quickly to the end of the hall and up the stairs on the third floor. He had kind blue eyes that always seemed on the verge of tears. The abbot had told him it was due to the injuries Meyer had received at the end of World War II. There were bullet fragments that had lodged too close to nerves and blood vessels to be removed, and for that reason the priest lived in constant fear that after more than four decades the fragments would shift and he would windup dead or paralyzed.

The young priest stopped before the plain wooden door with the cross, which was located at the end of the third floor corridor. He paused a moment before knocking. From inside the room, he could hear Meyer humming to himself. It sounded like a Brandenburg concerto. The young priest wondered why the abbot didn't give Father Meyer his own telephone. He was old and frail and received many telephone calls. Surely an exception could be made, the young priest thought, as he raised his hand and knocked gently on the door. It couldn't cost very much. Besides, the parish wouldn't have to pay for it for very long. How much longer could Father Meyer live?

"Come in," Meyer called.

The young priest opened the door and found Meyer sitting at a plain desk next to the window overlooking the Fraauenkirche.

"Phone call, Father," said the young man as he walked forward and stopped in front of Meyer's chair to offer him a hand up.

Meyer smiled and waved away the young priest's offer of assistance. He wasn't an invalid. They never seemed to realize that.

As Meyer got up and made his way to the door, he stopped for a moment and took a look at the picture of his son that hung on the wall. He had grown into a fine, handsome, powerful man—a man who stood on the verge of greatness. Meyer felt his heart tear a little, as it always did when he realized that his son would never know his true father.

That was impossible now. The mother of the man whose picture hung on the wall—the only other person who knew the truth—had died of a stroke a decade before. Now, only Meyer and God knew the terrible secret.

Taking one last glance at the picture, as he always did when he left the room, Meyer made his way down the stairs to the telephone, hoping that good news would take the edge off his physical pain.

The pain and weakness shifted from day to day, as did Meyer's memory and vision. It was the fragments, they told him. The Oberleutnant's bullets had shattered against his skull and against his ribs. There were six of them that could have been fatal had they gone another millimeter. He would be dead if Roten hadn't killed the Oberleutnant and if Summers hadn't gotten him to the American army doctors. He allowed himself a small smile as he carefully descended the stairs. In four decades he had learned not to make sudden movements that could encourage the fragments to shift.

Over the past forty years, he had had days when he felt perfectly well except for the blindness in his right eye. On those days, he wanted to ski or ice-skate again, but he knew that was toying with suicide. So he learned to treat his body with the gingerness of the elderly.

He reached the landing on the second floor and walked slowly down the long corridor toward the telephone. The young priest did not follow Meyer to the telephone. Instead he walked quickly to the abbot's room and rapped respectfully on the door.

"Father Meyer has another telephone call, your grace," the young priest said after stepping into the abbot's simply furnished room.

"Thank you very much," the abbot replied. And with a nod of his head, the abbot dismissed the young priest. The young priest was tempted to tell Meyer about the order the abbot had issued. He and the other novice priest were to notify the abbot or his assistant whenever Meyer received a call. No explanation. But then, explanations weren't expected by novices, just blind obedience. Still. The young priest thought, there seemed something . . . dishonest about the whole affair.

The abbot thought much the same thing as he pulled open the bottom drawer of his desk and checked to make sure that the small tape recorder the men from the Vatican had given to him was functioning. The men had first arrived there two days after Easter in 1962, just after Meyer had been assigned to the parish. The abbot had been a younger man then and had protested both the tapping of the hallway telephone and the order that he be forced to spy on one of his own priests. His protests were answered first by the archbishop of the diocese and later by a cardinal from the Vatican. Finally, when he continued to object, he had been called to Rome and told in no uncertain words that further protests would not be tolerated. And in the end they had told him nothing about the reason for the telephone taps.

He tried to deduce the reasons by listening to the tapes, despite the injunctions against it. The calls had been to a wide variety of people, art dealers and collectors—particularly an American named Summers and a Zuricher named Roten—police investigators and government officials. The calls that initially raised the abbot's eyebrows were the ones to or from former Nazis. At first the abbot thought the Vatican suspected Meyer of being a former Nazi himself. But that didn't reconcile with the way the priest had received his injuries. Then, as now, Meyer had seemed like a frail, harmless old man, unable to handle a full cleric's load, and who instead was allowed to indulge his hobby of trying to locate pieces of art stolen by the Nazis so he could return them to their rightful owners.

He had had some minor successes, and had even been written

174

up in the *Abend Zeitung* by a reporter, Johanna Kerschner, who had taken an interest in him and his work.

In the end, the abbot prayed and meditated, and concluded that God had placed a greater trust in the hands of the men above him, and that truly all that was required of him was his faith and blind obedience. So he had faithfully mailed the tapes to Rome every week since then. And over the years, other men had come and given him newer tape recorders and then gone. They had hooked up devices that automatically recorded all conversations on the telephone. But he didn't trust the device and he still liked to check on it each time to make sure it was working.

The abbot stared at the machine and saw that the cassette was turning. Then he sighed and slowly closed the drawer and went back to the paperwork. The paperwork, he thought in despair. He wondered if God's book of life were filled out in triplicate. He crossed himself and asked forgiveness for such irreverent thoughts and began to wade through the piles on his desk.

Seven thousand miles to the east, Derek Steele settled into the window seat on the upper deck of the KLM 747. He always flew KLM business class because they put the nonsmokers on the upper deck where the air always stayed clean. He plugged in his headset, put it on his head, adjusted the volume, and curled up next to the cabin wall as comfortably as he could with his seatbelt fastened.

He closed his eyes and saw Stephanie's face. She was there. He knew it in his heart. He knew she was still alive and that he was going to find her this time. He drifted off into welcome sleep as the giant 747 began to pull away from the gates. He had no inkling of the chain of events he had ignited halfway around the world.

CHAPTER ELEVEN

Stephanie shivered and tried to wrap the blanket more tightly around her. But every time she succeeded in covering one spot, the torn blanket exposed another. She sniffled and wiped her nose on the edge of the blanket. Damn it, don't cry, she scolded herself. Don't give them that satisfaction.

She sat up on the cot in a lotus position and pulled the blanket around her shoulders. The warmth began to creep back into her toes as she tucked them under her. She sniffed again, this time more from the cold than from her tears.

On the floor next to the cot lay the soaked wad of her T-shirt.

The man with the kindly eyes and sore feet—Czenek, someone had called him—had unchained her and then handcuffed her to the straightbacked chair. He threw ice water on her and slapped her. He threatened and yelled and slapped her again. He threatened to kill Derek. She cried and pleaded for Derek's life. He slapped her more and waved a propane torch in her face and said that if she didn't talk to him when he returned in a few minutes he would burn off her flesh with the torch, starting with her breasts and genitals and doing it in a way guaranteed to keep her alive and conscious for the longest possible time.

And then he went away. Stephanie remembered the way the man had said what he had said, and it still seemed to her that he seemed almost apologetic. He was different, she decided. The others who had questioned, drugged, and beat her had seemed to enjoy it. This Czenek seemed bored with it all. The others had beat her until she hurt even to the center of her bones. Not Czenek. His blows had been slaps, almost stage slaps designed for maximum noise rather than impact.

He was a strange man, she decided, as she shifted her weight to keep her right foot from going to sleep. They were all strange men.

On the other hand, she was a strange woman, she decided, or she wouldn't be in a predicament like this. She dwelt on the thought for a moment as she stared blankly around the room. It hadn't changed. Still the light that always burned, the desk, the chair. Czenek had left his heavy ankle-length greatcoat on the back of the chair. No one had ever done that before, left anything at all in the room.

She looked at the coat and the temptation grew. She could feel it around her, feel its warmth. She could imagine being warm, truly warm through and through. She could reach it. She knew she could reach it if she stretched the chain that bound her wrist to the wall out to its maximum, then performed a clumsy arabesque to reach the coat with her foot.

She shifted, then stopped. They would beat her for using the coat. She thought about the beatings for a moment. They would beat her anyway, she decided, and slowly unfolded her legs and stood shakily. She felt the icy linoleum freeze the soles of her feet. The blanket slipped from her shoulders, and as it did, she heard a small metallic clank.

Stephanie squinted her eyes in the dim light and searched for the cause of the clank. She saw nothing. She picked up the blanket, shook it, and heaped it on the cot. Still she saw nothing until she got down on her hands and knees, naked in the darkness, and searched the floor with her free hand.

When her dirty, cold fingers closed around it, she wouldn't believe her senses. Grasping it firmly in her fist, she stood up and opened her palm slowly. She didn't want to look at first, for fear it would turn out to be something else. But when she finally did look at the object, it turned out to be one of the three or four things she had prayed for most: it was the key Czenek had used to unlock her manacles.

Stephanie's hands trembled as she inserted the key in the lock of the cuff that bound her wrist to the chain. The lock gave a dull rasping sound and fell open. The chain clanked as it fell on the cot.

For a moment, panic rose in Stephanie's throat. She was free of the bonds for the first time in . . . in however long it had been since they had brought her here. But she had no time to worry about her sudden fear of freedom: from outside, she heard footsteps and voices. Had they heard the clanking of the chains? Thinking quickly, she sat back down on the cot and placed her wrist in the cuff that had bound her to the wall. She was naked and defenseless and right now was not the time to let her captors know she was free of her restraints.

Her hand shook and hesitated as she started to refasten the cuff to her wrist. Something psychological resisted. But finally, as the footsteps grew closer, she fastened it securely, and climbed back under the skimpy covers.

She pretended to sleep as someone opened the door for a moment and then closed it again. As she heard the footsteps recede, a thought formed in her mind that would nag her for the rest of her life: had Czenek just been careless to leave his coat and to drop the key? He had seemed to her to be tired: bored, weary, but not careless.

The plain was flat and sandy and distinguished only by a small stunted forest of six-pointed stars—together with occasional crosses—of wood, stone, and metal. The last rays of the setting sun colored the odd forest red. And among the crosses and the stars and the people who gathered awkwardly around a fresh mound of the ravaged earth, the wind blew foul and hostile, like the breath of death itself. It picked up small handfuls of sand and pea-sized pebbles and threw them in the faces of the mourners who had begun to straggle off into the gathering night. In the distance, the lights of Tiberias were blinking on.

Adam Gold and Nat Worthington were the last to leave. They had brought David Simon's body back from Vienna aboard a chartered El-Al flight just hours before, and now David had been buried before the sun set. Just.

They stared at the mound of earth, as if by sheer concentration of will they could shovel away the mound and the ugly accumulation of time that now bound him there, just inches away from the remains of his family.

"I think he always felt this was where he belonged," Gold said finally, his words barely intelligible over the complaints of the wind.

Worthington looked silently at Gold and nodded. He understood.

"Maybe we all do," Gold mumbled.

"What?" Worthington said. "I couldn't hear you."

Gold shook his head and turned away from the grave. "Nothing. It's not important."

Worthington followed Gold back toward the government Mercedes sedan they had ridden out in. Abraham, loyal Abraham, stood by the door of the Mercedes with his Uzi out and at the ready. This close to the Islamic sector, anything could happen.

They walked most of the one hundred fifty yards back to the car in silence. It was not so much a silence of respect, but one that came from a numbing of the soul.

"Why do you care about Jews, Worthington?" Gold asked, while they were still out of Abraham's earshot. "You don't have to do this. You've got family money. You're goy through and through."

Worthington looked at him oddly. "I never thought about it much," he responded. "Nobody ever asked me that before. It just seemed like the right thing to do."

They walked a dozen more paces before the silence was once again broken.

"Do you always do the right thing?" Gold asked.

Worthington almost smiled before he realized Gold was serious. The tough Mossad colonel had taken Simon's death personally. He had cried in Vienna. He kept telling anyone who would listen that this was to be Simon's last mission. They irony of it was lost on no one. Gold blamed himself for the death. If only he had tried harder, said the right thing, Gold told himself over and over, maybe Simon would have come out of the cold.

"Well," Gold said as they approached the Mercedes, "Do you? The right things?"

Worthington shook his head sadly. "Not nearly enough. Nobody does. But I guess that all we can do is keep trying and hope that by the time we die we've done enough of the right things."

Gold nodded and then stopped next to the Mercedes. He turned toward Worthington: "Enough for what?"

Worthington shrugged. "I don't know. Maybe that's what makes living such a mystery."

"And dying such an ordeal," Gold added. They climbed word-lessly into the rear of the Mercedes. After taking one last look at the sand-blown cemetery, Abraham flicked the safety on the Uzi, got into the driver's seat of the Mercedes, and drove away.

Anatoli Czenek sat before the mirror in his room at the Jura Hotel in Zurich and stared at himself. He loathed what he saw. No one had ever made him feel guilty before. But even now, the memory of the woman's words made him feel ashamed. Again and again in his mind's eye he saw her dignity, the quiet strength that had sapped his resolve and leached the conviction from his blows.

And try as he had for the past hours, he couldn't stop hearing her calm determined voice, whose unyielding dignity and honesty slashed at him.

"I am only doing my job," Czenek told the disheveled figure who stared back at him from the mirror. "And I will do my job because I have to."

But in the end, he knew he had not done his job that day.

Wearily, he stood up and shed his afternoon's clothes. They were wrinkled from the afternoon's exertion, and smelled of sweat and failure. He trudged into the bathroom and turned on the shower. When it was hot enough to interrogate a prisoner by, he stepped into the stall and closed the door.

Robert Maxwell was troubled. Troubled by what he was read-ing, troubled by what had been said.

Pragmatism had been his life's creed, yet tonight he had met a group of men whose pragmatism had sunk to malignant cynicism. But then, he knew people among the clergy who felt the same about him.

Maxwell pushed his chair away from the simple desk in his quarters at the ecumenical council's headquarters and stood up.

He walked over to the door and stepped out onto the balcony that overlooked the valley of the Inn River. The cold air cut through the pasty haze in his mind. The balcony had been cleared of snow. He walked over to the railing and leaned against it with both arms straight, looking like a preacher braced against the pulpit ready for a sermon.

He thought again of Braun's bizarre briefing in the meeting room. A second shroud, a woman, a murder—no, he thought, a mass murder—by a pope, the rewriting of scripture, the revision of history—easy enough to do those days when so little had been written to begin with—to cover up the existence of Veronica's Shroud.

After the briefing he had felt increasingly like a spy, the feeling intensifying during the evening's reception with Braun and the other members of the council. They were quite sincere and very convincing in their insistence that the existence of a second shroud made little difference to the world's worshipers. What was important was the symbol of resurrection and salvation and the belief in God. People weren't ready . . . couldn't, wouldn't accept a second Messiah.

The revelation of her existence would shake their faith in the Church, causing untold emotional suffering. The truth would not make them free, only unhappy.

And of course the talked about the sectarian violence and unrest that would follow such a revelation, how the Russians and the Communist Bloc would use the situation to expand and consolidate their influence, bringing even more of the world's population under the communist yoke.

Maxwell stared deeply into the darkness, searching for answers—answers that remained as elusive as the pinpricks of light arcing their way across the night sky.

His mind, his intellect, everything he had lived for so far, told him they were right. No truth was valuable enough if it would cause the violence, death, and upheaval that this would.

But his heart refused to listen. He could be pragmatic purely in church matters and doctrine, which usually boiled down to a bunch of old men debating whether or not to add or subtract a word from some creed or liturgy. But this was substance, not floss.

Maxwell turned away from the darkness, walked back into his

room, and closed the door. He stood there for a moment, looking at the thick volumes covering the desk top and resting on the floor. The complete history of Veronica's Shroud: the transcripts of the interviews with Veronica and the people of her village, the decrees of Pope Sylvester I and Emperor Constantine, and the travels of Veronica's Shroud as could best be reconstructed, until it disappeared from a Bavarian mansion in the mid-1930s.

Maxwell rubbed the fatigue from his eyes and looked at his watch. It was after midnight yet he was not sleepy. He sat back in the desk chair, picked up the yellow legal pad, and began to review his notes.

Following the murders, Veronica's Shroud and the documentation of its authenticity were placed in a large box made of gold and inset with precious stones. The top was placed on the golden box and its edges sealed with molten gold impressed with the royal seal of Constantine and the holy seal of Pope Sylvester I.

The box was then placed in a vault beneath what would later be Saint Peter's Basilica. And there it and its secrets rested in peace for seven hundred years.

It was monstrous, Maxwell thought, as he read the notes for what seemed like the thousandth time. It was like watching an old midnight horror movie where the archaeologist and his beautiful assistant open the mummy's tomb and set the curse free on the world. Only now, it was an ancient truth about God and murder that had come back to haunt them. He read on, trying to make sense of the nightmare.

The shroud and its documentation lay in the vault as Saint Peter's Basilica was built around it. And each pope passed on the secret of the shroud to his successor. The discovery of the box survived the sacks of Rome by the Visigoths in *a.d.* 410 and the Vandals in 455.

But the shroud's discovery could not survive politics and degeneration. As the end of the Christian Church's first millenium approached, the popes and the people around them grew to resemble the intemperate and profligate early emperors of the Roman Empire. Greed, sexual excess, and debauchery abounded in the Vatican, with tastes in perversion often rivaling Caligula's. The secret of Veronica's Shroud began to slip past the lips of drunken and licentious popes. And this, more than the debauchery, galvanized the church hierarchy to action.

In 1045, Gregory VI bribed his predecessor—Benedict IX—to resign from the papacy. But the abdication inflamed rather than soothed Church tensions. One faction convinced Benedict IX to retract his abdication, and thus there were two popes claiming the throne of Saint Peter. Efforts to negotiate the exit of one or the other of the popes failed. So a third faction of the church met to select a compromise pope—Sylvester III—to replace them both. But the choice of Sylvester was unsatisfactory to either of the other two groups, so by the end of 1045 there were three popes all battling for control of the hearts and minds of the Christian world, and not incidentally, the considerable wealth and power of the Church.

While the three popes battled one another, more level-headed bureaucrats within the Church removed the golden box with Veronica's Shroud, along with other priceless relics, to hidden places within the labyrinthine corridors of the Vatican, so that none could be stolen or used by the pretenders.

These same bureaucrats sent emissaries to Heinrich III, emperor of the Holy Roman Empire, asking him to intercede. In 1046, Heinrich III replaced all three rival popes with a fourth, Clement II. The emperor backed up his decisions with his army.

An unsteady balance prevailed for a decade until Heinrich III's death in 1056. He was succeeded by his son, Heinrich IV, who was six years old at the time of his father's death.

Maxwell closed his eyes and pinched the bridge of his nose between his thumb and forefinger. How in everlasting hell could any pope ever claim infallibility? Bestiality, necrophilia, orgies that would put the Romans to shame; greed, avarice, a lust for power. There was nothing that could be done that hadn't been done by a pope. And to believe they were infalliable made it necessary to believe that God had sanctioned it all.

He shook his head slowly. The infallibility of the pope was nothing more than apolitical agreement-between later popes and emperors that allowed both of them to rule with unbridled power, the pope by his blessing straight from God, and the emperors and kings by the blessings from the pope. It was all political, all greed:

men used the God as a convenient excuse, a powerful tool for their own purposes.

Opening his eyes, Maxwell returned to his scrawled notes. The words had begun to swim beneath his eyes. Sleep would come soon.

In 1061, Pope Nicholas II died and was succeeded by Alexander II. Alexander II was unpopular with the bishops of Heinrich IV's court and through a technicality—all popes at that time had to be approved by the emperor—the Imperial Synod at Basel declared Alexander II's election void and appointed instead its own pope, Honorius II.

The young emperor, now eleven years old, began to differ with the clergy among his court advisors, and so to make sure that the bishops continued to get their way, Archbishop Anno of Köln kidnapped Heinrich IV in 1062 and ruled in his name.

Heinrich IV, now growing into a strong-headed young emperor, was freed in 1066 and ruled his empire in harmony with the Church in Rome for nearly a decade. But in 1076, the German bishops who held so much sway in Heinrich's court disagreed once again with Rome. They refused to approve the election of Gregory VII as pope, and in the Imperial Synod at Worms, declared him deposed.

In reaction, Gregory VII excommunicated Heinrich IV and all the German bishops. Deprived of his holy warrant to rule, Heinrich IV faced civil war, a revolt by the peasantry, and the loss of his kingdom. The chastened young emperor repented and in 1077 was forgiven by Gregory VII, who also restored his power.

But Heinrich's confession had been a false one, constructed in league with his bishops to buy time. Later that year, Heinrich IV and the bishops again declared Gregory VII deposed and elected instead Clement III as their own pope.

Enraged, Gregory VII again excommunicated Heinrich and his bishops, and took the additional step of awarding the mantle of emperor of the Holy Roman Empire to Heinrich's rival, Rudolf of Swabia.

In 1079, Heinrich IV's forces killed Rudolf of Swabia, crushed the forces loyal to him, and invaded Italy. Four years later, Heinrich IV invaded Rome and drove Gregory VII into exile.

Once in Rome, Heinrich installed Clement III as pope and left, taking with him a gem-studded gold box as part of the booty from his victorious battles.

Maxwell pushed himself away from the desk and stood up. He had had enough reading for the night, and enough to think about for the rest of his life. He walked over to the bed, where the contents of his suitcase were spread from headboard to foot. But his mind wouldn't let go of the shroud.

The whereabouts of the shroud in the nine centuries since Heinrich IV took it from the Vatican were mostly unknown. From the skimpy records kept by Heinrich IV and his successors, it was apparent that none of them knew the true value of the box. It received neither special mention in the royal records nor any special treatment. It was, for all practical purposes, forgotten, along with booty from other raids and spoils from previous wars. Nothing more was heard of the gold box and its priceless religious relics until they turned up in Bavaria in 1935.

As Maxwell stripped down and pulled on his pajamas, he thought of the educated guesses made by Church historians on the probable history of the box. It was likely, according to the Vatican historians, that the box was given as a gift to a valued member of the royal court. The box was probably passed from one family member to another across the centuries. But someone in the long line of heirs to whom the box was bequeathed saw fit to sell it. Perhaps this person needed money, or perhaps had simply no use for a gaudy bejeweled gold box from the distant past.

Regardless of what happened during the nine hundred years that followed Heinrich IV's possession of the box, hard facts about it reemerged in the spring of 1935.

Acting on Hitler's orders, the German government began exacting onerous taxes from Jewish citizens of the Third Reich. Those unable to pay the punitive taxes were forced to sell their homes and businesses to Reich officials or to their friends.

Of course, most Jews did not have enough cash and savings to meet the outrageous Nazi demands, so they gave the government collectors their jewelry and family heirlooms, including art, rare books, antiques, and other times of value.

Maxwell finished buttoning his pajama top and walked across the room to turn out the lights. He stood by the switch for a moment, torn between fatigue and the remarkable discovery he had made that day. He looked at the books on the desk and then walked over to it and picked up his yellow pad of notes.

Sheldon Brucker was the man's name. Brucker had been a prosperous antique dealer in Bad Tolz, a small village south of Munich. Brucker had used a gold box inlaid with jewels to pay part of the Nazi government's tax.

Hitler had not yet formed the Sonderauftrag Linz—the organization responsible for the gathering of art for the Führermuseum in Linz, Austria—but even in 1935, he was aware of the need to scrutinize carefully the objects stolen from the Jews to make sure nothing of value was melted down or destroyed.

Objects from art dealers, antiques dealers, and the truly wealthy were all examined more carefully than the rest. The art experts and historians pressed into service by the Third Reich quickly recognized the extraordinary box with the seals of Constantine and Pope Sylvester I impressed into its metal.

The box had been opened carefully to avoid marring its beauty and the documentation inside quickly translated into German. From the moment the discovery was revealed to Adolf Hitler, Veronica's Shroud became the object of the most intense security ever. Ultimately, the shroud and its flawless documentation would be used by Hitler to assure the Vatican's silence on the treatment of the Jews. The Church would close it eyes to one evil, hoping to save the world from a second evil that might eventually prove greater.

Maxwell got up, turned out the light, and walked through the darkness of the unfamiliar room. Hitler had hidden the shroud well, Braun had told him. So well, that in the chaos following the fall of the Third Reich, it had disappeared as completely as if it had never left its vault in the Vatican nearly a millenium ago.

Now it appeared that modern-day fascists wanted the shroud. The Russians wanted it to blackmail the Vatican into silence on the unjustices of communism, to mute the Catholic Church's virulent criticism of communist regimes in Poland and throughout the world. And religious fascists—the Islamic Jihad, to name just one—wanted the shroud to destroy Christianity. Maxwell knew that there were others, both within the church and without, who would use the shroud for their own personal gain and power.

As he slipped between the crisp, cool sheets, he wondered where Braun and the ecumenical council fit in. Before he could fix on a precise answer, he dropped off to sleep.

CHAPTER TWELVE

Across the trolley tracks and a little west of the main train station in Amsterdam is a bar that has been serving gin for five hundred years. Not the effete gin favored by feverish English cricket players and American tennis dilettantes, but a richly flavored Dutch gin with an integrity its makers call genever.

The bar is old and dim and filled with dark wood, stained darker still by centuries of tobacco smoke. Its wooden plank floors are worn thin by centuries of feet, and the deep spaces between the planks are filled with a grime that has come off shoes worn by the likes of Rembrandt and van Gogh. Inside, it is always hazy with talk and tobacco.

Derek Steele sat at the mahogany bar nursing his genever and watching the man who had followed him for the past three days.

The man had a pale, ascetic face, wild dark eyebrows, and eyes that the old masters used to paint on the faces of the insane. The man's coat hung on a thin reedy frame. What little hair he had left on his head seemed to be a dull chestnut color.

Steele took a sip of the genever and let it roll on his tongue before swallowing it. In the image that played across the mirror behind the bar, he saw the man sitting alone at a small round table with a glass of lager in front of him, reading from a paperback novel.

Steele had first noticed the man at Schipol Airport, standing in the corridor just past the customs area. He had been dressed in an ill-fitting suit that looked as if it came from a secondhand shop. He looked like one of the tens of thousands of bums, street people, panhandlers, and genuine homeless attracted to Holland by its liberal attitudes and its even more liberal social welfare programs.

As Steele had walked past the man at the airport, he had looked directly at Steele and taken a single tentative step. Steele had looked quickly away and picked up his pace to avoid the expected plea for spare change.

Thoughts of the man had quickly vanished on the cab ride into downtown Amsterdam, as fatigue and jet lag leached the energy from first his body and then his mind.

But the man had been sitting in the lobby of the Hotel Victoria when Steele came down for breakfast the next morning. And he seemed to be always just a few feet behind, following Steele as he ran errands among the sleazy serpentine streets of the ZeeDijk section, where anything, it was said, could be bought for a price: drugs, sexual acts that stretched the best of imaginations, contraband jewels, and even firearms.

Steele downed the last of his genever and signaled the bartender for another. He shifted in his seat and heard the Smith & Wesson .357 Magnum in his coat pocket bump softly against the bar.

He had assumed the man worked for Anderson until he had called the NSA man from the Hotel Victoria to report in.

"My man?" Anderson asked with alarm. "I don't have a man in Amsterdam . . . at least not yet."

Steele had felt his legs go wobbly. He had let his guard down, had given the man plenty of chances to kill him, to hurt him. But the man *hadn't* hurt him. He told this to Anderson.

"That doesn't mean he won't do something," Anderson replied. "We've gotten some more information in the last twenty-four hours that indicates there are more players in this game than we originally thought. And they're all dangerous."

"Game?" Steele said. "Is that what all this is to you? A game? This is my life . . . and my wife's life, too. This is no game."

"It's all a game, Derek," Anderson replied calmly. "You really start getting into trouble when you begin to take it seriously . . . you lose your perspective. That's why you need to come into the fold. We can protect you. This isn't being a cop anymore, Derek. This is a different game, a very different game."

Steele had no ready reply for the agent. Maybe it was a game, maybe not. But Anderson was right: whatever this was, it wasn't about being a cop anymore. The painting that rested securely in the locker at Amsterdam's Schipol Airport was a secret too dangerous for him to handle. There was too much to Anderson's game, and Steele didn't even know all the rules.

"Stay in your room, Steele. Eat room service. Stay off the street. Wait for me to get there."

Steele remembered Anderson's words now as the bartender slid Steele's fresh glass of genever across the bar and took the empty glass. That had been two days ago. What had happened to Anderson? There had been no answer at the number the agent had given him and no messages left at the hotel.

Steele decided to map out his next move. He had expected to be in Zurich by now, and he didn't plan to wait for Anderson's next instruction.

He made a show of looking at his watch, then fumbled in his pocket and withdrew a multicolored wad of guilder notes. He rescued two of the notes, passed them across the bar to cover his drinks, then downed the rest of the genever in a single gulp. He slid off the stool and walked casually toward the door. The thin man with the insane eyes closed his paperback and started to rise.

Outside, the street was cluttered with traffic of every description: bicycles, trams, buses, and a mélange of autos from battered Fiats and Citroëns to brightly polished Mercedes, all dancing a delicate mechanical ballet with each other, trying to merge from one nonexistent lane to another in search of a turn, a parking space, or a break large enough to accelerate forward for a few lengths. Walking like a man who has an appointment to keep, Steele passed the display window of a diamond merchant across the street from the bar. Behind the display of raw diamonds and a few odd pieces of finished jewelry, a gaunt woman who looked like a Dachau inmate, clothed in what passed for high fashion, was looking down at the display.

Steele stopped abruptly in front of the window, as if something extraordinary had caught his attention. The gaunt woman looked up at him, gave him a smile that revealed teeth far too regular and white to be her own, then turned away and disappeared inside the store. In the reflection of the window, he saw the man with the insane eyes walk quickly out of the bar and then stop short as he caught sight of Steele.

Steele turned abruptly away from the diamonds and headed toward the central train station, a plan beginning to form in his mind. The man with the insane eyes had not hurt him. In the past three days, he had grown from an object of fear to one of curiosity. Who was he working for? If not for Anderson and not for the KGB, then who?

The question had preyed on his thoughts relentlessly as he sat stewing in his hotel room, trying to follow Anderson's orders. He had a plan for finding out who the man was.

Steele walked like a man with no time to waste, yet not so fast as to lose the man tailing him.

The crowds began to thicken as he drew closer to the train station and diminished his pace to match that of the other early afternoon pedestrians and Christmas shoppers, their arms bundled around gaily wrapped packages and shopping bags. Most of them were women, housewives from the suburbs who had taken the train in for a morning of shopping.

Christmas, Steele thought. Shit. He looked at the date calendar of his watch. Five days until Christmas. He thought of all the Christmases without Stephanie, before they had met: anxious family arguments as a kid, being alone as an adult. Then the joy of learning to love the holidays with her. And when he thought of Christmas without her ever again, bitter heavy sadness swelled in his chest.

The women with their shopping bags crowded tightly around him now as he stood at the corner of the Spuisstraat and the Prins Hendrikkade waiting for the light to change. Steele was surrounded by a million tiny rustlings of paper and wrappings and shopping bags that crinkled. The women chatted gaily in Dutch. Steele could only understand a few words, basically ones that resembled German, but he could tell that, other than tired feet, the shoppers were happy, satisfied, content, anxious to return to their homes and their families. He resented the hell out of all of their happiness.

The light changed, and the crowd spilled off the curve and cascaded across the great open spaces toward the station.

Steele flexed his legs and quickly outpaced the main body of the crowd, gaining the noisy, crowded interior of the Central Station far ahead of them. He walked past the newspaper stand to the train-schedule-covered kiosks with their yellow and white posters of arrivals and departures. He checked his watch again. It was 1:14. He quickly found the schedule for the new train line that connected central Amsterdam with the airport. There was a train leaving at 1:20. Steele noted the track number and turned alway from the kiosk.

Out of the corner of his eye, he saw the stranger pretending to look through the paperback novels at the newsstand.

Steele pushed his way through the crowds to the ticket window at the rear of the next ticket line. Overhead, trains rumbled and thundered, shaking the concrete floor beneath his feet.

When Steele got to the platform, it was sparsely scattered with people, mostly accompanied by suitcases. He walked down to the end of the platform and stopped. The clock overhead said 1:20, but there was no train. Unusual. Dutch trains were almost always prompt.

Steele turned to walk back toward the other end of the platform when he saw his shadow come up the stairs. He turned toward the adjacent track, which bore a sign informing him of a train to Haarlem scheduled to depart at 2 P.M. He looked at the man from across the distance. The stranger turned away quickly and tried to feign disinterest. But it didn't work. Either the man was inept or his superiors wanted Steele to know he was being followed.

The Schipol train rumbled into the station moments later and groaned to a halt in front of the platform. It lurched once and then loosed a great steaming sigh before the doors opened. Out poured a parade of weary faces, sitting atop bodies carrying pieces of luggage. The early afternoon flights from America had arrived.

Steele stepped aboard and looked out. The man with the insane eyes had already gotten on. Steele decided the man was no professional: he should have waited until the last minute.

The doors clunked shut and the train gathered speed. Steele glanced out the windows as the platform slowly slid away. Then suddenly they were back in the brilliant sunlight, snaking along between the harbor and the Oosterdok.

The train made its way southeast through a mostly industrial quarter for a couple of miles and then gently curved to the south. They passed the Amstel station and headed across the open polders.

Steele felt the palms of his hands tingle as he thought of the slim man with the insane eyes in the next car. What connection did he have with Stephanie, with the deaths in Los Angeles? A brief shadow of doubt passed behind his eyes as he wondered if he were doing the right thing. Should he have waited for Anderson? Steele had never been good at waiting.

The train slowed as it entered Amstelveen, a suburb just south of Amsterdam that was separated from the airport by a massive wooded parkland called the Amsterdamse Bos. Steele got out of the car with a half-dozen others who were not headed for the airport. He did not bother to look around. He knew the man with the insane eyes would be behind somewhere.

The traffic in Amstelveen was light compared to the jams in Amsterdam and Steele made good time as he walked directly east from the train station toward the Amsterdamse Bos. As he walked, he remembered the summer day he and Stephanie had picnicked in a green meadow beside a skyblue pond in the Amsterdamse Bos. She had still been a student and had come to study paintings in the non-public collection of the Van Gogh Museum. He had pried her away from her work and she had thanked him for it.

They had rented bicycles and ridden them around the park until it was nearly dark. The terrain they had covered, and the day, were still etched in his memory.

Steele made his way into the eastern boundary of the park. The ground was soft from the winter rains and carpeted with wet, pliant leaves. By now the deciduous trees had been stripped of their finery, but among the pale gray skeletons waiting for spring were stands of conifers that painted deep green smears across the winter drabness. He walked quickly as if late for some rendezvous. He wanted to be deeply in the woods before the man who followed him realized he was in a trap.

He reached the edge of a narrow tarmac road and waited as a lone cyclist passed and disappeared around one of the road's many bends. Steele quickly made his way across and down a short embankment into a copse of young cedar trees. He could see the road clearly from within the cedars. It was a good place to wait.

Time seemed to drag by. Steele gazed at the second hand of his watch. Once, twice around, and still no one crossed the road. Had he lost his man after all?

Steele waited, his warm breath hanging for an instant in the cold, damp air. In the distance he heard the urgent whines of jet engines decelerating, and moments later, the exultant roar of an aircraft breaking free of the earth. There were no sounds of traffic, no signs of cars on the road, and more important, no signs of the man with the insane eyes.

Then, just when Steele had nearly decided to backtrack to see if he could find his tracker, the man emerged from the trees on the far side of the road. He stood on the edge of the woods like a small wild animal afraid of the dangers of open spaces. Then he scurried across the road and plunged into the woods again, his head bent low. Steele realized the man was following the soft clear impressions his shoes had made in the earth.

The man seemed oblivious to all but the footprints before him, and he was almost to the small grove of cedars before he looked up. He stopped and looked at Steele with wide startled eyes. Steele realized then that what seemed wild in the man's eyes from a distance was actually a function of his face. The eyes were dark, almost black, and set deep within their sockets. The man's brows sloped outward over the eyes, making the sockets deeper still. Heavy tangled eyebrows seemed to cover half his forehead.

Steele trained his Magnum on the man's chest, watching with interest as fear flooded his face.

"Don't, please!" the man said raising his hands. "I don't mean you any harm."

"Why have you been following me, then?" Steele asked.

"To find out . . . find out what you are after." the man answered.

"Who wants to know?"

"Many people. Surely you know that?"

Steele nodded. "I know that, and I have a pretty good idea of who's on which side. I've talked to the people on my side and they don't know you."

"Perhaps you're on the wrong side," the man said gently.

"Perhaps," Steele replied, "but I don't think so." As Steele took a step forward, the frail man took a halting step backwards, tripping over the root of a large naked oak tree and fell into a sitting position with his back against the tree's trunk.

"Why have you been following me?" Steele asked again as he stood over the man.

"The people for whom I work are interested in you and the painting."

"How do you know about the painting?" Steele asked flatly.

"We know."

Steele stepped forward quickly and raised his hand to strike the man.

"Stop!" the man said with enough force to compel Steele into obeying. It was the voice of a man used to moral authority, of a man used to having people follow his orders.

"Very well," Steele said. "If I stop, I want something in return. I want information."

"I will tell you what you wish, Mr. Steele," the man replied. "But not at the point of a gun."

Steele looked at him for along moment and nodded. He stepped back several paces and put the Magnum back in his coat pocket. He could have it ready to use in a split second if needed.

The man slowly got back to his feet, taking a moment to brush off the dirt and leaves sticking to his coat.

"My name is Kent Smith. I'm ordained in the Catholic Church and work as an archivist for the Vatican."

"Jesus." Steele said. Smith winced almost imperceptibly at the blasphemy. "And *you* want the painting too."

Smith nodded. "I'm afraid the people I work for do."

"Everywhere I turn up there's somebody else who wants the goddamned thing." Smith winced again.

"And more people will turn up before you rid yourself of this painting," Smith said. "I suppose you thought this was another simple case of the Americans versus the Russians?"

Steele half nodded, not exactly sure of what he had suspected.

Smith shook his head ruefully. "Things are almost never that simple. The world is not binary, you know. Not in most cases. As much as we like to divide them into either and or, good and evil, hot and cold—"

"I don't want a philosophy lesson," Steele said sharply. "This painting is the reason my wife was kidnapped. I don't give a good goddamn about sides and paintings and this consideration and that one. I'm on *my* side. All I want is my wife back And I'll kill you and anybody else I have to—I'll do whatever I have to—to get her back.''

Fear flickered behind Smith's dark eyes.

"We can help you," Smith said finally.

"Who is we?"

"A small but powerful group within the Vatican dedicated to making sure both the painting and the priceless religious relic associated with it are not abused or used by people for their own personal gain."

"You're the good guys? Is that what you're telling me?"

"Don't trivialize things, please, Mr. Steele. We're dealing with things that could alter history—things that could easily upset the shaky balance between communism and the free world." Smith's voice grew strident and evangelical. "This is a far, far bigger thing than you realize, with implications that go far beyond you, me, or your wife."

"I told you I don't care about that crap," Steele said. "There's nothing more important to me than getting my wife back."

Smith studied Steele's face intensely. "I don't know whether to envy your dedication or to pity you."

"You don't have to do either," Steele said. "What you have to do is tell me something useful before I lose my patience."

"As I said before," Smith began cautiously, "there is a small but powerful group within the Vatican—we have the blessings of the Pope—"

"So did Torquemada," Steele said sarcastically.

"You're a difficult man, Mr. Steele."

"I've seen too many people suffer and die at the hands of people who were fulfilling what they thought were God's wishes."

Smith nodded knowingly. "But that doesn't alter the group to which I belong, or our purpose. Granted?"

Steele nodded his assent.

"Good. We're a group charged with trying to root out the worst of abuses, the political struggles and power plays that inevitably result from an organization of our size. Things . . . and people you see, are not always what they seem."

"Like Vatican archivists playing spy versus spy in Amsterdam?"

Smith smiled for the first time.

"Exactly," he said. "And likewise, there are people in high places within both your government and my church who are not what they seem."

"You're being cryptic again," Steele said. "I'd like some specific answers."

"I—"

It was as far as Smith got. For the smallest fraction of a second, Steele saw a luminous red dot on the front of Smith's coat. Its significance eluded him just long enough to make the dot a life and death matter. For, instants later, the crack of a rifle ripped through the silence of the crisp, bright afternoon. Only then did Steele recognize the red dot for what it was: the business end of a sniper's laser range-finder. Steele heard the slug slap through Smith's chest and watched as the frail man was hammered against the oak tree behind him by the impact.

For an instant Steele was paralyzed with fear. The nightmare had returned! Another time, another place, he had spoken with another old man . . .

Steele fought back the panic that clawed at his stomach and let the old police survival instincts take over. He grabbed the front of Smith's coat, brought the man to cover behind the cedars, then squatted down beside him as more rifle shots filled the woods.

Where were they? he wondered, as he pulled the .357 Magnum from his coat pocket. With high-powered rifles and laser scopes, they could be far away, anywhere, even outside the range of the Magnum. The woods were silent again. Steele strained to hear his enemies, but all he heard was Smith's laborious breathing. Steele bent his head low to hear what the man was trying to tell him.

"Brow . . . brun . . ." Smith's voice faded.

Steele bent low over the dying man, trying to snare his last words. But he was too late. Steele felt Smith's body go limp in his arms.

Brow, brun. Steele turned the ragged syllables over in his mind a few times, trying to make sense of them. He finally decided that the word Smith had been trying to say was "brown." Brown? What could it mean?

But Steele had no time to ponder the priest's last words. He heard a gunshot and then, a split second later, saw splinters explode in front of his eyes as a slug embedded itself in the tree trunk just inches from his face.

Steele dropped Smith's body and rolled away from the tree just as a volley of slugs smashed into the tree and the ground around it. Steele heard two of the slugs slap dull and wet into Smith's lifeless form.

Rolling to his feet, Steele raised the Magnum and whirled frantically, trying to spot the gunman. Where was he? How could you strike back at an invisible enemy? Before he could answer his own question, two more shots raised the leaves at his feet. Then he saw them: first two red dots and then three! Swarming about him, dancing about the ground and across his clothing like a flight of lethal stinging insects. There was more then one gunman. Steele's breath came fast and heavy now. He lunged away from the spots, and as he did, slugs, following the paths of the laser sniper sights, plowed into the ground and tossed wet earth and leaves into the air.

It was then that he heard them. From behind. No. In front. They were all around him, closing in. The red dots had returned and again Steele lunged out of their paths. But the gunmen were more methodical, more deliberate, this time. Steele pointed the Magnum in the direction of the first sound and fired. But there was no sound of pain, no cry of surprise. Just the crack of another rifle shot and the searing burning pain across his right side.

Christ! Steele thought, as his left hand touched the wound and came away red and sticky. A quick probe with his fingers assured him that the damage was slight. It was close, though. Too close. He couldn't afford to let the slugs get any closer. Steele jammed the Magnum into this coat pocket and scrambled away, up the short embankment in the direction from which he had come.

He had nearly gained the shoulder of the road when he saw the man step out of the woods on the other side. The man was too far away to identify, but Steele saw him raise a rifle to his shoulder. Reflexively, Steele fell to his face and reached for his Magnum. An instant later he saw a slug gouge pebbles and stone fragments from the road just in front of his face. Oblivious to the gunman behind him, Steele leaped to his feet and brought the Magnum to bear.

The man with the rifle saw him and tried to get off a shot. But a rifle, though accurate from longer distances than a pistol, is an awkward weapon. Steele sighted on the man's chest and squeezed the trigger. An instant later he watched with satisfaction as the slug hammered into the man's midsection, lifting him off his feet and twisting him around in the air. The last image Steele kept in his mind before he dropped on all fours was the sight of the red gaping hole in the man's back, trailing pieces of his entrails.

Steele tucked the Magnum back in his coat pocket and rolled toward a culvert. It was his only way to escape. To cross the road would give his killers a clear, sure shot at him.

Behind him, Steele heard the crashing sounds of men running headlong through the woods. Steele took a quick doubtful look at the culvert. His shoulders were broad and the culvert was narrow. If he got stuck or took too long in transiting it, he would be a sucker's target.

But it was his only chance.

Steele took a quick roll in the muck at the mouth of the culvert with an eye to being as slippery as possible, then plunged in. Inside, the pipe seemed to act as an amplifier; his quick desperate breaths came to his ears like frantic screams. It also snared and amplified the sounds of the man behind him. Steele inched his way through the culvert, pushing with his toes, wiggling his shoulders. The sounds of the men drew closer and closer. He heard their voices now.

"I can't see him anymore!" he heard one call to the other.

"Well, he hasn't crossed the road," came a second, more distant voice. "I have that bloody well covered."

"He must have hidden in the brush along the road," suggested a third voice.

Steele had made good time, but as he reached what must have been the middle of the roadway, the culvert seemed to narrow. He was stuck! Behind him, he heard footsteps crackling through the brush. He shifted his shoulders and still couldn't move. The weight of the roadway above must have crushed the culvert slightly as it settled.

"There's a pipe here that goes under the road." Steele heard the voice clearly. He felt his hands begin to shake and his breath flutter. He swallowed hard and tried to choke back the panic.

"Bring your light," he heard the voice call.

Desperately Steele twisted and turned in the pipe. He felt the edges of the metal tearing at his hands, ripping at his clothes.

"Here's the light," a voice said. "Be careful. If he's in there he'll have his gun ready."

"Maybe we should fire a couple of rounds in there just to be sure."

Straining until blue lights threatened to cover his vision, Steele felt his body move forward, slowly at first and then more easily. He was free!

But would he be in time? Any shot fired into the culvert would surely hit him.

He crawled frantically now, oblivious to the sharp edges of the culvert joints.

The bright circle of daylight ahead of him grew larger and brighter until finally his head emerged and then the rest of his body.

Gasping for breath, he rolled away from the pipe and lay there a few seconds.

"Don't move, Mr. Steele."

Steele froze. Time stopped.

"Turn over slowly and get up."

Steele rolled over slowly onto his back and then began to rise to his feet. In front of him was a man with a toothbrush moustache and a trilby hat. He held the ugly, stubby H&K MP5A machine pistol favored by the British SAS and the German commandos who had freed the Israeli hostages in Munich. It was a fast and deadly weapon at close range. The man saw him eyeing the H&K.

"Don't try anything foolish," the man said. "It will shorten your life considerably."

"Go ahead." Steele heard the voice at the other end of the culvert dimly, as if through an old-fashioned megaphone. An instant later a gunshot, followed by three more.

The man in the trilby jumped and looked at the mouth of the culvert. It was all the diversion steele needed. He leaped on the man, slammed an elbow into his face, and raised his knee into the man's crotch. Steele felt the man's testicles flatten out under the impact. The man's trilby hat flew through the air as he doubled up in pain.

Steele grabbed the machine pistol from the man's weakened grasp. Steele started to run. But the man began to scream.

"Over here! He's over here."

Steele emptied the clip of the H&K into the man, threw the gun to the ground, and sprinted through the woods toward Amstelveen.

CHAPTER THIRTEEN

The room had a view of Zurich, the lake, and the mountains. Mustafa Salem El-Nouty stood for a moment at the sitting room window of his suite at the Dolder Grand Hotel and watched the snowflakes settle on the ground. The snow had filed off the world's rough edges, leaving it with great rounded hills and gently undulating drifts that reminded him of the desert.

He missed the desert. All Bedouins, no matter how far they travel from the desert or how long they stay away from it or how rich they become, miss the desert and the crystalline silence of its hungry emptiness. Even the luxury of $400-per-night hotel suites and the first-class life that accompanied them could not completely blunt the pain of separation. The desert and the Bedouins—*Bedawi* in Arabic—would always be inseparable.

He had been poor in the desert, yet a part of him he could never understand persisted in making him yearn for the old life. Every brush with death and every passing year—time was its own flirtation with death—made the yearning grow stronger.

But he had a reason to return, and diversions to ease his homesickness until he did.

A frown wrinkled across his face as he remembered the reason he couldn't return to the desert. It happened the night Nathaniel Worthington had foiled his assassination of the Iraqi president in London. The scar tissue in his back and around the void where his right kidney had once been began to throb when he remembered the flight, the gunfight, and the frantic scrambling hands of the people at the Libyan embassy who had pulled him inside after he had fallen, critically wounded by Worthington's bullets, on the front door step.

He had failed visibly. The Iraqi president had escaped, and that had upset Colonel Qaddafi. He had been defeated by an American, and that had further blackened his face.

El-Nouty felt a rising anger now as he thought of the debt he must pay before the Colonel would let him live in his beloved desert again: Nat Worthington must die, and he must die by the hand of the one he had shamed. For a Bedouin's *wajh*, his face, is the most important element in his life next to Islam.

Only Worthington's death could erase the darkening of his face—only Worthington's death could obtain the Colonel's forgiveness. El-Nouty had burned Worthington's farm near that godforsaken village in New Zealand and driven him and his wife into hiding. But that wasn't enough, not nearly enough. Worthington had to die. And after him, his bitch wife for her insults to him. His face burned with anger as he remembered the humiliation and pain.

Then, from behind him, El-Nouty heard low sexual laughter filtering from the bedroom of the suite. He felt himself growing hard, and began to forget Worthington, the desert, and the Colonel. Diversions were necessary to make his exile from Libya bearable. The trio in the bedroom had charged him exorbitantly, but they had made life distinctly pleasurable. You could buy anything you wanted, anywhere you wanted it, if you had enough money. And as the world's highest paid assassin, El-Nouty had enough money.

Money was the perfect disguise. It blinded people to your faults, crimes, and sins. They saw only the money.

El-Nouty turned from the window and padded barefoot across the lush cut-pile carpeting toward the bedroom door. He passed a full-length mirror and stopped to look at himself. He smiled as he untied the cord around his waist. His erection pressed at the fabric of his brown velour robe, standing free as the front of the robe parted. He let the robe drop to the floor, leaving his smooth alive skin framed in the mirror.

He admired the way his 215 pounds covered his elegant six-foot-seven-inch frame. Veins throbbed on his arms, his legs, the washboard ripples of his stomach, and along the shaft of his hard penis, which bobbed up and down in time with his heart. He turned toward the bedroom.

When he opened the bedroom door, he saw a young woman with blonde hair and large breasts kneeling between two athletic men in their mid-twenties, fellating them both by turns. She looked up when El-Nouty opened the door, slipped a penis from her mouth, and gave him a large smile. El-Nouty noted with satisfaction that her eyes went immediately to his crotch, and that her smile broadened as she did. She stroked both of the men's penises, one in each hand, as she looked at him.

"Continue with what you were doing," El-Nouty commanded as he stepped toward the trio. He walked over to a large armchair in front of the drawn curtains and sat down to watch. He had seen the trio perform their live sex act on the stage of a small and exclusive club just off the Niederdorfstrasse and had hired them to perform for him during his spare moments. They had earned their money well, offering him all their orifices for his penis to enjoy.

El-Nouty stroked himself slowly as he watched one of the men lie down on his back and pull the girl down to him. She eagerly sat on his erection and slid langorously up and down along its length. The other man walked around and, straddling his companion, offered his penis to the girl who immediately took in in her mouth and began to suck it.

El-Nouty stood up slowly and walked toward the trio, still undecided as to how he would enjoy himself. He walked up to the man who was standing, grasped his penis, and pulled it from the girl's mouth. She looked up at him and smiled. El-Nouty thrust his erection in her mouth, and—still holding the other man's penis in his hand—began to thrust his hips. She took all of his shaft and did something wonderful to it with the back of her throat. El-Nouty stroked the man's penis as he closed his eyes and enjoyed her ministrations.

After a moment, he pulled the other man closer and offered his penis to her. She took them both into her mouth, each thrusting at her from opposite sides while her body moved up and down from the third man who moved inside her.

El-Nouty felt his penis sliding against her tongue and against the other man's shaft. His mind spun with the possible combinations of their bodies and how he would use them. He remembered how he and the two men had filled all of the woman's orifices, taking turns until each had completed a full circuit. He remembered slipping his penis up the men's rectum as they thrust their shafts into the girl. He wanted it all at once.

The telephone rang twice and then stopped. The girl seemed to tense up, but then relaxed instantly. El-Nouty thrust harder against her mouth and then decided.

He slid his penis out of her mouth. He walked around behind her and knelt on the floor between her legs and those of the man pumping into her so energetcially. El-Nouty reached in and pulled the man's slick penis out of the woman, licking the bottom of the shaft before re-inserting it. Then he spread the girl's cheeks and probed at the tight pink rosebud of her anus with his tongue. He inserted first his little finger and, successively two and three, and finally with a fluid shove of his hips, slid in his penis. He heard her gasp as he began to pump. He could feel the other man's penis sliding against the narrow tissues that separate the rectum from the vagina. El-Nouty liked the sensation.

El-Nouty closed his eyes and enjoyed her young tightness. He felt his heart pounding and his breath coming in quick audible gasps as he pumped faster and faster. He could feel the fluid rising in his groin when the door of the suite exploded inward. He withdrew from the girl and started to rise. He heard someone at the door yell in Hebrew: "Get away from him!"

Time seemed to telescope into the slowest of motions as El-Nouty's brain raced. The two rings from the telephone moments ago: a signal. The performers' willingness to come to his suite. The men were circumcised. He had dismissed that as common today even among non-Jews, the order just now in Hebrew. He looked around him and saw that his naked sex partners had rolled away from him, leaving the intruders a clear shot at him. The signs had been there all along, and he had failed to recognize them. It had been a trap all along. A Mossad trap.

Turning to face his attackers, El-Nouty heard the first muted phut from a silenced weapon. An instant later, he felt the slug slam in to his right shoulder and spin him around. He shoved with his left leg, trying to spin himself further out of the line of fire. As the room whirled about him, he caught a glimpse of two men at the door, in dark three-piece business suits with ski masks over their faces and tight black leather gloves on their hands. He heard other silenced shots as he stumbled away from the door, but all of them missed.

There was a Graz-Burya automatic in the drawer of the bedside table, and as El-Nouty spun away from his attackers, he rolled across the bed and off the other edge toward the table.

The pain burned in his shoulder as he reached for the drawer in the beside table. He bled freely on the lush cut-pile carpeting.

Across the room, he could hear their voices clearly now. One in particular.

"Get out of here quickly!" He heard the voice ordering the two naked men and the woman from the room. "You've done your job." It was Nat Worthington's voice!

El-Nouty lunged for the drawer and pulled it open. Grasping the Graz-Burya with his left hand, he flicked off the safety and began to turn toward the man who had to die for him to erase his shame.

Nat Worthington watched the bloodied Libyan turn suddenly toward them.

"Watch it!" Gold warned.

But Nat had seen the gun in El-Nouty's hand. He quickly changed the Uzi's fire selection switch from single shot to full automatic. Nat fired from the hip as El-Nouty brought his own gun to bear.

Slugs from Nat's Uzi walked a crooked line across the wall beside El-Nouty, pocking the carefully smoothed plaster and sending a small geyser of dust and fragments from each impact. And then the hard dry thuds abruptly turned dull and wet as three slugs stitched across the smooth olive skin of El-Nouty's chest, plowing into the lean, perfectly formed pectoral muscles.

The shots hurled El-Nouty's body against the wall, a single wild shot from the Graz-Burya gouging a jagged hole in the ceiling. The unsilenced handgun sounded like a cannon in the room.

"Shit," Worthington said. "Everybody and his aunt'll be up here in a minute."

They rushed over to El-Nouty. The Libyan's eyes were closed. Red froth bubbled at the holes in his chest. The assassin was dying, his lungs filling with blood.

"I'll go make sure the others are dressed and out of here before the police come," Gold said as he headed for the sitting room of the suite.

Worthington sat on the edge of the bed and stared down at his old enemy. And suddenly the horror of the business he was in rushed out at him. He felt weary, tired of the whole sad mess. It wasn't supposed to be like this, he thought. He was supposed to be the jubilant victor, the triumphant warrior. Worthington felt a brief stab of remorse, then reminded himself of the death he might have had at the Libyan's hands.

Then El-Nouty's lips began to work. He was trying to say something.

"What did you say?" Worthington asked, as he leaned closer. "I can't hear you."

"How?" El-Nouty's eyes remained tightly shut against the pain.

"How did we find you?" Worthington said. "You got set in your ways. That's why spying's a young man's job. You got old enough and set in your ways. Your sexual habits didn't change. Your love for fine hotels and elegance didn't change. There are only so many elegant hotels in the world, especially ones where you can conveniently buy the kind of sex you like. A lot of people want you, El-Nouty. We set a lot of traps. It was only a matter of time before you fell into one."

El-Nouty tried to say something else, but the words were indistinct. Worthington leaned closer, his face almost touching the Libyan's.

"What's that?" Worthington said. "I can't hear you." He leaned closer.

In an instant El-Nouty's powerful arms were about him. The awesomely strong fingers of his left hand, strengthened grotesquely by a lifetime of compensating for the lack of a right hand, closed around Worthington's throat. At the same time, El-Nouty passed his right arm around the back of Worthington's neck and caught it in the crook of his elbow. He forced Worthington's head into the grasp of the left hand, which probed and strangled.

Nat twisted but could not get free. He pushed against El-Nouty's body, but his hands found no purchase against the slippery wetness of the blood from the Arab's wounds. Worthington tried to reach the Uzi, but he had set it down purposefully far away so

El-Nouty wouldn't be able to grab it. He tired calling for help, but the Libyan's grip throttled back even small choking sounds.

A constellation of blue pinlights began to fill Worthington's vision; the room began to grow dimmer. How long could the Libyan go on? His strength was not human!

Worthington twisted and wriggled, but El-Nouty's grasp was unflagging. Nat pummeled the Arab with his fist, to no avail. He found the Libyan's genitals and struck at them, he pulled at the penis, tried to crush the testicles, but still El-Nouty's grip tightened. His hatred had taken him to a place beyond pain. He should be dead by now, but some mystical force seemed to drive El-Nouty on.

Nat continued to pound at El-Nouty's most sensitive places, but his blows grew weaker as the blue lights filled his vision and the world grew darker. He sat on the edge of infinite darkness.

Then from somewhere in the darkness, Worthington heard a sound. Instants later, he felt warmth splatter across his face and the vise around his neck ease.

When he came to, Gold was standing next to him and El-Nouty's body was slumped against the wall, the pink grayness of his brain showing through an open crater in his head. Gold helped him to a sitting position on the bed. Worthington probed gingerly at his neck. It would be sore for a long time. He wiped at his face with his hand. The hand came away with jellied blobs of El-Nouty's brain tissue clinging to it.

He almost made it into the bathroom before vomiting.

Adam Gold stood by the bedside, listening to Worthington, looking at the wasted body of a man they had hunted for more than a decade. Unlike Worthington, Gold felt a glimmer of triumph as he remembered the faces of the agents that El-Nouty had killed or maimed. Gold protected his agents and he had taken each death and injury personally. Now it was over.

He turned away from the body, walked quickly to the bureau, and began pulling open the drawers. As he pulled out El-Nouty's hand-tailored, fitted shirt, he heard the faint sounds of excited people. Someone had heard the shots and would arrive in minutes.

He thought for a moment of the three people he had hurried out the door moments before. They had earned their pay and in their own way had contributed to the security of Israel. When he had approached them, one of them had even asked about immigrating there. He would help her.

Closing the first drawer, he pawed through the second, third, and finally the bottom one. He found nothing helpful.

Gold stood in the middle of the room and looked around. Even the best agents, the most careful, leave clues behind as to where they've been. It's usually just a case of recognizing them.

The barely audible whine of a siren made its way through the soundproofed rooms of the hotel. They had to get out of there, Gold told himself. His attention was attracted to El-Nouty's wallet and a pile of change and loose paper on the dressing table.

Rifling through the wallet, Gold found several large bills in the currency of half a dozen countries, the usual complement of credit cards found on international travelers, and membership cards in several exclusive clubs in Switzerland and London. But, again, nothing helpful. He slipped the wallet in his pocket. Using the credit card numbers, they could trace his whereabouts from the transactions. And they'd surely trace the club membership to find out who sponsored El-Nouty. When they found out who—and what—he had really been, those people might turn out to be valuable allies either through blackmail or, preferably, cooperation borne of the outrage of being deceived.

Gold turned his attention to the loose papers. They were all short cash register tapes for various small amounts not exceeding the equivalent of six U.S. dollars. All of them were torn half in two as was the custom at European cafes when a customer paid the tab.

None of the tapes had a name on it. Gold started to toss the tapes back on the dresser surface when it came to him.

He picked up one tape and noted the string of numbers across the top. There was a serial number, followed by the date and time of the transaction. He looked at the second tape. Same serial number, different date. With growing excitement, Gold noted that all of the tapes had the same serial number. He shoved the tapes in a side pocket and rushed to the bathroom.

Worthington had washed his face with cold water, and except for his paleness, looked fit to Gold's eyes.

"Where's your mask?" Gold asked as he pulled his own off his face.

209

"Stuffed in to the back of my pants," Worthington said. Gold nodded and slipped his along the small of his back where the tension from his belt hid it from sight.

They walked to the door. From outside they heard voices hurrying up some distant flight of steps.

The telephone rang as Gold turned the knob. They hesitated. Both knew that skillfull handling of the caller might yield invaluable information. The telephone rang again. The voices from the hallway grew louder. In moments the killing would be discovered. Again the telephone rang.

"Let's go," Gold said, opening the door. The telephone was still ringing as they entered the hallway and closed the door firmly. Both men peeled off their thin black leather gloves and stuck them in side pockets of their coats as they walked briskly away from the babble of excited voices.

CHAPTER FOURTEEN

Anatoli Czenek stood next to the desk in the warehouse office and shivered imperceptibly as he listened to the telephone ring for the ninth time. He was about to hang up when the line clicked at the other end.

"Hello?" The voice answered in German.

Czenek didn't recognize the voice. It certainly wasn't El-Nouty's.

"Ah . . . yes, hello," Czenek replied in German. "May I speak to Mr. El-Nouty?"

"Who is this?" the voice asked suspiciously.

"I should ask you the same thing," Czenek replied sharply. "I called for Mr. El-Nouty. Please put him on."

"That's quite impossible," the voice said. "And I think you should identify yourself. I am David Bratz, chief of security for the Dolder Grand Hotel."

Czenek hung up the receiver. He looked at the four men assembled in the office. There was Pyotr Sergiev, the KGB operative who ran the warehouse and its shipping business as a front for smuggling Western technology into Russian. Next to him stood George Molotov, chief of the KGB's Zurich station, who posed as the consulate's cultural affairs officer. Behind them were two KGB thugs who looked as if they had seen too many American gangster movies.

Molotov spoke first. "What's the matter?" he asked, as Czenek slowly replaced the telephone receiver in its cradle.

"I'm not sure," Czenek said slowly. "The telephone in El-Nouty's room was answered by the hotel's security chief."

"Oh, damn," Sergiev began to shout. "Now you've done it. You've gone and ruined all that I've worked for all these years. You and that sleazy Arab and your fucking paintings and religious mumbo-jumbo. I ought to—"

Molotov raised his hand and shot Sergiev a look that would blister paint.

"You'll do nothing, Comrade Sergiev," Molotov said ponderously. "You have performed a valuable service. But the task given to Comrade Czenek and to our Third World brother, Comrade El-Nouty, is one of the highest importance, which our leaders in Moscow have seen fit in their wisdom to keep mostly to themselves. My orders state that we are to do whatever is necessary to see this operation to a successful conclusion, even if it means sacrificing your operation here or"—his voice dropped "—any of us present."

Sergiev's eyes widened momentarily. "Yes, Comrade," he replied in a chastened tone of voice. "I am sorry for my outburst."

"Good." Molotov said, satisfied, and then turned his attention to Czenek. "What do you make of this man being in El-Nouty's room?"

"It could mean many things," Czenek began carefully. Molotov was one of those party apparatchiks who could make a man's retirement very, very miserable, or at least extremely uncomfortable. Good results that compromised political purity were a failure in the man's eyes.

"There could, perhaps, have been a burglary, or perhaps a fire in El-Nouty's room," Czenek offered carefully. "But that's doubtful."

Molotov nodded his agreement.

"Whatever's happened seems to be either a local hotel matter or one which the Zurich police have not yet had time to respond to."

Molotov nodded again.

"In any event, I believe we should assume to worst," Czenek said. "That one of the many foreign intelligence services that have been looking for El-Nouty has finally succeeded in finding him."

Molotov's head bobbed in pensive agreement before he said, "In which event, we should withdraw all our personnel here."

It was Czenek's turn to nod his agreement. Sergiev's eyes widened in horror.

"But . . . but . . . but—" Sergiev's stuttering attempt to object made him sound like a faulty outboard engine. "But all the . . . my time . . . the, the—"

Molotov's voice was soothing when he spoke: "You have made your contribution. You will be well rewarded. But it's time to bring this operation to a halt before the West discovers it."

Sergiev took a deep breath, looked as if he were going to speak, then decided better of it. He loosed the breath in a defeated sigh. "Yes, Comrade."

"How long will it take to . . . wind things up here?" Molotov said.

"Not very long," Sergiev replied. "The warehouse is nearly empty, due to the—" He shot a resentful glare at Czenek. "Due to the exigencies of the present operation. The crating of the art has been completed. The crates—marked as tractor parts—are being loaded at this very moment. That task should be completed within the hour. We can transport our files to the consulate to be designated as diplomatic baggage. That will take less than another hour. The only piece of loose baggage is . . ." He nodded toward the room in which Stephanie was kept.

"Yes," Molotov said simply. "That's why I've brought my two assistants from the consulate." He turned and smiled at the two brawny men, who had started to run to fat.

"I understand the girl is quite attractive," Molotov said.

Czenek acknowledged the fact with a reluctant nod. He could see where it was all leading.

Molotov smiled broadly. "Good, good. That's very good." He turned to the two men behind him. "You will telephone the consulate for a truck and then make sure that all of the files in Comrade Sergiev's operation are carried safely down to the truck and the vehicle sealed. You will then dispatch the girl in an untraceable manner. I do not care what you do with her before that, but I want to be sure she has disappeared by . . ." He looked at his watch, "by six o'clock at the latest. That gives you three hours."

"Three hours will be sufficient," the larger of the two said.

Czenek felt his anger intensify as he saw the two thugs exchange smiles and walk out of the room. He thought again of their woman captive and how much she resembled his wife. And suddenly he hated all the men in the room very, very much. He included himself.

Braun had erected a large map stand on a tripod. On it now was a topographical map of southwest Austria. Braun was using a pointer to trace the movements of gold and art looted by the Nazis.

"It is somewhere here." Braun made a small circle on the map with its center near Altaussee. "We know from captured records that the truck carrying the shroud reached Bad Ischl. But beyond that, it could be anywhere. The hills in this area are honeycombed with natural caves and salt mines."

Ten men—the ecumenical council still had a single vacancy caused by the murder of the Polish priest—sat around the table watching Braun, their expressions ranging from polite but bored disinterest to extreme fascination. Robert Maxwell was engrossed.

"I realize several of you already know most of this," Braun said, looking at the Anglican bishop who looked as if he would fall asleep any minute; the late afternoon's fading light helped the man's attention to wander. "But there are good reasons for reviewing the situation." Braun stood with his hands behind his back, like tank commander delivering the briefing prior to the final battle. "We are close now, very, very close. We should have all of the facts firmly in mind. My sources have been transmitting information on a daily, sometimes hourly, basis. Most of you have not been here for nearly three months and much has happened since then. Most significantly, the painting of The Home of the Lady Our Redeemer has surfaced, albeit briefly."

"Good Lord." The Anglican stirred to life. "I had almost begun to believe it was just myth." The other members looked at him with special tolerance. He was insufferably upper British crust, but he was also extremely powerful. He had spent World War II in military intelligence behind enemy lines and had accumulated a treasure of favors from the men who now ran the British government. Most of them would dispatch and agent on the bishop's word without asking embarrassing questions. The council had re-

214

lied on those agents many times in the past, and all present knew the wisdom of not antagonizing him. He was very valuable to them.

"And why now?" the bishop asked.

"Why now indeed," Braun echoed remotely. His thoughts seemed to wander for an instant to a place far beyond the room. With a visible effort, he brought his focus back to his audience.

"Why not? Because of an old man with a lifetime of guilt and a painful secret."

Puzzled faces stared back at him.

"I'm only now piecing together part of the answer to that question," Braun began, as he paced slowly in front of the map. "The information seems to come in almost hourly. But I'll tell you what we've learned. One of the faithful of the Catholic Church had been a sergeant in the SS in World War II. He had been assigned to work in some secret installation near Altaussee. The Shroud of Veronica, gentlemen, was hidden in that installation. The sergeant served as adjutant to the installation's commandering officer, and as such was one of only three or four people at the installation who knew what they were really guarding. Most of the troops thought they were there to guard Hitler's personal art treasures, many of which were also stored in the same place.

"It seems our sergeant had an attack of conscience when a young man was shot skiing near the perimeter of the installation." Braun pulled his chair away from the table and sat down. "Although troops at the installation were forbidden to visit the town of Altaussee, the sergeant felt the need for confession, and for that reason entered the town surreptitiously to see the local parish priest, a man named Werner Meyer.

"The sergeant told the priest about the shooting, and then he blurted out the secret they were guarding." Braun paused as he looked around the table. "I am not sure what happened after that. I do know that several days later, there was a massive explosion at the mine just hours before the Allied forces marched into Altaussee. Father Meyer was shot several times by the retreating Germans. Meyer survived, though, due to the good skill of the American army field hospital."

"I remember you telling us about this priest before," said an ascetic-looking Dutch Orthodox minister who sat at Maxwell's left.

"Please refresh my memory as to why we haven't interviewed him."

Braun smiled. "Father Meyer, though he has expressed a deep interest in the recovery of looted art and relics, sustained severe head injuries in the shooting by the Nazis. He managed to survive with his considerable intellectual abilities intact. But the surgeons, in removing some of the damaged brain tissue, destroyed much of his memory. Poor father Meyer suffered from almost total amnesia for nearly two years. And when his memory flooded back, he was still left without any knowledge of the sergeant or the location of the installation. He wandered the hills with others after the war, but there were so many Nazi encampments guarding the entrances to so many mines that it was impossible to determine which one might have held the shroud.

"In any event, as the Allied forces approached, the sergeant and many of his comrades deserted the camp, taking with them as much of the precious art as they could carry. In a country where paper currency was worthless, only gold or valuable antiques and paintings could be used to barter for food, safety, and transportation. It's unlikely that the shroud was among the items taken by the deserting soldiers, since it was protected by a heavy vault, much like the time vaults banks use today.

"As best I can piece things together, the camp commandant, when he discovered the looting and desertion, set off special explosive charges to seal the mine. Troops were sent to comb the woods and kill the deserters.

"It was not known until recently who among the deserters had survived," Braun continued. "But the sergeant had, and apparently in fine style. He and the bulk of the art he had stashed in a stolen jeep managed to make it to Konstanz, where he had relatives. They in turn, smuggled him across the border into the neighboring Swiss city of Keuzlingen, where he was hidden from the authorities by sympathizers.

"With help from his friends and family, and through the use of considerable business acumen, he built a small fortune in valuable paintings into a huge fortune in art. He bought, sold, and bartered fine art. But in all those years, he did not sell or even tell anyone about a small painting he had taken." Braun looked around the table at his audience. "Yes, gentlemen, The Home of the Lady

Our Redeemer has resided in a baronial mansion in Kreuzlingen all these years.''

"But, as I asked before,'' said the Anglican bishop, "why has it surfaced now?'' The bishop's daydreams were gone.

"After a lifetime of living with the secret, the sergeant decided he needed to get it off his chest. So he did what he had done forty years before. He used his wealth to track down the priest who had given him absolution in Alt Aussee.''

"Meyer,'' Maxwell said softly.

Braun nodded. "Correct. Werner Meyer. We—the Vatican—had given Meyer a fairly free hand to pursue his hobby of tracing lost art and treasures. He concentrated on those of religious value and had had some minor successes in recovering objects from a variety of faiths. We have also . . .''—Braun searched for the correct phrase—"kept close tabs on Meyer, in the event that he should develop helpful information on the whereabouts of the shroud.

"Well.'' Braun picked up the pace of his soliloquy. "In April of this year, the sergeant contacted Meyer by telephone—Meyer lives in a small abbey in Munich—and made a clean breast of everything. The sergeant had lived an assumed life for four decades, and, suddenly, the specter of dying caused him to throw caution to the wind. He asked Meyer—no, he begged Meyer—to come get the painting. He offered to pay transportation and expenses. But only if Meyer would agree to make the shroud's secret known to the world. Meyer, being the sort of person he is, agreed.

"Meyer's request to travel was, on the Vatican's orders, refused. In the meanwhile, we tried to arrange for the purchase of the sergeant's entire art collection—including the painting in question—through a disinterested third party.

"But things went sour. The sergeant's manor burned, destroying—we were told by the local authorities—all of the art contained in it. The sergeant died of a heart attack suffered during his attempt to save his collection.

"But now we learn that Russian and Polish agents probably got to the sergeant first,'' Braun said. "They interrogated him, took his paintings, and burned his mansion down to cover their tracks. There is a supreme irony here; the paintings have now been looted three times in the past half century.

"But we have good reason to believe that the communists didn't get the painting of The Home of The Lady Our Redeemer."

"But where could it be?" Maxwell asked.

Braun shrugged. "As best we can tell, the only person who knows is an American professor named Derek Steele, or perhaps his wife, if she if still alive."

CHAPTER FIFTEEN

The mechanical thunder of Zurich's huge rail switching yard rumbled through the thickening darkness as Adam Gold and Nat Worthington trudged along the Geroldstrasse toward the panel truck Gold had rented at the airport. In their rough clothes and boots, they could be two workers leaving work . . . or arriving for the night shift.

"They've got to be here somewhere," Worthington said doubtfully.

They had been able to trace the model and serial numbers of the cash register receipts to a small cafe just off the Geroldstrasse. The cafe was nothing exceptional in looks, but when they stopped in and ordered coffee and a late lunch, they discovered simple but outstanding fare. Even so, it must have been conveniently close for El-Nouty to stop here so frequently. He preferred eating establishments with white linen tablecloths and extensive wine lists, not paper napkins and beer in bottles.

The owner had remembered El-Nouty well; "the snotty Arab," as he referred to El-Nouty, had come in once or twice a day for the past week or so. He always seemed to arrive on foot. "Which I found odd," the cafe owner volunteered, "since he was always wearing those pointy Italian loafers with the thin soles. They don't hold up the snow and rain very well, I wouldn't think. Most of the men who come in here work in the warehouses and wear boots with steel reinforcements in the toes."

They thanked the man for his information, ate his food, paid him for it, and left. And for more than three hours now, they had scoured the industrial quarters around the cafe in every direction. And in three hours, they had found nothing. The warehouses all looked the same. They were all anonymous and cheerless and dimly lighted, revealing nothing about the activities inside. They had even walked the tracks behind the warehouses, but there was nothing to distinguish one from the other, certainly no sign of a woman being held as a hostage.

The clear cold wind ranted through the dusk. Gold tugged his jacket tighter at the neck after encountering a particularly sharp-tongued blast.

"I guess we go back and ask for more help," Worthington said.

Gold shook his head. "I can't justify using anybody else. They'd never approve it back in Tel Aviv. The only reason we're here now is that I got approval to see if we could trace any of El-Nouty's associates. But now that he's dead, they don't care a lot back in Tel Aviv. They want us back immediately. There's no way they'd give me a helluva lot more help, and for sure, no more people. I'm the one who owes it to David Simon, not the rest of the Mossad." He stopped and looked at Worthington. "Not even you. You don't have to come along with me. You can go back to Tania now. Your farm's safe now that El-Nouty's dead."

Worthington nodded. They walked along in dejected silence for another half block before Worthington spoke.

"I know. We already talked about that. I can't let you do this alone. You do it for Simon. I'll do it for you. Okay?"

Gold smiled warmly and they continued their walk. In the distance they could see the panel van.

"Besides, I want to have a chance to use those toys we've got in the back of the van," Worthington said, trying to cheer them both up. It didn't work.

The van contained a variety of weapons and explosive they had brought with them from Tel Aviv after being notified of El-Nouty's presence. They had overprepared, knowing they would have to have everything on hand to handle any situation that might come up. The materials had arrived via Lufthansa air freight in wooden crates marked "Kosher Chablis."

"I don't think you'll get a chance to see the gadgets work," Gold said glumly. He wanted badly to use them or whatever it

220

took to free the girl. He had felt too guilty for too many years, sitting in Tel Aviv with his colonel's rank and sending young men to die for their country. Most of them had deserved more to live than he. Gold had gradually grown apologetic about the lack of serious injuries sustained during his early years in the field. Finally he told Worthington: "I've just got a feeling we're too late for the woman that David Simon told me about."

"I hope you're wrong, but—"

Worthington stopped as they reached the corner across the street from the cafe. To their right, about half a block down, they watched two burly men carrying a filing cabinet from one of the warehouses. Both men were wearing suits.

"Hello," Gold said as he watched. "What do you suppose we have here?"

Worthington turned down the street toward the truck. Gold followed.

Worthington felt his pulse accelerate as they neared the truck, trying to appear nonchalant. They switched into German, and talked about football and the damned influx of *Gastarbeiteren*—imported foreign workers.

As they drew closer they noted that the suits worn by the two men wresting with the filing cabinet in the back of the truck were dark, and poorly tailored on their massive fleshly bodies. As they passed, Worthington caught a glimpse of a shoulder holster as one man twisted, trying to position the cabinet. One of the men glared at them and returned to his work.

Gold and Worthington reached the end of the block and turned the corner.

"That's it!" Gold said excitedly. "That has to be it! Those apes have KGB written all over them."

"Yes, but that's hardly enough reason to blast our way into the warehouse," Worthington cautioned.

"I agree," Gold said, his enthusiasm unslaked. "But did you notice the truck?"

"What about it?"

"The plates," Gold said. "The license plates were diplomatic plates. And I'll bet they belong to the Russian consulate."

* * *

221

Anatoli Czenek lounged uneasily in the hardbacked wooden chair in the warehouse office. Sergiev sat in an indentical chair behind the desk and glared at him as Molotov's two brutes carted the last of the filing cabinets from the room. Sergiev chain-smoked the most disgustingly foul cigarettes, and the hair hung heavy and blue between them, like a smokescreen between two warring battleships.

The smoke made Czenek want to cough, but he wasn't going to give Sergiev that satisfaction. Besides, a bubbling indigestion almost made him forget the smoke. It burned under his ribs like a fire. He should never have eaten the second helping of *Rösti* at the little cafe. It had never disagreed with his digestion before, Czenek thought, but then he *was* getting older. It hurt to admit it.

It hurt even more to feel so lost for a direction. For the first time since he had been a young man and trying to set a course for his future, Czenek now felt rudderless and morally invalid.

Damn her! God damn her to hell! He cursed to himself and he couldn't decide whether he was cursing his wife or the woman in the next room. Together, they had unwittingly conspired over distance and time to unhinge his self-confidence and undermine his judgment.

What could he have been thinking? Damn you, you romantic dreamer. He cursed himself now. What possible insanity had seized him when he had left his raincoat and the key to her manacles. Did he really think that she would unlock herself, put on the overcoat, and push past the guards to a successful escape? Damn the fantasies. Fantasies hadn't kept him alive all these years. Reality had done that. Reality had kept him alive in the field longer than some men live as office clerks.

But as he thought about his wife in the institution, about the woman in the next room, and about the plans that Molotov's animals had for her, his long years of survival seemed to add up to a worthless sum. But it was too late to recalculate all the integers that formed the sum. It was too late for him, too late for his wife, too late for the woman in the next room.

The winter night filled the streets of Zurich. Nat Worthington locked the door of the panel van securely, picked up the large box

222

tied with twine, and joined a stream of pedestrians as it flowed back toward the warehouse Gold was convinced held the woman. Behind him, the van's engine idled smoothly.

The sidewalks were thronged now as the men who worked in the warehouses went home for the evening. In half an hour, things would be completely deserted. Worthington glanced at his watch as he walked. In another half an hour—at quarter to six—different men would be pouring into the warehouse district for the night shift.

The box rattled softly with each step as Worthington lugged it back toward the narrow alley he and Gold had turned into their staging area. The alley ran along one short end of the rectangular warehouse and connected the street with the rail yard behind it. Both ends were secured with a chain link fence that had yielded easily to their wire cutters. The cuts wouldn't be visible until morning, and by then it would make no difference.

The sidewalks thinned as Worthington turned the corner. The night was thicker here, held back only by the glow of electric-arc streetlamps that splashed bright circles of daylight on the sidewalks and along warehouse walls and then faded back into the night. Ahead of him now just half a block, he could see the truck with the diplomatic plates. The lights were out and the vehicle was unattended, as it had been for more than half an hour now.

Across the street, Worthington watched a man detach himself from the stream of homeward-bound workers, step off the curb, and head directly for him. As the man drew closer, Worthington shifted the heavy cardboard box to his left hand and slid his right inside his coat. His hand closed around the grip of the mini-Uzi which hung in its leather holster under his left arm.

The man was out of the range of the streetlights now, and was a night-on-night shadow steering a collision course with Worthington's own. The man was almost close enough to have to shoot when Worthington realized it was Adam Gold.

"Relax," Gold said as he fell into step next to Worthington. "It's going to go okay." Gold's voice was filled with the eagerness of men who have taught themselves to forget, if only for a moment, the memories of past violences and the sounds of people dying.

"What were you doing over there?" Worthington looked across the street.

"Diversion." Gold said. They walked two more steps and he explained. "When we start up at the warehouse, the street's going to be crawling with police, firemen, spectators . . . maybe even a few reinforcements for our two apes with their poorly cut suits." They walked several more paces. "I wrapped some C-4 around a huge gas valve in the alley between those tow buildings back there."

C-4 was plastic explosive.

"When it goes, we'll have an explosion to keep the authorities out of our hair." Worthington's step faltered for a moment. Gold sensed Nat's concern.

"Don't worry," Gold stopped and laid his hand on Worthington's arm. "It's not going to hurt anybody. The valve's on a concrete pad a good twenty feet away from the walls of the two warehouses. The valve'll go straight up and so will the flames. It'll be spectacular—loud and bright—but not very dangerous. The police and the firemen will stand around looking at it while they wait for the gas company too locate the main shutoff valve. By that time, we'll be gone."

Worthington nodded reluctantly and they continued their walk. Gold was right, Worthington conceded. They were two men against at least half a dozen—maybe more, counting the workers they had seen loading the crates on the boxcars at the rear of the warehouse. To survive and to rescue the woman—if she was indeed inside—they would need surprise on their side, surprise and cunning. They had both of these elements, Worthington thought with some satisfaction. And they had an additional advantage. Overkill.

The van contained enough C-4 to level a city block. But they had used only small amounts placed in strategic locations around the warehouse. A few ounces here, a few there. All connected to timer detonaters constructed of cheap digital watches. The alarm times on the watches varied. All of the charges were designed to startle and distract rather than kill and destroy.

As they approached the warehouse, both men strained to find any sign of sentries who might catch them sneaking through the cut fence into the alleyway.

"You see anything?" Gold asked Worthington, as they continued to walk.

"Nothing."

"Me neither," Gold replied.

As they approached the breach in the wire fence, Gold walked quickly ahead and bent low to grab the cut edge. Worthington slid the box through the hole first and then sidled through himself. Gold followed moments later.

Silently they made their way into the darkest recess of the alley, a thicket of blackness untouched by either the streetlamps behind them or the glaring kleig lights atop towers in the rail yard beyond. Worthington set the box down and massaged is cramped fingers.

Both men stood for a moment, their breaths floating white and opaque in the cold. The wind hummed through the high-voltage wires overhead.

Then Gold moved. He used a folding woodsman's knife to slice open the box Worthington had carried from the van. From it, he pulled two breadloaf-sized packages wrapped in plastic, and laid them on the concrete alley floor. Then he pulled out a shoebox that rattled as the contents shifted. Next he turned the large box over to use as a work surface. On it he placed the two gray loafs and the shoebox. He cut the tape on the shoebox lid and opened it. Inside, it was filled with digital watches, the wristbands having been removed. Each of the watches had a twisted pair of wires leading from it to a small detonator box.

Gold palpated the two loafs.

"We've got to work quickly," Gold said. "It's already starting to get hard."

"I've got the van's heater going full blast," Worthington said.

"Yeah," Gold said as he pulled the plastic wrapping from the doughlike loaf of C-4, "but the outside air has to be close to zero . . . Fahrenheit, not centigrade. In ten minutes, this stuff'll be so hard we'll have to use the whole package in one whack."

Worthington looked at him sharply. The entire loaf would level the warehouse.

"Just a joke," Gold said. "Just a joke." Gold winked, then tore a handful of C-4 off the loaf and molded it in his hands into a wad the size of a handball. As he did, Worthington stood silently by his side trying to screw up his courage. His resolve had died with El-Nouty. With the Libyan no longer a threat to him and to Tania, he was suddenly afraid for them . . . for him: he wanted nothing more than to take her back to New Zealand and rebuild their lives and their farm. And so he had no more courage, no more daring.

And yet, a small part of his mind told him that he had never been very brave until all hell broke loose.

Gold finished one ball of C-4 and pressed a timer and detonator into it. Then he repeated his actions until there were two hand-molded bombs. Gold squinted at his wristwatch, held it close to his face, then took a small penlight from his pocket, turned it on, and held it in his mouth as he carefully adjusted the alarm settings on both. When he was finished, he looked up and handed the devices to Worthington.

"Put these at the bases of the fences at both ends. I want to make sure there's nothing in our way if we have to get out of here in a hurry."

Worthington took the devices without comment and walked to the fence nearest the railyard. Before he pressed the still-pliable explosive to the base of the fence post, he examined the timer closely and noted it was set for 6:01. The rest were set for 6:00. He looked at this own watch. It read 5:37.

As Worthington walked back through the darkest part of the dark alley, he noted that Gold had already attached a half-dozen small charges to the warehouse wall. The charges formed an arc that led from the ground to an apex about six feet high. Worthington walked past without comment as Gold continued to slap more charges on the wall, eventually completing a ragged circle. The C-4 would blast an opening that would take the defenders inside by surprise. Few people ever prepared themselves to defend against an attack that came through a concrete wall.

Gold was now running twisted pairs of timing wires from their detonators to a single timer. When the moment arrived, the tiny electrical charge from the digital watch's alarm circuits would travel along the wires and trigger a sensitive relay in the detonator. The detonator's central capacitor—much like the charging devices in a camera's electronic flash—would then discharge a brief surge of fifteen thousand volts into the C-4. And a split second after that, a segment of the wall would disappear. It would also kill or maim anyone on either side of the wall within a radius of twenty or thirty feet. Gold just hoped it wouldn't bring down the entire wall, which would also collapse the roof, probably crushing them in the rubble.

"All set, partner," Worthington said calmly. "What's next?"

Gold stood back and looked at his handiwork. He glanced at the fences at either end and then back at the arc of explosives on the wall in front of him.

"Only this," he said, as he leaned over and plucked a golf-ball sized blob of C-4 from the surface of the overturned box. He pressed a detonator into its surface and handed it to Worthington. "Go stick this on the electrical supply box." He nodded toward a huge gray metal trunk hanging on the warehouse wall near the railyard fence.

As Worthington walked briskly toward the end of the alley, Gold rummaged about in his toolbox and pulled out a small metal container the size of a package of cigarettes. Two prongs protruded from its bottom end. Gold took the remainder of the C-4—and untouched loaf and part of the second—and placed it on the ground. He pressed the prongs of the small metal box into the untouched loaf of C-4. He then pulled a small piece of stiff wire from the box; it telescoped up precisely four inches. Next, using the penlight to illuminate his handiwork, Gold flipped a switch on the box to "TEST." A small amber light shone in the darkness.

This done, Gold walked back to the toolbox and pulled an almost identical metal box from the interior. He pulled out a four-inch length of stiff wire, and pushed the switch to "ON."

Standing next to the loaf of C-4, Gold pushed a small flat button on the box in his hand. The amber light on the companion box blinked rapidly. It was operating.

Gold then turned off the switch on the unit in his hand, pushed the wire down inside it, and slipped it into his coat pocket. He then leaned over and flipped the switch on the second box to "ARMED." A red light shone. It was now impossible to turn the switch off without detonating the entire block of C-4. Worthington returned as Gold placed the overturned box on top of the loaf of C-4 and its detonator to hide them.

Worthington looked at his watch. "And now we wait?" he asked.

Gold nodded solemnly as he walked toward the fence through which they had entered the alley. Gold hoped they would be out

227

of danger there when the main explosion blew a hole in the wall, and away from the smaller one that would blast the electrical box at the other end of the alley.

Worthington followed him. They squatted in the shadows next to the fence, and, like paratroopers waiting for the final buzzer, silently pulled out their weapons and checked them: mini-Uzis—more compact versions of the famous battlefield weapons; clips taped back to back, ready for quick reloads; and spare clips tucked into their belts and in their coat pockets.

They checked their sidearms. Both opted for the familiar Colt .45 automatic, M1911, which would tear a man's arm off if you could just wing him in the biceps.

And the bulky cargo: stun grenades, designed to flash and disorient; smoke grenades to provide cover where there was none; fragmentation grenades to kill; incendiary grenades to burn. both men had been outnumbered enough times to know that survival meant being ready for unexpected situations.

Their weapons checked and rechecked, both men squatted on complaining knees and stared at their watches as the second hands crawled like glaciers.

Worthington broke the silence. "Waiting," he whispered. "The soldier's curse."

"And prayer," Gold added as he bowed his head. "Prayer. The soldier's deliverance."

Nat bowed his own head and waited.

Stephanie felt oddly calm. An icy numbness gripped her body when she finally realized she was about to die. The dull realization spread like an anesthetic, deadening her emotions and honing her wits.

She sat on the edge of the bed, absentmindedly caressing the bruises their brutal hands had left on her breasts and the insides of her thighs. They had come in and torn the T-shirt from her body. She had not resisted physically, but she had glared defiantly at them both. As she limply let them handle her body, her eyes had worn a look of triumph that told them they would never break her dignity no matter what they did to her physically.

Her defiant passivity infuriated the two KGB brutes, and instead of raping her they beat her for several minutes before the tall one pulled his comrade away and whispered something to him in Russian that Stephanie couldn't understand.

Then they left the room.

How long ago had that been? Stephanie wondered but didn't care. Lifetimes could pass in a second; she recently had known seconds that seemed to last for lifetimes. It didn't matter, not here and not . . . not in the other world beyond the boundaries of the warehouse. If that other world still existed. She had been caged for so long that a normal world with normal people and normal food served on plates and normal hot showers and toilets that flushed—that world seemed no more real to her now than the storybooks she used to read as a child.

Stephanie shook her head to clear the thoughts that were headed for self-pity. She was beyond pity, for herself or others. There was only the damage she would inflict before they would kill her.

In the chilled numbness of her mind, she was in the final moves of a long and nearly stalemated chess game. She remembered playing games like that with her brothers. Moves and countermoves, pieces dancing about each other, each player waiting for the other to make the fatal error. Only this time she had started the game in check; mate had always been just one move away for months now. And now at last, she saw the final moves sliding into place.

She had been a brutal chess player—determined, even when she could see the game was lost, to inflict the maximum damage on her opponent. And she would do that here as well, she told herself as she used the key to unlock the manacle that attached her to the wall. She walked quickly to the chair, picked up the overcoat Czenek had left there, and swiftly put it on and buttoned it up.

Outside she heard voices. Her tormentors would return soon; she could sense it. Calmly she surveyed the room, as if for the first time. She had lived in the room for months, but only with the clear vision granted by the certainty of her death was she able to see it as a place filled with potential weapons.

It was dismally bare, as if someone had foreseen her present circumstances. Her motions were sparse and unwasted as she determined that all of the drawers in the desk were empty, that the chair was too heavy for her to swing as a weapon, and that the wooden frame of the cot she had slept on for months was fasted together with bolts and wingnuts for portability and quick assembly.

Moments later, she had the cot upended, its legs sticking rigidly in the air like the limbs of a dead horse. She unscrewed one of the legs. It was a piece of wood two inches square and about eighteen inches long. She stood up and hefted the stick. It felt good. But she needed an edge to make the stick lethal. Quickly she spotted the end of the bolt sticking from the frame. She worked it loose, inserted it in the hole in the end of her club, then fastened it tight with the wingnut. She would have liked to put a point on the end of the bolt, but there was no time. She hoped she could swing the club—perhaps at the temple where the skull was thin—with enough force to penetrate the bone. She could see the three-inch length of bolt hammered into the tall man's temple, could see him toppling to the floor. She was the white king, cornered by the black pieces, striking back in her last moments. The thought pleased her.

She walked over to the door and tested the knob. It was locked. She waited behind it.

The wait was not a long one. In moments she heard their voices—laughing voices—and along with it a sharp metallic snapping sound she couldn't identify.

Outside Stephanie's quarters, the two bulky KGB agents walked along the catwalk that faced both offices on the mezzanine level. Below them, workmen loaded the last of the crated art into boxcars. In one hand, the short agent held a length of lamp cord with a plug at one end and two bare wires at the other. In his other hand he held a roll of adhesive tape.

"This will be interesting," the taller agent said in Russian as they approached the door to Stephanie's cell. In his hand he held a staple gun. He pulled the handle and watched as a half-inch staple flew from the end. "It will easily penetrate the flesh. I have used it successfully in many interrogations. It is most effective when the staples embed themselves firmly in the bone."

They walked another two paces before the shorter one spoke. He held up the lamp cord and asked: "And this, comrade?"

The tall man smiled.

"We have many options," he said. "We can tape the wires to her body, or we can staple the bare wires to her. The second method makes for a far better electrical connection." Both men

230

grinned as up ahead the locked door to Stephanie's room loomed before them. As he reached the door, the tall man pulled a key from the side pocket of his jacket and inserted in into the lock.

Stephanie shouldered her club like a baseball player stepping up to the plate. She heard the lock click and stood back in the shadows as the handle of the door turned slowly. Her fear returned and felt like a cold heavy stone against her heart. The door opened. She heard them babbling in Russian.

As the door swung open, she stepped out to make sure her swing would reach its target unimpeded. Suddenly the men stopped talking. They must have noticed her absence. Now! She swung the club forward with all her might, the muscles in her legs and back straining to the utmost, concentrating all of her strength into the point of the bolt as it homed in on the short man's head.

Then she felt her stomach knot into a slick tight fist as the short man's head started to turn. Time distilled itself into stop framed she would remember the rest of her life: The short man's eyes widening as they fixed on the club. The contorted anger carved into the tall man's face when he spotted her. The deadly end of her club arcing down on the short man's head. The short man's head as it twisted frantically out of harm's way. The grimace on the short man's face as the blunt end of the club smashed into the bridge of his nose. And the final frame, the satisfying vision of the blood spurting from the short man's broken nose just before the hamlike fist of the other man hammered into her own face and brought the warmth of darkness to her thoughts.

CHAPTER SIXTEEN

Serge Petrovich opened the front door to the warehouse and stepped into the steadily chilling night. Behind him, Sasha, his three-year-old Alsatian, rushed outside and dashed halfway down the block before Serge's whistle brought her back toward him in quick dashing circles. Technically, she wasn't a trained guard dog. But she was large and had an intimidating bark and growl. And she kept him company during the long lonely hours, usually in the dead of the night when the embassy assigned him to sentry duty.

The warehouse hadn't been bad duty as it went, Petrovich thought as he closed the door and walked stiffly toward the embassy truck parked at the curb. He had watched the truck from the peephole in the door for hours now, ready to shoo away the hostile or the merely curious. He considered it the ridiculous paranoia of that prissy embassy stuffed shirt Molotov who—through his family connections, favors, and shameless ass-kissing—was his boss.

Serge watched Sasha loping her way back toward him, stretching her young legs in the crisp night air. He had gotten Sasha as a puppy three years ago, right after the embassy had posted him to the warehouse. They had let him put an old blanket inside a wooden packing crate for her to sleep in. And Sergiev, bastard that he was, was a sucker for animals. He tried to tell everyone that is was good for security to have a dog in the warehouse. But Serge could see the affection in the man's eyes for the puppy that had grown into an Alsatian the size of a small pony. Sasha owned a corner of the warehouse now. In it were food and water bowls and a handsome doghouse made of a large wooden shipping crate.

Cursing at Molotov under his breath, Petrovich checked the passenger side door of the van. It was still locked. No surprises there.

Molotov, the bastard, was closing down the warehouse operation. Serge didn't know what they did at the warehouse. He didn't care. He only knew that he'd probably not find another posting as comfortable, and one where Sasha could stay so close by. He walked around to check the rear doors. Locked. So was the driver's door.

So where would they send him next, he wondered as he stood on the sidewalk between the truck and the warehouse and stretched. He was still young, only twenty-eight, and still unmarried. They sent people like him to places they wouldn't send a man with a family. Serge had only his mother for family, and mothers didn't count with the KGB.

He looked at Sasha now, sniffing along the perimeter of the warehouse, using her nose to read an invisible history book of people and other animals long since gone. Serge leaned against the rear-quarter panel of the embassy van—gently so as not to set off the motion detector—and fumbled around inside his coat for the pack of American cigarettes.

He pulled the pack out, shook out a single cigarette, and placed it between his lips. Sasha was barking now, not angry challenging barks, but the high-pitched playful yips she made when she was on the hot trail of one of the cats that belonged to the embassy's kitchen staff. Serge looked at her, down near the corner of the warehouse building by the chain link fence that blocked off the alley between it and the next warehouse.

With a disposable American lighter, Serge lit his cigarette and coughed violently after the first puff. He coughed again and spat a firm blob of phlegm from deep in his chest. Again he resolved to quit smoking, drawing heavily on the cigarette as he pushed away to see what Sash was so excited about.

"Damn! Go away! Go away, damnit!" Gold whispered as he tried to shoo away the dog. He looked at his watch. There were still ten minutes to go before the first charge was set to explode.

Worthington placed his hand on Gold's shoulder and moved over him toward the dog.

"Hey puppy," Worthington said as he scrambled over to the hole in the fence. "Come on boy, shu-u-u-sh, shu-u-u-sh." Worthington watched as the dog stopped its high-pitched yips and looked at him, its bright eyes reflecting the streetlights. It was a beautiful Alsatian, whose glistening coat shone black and silver under the artificial night lighting.

Tentatively, Worthington bent the cut edge of the wire fencing back and extended his hand. The dog stepped forward and licked the hand. He reached out and stroked the dog's head. The fur was soft and rich. The Alsatian had an owner who cared for it well. The dog quieted down. Worthington looked at his watch—eight minutes to go. He relaxed a bit. All they would have to do was keep the dog quiet for another eight minutes and then—

Gold smelled the cigarette smoke first. He pulled his mini-Uzi from hits holster and held it at his side. The sound of quiet gritting footsteps came to them from just around the corner. Worthington was reaching for his own mini-Uzi when he looked up and saw a man pointing a large caliber revolver at his face. He held a cigarette between the second and third fingers of his left hand.

"Don't move!" The Russian ordered in Russian, and then again quickly in German.

Gold calculated the odds. It would be possible to bring the Uzi to bear on the man, but he clearly had to drop on Worthington and would most probably shoot him before Gold could pull the trigger. Gold froze.

The tall agent who worked for Molotov leaned over Stephanie's face and leered down at her. He had tied her naked and spreadeagled her to the top of the desk. Ropes from her wrists and ankles ran to the legs of the desk. In the corner of the room, the smaller man sat on the desk chair, hunched over, elbows on his knees, staunching the flow of blood with a handkerchief.

"We are not playing games anymore," the tall man said to Stephanie is passable English. "You are going to die, but before you die you will experience great pain." He smiled as he ran his rough calloused hand along the inside of Stephanie's thigh.

Tears of frustration streamed down Stephanie's face.

"I could kill you quickly," the tall man said, "but it is much more satisfying to kill you slowly." He leaned over and came up with a length of electrical wire.

"You will dance for me," the tall man told her. "When the current goes through your body, you will ask me, beg me for mercy. You will want me to kill you quickly. But I won't. Do you hear me? I won't." The tall man smiled to himself, dwelling for am moment on "interrogations" he had conducted in the past. "You will lose control of your bladder and bowels and the excrement will collect beneath you. But I will stop only to make sure you do not die too soon. You are a young and healthy woman. You might live for hours."

He picked up the staple gun from the floor. Straightening back up, he held it in front of her eyes. For an instant, she thought he was going to put her eyes out with it. She felt a bitter scream welling in her throat. But he turned instead and walked to the other end of the desk.

Stephanie raised her head and watched as the tall man lifted her foot. She tried to kick at him, but the ropes were too tight. She felt the tough ends of the wires on the electrical cord as he placed on of them against the ball of her foot, and she watched as he brought the staple gun up and placed it against her flesh.

She screamed when the first staple ripped through the skin and embedded itself in the small metatarsal bone behind her middle toe. She screamed louder when the second staple stabbed home and louder still with the third.

The first scream interrupted Molotov. The embassy's chief KGB officer stopped talking for a moment and raised his eyebrows. Apparently Lubchek and Sanyev had gone back to work. They were efficient, those two. Especially Lubchek. As he stood there, seeming to gather his thoughts, Molotov wondered what combination of circumstances had produced a man like Lubchek, a man so in love with torture. Molotov's contacts in the home office had spoken of certain childhood deprivations, a brutal gang rape when Lubchek was only six, but still, none of what he had heard accounted for the agent's extreme sadism. Molotov thought for an-

235

other moment, then gave a dispassionate shrug, counting himself lucky that he would never be one of Lubchek's victims.

He resumed his final briefing to Czenek and Sergiev, telling them about a message from Paris, an intercepted telephone call to a Zurich art gallery and frame shop, and a man named Derek Steele, who had escaped from Czenek in a blinding rainstorm days before.

Steele, Molotov continued accusingly was the man Czenek had not stopped. Sergiev's eyes flashed at Czenek, dark and victorious. And now, Molotov said, Steele would be here in Zurich—a final chance for Czenek to correct his earlier mistake.

But Czenek had stopped caring about Steele or Molotov or Sergiev or even whether they posted him home and chained him to a desk in the basement of state security's drab headquarters in Warsaw. All Anatoli Czenek could think of was the nausea and the pain that burned in his upper abdomen and the screams from the next room that bleached the meaning and threat from Molotov's words.

Beasts, Czenek thought, as he sat there and nursed the indigestion that just kept getting worse and worse. Perspiration ran down his face. Beasts, all of them. For the first time he considered the possibility that the indigestion that burned in his chest might be more than a tainted meal. He wondered if maybe his soul had finally had all it could take of a tainted life.

He shivered now as he listened to the tortured cries for mercy. They were cold and cut him deeply in places knives could never touch. Somewhere among the strains of agony he thought he heard a cry from within himself. The worst beasts, he thought, are the ones we all struggle to keep inside ourselves.

"Out!" Serge Petrovich demanded in German. "Come out now!" He waved his revolver menacingly. Behind him Sasha looked on in bewilderment. The men were angry at each other, his master at the pleasant man who had rubbed her head with genuine affection. Sasha paced unevenly behind her master.

"But all we wanted was a dry place to sleep, sir," Worthington responded in the most grammatically fractured German he could muster. "If you turn us over to the authorities, they will deport us back to Hungary. We have jobs here, send money back to our families.''

Worthing swallowed hard against the fear that rose in his throat. Would the man buy their story? Two *Gastarbeiteren*—guest workers—in the country illegally, working for money to send back to their families in Hungary. Gratified, Worthington watched the man's gaze waver. It must be close to the time now, Worthington told himself. All they had to do was stall until the first charges detonated.

"Your dog is very pretty," Worthington said genuinely. "And such a nice smooth coat. You must take very good care of her."

Serge Petrovich smiled involuntarily at the compliment. Yes, he did care for her very well. He loved the animal as much as many people loved brothers and sisters. Then he remembered Molotov, just meters away inside the warehouse, and Petrovich's smile dissolved. Molotov would shoot these two guest workers in an instant. He would find a way to call it self-defense, to brand the men as agents—provocateurs from the West. Molotov was a man like that. That was why he was the head of the KGB in Zurich and Serge Petrovich was a simple guard whose best friend was a three-year-old Alsatian called Sasha.

"I don't know . . .'' Serge said uncertainly. "Perhaps we—''

The Serge saw the Rolex on Adam Gold's wrist. He tightened his grip on the revolver and looked at the man more closely. Guest workers didn't wear Rolexes. But some foreign agents did.

Serge felt his heart thumping in his chest as he stepped back and pulled back the hammer of the revolver. The sound of the revolver's cocking mechanism reverberated menacingly as it advanced the cylinder to a fresh round, placing a split second of air between the hammer and Worthington's death.

When Serge recovered his voice, his words contained a strength and menace he had not believed he was capable of: "Do not make any sudden moves or I will kill you quickly.''

Stephanie cried out in agony as the taller man continued to abuse her. Both her feet burned with a hellish pain that ran like molten steel up both legs to her head and back. But she refused to beg for mercy. She would not give him that satisfaction.

Then the assault of new pain gave way to the dull throbbing of the old as the man dropped the staple gun and approached the end of the desk where her head lay. He held the plug end of the electrical cord at her face like a snake handler brandishing the fanged, open-mouthed head of a rattler.

"You will beg me," the man said. "You will beg me when the volts singe your flesh. Then you will dance. Maybe two dozen times you will dance with me. They all beg sooner or later."

He walked over to the wall next to his comrade with the bleeding nose and knelt on one knee next to the electric socket.

Gold and Worthington were standing in front of the fence now, hands on top of their heads. The Russian had stepped back and was reaching for the radio at his belt. Holding the revolver steadily in his right hand, the Russian brought the radio to his mouth and pressed the transmit button.

As hard as he tried to remember in the following years, Serge Petrovich could never recall the exact moment the radio had been ripped from his hand. Nor could he recall his revolver flying across the sidewalk. All he could remember was the terribly explosion that ripped through the night just before he pushed the button. There was the explosion behind the two men he had held at gunpoint, and there was also another, simultaneous one behind him, across the street, and down the block.

The first blast knocked his feet from under him and set him backwards onto the pavement. He hit his head and lost consciousness for a moment.

Then there was Sasha standing over him, licking his face and pawing at his shoulder. The blast had numbed his ears and produced a physical pain behind his eyes. He sat up and shook his head, trying to clear the fireworks from his vision. Struggling to his hands and knees, he finally stood and looked around.

The two men he had held at gunpoint were gone. Beyond the fence, he could make out a gaping hole in the side of the warehouse.

Molotov was going to be furious, very, very furious with him. He would know that Serge Petrovich had failed to prevent an attack by two agents from the West. Serge didn't know how, but

Molotov always knew. And what Molotov didn't know, he made up—stories that were accepted as the truth because he was the head of the KGB in Zurich. The head of the KGB always found someone else to blame things on. And Serge Petrovich knew he would get the blame for this.

As the dizziness cleared, it was replaced by seething fear and uncertainty. He felt Sasha rubbing against his leg. He looked down at her and she seemed to be trying to tell him something.

Molotov would probably have him shot. And there would be no one to care for Sasha.

On shaky legs, Petrovich turned in a short circle, surveying the world around him. Across the street a pillar of flame shot into the night sky like a message from hell. A message from hell. Molotov's hell.

Serge Petrovich knew then what he had to do. He ran. With Sasha pacing alongside him, Serge ran away from the flames and the explosions and the first twenty-eight years of his life. And in his mind's eye, he saw the smartly dressed marines who stood guard just outside the entrance to the American consulate. They would know what to do with a Russian seeking asylum.

CHAPTER SEVENTEEN

Fragments of the concrete wall shattered by the blast skidded and clattered around them as Worthington and Gold stood just inside the hole blasted in the warehouse wall and surveyed the interior. With the power out, the only illumination in the warehouse was a ghostly yellow flickering that came from a small fire started by the main explosion in a pile of cardboard and wooden crates filled with packing material. It was enough light for them to see where they were going but not enough to make them sitting ducks.

It was nearly empty. Near the front, tucked in a corner, they saw a desk near a large wooden crate with a hole in it. At the rear, the large loading dock doors were all closed except for one that looked out on the open door of a boxcar filled with crates.

Ahead of them, the warehouse floor was bare save for a forklift. The flames flickered off the silver propane fuel tanks behind the driver's seat.

"Up there." Worthington pointed toward a balcony-like mezzanine level two doors and two large glass windows. It had obviously been placed high off the floor to avoid occupying usable warehouse space, and to give the warehouse foreman a good view of activities below.

"Got to be it," Gold said as he looked around the warehouse again. "There's nowhere else to keep anybody, unless . . ." He let his words trial, unwilling to consider the possibility that their efforts had been in vain. What if they were too late to save the woman David Simon had felt so strongly about saving?

As the ringing of the blast subsided, Worthington and Gold suddenly heard cries of pain and surprise from the mezzanine offices. There were shouts—angry, surprised shouts—and mixed in with them, the high-pitched screams of a woman.

Molotov let loose a string of invective as he got first to his hands and knees, then stood shakily in the darkness. He shook his head to clear his thoughts.

Czenek shakily grabbed the edge of the desk and struggled to his feet.

Sergiev's panicked shrieks filled the darkness, rising and falling like a siren, the sound trapped in the confined office. The shrieks stirred old fears in Czenek's mind and sent wild panic tingling through his body. The pain beneath his breast bone had intensified.

Czenek wrestled with his panic as he watched Molotov's pale ghostly outline move shakily toward Sergiev. Czenek moved closer himself, and saw that Sergiev was bent in a fetal position on the floor, holding his face. Moving dumbly like a sleeper pursued in a nightmare, Czenek fumbled in the middle drawer of the desk, pulled out a small electric flashlight, and shined it on Sergiev.

The floor around Sergiev was puddled with blood. Czenek stood transfixed as he watched Molotov grasp Sergiev's wrists and forcibly pull them away from his face. It was a sickening sight. Sergiev had been sitting next to the window when the blast rocked the warehouse and blew in the window. The shards of glass had sliced away most of his nose and carved a huge piece of flesh away from his right cheek. The white of the bone shone bright and glowing under the flashlight's beam. But what made Czenek shut his eyes and turn his head was the sight of Sergiev's bloody eye sockets. Both of them were gaping holes filled with the remains of eyes that would never see again.

Sergiev was screaming louder now, screaming in pain, screaming at Molotov to leave him alone, to get him to a doctor, to do something to save his eyes, his sight.

Czenek felt like screaming a long with Sergiev. Instead, he pulled his pistol from its holster, made his way to the gaping window, and looked out on the warehouse below.

The fire caught his attention first. Then the gaping hole in the warehouse wall. Then the two men illuminated by the flickering light of the fire.

"Molotov!" Czenek shouted over Sergiev's screams. The KGB chief was immediately at Czenek's side.

"Down there," Czenek pointed at the two figures. They were obviously carrying some sort of automatic weapons."

"Uzis?" Molotov asked.

Czenek shook his head. "Too far. Can't tell." Czenek winced as the pain from his indigestion or whatever it was burned white-hot.

"You take the one on the left," Molotov commanded as he whipped out his Graz-Burya automatic. Oblivious to Sergiev and to the cries for help from the next room, Czenek and Molotov braced their elbows on the sill of the bombed-out window and brought the muzzles of their guns to bear on the two figures passing before the flames.

"Now!" Molotov said.

Stephanie's legs spasmed for an instant as the electricity coursed through her body. Then the warehouse shook with a deafening blast and everything went dark. The desk rocked for a moment, then settled down. Small slivers of glass filled the darkness and pricked her side. In the back of her mind, she said a word of thanks that the Venetian blinds were always kept closed. They had screened out most of the shards.

With the electrical shock gone, the pain from the wounds in her feet once again throbbed.

In the strange yellowish light that filtered through the mangled blinds, she watched her two tormentors pull their guns and move swiftly toward the door. That was when she started screaming for help.

"Shut up, you!" the short man said viciously as he rushed to her and struck her alongside her temple with the barrel of his gun. She twisted way from him. "Shut up or I'll kill you now." He brandished the muzzle of the gun in her face, then turned abruptly to rejoin his partner at the window.

From the room next door, the sharp reports of two shots cut through the night.

"Let's go!" Gold said eagerly, as he ran toward the stairs that led up to the mezzanine offices. But just as Worthington sprinted to catch up with him, two shots echoed across the warehouse and scraped long white gouges in the concrete floor behind him. Gold caught sight of the muzzle flashes and loosed a wild volley from his Uzi as he took cover behind the forklift. Two more shots issued from the mezzanine, following Worthington as he dived for cover beside Gold.

"Warm welcome," Worthington said as he crouched at the front of the forklift and gazed up at the mezzanine offices.

"You expected maybe eggnog?" Gold replied as he peeked around the rear of the forklift.

Just then two new guns opened fire from the other window.

"That makes four," Gold said, jerking his head back into the safety of the forklift's heavy bulk.

"At least," Worthington said. "Why is that rear door open to the boxcar? I can't imagine they'd leave it unattended."

Worthington's doubts were confirmed when two men stepped through the loading door from the boxcar, firing Kalashnikovs with their distinctive banana-shaped ammunition clips. Slugs slapped and scraped the concrete all around Worthington and Gold and slammed into the body of the forklift with dull metallic thuds.

"Behind the wheels," Worthington yelled. "Quick!" Worthington lunged for the front wheels of the forklift as the gunmen from the boxcar lowered the aim of their Kalashnikovs and began skipping slugs under the carriage of the machine. To his right he heard a sharp cry of pain.

"Gold!" Worthington said. "Are you all right?"

The Mossad colonel clutched his ankle, rocking back and forth as he cursed under his breath.

"I'm all right." Pain colored Gold' words. "Just slower than the bullets."

Around them the gunfire intensified. Slugs continued to pound the forklift both from the men out of the boxcar and those in the mezzanine area. The forklift sagged wearily on its shot-out tires as it settled down, its metal rims grinding against the concrete floor.

Then, as if a signal had been given, the firing stopped. In the relative quiet Worthington heard the roar of the gas fire down the block, the hungry crackling of the fire that fed greedily on the pile of packing material inside the warehouse, and, almost lost beneath them both, the thuds of running feet that swiftly grew louder.

Worthington stretched around the front of the forklift to get a look. Gunfire erupted instantly from the mezzanine. Worthington felt the soft etheral breath of one of the slugs as it ruffled the graying hair at his left temple. He threw himself back into the shelter of the forklift. The running footsteps became still louder. The men with the Kalashnikovs would be on them in an instant.

From outside the warehouse came a dual *crump-thud* as the charges Worthington had set on the fences at each end of the alley detonated. For an instant the footsteps faltered, the sounds of men startled by the unexpected explosions.

Worthington seized the opportunity and lunged past Gold. Still protected from the bullets of the men in the mezzanine, Worthington crouched at the rear of the forklift and had a brief impression of two men, caught in mid-stride, their heads turned not toward him but toward the source of the explosions.

As their heads started to turn back, the man on the left spotted Worthington and brought his weapon to bear. With a reflex action born of years of training, Worthington flicked his Uzi's fire selector to full automatic and pulled the trigger. He raked both men with the Uzi's withering fire, bringing the muzzle down to follow the men as they hit the floor.

As the Uzi's clip ran out, Worthington ejected the empty clip and rolled back into the protective shadows of the forklift. In an instant he slapped a fresh clip into the Uzi and stepped back to finish the job he'd started.

But the first clip had done the job. In the warm flickering light of the flames behind him, Worthington could tell that the two men would never be a threat to anyone again.

Worthington stepped back and turned to Gold, who now sat on the floor with his back propped against the rear wheel of the fork-lift. The Israeli had his pants leg pulled up and was binding a nasty wound from a slug that had torn through his calf.

"How bad?" Worthington asked as he knelt down.

"When I die, it won't be this that kills me," Gold said as he pressed a gauze pad into the wound and fixed it to his leg with a strip of adhesive tape. "But, I'm sorry to say, I won't be much of a dance partner."

Worthington nodded gravely. The wound had destroyed the Mossad officer's mobility; Worthington would have to assault the mezzanine area alone. But there was no longer any doubt, any question. The operation had began and it would be finished.

A new sound had begun to lace itself into the patterns of fire and explosion: sirens.

"They'll be here in minutes," Gold said. "Firemen, too." The mission had to be wrapped up almost instantly. There was no legitimate way for either Gold or Worthington to answer the questions that would be asked. And there was the woman, if she was still alive up there somewhere. How long would they let her live before they killed her to eliminate excess baggage?

"All right," Worthington began. "Can you stand?" Gold nodded. "Good. You can give me the covering fire I'll need to get up the stairs. See if you can keep them occupied."

"You're the boss now," Gold said, letting Worthington help him to his feet. Pain deepened the age lines on his face as he struggled to get up. Then, as Gold raised his Uzi and began firing, Worthington stepped from behind the forklift and ran toward the stairs.

The darkness closed in on her as Stephanie struggled to make sense of what had happened. There had been the big explosion, then another one. Gunfire. One of the men had hit her. Her temple throbbed now, the pain almost as intense as that in her feet.

Her temple exploded white hot as she raised her head to survey the room. She was alone again. The two thugs who had tormented her had been ordered in to the other office by the man called Molotov. They had left quickly, slamming the interior door that joined the two rooms.

Slowly, she turned her head toward the window, every small movement of her neck muscles a torment to the blow on her head. The light was growing brighter outside the office. She smelled smoke, and for the first time realized the light must be coming from a fire.

Fire! She trembled. Not fire! Please God! Not fire! Anything but fire!

And suddenly she was seven years old again and the flames and the smoke, the blinding, choking smoke, roiled about her. She struggled out of her bed on the second story of the modest colonial home on the tree-shaded lot her parents had bought in Westwood.

She stumbled to the door and opened it. In the hallway the flames and the smoke roared at her, but she wanted her mother and her father and she crawled along the baseboards toward their bedroom, hoping they'd be there.

The floor grew hotter under her hands and knees until the flesh blistered.

And just a few scant feet from the door to her parents' bedroom, where the fire had started, the floor collapsed under her, pitching her into a funnel of burning cinders that ended at the living room below.

When she regained consciousness, her grandmother had been there to tell her that the fire had started in her parents' bedroom, had been caused by a smoldering cigarette. Both of her parents, she was told, were dead.

The crackle of gunfire dragged Stephanie back across the decades, back to the warehouse in Zurich, back to a mortal dread that, until now, had lain buried: the fear of being burned to death. And, like a woman possessed, she tore at her bonds without regard to the damage she might wreak on her flesh. Somehow . . . somehow she had to get free.

Molotov jerked his head around at the wailing from the next room.

"Screamers and whiners!" Molotov spat. "All around us! Nothing but screamers and whiners." He looked at Czenek. In the far corner of the office, Sergiev's screams of pain had damped themselves to whimpers of self-pity. Next door, Stephanie's screams continued unabated.

"Get rid of that awful screaming!" Molotov told Czenek. "Kill her. If they think they've come to rescue her, we'll show them a

246

thing or two." Czenek hesitated. The indigestion felt like pincers crushing his insides now. His face was covered with cold sweat.

"Well, move it man, kill her!" Molotov's eyes brimmed with glassy fury.

Dumbly, Czenek turned away from him and opened the door into the adjoining room with his left hand; he carried his pistol in his right.

Stephanie stopped screaming and jerked her head around as the door opened.

"Please, anything," she begged. "I'll do anything, *anything*— just don't let me burn to death." She began to cry.

Czenek stood numbly in the doorway, staring at the naked woman tied to the desk. He felt a profound sorrow, for she had finally lost her dignity and was begging for mercy. Even under the torture and stress and questioning of the past six months, she had endured their words and actions with a stoic dignity he had come to admire and respect. Nothing they had done had shaken that dignity. Now, in the last minutes, some internal fear they had been unable to touch had driven her to beg.

He looked at her now, the pain growing in his chest.

"Come on, you worthless Polack."

Czenek heard Molotov's rantings behind him, but they no longer seemed to matter. The woman they had savaged still looked like his wife, his only love, and in an instant something inside him seemed to snap.

"If you don't kill her this instant," Molotov's voice roared, "I will kill you!"

Czenek walked over to Stephanie and placed the muzzle of his pistol at her temple, the unbruised one. He looked into her eyes. They seemed to thank him. A brave woman, he thought. Czenek said a small prayer to himself, and tried to convince himself that he was saving a condemned woman from a worse death.

The machine-gun fire from outside intensified, filling both rooms with stray rounds that entered the windows at an acute angle and embedded themselves in the ceiling above their heads. Seconds later, the floor of the office bean to vibrate with the running steps of someone mounting the outside stairs two at a time.

"They're coming!" Molotov bellowed. "Shoot her quickly. I need you here."

Czenek closed his eyes and began to squeeze the trigger of his pistol. Stephanie closed her own eyes and thought of Derek.

Suddenly Czenek felt a savage crushing blow hammer at him from his breastbone and set him afire. He clutched at his heart, feeling hot knives flay the flesh away from the bone. His breath left him. He gasped, but he couldn't fill his lungs with air.

As his grip on the trigger loosened, Czenek realized that not even the food at that little restaurant where he and El-Nouty had eaten was so bad that it could produce indigestion this intense. His heart fluttered wildly, then weakly, overcome by the massive infarction that had been building for more than five decades.

"Czenek! Shoot her! Now!" Molotov screamed from directly behind him. Painfully, Czenek turned and focused the pain on the Russian.

"No," Czenek said.

"What did you say?" Molotov stood stunned, a look of bewilderment on his face.

Czenek raised his pistol, his hand unsteady from the crushing pain. Oh please, he prayed, please God, let me live long enough to kill this Russian pig. "I said no," Czenek answered. His pistol arm waved. "I won't kill her." He pulled the trigger but saw the shot go wide of Molotov and crash into the wall.

Molotov lifted his automatic and fired it, but the bullet hit Czenek too late to inflict any pain. His heart had already stopped.

Stephanie heard the gun clatter to the floor, and moments later, the softer thud of Czenek's body. Molotov now turned to shoot Stephanie, but was distracted by a volley of shots that whistled overhead. He stepped into the next room to see what was happening.

"Where are they?" Molotov asked.

"Not sure," the short agent said. "There's one down on the floor. I lost sight of the other."

Under a hail of bullets Molotov made his way across the room and peered out the office window. He saw muzzle flashes down below, but they originated from only one source. Where was the second man?

"Go kill the woman," Molotov said to Sanyev. "Then get the hell back here."

Sanyev turned from his position at the far end of the window and made his way across the room in a crouch. His nose still throbbed where the woman had hit him with the cot leg. He was glad that he would have the chance to complete the job Czenek had left unfinished.

Worthington made his way up the welded metal stairs, slowly now as he approached the landing. Less than a yard over his head, a steady stream of slugs from Adam's Uzi poured into the windows of the mezzanine offices.

Wiping the sweat from his face, Worthington looked out over the warehouse floor. The flames from the fire were brilliant now as they spread, feeding on electrical insulation, the paint on the walls, and the roof. Below him he could see the two men he had killed moments ago. They were sprawled less than ten feet from the forklift.

As Worthington pulled a stun grenade from its clip on his belt, he heard the reports of two, perhaps three different guns above him, answering Gold's incessant covering fire. The grenade was to be the signal to Adam to stop firing so Worthington could begin his assault. The grenades were identical to those used by anti-terrorist squads to stun and blind airplane hijackers without injuring them or their hostages. They caused a brilliant flash and loud explosion with a minimum of shrapnel.

He pulled the pin from the grenade, holding the arming handle down, and craned his head to get a good look at the windows above him. He'd toss the grenade in the first room, storm it, and, if the woman wasn't there, try to repeat the actions for the second room.

Worthington now pulled the grenade's arming lever, held the missile in his hand, and counted. One-one thousand. The grenades had a six-second fuse. Two-two thousand. He wanted to make sure no one had time to pick it up and throw it back. Three-three thousands.

Stephanie watched as the short KGB agent named Sanyev approached her.

Four-four thousand.

In the other room, the tall KGB agent pushed the desk in to the corner and stood up on it. If he stretched, he could reach the small square in the ceiling that resembled the kind of accessway used to enter the attics of most homes.

Five-five thousand, Worthington counted, and then lobbed the grenade up toward the window above him.

A second later the bright flash bleached all color from the world, and for a fraction of a second the thunderclap blotted out the sounds of gunfire. Worthington didn't wait for the ringing to clear from his ears before he raced up the steps, his Uzi at the ready in his right hand.

Stephanie thought she had been shot. There was the incredible explosion and the brilliantly painful supernova of light that she knew must surely be the bright flashing of her last mortal thoughts as the bullet plowed through her brain.

But the pain in her head and the pain in her feet continued to remind her that she was still alive. The first bullet hadn't killed her. She steeled herself to accept the coup de grace that she knew would surely come.

She opened her eyes and instead of staring into the face of her executioner, found him with both hands covering his own eyes. An instant later, she stared in stunned amazement as the outside door of the room crashed inward and slammed back against the wall.

She watched as a man of medium height stood in the doorway for just an instant, surveying the room. He was a faceless black shadow silhouetted by the orange and yellow flames behind him. He rushed forward into the room, firing his gun. He heard the KGB agent named Sanyev violently exhale his last breath and crash backward against the wall, driven before the relentless power of the Uzi.

The man whose face she couldn't see was closing the door to the adjoining office. She was struck dumb as all of the questions she wanted to ask him flooded in to her mind, carried along by a tidal wave of relief and the impossible hope that she might survive.

Then, as soon as the man had closed the door to the next room, he was turning the desk over, exposing its underside to the next room.

"Don't worry," he said as he rushed to her side and crouched down beside her. Just as he did, the door to the other office exploded in a mist of splinters and slugs, all of which harmlessly embedded themselves in the desk or bounced off it.

Swiftly, he took a long knife and cut the ropes binding her arms and legs to the desk.

"Are you all right?" asked Worthington as he reached for an old overcoat on the floor nearby.

"I . . . I—" Stephanie struggled with her thoughts and her words, but all she could manage were tears and a grateful sob.

There was the sound of movement from the other room. The man raised himself for just an instant and fired a long burst of bullets at the next room. The next few moments would always seem like a blur to her. He dressed her in the overcoat Czenek had left for her and helped her button it up. The wounds on her feet were too severe, with the staples still embedded in the bone, to allow her to walk. She was amazed at the man's strength as he threw her over his left shoulder and, firing his gun in his right hand, raced out of the office and down the steps.

"Where are you going?" Molotov demanded anxiously as he watched Lubchek disappear through the small hatch in the ceiling.

"To get a better shot, sir," the tall agent answered quickly. "To see if I can get that bastard behind the forklift."

Before Molotov could formulate a protest Lubchek disappeared.

The space between the office ceiling and the warehouse roof was foul with smoke and hot with gases from the fire. As Lubchek crawled across the surface, he cautioned himself to inhale and exhale shallow, even breaths to avoid choking. He edged himself to the boundary of the offices and looked down in time to see a man carrying the woman down the stairs.

Lubchek quickly pulled out his gun, but before he could even aim it, the roof beside him exploded with gunfire from the man behind the forklift. A huge splinter erupted from the roof and slashed his cheek. Bellowing with rage, he rolled quickly back out of the gunman's sights. Slugs continued to chew at the edge of the roof for yards on each side of his position.

Worthington was amazed at how light the woman seemed. She was no burden as he made his way down the stairs, careful to descend slowly enough to avoid tripping. A stumble at this stage would probably be fatal. He took the last two steps in a leap and hit the concrete floor running as he made straight for the forklift just over fifty feet away.

Molotov was alone and it frightened him. He was a leader, and what were leaders without men to lead? Fighting the desperation that clawed at his chest, he crawled to the window. The man behind the forklift kept up his incessant firing, but to Molotov's relief the gunfire seemed directed toward the roof.

Fine, Molotov thought, as he sighted in on the muzzle flashes from the forklift. He began to squeeze the trigger and then stopped. He could only be calling attention to himself and draw the man's atutomatic weapons fire.

Molotov lowered his gun for a minute as he studied the forklift. It seemed as impregnable as a tank. He looked at it for several more moments. He felt almost giddy when the thought came to him.

Worthington's heart pounded as he sprinted across the open warehouse floor, expecting to hear pursuing gunfire any second. In seconds he would be close enough to the forklift so that he would no longer be blocked from the view of the mezzanine offices by the catwalk that ran in front of them.

Molotov allowed himself a tiny smile and squeezed the trigger of his Makarov. An instant later the gun's slug ripped into one of the three propane tanks that powered the forklift's low-pollution engine. A ball of flame that reached almost to the ceiling erupted from the tank.

Worthington felt the flames singe the side of his face as he veered sharply away.

CHAPTER EIGHTEEN

Adam Gold had been crouched next to the propane tanks of the forklift, his shoulders propped against the one on the end to steady the aim of his Uzi. He had heard Molotov's single shot, but paid it no special attention. It was just one more round in the withering firefight.

He was about to lose another volley at the man on the roof when the slug from Molotov's gun ripped into the propane tank at his shoulder. The propane gas, used to power a low-pollution engine for indoor use, instantly became a bomb. The metal of the propane tank exploded outward, spraying metal shards that were accompanied by a huge ball of fire.

The flames burned him first. A flash of pain that transcended comprehension enveloped him and he screamed. Then Gold felt rather than heard the explosion. He remembered the pain, the boom that resonated in his chest and in the pit of his stomach, and the sensation of being plucked up and tossed like a sack of rice.

He must have passed out after that.

Gold regained consciousness for a dim instant, and there was someone kneeling beside him, cradling his head. He could feel that his insides were freezing and wondered how the cold could get inside a man so quickly. He felt drowsy, like the time he had the measles as a small boy. The fever had burned dangerously high and led him by the hand through a world of hallucinations and dreamy semi-consciousness pleasure that he felt again only as an adult during a trip to a hashish parlor in Cairo.

He could hear a voice speaking to him faintly from the dimness.

"Sorry Adam. I'm so sorry, so sorry, so sorry . . ." And the words kept time with the rhythmic rocking of the man who cradled his head. Gold tried to open his eyes, and realized with a sanguine acceptance that they were open and he could not see.

But in the darkness, he knew the voice. It was Nat Worthington's. It must be all right, he thought, if Nat's here.

Suddenly, he was a boy again, before Israel was special to him, before he realized that being a Jew made him different, before he left his native land to be a soldier for Israel.

And he was lying on his back, swinging in a hammock his father had thrown between two gum trees in the backyard of their home near Los Angeles. An early June sky bled slowly into colorful dusk and then into night. He could smell the eucalyptus from the trees' leaves and berries around him, and in the distance, he could faintly hear the sea as it marched in from Australia and threw itself against the sand. It was good to be home again, he thought, good to be a boy again. Then a peace like none he had never known settled into his heart and mind. Adam Gold closed his eyes and died.

"Damn it, Lubchek! Get down here immediately!" Molotov shouted over the roar of the fire. "We have them! We mustn't allow them to escape!" Overhead, Molotov could hear the scraping and thuds of his agents returning. Moments later the man's shoes, then his legs, and finally the rest of his body emerged from the accessway in the ceiling.

"Down there!" Molotov said, rushing out of the office. He leaned against the steel bars of the catwalk's guard rail and waited as the agent came up beside him. Below them, mostly hidden from their view by the burning hulk of the forklift and the smoke from both fires, they saw three figures. Lubchek raised his gun.

"Don't!" Molotov ordered as he brought his hand down on the agent's gun hand. "It's a poor shot. They've been motionless like that for a long time now. If you shoot now and miss, they'll probably get away before we can reach them. We must go down and make sure they're finished off properly." He looked at his man. "Do you understand?"

Lubchek nodded, then turned and descended the stairs. Molotov followed him as far as the stairway's foot.

"You go to the left," Molotov ordered. "I'll circle around to the right to cut off their escape." Lubchek smiled, then set off quickly toward the burning forklift.

Worthington gently set what was left of Gold's head down on the floor. It was the first time anyone had every died in his arms. He gazed down blankly on the maimed body of his old friend, ally, comrade, the man who had made it possible to escape El-Nouty and the rest of his enemies, a man who had once saved his life and now gave up his own. The flames roared around them, but the sounds had little success penetrating Worthington's grief.

A cry of pain finally brought him back. Next to him, the woman was sitting crosslegged, bent over her right foot. Worthington looked closer and saw that she was pulling staples from the bottoms of her feet.

"Sorry," she said apologizing for her cry of pain. "That was the last one. It hurts like hell." Worthington nodded, partly in understanding, but mostly in admiration for this strong woman.

Molotov kept to shadows as he moved slowly around the front end of the forklift. Across the way he could see Lubchek making his way toward the rear. It would be over in moments.

Worthington was struggling with Adam's battered and twisted body, wondering how to get it out of the warehouse, when a movement caught the corner of his eye. At first, he thought it was a flicker of the fire. But when he looked up, he saw a thick man with a gun.

"Look out!" Worthington yelled as he propelled himself at the woman. He heard the sounds of gunfire beside him as he slammed into the woman like a downfield blocker. Slugs plowed up the floor next to his feet and peppered them with fragments of concrete.

In the next instant, Worthington rolled to his feet and came up firing the Uzi, sweeping it blindly in broad arcs around them. He saw shadows recede into shadow. Gunmen taking cover? He had no way of knowing.

"Come on!" Worthington said as he leaned down and pulled the woman to her feet. "Can you run?"

"Yes, I think—" A gunshot cracked loudly in the shadows. Instants later, the slug slammed into the forklift with a metallic thud. Worthington turned and fired toward the sound, then propelled the woman toward the hole in the wall.

Gunfire pursued them.

"After them!" Molotov shouted. He watched Lubchek follow them directly as they went through the hole and turned toward the street. Molotov made for the door leading to the street, in hopes of cutting them off.

Pain like sharpened nails pounded into Stephanie's feet with each panicked step. They burst into the alleyway and ran no more than ten yards when the man grabbed her arm and jerked her to a halt. She watched as he turned toward the hole in the wall and hammered the opening with a long burst from his machine gun.

"That ought to make them think for a moment or two." He said and again they were running.

He helped her over the twisted wreckage of what looked like a wire fence, and then guided her left, away from the warehouse.

"Uh! No! There!" She struggled with him and pointed back to the right, at a police car with its lights flashing. Behind it a fire-truck was pulling to a halt, and behind it, another police car.

"Uh-oh!" Worthington said as he cast a watchful glance into the alley behind him. "Let's not deal with them right now. Trust me. You don't want to answer the questions they'll want to ask you."

She looked at him doubtfully for a moment. Who was she to argue with a man who had just risked his life to save her? She nodded her assent.

Worthington led her in the opposite direction, toward the parked van.

Inside the warehouse, Molotov struggled with the bolt lock on the front door. He cursed at the lock and the steel door, and finally stood back and fired five shots around the deadbolt. He kicked at the bolt and it dropped neatly outside.

He pulled back the door like a madman and shot into the street. He saw them half a block down and running away. They were unmistakable, with her limp. He planted his feet and took careful aim. It was almost impossible to miss a target that was running directly away from you.

Moments after Worthington had fired the burst at the hole in the warehouse wall, Lubchek had come flying out in pursuit. He stumbled on a piece of debris and almost lost his footing. But he quickly regained his balance, knocking over a cardboard box that rested against the wall of the adjacent warehouse.

Inside the box, the movement jostled contact switches on the tamper-proof detonator Adam Gold had attached to the extra loaf of C-4 explosive. Gold had intended to set the explosive off with the radio control unit he had put into his coat pocket. He had planned it as a last-minute escape diversion.

The diversion worked, although not as Gold had originally planned it.

When Lubchek tripped over the box and set off the motion sensors, the C-4 exploded with a force sufficient to demolish the supporting walls of the warehouses on both sides.

Out on the street, the blast threw Molotov to the ground and ripped the Makarov from his grip. He never found the gun.

Rescue workers also never found Lubchek. Even though they sifted carefully through the rubble that filled what had once been an alleyway, all they ever found was a few singed swatches of cloth, which collectively were smaller than a man's hankerchief.

The explosion and fire were awesome, Derek Steele thought, as he sat alone in his compartment on his stationary train with his cheek pressed against the cool glass to give him a better view of the flames that burned to his right, and just head of the train by perhaps a quarter of a mile. The train's announcer had come over the loudspeaker fifteen or twenty minutes ago to tell them that, because of an industrial accident involving a natural gas main, the rail yard controller had ordered that all trains be stopped as a safety measure.

And then there had been the explosion about five minutes ago. Brilliant flames, and instants later, rolling thunder. As a policeman, Steele had heard gas explosions and he had heard dynamite go off. The last explosion surely sounded like dynamite.

Steele kept his eyes on the bright flames as he slowly got to his feet to stretch his legs. It had been a long train ride, more than ten hours. And though it was barely 6:30 in the evening, it felt more like 3 A.M. to him.

He dragged his eyes away from the flames and scanned the

blackness of the night with its myriad lights burning small temporary holes in the darkness.

"Where are you?" Steele said softly to himself as he stared through his own dim, ghostlike reflection in the window's glass. The fire was forgotten, and as it had been for half a year now, he thought only of where Stephanie might be, and whether she might be alive.

Are you out there? he wondered. Can I see the light that shines on you right now?

Rubbing his eyes wearily, he sat back down, closed his eyes for a moment, and let the knotted ropes behind them unwind a bit. Once again he was thankful he had booked all six seats in the compartment for himself. He needed the time to think and he'd wanted no distractions from other passengers. He had also wanted to be sure that a killer didn't sit down next to him. It had been expensive, but worth it. Davidson's money had covered that and would cover many more contingencies. Somehow it didn't seem like real money.

Just as the last six months or the last twenty-four hours didn't seem real.

Twenty-four hours. Christ! A day ago—it seemed like centuries—he had clawed his way out of a culvert pipe and killed a man. Unreal.

Brown.

The last word of a dying priest. Unreal.

He had thrashed his way out of the woods and into the streets of the small Amsterdam suburb of Amstelveen. He hid in a dumpster and watched through a crack as the killers raced by. Unreal.

The next hours were as unreal as a dream. He wandered through the streets until he found a men's clothing store. The clerk had been shocked at Steele's appearance, but his shock turned to dismay when Steele explained that he had been mugged.

Which was true in its own way.

"I am so ashamed," the shopkeeper kept saying. "This is not like Holland at all. We are a peaceful people." The man kept apologizing as he helped Steele select a new wardrobe, then took him by the hand down the street to a luggage shop owned by a friend. Steele had to force money on the man for the two pieces of luggage he bought, both soft-sided and made of a rugged nylon fabric with leather trim. One was a shoulder bag, the other full-sized, also doubling as a hang-up suit bag. Back at the clothing store, he put his new wardrobe in the suit bag, and into the shoulder bag he placed his dirty coat and clothes, all carefully wrapped to conceal the ugly but effective Smith & Wesson .357 Magnum.

He repeated the scene with a sympathetic woman at the small commercial hotel near the train station. She clucked over him like a mother hen, insisting that she press the wrinkles from his newly purchased clothes, and like the clerk, apologized for the violence because, after all, "This is not America, where things like that happen all the time."

Following a long bath, he hired a taxi to take him to Schipol Airport and wait as he retrieved the painting and the rest of Davidson's money from the locker where he had left them. From the international telephones at the airport, Steele managed to get through to Gordon Highgate, Anderson's assistant, and file a report on what had happened and where he was headed. He failed to mention his possession of the painting or his appointment with Joseph Roten.

And after that, he had drunk the hot chocolate the hotel desk clerk had brought up to him, and sunk into the crisp, clean sheets. He slept a ragged sleep, haunted by recent scenes of dead people who all eventually wore his face.

His decision the next morning to cancel his flight to Zurich and take the train instead was an easy one. He didn't want to risk a search turning up his gun. And trains were harder to watch: no security gates controlling the crowds, no single queues for boarding, no centralized boarding areas. And they were easier to get off, which was why Steele had taken a local train with stops every twenty or thirty minutes.

Still, he felt as if he should have done more.

But what? It was hard to run from people when you didn't know who you were running from. Hard to hide from danger when you didn't know its face. How had they found him? The question continued to hammer away at him. The telephone call from the airport? He ruled that out. There was no way they could have known he would use that telephone.

Someone unseen by him or by Anderson could have shadowed

him. Unlikely. His neighborhood in Playa del Rey didn't lend itself to hiding strangers well. It was not an anonymous street.

Anderson? He had told Anderson's man—the one keeping a vigil at Steele's house in Playa del Rey—that he was going to Amsterdam. But that would mean that—

A chill spread through his body like ice water. Suppose Anderson's man, or the man he had assumed was Anderson's, worked for someone else?

"Brown?"

The man in Amsterdam Steele had initially assumed worked for Anderson turned out to be a priest. A priest working for whom? Why was a priest involved?

"A small . . . powerful group within the Vatican . . . far, far bigger thing than you realize . . . the blessings of the Pope . . ."

Steele heard the priest's last words, the implications staggered him.

"Things . . . and people, you see, are not always what they seem . . . There are people in high places within both your government and my church who are not what they seem."

The words ran like a refrain through his fear. *Who* were not what they seemed? Was Anderson something other than he had represented himself to be? Or was the priest? Or Davidson?

And who was involved? Anderson said the people who had killed Davidson had been Polish agents working for the KGB. So whose interests were they looking after? Poland's? Russia's? Were the Russians using them to disguise their own activities, or because the Polish security forces had a special grudge against priests? And why was this priest involved?

"We're a group charged with trying to root out the worst of the abuses, the political struggles and power plays . . ."

So what did they want with a painting by an obscure Nazi artist?

Steele shook his head as the thoughts twisted around each other. Every time he answered one question, two or three arose to take its place. It was as if he—

Steele was suddenly aware of a man who had stopped in the train corridor outside his compartment. The man was about six feet tall, his build hidden under a long wool coat. A long woolen coat, Steele thought, bulky enough to conceal almost any kind of weapon. The man's hair was light brown and there was nothing remarkable about his face save a nose that looked as if it has been broken badly at least once. Their eyes met for an instant. The man nodded a polite acknowledgment, then turned his back on Steele and stood in the passageway looking out the window at the rail yard.

Startled, Steele got to his feet and pulled his new shoulder bag from the overheard rack and set it on the seat beside him. He replayed the man's look again in his mind. Was it a look of recognition, or merely the courtesy of one stranger acknowledging another? Did the man know him? Did *he* recognize the man? Steele tried to remember the past days, trying to single out a face from the crowds he had drifted through in airports, on the street, at the train station. But the man's face remained that of a stranger.

But that was why men like this were always selected as killers and spies. The nondescript make the best killers because they are hard to remember, hard to spot in a crowd. Was this man a killer? Was this a killer sent to finish off the jobs botched in Los Angeles and Amsterdam?

Steele was taking no chances. He unzipped the shoulder bag and worked the Magnum from its concealment in the middle of his old clothes. He placed it on the top, where he could get to it easily, and then pulled the unzipped edges of the bag together. He sat down next to it and pretended interest in the *International Herald Tribune.*

The man didn't move, but instead stood in the corridor with his hands in his pockets for a moment before taking one hand out and reaching into the open front of his coat, where Steele couldn't see. Was he reaching for a weapon? Steele's hand jerked into the shoulder bag beside him and quickly found the Magnum. His fingers closed around the wooden stock, the index finger curling on the trigger.

The man's other hand came out of his pocket. Moments later, the man started to turn sideways. Steele tensed, ready to bring the Magnum out. As the man finished turning, Steele saw he had a package of American cigarettes in one hand and a cheap disposable lighter in the other.

The man noted Steele's gaze and smiled. He held the pack up to offer Steele one. Feeling foolish, Steele shook his head and smiled back, the courtesy of one stranger to another. The man shook out a cigarette, placed it in his mouth and lit it. He then walked through the pale blue cloud of smoke toward the end of the car.

Heart pounding, Steele slumped in his seat and closed his eyes. He felt the sweat trickling down his forehead. He opened his eyes and wiped at the sweat. The corridor was filled with pale blue cigarette smoke, like the remains of a magician who had just stunned the audience with his vanishing act.

He was seeing demons where there were none, shadows where there was only light.

Christ! He was getting paranoid!

Then for an instant, he was back in a patrol car at Manchester and 189th Place and it was dark and scary and the night was filled with death and the veteran behind the wheel had only half laughed when he told Steele: "Listen kid, just remember you've gotta be paranoid when everybody's out to get you."

Steele remembered not laughing at first.

Suddenly the train jerked and groaned as it gathered forward momentum and slowly passed the fire and gutted warehouse.

Robert Maxwell paced his room angrily. He had barely been able to contain himself in the last session of the ecumenical council's meeting, and he was unsure that he could continue to do so. Even his renowned capacity to absorb without striking back was being tested by Braun and the other members of the council.

He reached over and turned out the light next to the bed, then settled back for what he knew would be a fitful sleep.

Of course, he had been manipulative, pragmatic—sometimes cynical—in his actions and decisions. But he had always been convinced that he had behaved as he did in the interests of the hundreds of millions who believed.

In all those matters, he had been a fixer of church doctrine and a mediator in power struggles among men. He had fixed, tinkered with, adjusted, and refined human institutions and human emotions—the imperfect, usually petty, but inevitable secular organizations that spring up around the spiritual.

Never before had he been called upon to deal with crucial, basic issues that struck at the very heart of religion. Which is to say that his integrity, his faith, had never been truly tested.

Maxwell pulled up the covers against a chill that transcended the room temperature. He had always believed in the basic integrity of the faith. That the Bible's word was basically sound, even though it had undoubtedly been translated and edited over the centuries to reflect changes in the Church, and in power struggles among its members.

But now . . . now he had to face the possibility—no the fact, absolutely documentable fact—that major parts of its history, and of its basic religious content, had been edited out, censored, covered up, in order to support the established religious order.

Maxwell twisted, trying to get comfortable without realizing that his discomfort came from within.

He was being asked to join a conspiracy to cover up the documentation of a second Messiah, killed before she had time to be recognized, to develop a following. How might today's world be different if she had been allowed to live?

Never before in the history of man had there been such incontrovertible evidence of resurrection, of an afterlife! The documentation was absolutely irrefutable. It was what the nonbelievers needed, a tangible sign that God was real, that no matter how perverted every religion had become, no matter how deeply the true message had been buried under Church bureaucracies and power plays and liturgies and interpretations of the Bible or the Koran or the Talmud, no matter how far the men who cared for the churches had strayed from the teachings of their founders—all of this didn't matter at all. The only thing that mattered was the believing.

If it were possible, Maxwell thought, this might be more significant than the resurrection of Jesus.

But the other men sleeping in this _château_ on the Nockspitze wanted to suppress the word of Veronica's resurrection, because it threatened the order of their established religions. Maxwell wondered what else had been suppressed over the ages by men like them.

Men like them.

It was hard to believe they were evil men. They were reasonable, rational, intellectual men who honestly believed they were taking the right course for the believers of the world. Their convictions were rooted in a studied decision-making process that took current world instabilities into consideration, in an examination of history, and in the potential religion had to either bring peace and order to the world, or be used as a force for violence and chaos. The imams of Iran and the Middle East, the bombers in Belfast, the violence between Sikhs and Hindus in India were all the evidence any rational person needed to know that religion could be used by those in the last fifth of the twentieth century who would first divide and then conquer for their own gain.

None of the members of the ecumenical council were wild-eyed fanatics or corrupt manipulators of history. They were all quiet prophets of reason and order. And they all had persuasive arguments to back up their actions.

Maxwell continued to twist his sheets around him as he struggled with his dilemma. They were right, these men of the ecumenical council. The revelation of the truth, of the documented existence of this woman from history, would rip apart established churches in the West, start fiery theological arguments among church members and leadership. The Church leadership would fragment, causing a resultant diminution in the moral force needed to oppose the expansion of communism and religious fanaticism.

Only history could ever make the final judgment, but loosing the secret of Veronica's Shroud upon the world could be the linch-pin of the last fifty years of the twentieth century. Just as the assassination of the Archduke Francis Ferdinand in Sarajevo had begun the unravelings of civilization that led to World War I, there was a definite probability that Veronica's Shroud might unravel the fabric of modern history to an even more disastrous degree.

But somehow, though his mind told him the men of the council were right, his heart spoke to him of their mistake. His heart told him that the truth had to be known, that the affairs of men had always been precarious and that no manipulation of history could make them more secure.

"Ye shall know the truth," Maxwell had read in the Bible, "and the truth shall make you free." Maxwell wanted to believe this, but his intellect would not let him.

He followed the old arguments around in familiar circles, caught between his heart's desires and the past thirty-seven years of traditional religious training that wanted to reject Veronica as blasphemy and myth.

He fell into a deep but troubled sleep, detesting the fact that he was such a product of his past.

CHAPTER NINETEEN

Stephanie viewed the night and its lights through half-closed lids as Nat Worthington drove the Volvo skillfully through the snowy streets of Zurich. Though her eyes were heavy with fatigue, pain, and the accumulated weight of the last six months, she was too excited to sleep.

The last two hours had seemed like scenes from a surreal spy movie. First they had driven away from the fire in a panel van. The man had identified himself only as Nat Worthington, nothing more, and refused to talk as he drove, warily, his eyes drifting constantly to the rearview mirrors as if he expected to be followed.

Fifteen minutes passed on the dashboard clock before he pulled the van into an underground parking structure on the outskirts of Zurich. He helped her out of the van and into the front passenger seat of a steel-gray Volvo, then pulled a blanket from the trunk and wrapped her gently in it. Still, he refused to answer her questions. Why weren't they going to the police? Who did he work for? Why had he saved her life? Was the man who died at the warehouse a friend? From the way Worthington drove silently, tears glistening in his eyes but not falling on his cheek, she thought they must have been friends, good friends.

And so she stopped asking him questions, letting him be alone with his grief.

Worthington stopped once to make a telephone call from a box on the side of the road, then drove straight to a clinic near Opfikon. The doctor was like Nat: silent but friendly. He X-rayed her feet to make sure nothing remained embedded in the bone. Then he cleaned and dressed the puncture wounds on her feet and gave her an antibiotic injection, a tetanus inoculation, and a large bottle of pills to prevent infection.

During the examination, he asked her a steady string of questions about her diet and sanitation during captivity. He asked her about the drugs that had used on her. The questions were so perceptive she was sure the doctor had either used the same drugs himself, or had them used on him. She was not shocked when the doctor told her she had survived in remarkably good condition for someone who had been held prisoner by the KGB for more than six months.

Six months! She thought about it for a few moments then Worthington and the doctor had entered the hallway to talk in subdued voices. They had stolen six months, a half a year from her life! She felt anger mixed with giddy relief—relief born of finally being free. Then she thought again of the pain she had endured and began to hate the people who had held her. And to hate even more the people who had gotten her into the trouble in the first place. Even in her fatigue, she began to think of what she had to do, both for herself and to them.

When they came back into the room, she was sure they had been talking about her.

"I think you ought to go with Nat, here, and stay in a safe place for a few days," the doctor said, as if the suggestions were part of her prescription.

She shook her head. "I've been held a prisoner for six months," she argued, "and the only place I'm going now is to the most luxurious hotel I can find."

They argued with her for the best part of ten minutes. The KGB might be looking for her. Her life might be in danger. But she had had enough of being held against her will, she responded. She had to have the right to make her own decisions. If they forced her to some place against her will, they were little better than the KGB.

The force of her argument and the vehemence of its delivery startled them all, including Stephanie.

Finally, Worthington and the doctor went back into the hallway and conferred in the low mumblings of men who took events seriously. For a moment, she considered trying to run away from the clinic and then quickly dismissed it as absurd. You just don't run away from people who have saved your life, she told herself. She was a lone woman those only clothes were an old overcoat and the cotton examination gown the doctor had given her. Her feet were bandaged, she had no shoes and no money. She decided to wait.

Reluctantly, they consented to her demand, but only if she would accept a bodyguard until they were sure she was safe. And would she consent to talking to a man, a sort of detective who would like to learn as much as he could about her experience?

Eagerly, she agreed.

But before she could leave, Worthington told her, she had to have clothes. He took her measurements while the doctor called several stores to find one that was still open. Fortunately it was the Christmas season, and stores had extended their hours to accommodate the wallets and purses of last-minute shoppers. The doctor located a women's boutique a few miles away and gave the directions to Worthington.

While Worthington was shopping for her wardrobe, the doctor let her use his telephone to call Derek. Three times she called, and each time she got the answering machine. Where was he, she wondered, then realized it was ten hours earlier in Los Angeles; it was only eleven in the morning there. So she called his office at UCLA. There was no answer.

"What day is today?" she finally asked the doctor.

"Saturday."

Of course, she thought, as she tried to force her mind out of the habits of a prisoner and back into those of a normal person. He must be at the boat.

But there was no answer there. Damn! Damn! She wanted *so* to talk to Derek, to hear his voice again. Instead, she swallowed her disappointment and called the house again and left him a message on the machine. "I love you," she said over and over. And finally, before the message tape ran out, she left him word to call her at the Eden au Lac Hotel. There were others she should have called, she thought, but suddenly her energy seemed to drain from her body . . .

That seemed like hours ago, she thought now, as her head lolled gently against the headrest of the Volvo's seat. She closed her eyes and visualized Derek's face when he returned and checked the message. She hoped he wouldn't call before she got checked in at the hotel. What a perfect place. They would begin where they had left off six months ago.

He would fly over to see her, and before he got here, she would buy new clothes and she would make herself beautiful again—at least, she would try. She would pamper herself, have the hotel's hair designers and manicurists and nail specialists and everyone else she could think of come to her room and indulge her, help her wash six months of neglect from her hair and from her body.

She felt so giddy from her freedom now, at her second chance at living, that even the pain in her feet reminded her of her good fortune. She opened her eyes now as Worthington guided the Volvo around the perimeter of the lake.

He had grown more talkative since leaving the clinic. He was as American, he told her, and he was working for the Mossad, Israeli intelligence. The man who had been killed at the warehouse was named Adam Gold and had once saved his life. He talked a bit more, about his wife, Tania, about a Libyan and about another agent for the Mossad, a man named David Simon, and how a telephone call Simon had made just before his death had eventually saved Stephanie's life.

She listened with a morbid fascination as he talked casually of killing and assassination and torture and how it had swirled around her for more than six months now. His tale blunted the intoxication of her newly achieved freedom. She realized that hers, like all freedoms, had an expensive price. Nat grew silent again as they reached the lake. It was icier here, and the snow had blotted out the road. His face grew intense as he concentrated on his driving. After a quarter-hour or so, she caught a glimpse of the hotel's lights, and as they got closer, each bend in the road gave her a better and better view.

Stephanie's eyes were nearly closed when Worthington pulled the Volvo to a halt on the cobbled auto court in front of the Eden au Lac's lobby. She opened her eyes and sat up.

In front of them, a uniformed porter with more gold braid than a Russian general was unloading expensive leather bags from the trunk of a Mercedes. Across the entryway from him, a similarly uniformed doorman was opening the door for a gray-haired gentleman and a woman wearing a battalion of sables. Through the doors, Stephanie could see the warm glow of lights and the un-hurried movement of guests with no appointments to keep. She and Derek had parted here, and there was no better place to begin putting themselves back together.

Her hand went automatically to the door handle.

"Wait a moment," Worthington said.

Stephanie felt the blood draining from her face. "What's wrong?" She asked anxiously. "Has someone followed us?" Oh God!, she thought. Not here. Not this close to rest, to warm, soft, comfortable *safety*. She couldn't take it *anymore*. Why wouldn't they leave her alone?"

"No, nothing like that," Worthington said soothingly. "I'm sorry I startled you."

Stephanie relaxed.

"I just want to find my man before I go in and register." He twisted in his car seat and scanned the immediate area. She looked along with him.

Long-term parking wasn't allowed in the driveway, but there were a handful of cars stopped nearby, some occupied by drivers waiting for hotel guest, others empty, waiting for the valet parking attendants to ferry them away.

Worthington turned the other way, and as he did, a flame glowed behind the windshield of an older but well-kept Mercedes parked behind the Volvo on the other side of the driveway. The flame lingered as if the man were lighting a cigarette. Stephanie could see that the man had a cigarette in his mouth, but he didn't light it. After a few seconds, he pulled the cigarette out of his mouth— someone trying to quit smoking who had nearly succumbed—and flicked the light off.

"That's him," Worthington said as he reached for his door handle. "Wait here for me. If anything happens, Rich will take care of you. He's 290 pounds of trouble for anyone who might try to harm you."

"Rich?"

"Rich Seeley," Worthington said as he opened his door and started to get out. "British, former member of the SAS—Special Air Services—and tough as they come. He's a freelance, but only for the right side. He'll be your companion until things sort them-selves out."

Without further explanation, Worthington shut the door and walked toward the lobby. He stopped to exchange a few words with a parking valet and then disappeared into the lobby.

Stephanie craned her head to look toward the older Mercedes, but could see little more than the gray shadow on the black shadow of Seeley's outline behind the windshield. She thought she saw a hand wave in greeting. She waved back, then turned around and rested her head on the seat. She fell asleep almost immediately. They would take care of her, she thought, just before drifting off. She was safe.

Stephanie fell immediately into a deep dreamless sleep. Not even the bright headlights of a Peugeot taxi could wake her up as it swept past the Volvo and pulled to a stop at the curb in front of her.

Derek Steele cursed under his breath as the taxi pulled to a halt in front of the Eden au Lac's lobby. Of all the goddamned places he'd like to avoid, this would be the only decent hotel in Zurich with a reservation. Damn. He'd called hotel after hotel from the train station. "We're sorry, *Mein Herr,* they all told him. "But the pre-Christmas season is upon us. Parties, visiting, people coming from the country to shop and celebrate. I'm afraid we have no vacancies until the night of the 24th. Perhaps then . . ."

Steele had thanked them all politely and hung up to call another number. Then he had tried visiting them in person. With the same results. The Schweizerhof had been more helpful than most. The clerk behind the desk called several of his counterparts at other hotels and finally found Steele a room.

"It is at the Eden au Lac," the clerk said proudly. "It is a fine hotel, but they are a bit farther away from our main shopping area. It is for this reason I was able to get you a room."

Steele had tried to look enthusiastic for the clerk's sake, tipped him generously, and walked back outside to his waiting taxi.

They didn't go immediately to the Eden au Lac. Steele just didn't want to face it. It would be lonely, depressing without Stephanie. It was a wonderful romantic establishment they had enjoyed together. He knew he'd never be comfortable there without her.

Putting of the inevitable trip to a hotel he didn't want to stay at, Steele took his cabdriver to dinner. They left the meter running in the cab, and Steele paid for it all. The man was a Turkish immigrant who spoke little German and no English. His family was still back in Turkey and he sent them most of the money he made from driving the cab. He had a wife and seven children, the oldest a boy of twelve. He missed them all. Beyond that, the language barrier prevented anything approaching real conversation.

So they muddled through the meal, using hand signs and facial expressions to communicate. They had toasted each other from the bottle of Saint Julien Steele had ordered. Neither understood the toast of the other, but both felt honored. And they shared the universal language of strangers alone in a foreign country, separated from the ones they love.

But time finally ran out. Steele had to get to the hotel before the front desk gave his room to someone else.

Steele's taxi driver leaped out of the cab as soon as he had braked to a halt and opened the door for him. Then he opened the trunk and signaled for a porter. In one of the few phrases of German the driver knew, he told the porter to be careful with the bags. Finally Steele pulled a wad of Davidson's money from his wallet and counted off the amount on the meter, doubled it, and gave it to the driver.

"Merry Christmas," Steele told the Turkish cabdriver. The man hugged him, kissed him on both cheeks, then got back in his cab and drove away.

Steele was unaware of the curious looks of the porters and doormen as he turned and walked toward the entrance. He hoped the money would make for a better Christmas, and maybe a better life, for a hard-working husband in Germany and a wife and seven children in Turkey.

In his fatigue Steele took no notice of the Volvo parked at the curb, or of the woman asleep in the passenger seat. He continued past it and through the door opened by the man in the uniform with all the gold braid.

Across the driveway, Rich Seeley lowered his silenced Uzi and placed it back on the seat beside him. Seeley took no chances. If the man who had just gotten out of the Peugeot had tried anything, he would have been dead before he could get the door of the Volvo open.

A bellhop with the imperial bearing of Russian nobility carried

Steele's bags up to his room, hung up the clothes, adjusted the thermostat, turned down his bed, and demonstrated the dry bar stocked with full bottles of whiskey and cordials—and the refrigerator with its champagne, white wine, fruit juices, and bottled water. His name was Klaus and he spoke impeccable English.

Steele tipped him well enough for the man to remember him if the time every came to ask him a favor. Steele briefly considered opening one of the bottles of orange juice and lay on the bed to think about it. He fell asleep with his clothes on.

The wind shrieked up off the valley of the Inn River and heaved its icy shoulders against the lodge's stout timbers. The half-century-old wood creaked and complained with the stronger gusts. It was after 2 A.M. and lights shone in only one set of windows, high on the former resort hotel's top floor. Behind those windows, Archbishop Cardinal Neils Braun paced his bedroom angrily as he listened to the man on the other end of the telephone line.

"What do you mean you lost track of him?" Braun demanded. "I provided you with a great deal of money to hire the best men possible. Is it possible that you decided to keep some of that money to yourself and hire inferior personnel?"

Braun shook his head as the man tried to explain why they had not recovered the painting from Derek Steele in Amsterdam. Braun winced as the common, almost Cockney accent grated in his ears like fingernails along a chalkboard.

As head of the Secretariat for Non-Believers, Braun had a great deal of discretionary money to pass along to shadowy anticommunist groups, in ways that were mostly unaccountable and always untraceable. Those activities and the importance the Vatican placed on recovering the Shroud of Veronica put his use of those funds beyond the usual purview of the Holy See's auditors. Even the tightened auditing procedures following the Banco Ambrosiano scandal failed to touch his accounts. He had used more and more of the money of late trying to pay for the secretariat's efforts to recover the shroud. While a telephone call from any of the ecumenical council's members could enlist the assistance of senior members of hundreds of government agencies in dozen of countries, those senior men—like the one to whom Braun now listened—sometimes resorted to using hired assassins in order to keep their departments' noses clean.

Braun let the man on the other end of the line stammer and stutter his explanations. The man was a ranking member of the British intelligence establishment who owed a great debt—his life—to the Anglican bishop who sat on the ecumenical council. While the bishop slept in his quarters two floors below Braun's bedroom, the British spy's list of excuses as to why they had let Steele slip through their net gradually degenerated to a whining plea that the bishop not be told about the abject failure in Amsterdam.

Braun let the man blather on until he had talked himself into a corner. The cardinal believed that mistakes, particularly when they were made by other people, were usually opportunities for him. He saw a chance to undercut the Anglican bishop's recent bids for more power and influence within the ecumenical council.

Though the Anglican bishop had always been an insufferable, power-hungry, upper-caste bore, Braun had chosen him both for his influence within the NATO intelligence community and his ability to call in favors for the council's activities. Within the last two years, however, the bishop had demanded more and more power for his influence. Braun now saw the opportunity to drive a wedge between the bishop and the men he controlled.

Braun had done it time and again. In the beginning, people in powerful government positions performed favors at the behest of one council member of another. In the end, they found themselves indebted to Braun, and wound up using the power and influence of their offices and agencies at the request of the cardinal archbishop.

It was a question of charisma that permitted him to command others, Braun thought now with more than a little pride. The force of his personality allowed him to win their confidence and to secure their allegiance. Where others had to rely on power derived from their offices to lead men, Braun knew he needed only his character.

Braun held the cordless telephone to his ear as he walked into the darkened coolness of his personal study. The light from the bedroom cast the shadow of a giant as he still listened to the verbal grovelings from the British spy in Amsterdam.

Flipping on the overhead light switch, he looked about him, at the walls lined with books, at the bound copies of his own books, seven of them, all published by commercial publishers of international renown. Philosophy, theology, history. The works had accounted in large part for the spread of his influence beyond his own important—but clerically insular—niche in the Vatican hierarchy.

Still listening to the frantic man on the other end of the line, Braun walked over to the book shelf and pulled out a copy of the book that had put his name on the lips of people around the world and elevated him from the obscurity of the Curia to a serious contender for the throne of Saint Peter.

He pulled the book from the shelf and looked at it absently. *Communism As the Antichrist*. Based on years of solid research and on his own secret experiences as head of the Secretariat of Non-Believers, the book had been written for laymen and clerics alike. It had become a text for serious scholars of the conflicts between church and state. And it had also become a popular best seller in every country in the free world, making him a prime target for communist assassins.

Upon publication of the book, he became a sought-after guest on television and a popular speaker at religious and secular anti-communist events. It had not hurt his climb within the Vatican's byzantine hierarchy.

And with its success, he had no trouble recruiting the most powerful men for the ecumenical council. He replaced less powerful members with those of more influence. Those who refused to resign and allow others to take their place usually grew too ill to serve any longer. The ecumenical council's influence grew along with his own. He became an increasingly bitter focus of virulent propaganda and denouncement by the Soviets. And with each attack, and following each assassination attempt, his own support within the church had grown. Cardinal after cardinal came to him and they all said the same thing: Neils Braun would be the next pope. It was just a matter of time.

But it hadn't been a matter of time, Braun thought, as he angrily shoved his book back into its slot on the shelf, and with the Cockney still whining in his ears, walked toward his desk. He avoided looking at the portrait of the Pontiff that hung behind the desk. Looking at it made him angrier. The portrait should have borne his image.

Braun turned his back to the portrait and pulled the chair from the desk's kneehole. Oh, he had never let the anger show! Not even to his closest allies on the Curia had he been anything but magnanimous in defeat. He was a young man, his supporters said. There would come another time, another day, another vote.

As he sat behind his desk, Braun cursed silently as he thought of his defeat. Time was too short! The communists were all around them. Every day, the faithful suffered more and more—in Poland, in Cuba and across the rest of Latin America, in China. The communists gained ground every day; the Church lost it every day. None of them realized there might not be another day for the Church. No time for another pope. No one realized it: not the present pope, not the College of Cardinals. None of them knew how little time they really had to be patient. And even that little time would evaporate if the communists got their hands on Veronica's Shroud. Something had to be done, and Braun knew what that was.

His ruminations were interrupted as new, deeper notes of desperation seeped into the words of the man from Amsterdam. Anything, the man was saying; he'd do anything to make sure the Anglican bishop didn't learn of his failure.

"Of course," Braun replied, in his most soothing pastoral voice. "Calm down, all is not lost. All is never lost as long as we continue to hold fast to our faith in Jesus Christ."

Then Braun talked, the charisma flowing from his voice. At the other end of the line, the high-ranking intelligence official from Great Britain readily agreed that, in exchange for the cardinal archbishop's silence on the Amsterdam failure, instructions for all future missions on behalf of the ecumenical council would come directly from Braun and not from the Anglican bishop.

By three A.M, both men were asleep in beds six hundred miles apart, each believing that he had won a great concession from the other. Braun knew who the true winner was. He always did.

CHAPTER TWENTY

Zurich's Bahnhofstrasse runs for less than a mile from the train station to the lake. But along its length, the visitor can see almost everything that has given this small Swiss city such an international reputation.

The Bahnhofstrasse is lined mainly with banks and jewelry stores. The banks store money, precious stones, gold, and objects more valuable than gold; the jewelry stores sell gold and precious gems in exchange for money, gold, and sometimes for things more valuable than gold. Bankers and jewelers have long been allies, but nowhere are the bonds tighter than on Zurich's Bahnhofstrasse. All the big ones are here: Swiss Credit, Union Bank, J. Vontobel & Co., A. Sarasin & Cie., and more.

And between the impressive bank buildings, with their bold public facades and polished mahogany doors lines with armor plate, are the small private banks: small, exclusive, the most secretive among a secretive bank industry. The brass plates on their doors bear single muted names—such as Bertholdier et Fils—or perhaps a string of names like a law firm. Nowhere is there an indication that a bank may be behind the door. If a visitor does not know it is a bank, he has no business there.

The jewelry stores that separate the banks from one another operate in much the same way. The large ones have public displays designed to appeal to the bourgeoisie, and—accessible only by private elevators and authorized escorts—salons for those who in all probability have just come from a small establishment with an armor-plated mahogany door.

Steele paid off his taxi at the foot of the Bahnhofstrasse where it ended at the lake. It was a brilliant day and in the cold, clear distance, a lone sailboat braved the chill waters. From Steele's vantage point the sail looked like a bleached wizard's cap sliding across the water. He paused for a moment and thought of a summer day, more than six months ago, when he had taken a small rental boat up the lake as far as Zollikon while he waited for Stephanie to return.

He turned abruptly, from the thoughts of that day as much as from the physical sight that reminded him of it. Walking briskly now, Steele passed a small park and plunged into the thickening crowds of Christmas shoppers. It was December 22; two more shopping days until Christmas.

The sidewalks lining the Bahnhofstrasse were crowded with shoppers, shopkeepers, a straggling of tourists, schoolchildren out for the holidays, and a sprinkling of immaculately groomed men and women—most of the women wrapped in furs—making their stately ways between limousines and banks and jewelry stores.

Steele slowed his pace to match the crowds as he made his own way toward the Bahnhof, the train station. He paused briefly in a small triangular plaza next to a tram stop to consult a tourist map the front desk had given him before he left that morning. He looked about him and oriented the map to his direction of travel.

To his right was the old city of Zurich, with its serpentine cobbled streets lined with medieval and Renaissance buildings. Roten's shop was off one of the narrow lanes that intersected the Bahnhofstrasse two blocks up. As he shoved the map back in his overcoat pocket, Steele felt the lethal chill of the Magnum's metal cylinder.

Christ, he thought as he pressed on into the crowd, death followed him like a shadow. First Davidson on his boat, then Claude Tewles. Then the priest in the park in Amsterdam.

And Stephanie.

Stop it! He told himself. She's alive. She has to be alive. *Death. Death follows you. She's dead. Dead. Admit it. You're fooling yourself.*

Steele burrowed his hands deeply in his coat pockets and pressed on, head down, hurrying now as if he could outrun the thoughts that haunted him. If she was dead . . . he tried to think of an if, but he couldn't conceive of life without her. He pressed on.

He was about to turn right on the street that led into the old section when he heard a low, arresting sound, a haunting musical note that seemed to fill the air around him and appeal to every part of his body, not just his sense of sound. He stopped and turned around, trying to find the source of the tones that came from everywhere, and from nowhere in particular. Most of the people around him stopped also.

Beside him a woman bent low and spoke to her daughter.

"There," she said in German. She pointed, and the daughter immediately pushed through the crowd ahead of her mother. Steele followed them.

Across the street, his hat lying on the sidewalk, a bearded man of perhaps twenty, dressed in traditional alpine garb, blew into the mouthpiece of an Alpenhorn. The wooden instrument, a good ten feet long and shaped like a stretched-out Meerschaum pipe, seemed to glow with sound as the youth played a series of notes that resonated among the buildings.

A well-dressed woman walked up to the youth's hat and tossed in a banknote and then rejoined the edge of the crowd. Soon several other people repeated her gesture as the youth played the simple melodies and messages that the isolated alpine people had used to communicate with each other from ridge to ridge before the birth of the telephone.

Steele listened with his whole body. First one note would please his ear, then another would seem to vibrate in his chest, and another in his head. Finally, he dropped an American five-dollar bill into the youth's hat and turned reluctantly toward the street that would lead him to Roten's shop and—he hoped—some answers.

Less than ten minutes later, Steele found Roten's shop at the address on the back of the painting, which now rested in a safe deposit box at the Eden au Lac. The shop had undergone several expansions in the past forty years, taking over a number of the adjoining shops, and Steele found the entrance now at Number 13 Augustinergasse, just down the street from the original entrance.

Steele stood back at the edge of the sidewalk and looked at the front of the store. He had expected a slightly cluttered and dimly lighted shop with a display window filled with elbows of framing molding that had faded in the sun. Instead, he found an establishment that looked, for all he could tell, like one of the jewelry stores down on the Bahnhofstrasse. "Joseph Roten & Sons, Fine Art" read the discreet polished brass letters set into the cut-stone walls of the first floor of a Renaissance-era structure. It was a gallery now, not just a frame shop. Set into the stone facade at window level were half a dozen glassed-in display cases containing framed works of art. There were no prices on any of them. Either they were not for sale or they were for people who knew how to bid on fine art.

Doing his best to quell his excitement, Steele stepped quickly across the sidewalk to Roten's gallery and pushed through the double glass doors.

Inside, Steele found an elegantly warm room whose high-ceilinged walls were hung from floor to ceiling with art of every description. The fact that each work looked extravagantly expensive was the only unifying characteristic that ran through the art. The floor space of the room was empty save for a collection of dark mahogany furniture: half a dozen chairs upholstered in wine-red velvet, several pie-crust end tables, and a marble-top casual table in the middle to unify it all. Two of the chairs had fur coats draped over their arms like dead animals.

A cut-crystal decanter filled with what looked like sherry rested on a silver tray in the middle of the marble-top table surrounded by a circle of crystal sherry glasses. The circle of glasses had two gaps in it, and as Steele scanned the room he quickly spotted two white-haired women lifting glasses to their lips. They stood on either side of a short, fat man in his thirties who pointed at first one picture and then another, speaking in hushed, respectful tones. Both women nodded as he spoke.

"May I help you, sir?" asked a voice in English.

Startled, Steele whirled toward the voice. A younger but equally fat version of the man who guided the two women seemed to have materialized from the right. The man's formal dark suit and muted tie made him look like an undertaker. Steele stared at the man for a long moment, trying to collect his thoughts. He hadn't expected Joseph Roten and Sons to be anything as elaborate and . . . elegant as this.

"I'm sorry if I startled you," the man said and then he paused. "You *are* American, aren't you?" His eyes appraised Steele's casual attire: gray wool slacks, black leather walking shoes, navy-blue crew-necked sweater under a red down ski jacket. The man's eyes said that while he didn't approve of such attire in his establishment, he respected the eccentricities of Americans who might very well be rich.

"Yes," Steele finally managed as his pulse pounded in his ears. "I mean, yes . . . I am American, but I understand German clearly, if that would be more comfortable for you."

The man shook his head and extended his hand. "I am Felix Roten," he said. "I studied for two years in the United States, at the Getty Museum in California." Steele took the man's hand and shook it. Roten's grip was fleshy but firm and warm. "I welcome every opportunity to maintain my fluency in your language."

Steele nodded. "I'm Derek Steele," he said. "I called several days ago and spoke with your father about . . . about a painting." He watched the beginnings of a frown start to appear and then vanish from Roten's face. Steele reached for his wallet and pulled from it the snapshot of the painting that Davidson had given him.

"I wish to speak to your father about this painting." He handed it to the fleshy young man, who studied the photograph with hooded eyes. There was a long silence. From across the gallery floor, Steele could hear the two white-haired women arguing. One wanted a painting because it was a valuable investment. The other called it an eyesore.

"But dear, what a remarkably valuable eyesore," her friend replied. They continued in this vein as the silence between Steele and Roten grew increasingly uncomfortable. The young man seemed reluctant to look up from the photo.

"When I called earlier, I was told your father would be happy to meet with me," Steele said finally

What Felix Roten did next took Steele completely unaware.

"Here!" Roten hissed as he thrust the photograph back at Steele. "Take your filth and leave us alone."

Steele took the photo and stared blankly at Roten.

"Are you deaf?" Roten asked. "We are decent people and we will not be forever haunted by one mistake forty years ago. Get out of here. Get out of here now or I'll be forced to call the authorities."

"But . . ." Steele searched for the words that wouldn't come to mind. What had gone wrong? The name on the back of the painting was his only clue to Stephanie, his only way to find out what the painting meant! What had changed Roten's mind? Had someone talked to him? About what?

Roten had grabbed Steele's upper arm and was trying to steer him out of the store. "Please, Mr. Steele, or whoever you say you are, please leave! We don't want any trouble and we therefore want nothing to do with the painting of which you speak."

"But why?" Steele shook his arm loose from Roten's grasp and turned to face him. Roten was a full head shorter than Steele. "I don't know anything about the painting except that it's connected with the disappearance of my wife and with the deaths of at least three people."

Roten's eyes widened as Steele spoke. "That precisely is why we wish nothing with this painting to do." Roten's fluency in English degenerated into patterns of German grammar as his agitation increased. He grabbed Steele again and shoved him toward the door.

"Please not to make me call the police," Roten pleaded. "But I will if you do not leave."

Steele shook himself free of Roten a second time and stood with his back to the door, shaking with anger and frustration as he stared down at him. His mouth worked furiously, like that of a fish out of water, as he tried to clear the inarticulate rage from his head.

Finally, Steele put his right hand in the middle of Roten's soft fleshy chest and pushed him so hard the chubby man stumbled backwards, arms flailing the air like a windmill, and crashed rump-first into the cut-crystal glasses and decanters on the marble-topped table.

The high-pitched tinkles of breaking crystal followed Steele out into the bright sunshine and stopped only when the door slammed shut behind him.

"I've found him."

"Good," replied Neils Braun, as he paced his office in the lodge high atop the Nockspitze overlooking the Inn valley. Braun squinted as he walked to the window with his favorite view, and surveyed the landscape with a proprietary gaze. He was feeling decidedly better since he had answered the telephone. "You've done much better than our British allies."

"So what else is new," the man on the other end of the trans-atlantic call replied. "It's been that way since we pulled them out of the first war."

The arrogance, Braun thought as the lines of his face dug themselves deeper into a frown. Americans were so arrogant.

"How did the Brits screw this one up? What with all the information they had?"

"I'm not willing to discuss that," Braun said, fighting back his anger at the American's impudence and lack of respect. "We have better things to do than discuss such things at present. Suffice it to say that our Mr. Steele is quite resourceful."

"He's a regular hellhound, is what he is," the American replied.

Braun said nothing.

"I'm on my way," the American said. "I had a little trouble in Washington, a snoop who I had to . . . make arrangements for."

"Is everything secure?" Braun asked, too eagerly. For the first time, his anxiety seeped into his words. The American's connections were too valuable to lose, especially when they were so close.

"It will be in a day or so," came the reply. "Remember, I'm using a lot of computer time and manpower. It's not as easy as you think to cover them up with false computer entries. I have to enter the computer at the very basic levels, in machine language, to avoid the auditors. And they go through the records every—"

"I'm not interested in all that," Braun said. "I just want to know if everything is secure."

"Yes, your grace."

"Good. When will you be here?"

"I'll be in Zurich on a flight that arrived there just before midnight. Are you sure he has the painting?"

"I'm sure." Braun said. "If he didn't, why the sudden trip to Europe? And that telephone call to Zurich?"

"It's the best explanation I can think of, but that doesn't prove that he's got it with him. All he said to that guy was that he wanted to talk to him about a painting. He could just be fishing for information."

Again, Braun hid his disdain from the disrespectful American. Where? he wondered. Where are the men who can follow orders? They seemed to be all gone.

"Well," the American said, with doubt in his voice, "if he's got it, I'll get it."

"That's what I'm paying you for," Braun said dryly. "So why don't you get to it."

"Sure, sure," the American said. "Don't get upset, your grace. I'll be there by midnight. Goodbye."

But the receiver on the Austrian end of the line crashed down in the middle of the American's "goodbye." The receiver clicked rudely across half the European continent and the Atlantic Ocean.

"What's his problem?" Gerry Anderson asked himself as he hung up the receiver of the pay phone. He reached down, angrily snatched his briefcase from the floor, and then made his way across the vast open spaces of Dulles International Airport toward his boarding gate.

"He's gone!"

The abbot flinched visibly as he heard the young priest's words. The abbey's shabby financial condition faded from the abbot's thoughts now as he looked from the window of his office at the twin towers of the Frauenkirche towering over the roofline of Munich's old town. He turned slowly to face the young priest.

"What do you mean, 'gone'?" the abbot asked slowly, his words carrying the edge of a razor. The young priest's face looked as if it had been dusted with flour.

"I—" The priest tried to clear his nervous throat.. "We knocked at his door with his lunch. He . . . he said he wasn't feeling well; he spent the morning in bed. He's . . . he's very—"

"Sick, yes, I know his medical history," the abbot said impatiently. "I know more about his medical history than I do my own, so get on with it!"

"He asked to be left alone this morning, and we . . . we assumed he was sleeping. He's done that in the past, you know." The young priest looked hopefully for some sign of flexibility in his master. Finding none on the abbot's chilly face, he continued.

"We knocked just a few minutes ago," the young priest said.

"And when we got no answer we—we were afraid he had . . . died or something—we entered the room and found he had gone."

"Gone? Just like that? Gone?" the Abbot asked.

The young priest nodded.

The abbot's reply began low, like rumbles on the distant horizon, and rose steadily until his words thundered at the young priest, so forcefully that he flinched under their blows. "I give you and five other incompetent human beings who call themselves priests the task of looking after a feeble, half-crippled old man and you've come to tell me that he has somehow disappeared right from under your keen eyes in the middle of the day! I—" the abbot choked on his rage. His face burned red with anger and his fists trembled at his side. For a long moment, he glared at the young priest. Then: "Get out! You and your fellows are confined to your rooms. I will deal with you later."

The young priest seemed petrified.

"Out! Out now!"

The priest abruptly came to life and ran from the room.

The abbot walked to the door of his office and closed it quietly. Then he went to his desk and sagged heavily into the chair. Why him? he wondered through closed eyes that he rubbed with the heels of his hands. Why?

He reached for the telephone. As his hands neared the receiver it hesitated for a moment, almost as if the instrument were a venomous reptile. His hands shook, from fear now rather than anger, as he dialed the Innsbruck number of the archbishop cardinal of Vienna. Neils Braun was not a man who took failure with equanimity.

CHAPTER TWENTY-ONE

How had they ever found him?

Andrei Malenkov, M.D., watched the two men climb into the dark blue Mercedes. He stared numbly at the modest parking lot in front of his clinic as the Mercedes skidded through an icy patch left by last week's snows. The tires made a quick squeal as they found purchase on the pavement. The car and the two men inside disappeared in the direction of Zurich.

How had they ever found him?

He had changed his name. He had never even written home to his mother to let her know if he was still alive. He had avoided all of his old friends and even stayed away from medical meetings and conventions, fearing that a colleague might recognize him in spite of the plastic surgery that had altered his face and erased a decade from his features. Even when he went to temple, he was always careful to sit in the back, away from others. And he left immediately after the services, never lingering long enough to talk with anyone. Oh, his practice had suffered from his antisocial behavior, but he had stayed alive, and his mother had not suffered at the hands of the KGB. Until today, he was convinced that both his mother and the KGB had accepted the newspaper accounts of his drowning at that resort in Czechoslovakia.

But he had been wrong.

Malenkov turned from the window and walked down the long hall of his clinic, looking into each examining room like a departing tenant.

How long had they known about him? They must have been

waiting for a very long time, waiting for the right moment. The KGB was like that. They were good waiters. Many people had made the fatal mistake of assuming that KGB patience was stupidity.

Malenkov paused at the doorway to the laboratory. It was one of his prides. No other clinic of its size anywhere in Switzerland had such a complete laboratory. It saved his patients money. And it saved them worrying time. The results of their tests could be known in minutes or hours, treatment begun sooner, worrying ended sooner.

He turned from the door and continued toward the rear of the clinic.

The KGB had the patience and the methods. Computers—mostly stolen from the United States—and manpower. He had read about the millions of people who worked for the KGB, willingly or unwillingly. Was one of those millions working for the Mossad?

Reaching the very rear of his clinic, Malenkov pulled a key from a ring, unlocked the bolt on the door, and stepped in, closing the door behind him. He flipped on a light. The walls were covered with glass-fronted cabinets, some of them refrigerated, behind which sat vial after vial of pharmaceuticals, some antibiotics, others narcotic, others for adjusting hormones, blood pressure, digestion.

They had found him.

He looked about him until his eye fell on the vial he was looking for.

It didn't matter how they found him, for he could do nothing. If he warned the woman at the Eden au Lac, or if he warned the Mossad, they would kill his mother. Slowly. And they would send him pictures and tape recordings and they would come back to him and make him listen to her cries and view the damage to her face and body. The KGB agent with the bandage on his face had smiled at him when he described what they would do to his mother.

Malenkov opened the cabinet and pulled from it a vial of succinylcholine hydrochloride. He took the vial and walked back into the clinic. He carefully locked the door of the drug room behind him. He walked into the first examining room he came to, went to the supplies cabinet, and pulled from it a hypodermic.

He had told them and he was ashamed. He had told them where she·was because the woman with the staples in her feet didn't matter to him as much as his mother did. Neither did the state of Israel, for whom he had worked for nearly fifteen years now.

Nothing mattered anymore, Malenkov thought as he rolled up his sleeve. The KGB had used him. And they would be back. Oh, yes. He knew how they worked. They would be back and they would use him to lead them to others. And they would kill and torture the others, just like they had tortured and would now kill the American woman.

That he had caused her death was too much to bear.

Malenkov stuck the needle of the hypodermic into the vial and filled the barrel of the syringe. Succinylcholine hydrochloride in infinitestimally small doses is a superb anesthetic. By the syringe, death comes quickly.

As he plunged the needle into his arm and emptied the syringe into his body, he only regretted he couldn't make the woman's death this quick, this painless.

Darkness covered the bright Swiss morning.

He was being followed. There was no longer any doubt about that. Derek Steele brought his glass of white wine to his lips and gazed over the rim at the man across the cafe from him. He was a tall man, six-two or more, with wavy brown hair cut almost short enough to suit a police force or a military organization. His face had the lean and angular agelessness found usually in combat officers who have devoted a lifetime of physical effort to staying in superb physical condition. Steele was suddenly conscious of the fifteen pounds he had added since Stephanie had disappeared, of the roll of flab that girdled his waistline.

The man carried himself with a physical precision and confidence that conveyed strength hidden beneath the bulky wool overcoat. He wore a business suit now, with a tiny, precisely knotted tie and a coat that could easily conceal a firearm. And even from across the main dining room of the crowded cafe, the intensity of his glacier-blue eyes was apparent.

Steele set his wineglass down slowly and pretended interest in the *Rösti* on his plate. The man was no professional at tailing people, Steele thought, as he chased the potatoes around his plate with a fork; he was too obvious, looking too hard, following too closely, making eye contact accidentally. Unless, Steele stopped to think, unless someone wanted him to know he was being followed. But who could that be? Someone associated with the priest who had followed him in Amsterdam? Or someone who wanted to kill him?

He rejected this last notion. If that had been the man's intention he would have done it sooner, back when Steele had walked along through the deserted park alongside Saint Peter's Church. He had first seen the man there, just minutes after shoving Felix Roten into his sherry and crystal.

Steele had begun to regret his display of temper as he climbed the steps at the end of the In Gassen. He had just about decided to go back and apologize to Roten and offer to pay for the damage when he saw the man.

Steele had stopped, and unlike a professional tail, who would have continued on past him, the man stopped too, startled and uncertain of himself.

Continuing on up the steps, Steele dismissed the encounter as coincidence. But the man followed him across the courtyard at the top of the In Gassen, around the church, and through the courtyard on the other side. Steele took the glove off his right hand and kept a firm grasp on the Magnum as he walked along. The man might have a silenced weapon, or accomplices could be waiting around the next corner. They would suffer for whatever they might have in mind. But nothing happened.

The man had had plenty of opportunity to kill him and escape without being seen. Yet he had just continued his clumsy surveillance. Steele sneaked a look at the man across the cafe again. He was amateurishly trying to hide behind a copy of the *Neue Züricher Zeitung*. Steele read the headlines from across the room.

Suddenly Steele knew what he had to do. Letting his fork drop abruptly on his plate, he fumbled about in his pockets for currency to cover his meal, dropped the money on the table, then swiftly got up and walked across the room. Quickly, Steele plunged his right hand into the deep pocket of his ski parka and found the grip of the Magnum. He grabbed it and slipped his index finger through the trigger guard, curling it around the lithe coldness of the trigger.

Steele heard the man's newspaper rattle loudly and saw the expression of surprise and confusion on the man's face as he caught sight of him approaching. Startled, the man knocked over the cup of tea he had been nursing as he made an effort to rise.

"Don't bother getting up," Steele said in German, as he held up his left hand in a stop gesture. The man froze, half in, half out of his seat. "Go ahead, sit down," Steele said.

Then, in a lower voice, Steele continued: "I have a very powerful handgun in the pocket of my coat." He watched the man's look flicker down to Steele's concealed hand, immediately, his eyes widened with fear. "It's pointed at you and will tear a hole in you the size of that tea saucer if you so much as think of doing something I haven't first told you to do. Have you got that?"

The man nodded cooly. "What do you want?" His voice was calm, confident. He might be an amateur at tailing people, Steele thought, but he had an uncanny calmness when faced with danger. Only people who had faced danger and survived were capable of that.

"I should be asking you that," Steele said. "And since I have the gun, why don't you start first?" He pulled out the chair opposite the man and sat down.

Steele said: "My life is in danger and if I think you're part of that danger, I'll pull the trigger. Got that?" The man nodded again. "I'm nervous, so don't force me to make a mistake." The man nodded again. "Hand me your wallet," Steele commanded. The man's hand moved quickly toward his coat pocket. "Slowly! Slowly," Steele said. "I want to make sure you don't pull any surprises from your pockets."

The man nodded calmly, his head tilted slightly to one side, and pulled a slim leather wallet from his inside coat pocket and slid it across the table to Steele. He then leaned casually back in his chair and looked appraisingly across the table as Steele, using only his left hand, opened the wallet on the table and began to sort through its contents. There was currency, the equivalent of less than $100 in Swiss francs, the card key to a parking lot, a collection of credit cards, and a Swiss driver's license in the name of Joseph Roten. Steele glanced sharply at the man across the table.

"You're Joseph Roten?" His voice betrayed his incredulity.

The man nodded. "I am the son of the man you called several

days ago. I am Joseph Roten the second . . . or junior, as you Americans refer to it.''

Searching for words, trying desperately to collect his thoughts, Steele replaced Roten's driver's license in his wallet and slid it back across the table. "I . . . I don't understand,'' he stammered. "Why would you . . . Why follow me like this?''

"Because someone who said he was you came to our house last night. He had men with him and he wanted to hurt my father. The man is not alive. Neither are his friends.'' Roten's voice was matter-of-fact.

"But who? Why?'' Steele asked.

"They had no identification,'' Roten said, "and they spoke German with Russian accents. I believe they worked for the KGB.''

Steele nodded knowingly. "That makes sense,'' he said, and then stopped himself. "No, that doesn't make any sense at all . . . none of this does. But at least it fits. They tried to kill me before. I thought you . . .''

"Might be one of them?'' Steele nodded. Joseph Roten smiled for the first time. "No, Mr . . . Steele?'' Steele nodded. "We are both on the same side.''

Roten extended his hand across the table. Steele looked at it warily. Was it a trick? A clever ruse to disarm him? Identification can be faked, Steele reminded himself. And the best of killers are also the best of actors. As he looked at the proffered handshake of friendship, he thought of Davidson, of the priest of Amsterdam, of Gerry Anderson. They had all come to him in friendship and they had all proved they were worthy of trust . . . Anderson had saved his life; the other two had died.

Like a small boy edging his way to the end of the high dive for the first time, Steele decided he had to trust this man. He stifled a chill that skated down his spine as he slowly relaxed his grip on the Magnum and pulled his hand from his pocket.

"All right,'' Steele said finally as he took Roten's warm, dry grip and shook it. "We're on the same side.''

"That's good,'' Roten said, shaking Steele's hand and then letting it go. "Because the man at the next table,'' he nodded to his left "has a gun more powerful than your own, pointed at your head.''

Steele whirled to his right and saw a stocky man with long straight brown hair. The man smiled at him, looked down at his lap, then quickly back up at Steele again. Steele followed the man's eyes downward, and immediately spotted the muzzle end of a silencer hidden under the folds of a paper napkin.

Steele looked back at Roten and watched as Roten nodded at the man with the long hair. The man nodded back, reached down, and plucked a forest-green knapsack from underneath the table. He then slid the silenced gun into the knapsack, placed a banknote on the table, and left without further communication.

"You don't take many chances, do you?" Steele remarked, his question more of a statement.

"I am a very, very careful man, Mr. Steele," Roten said. "I don't like to take chances."

"But you're taking one now, aren't you?" Steele asked, as he turned his full attention to the man across the table from him. Roten's raised eyebrows described the arc of an unspoken question on his forehead.

"You're taking a chance right now with me," Steele answered Roten's unspoken question. "How do you know I'm not just a clever KGB agent?"

Roten's eyebrows knitted themselves into one long mass as he considered Steele's question. The thoughts shifted behind his eyes. Finally: "The same way you knew to trust me, Mein Herr," Roten began slowly. "If you were not who you say you are, you would never have dropped your guard with me. You would have dealt with me differently. Do you agree?"

Steele nodded thoughtfully.

"Good," Roten said. "We have some important arrangements to make . . . questions to answer, before you meet my father tonight."

Brilliant sunlight cascaded through the windows of the sitting room that separated Stephanie's bedroom at the Eden au Lac from Nat Worthington's. The three of them—Stephanie, Nat and Rich Seeley, the bodyguard Nat had hired until the Mossad arrived to assume the duties of protecting her—sat at a small round table next to the window, eating from a tray of sandwiches brought up by room service. A bottle of red wine sat uncorked and half empty in the middle of the table. Only Stephanie and Nat drank.

The suite had been a last-minute cancellation and had simplified Nat's plans for Stephanie's security. He had barricaded the door to her room, and availing himself of Rich Seeley's prodigious strength, moved a Louis XIV armoire in front of it. Except for the windows that faced a sheer drop—no ledges or fire escapes nearby—the only way to get to Stephanie was through the door that connected to the sitting room. And Seeley, the huge former paratrooper, slept in the sitting room at night.

Stephanie stretched lazily now and closed her eyes for a long moment. Except for a minor ache in her feet—the wounds had not been serious after all, more pain than damage—she felt the inner rapture of the condemned prisoner who has been granted a miraculous reprieve.

And although it was only slightly past one o'clock in the afternoon, she had already run the gamut of the Eden au Lac's beauty salon. After a long luxurious bath, the hairdresser had cut and styled her hair, tsk-tsking all the while, but too discreet to actually come right out and ask madame how her hair had managed to fall into such a shabby state of repair.

And while the hairdresser fussed, the manicurist labored over her nails with the fervor and energy of a sculptor attacking a virgin block of marble.

Next had come the woman with the facials that smelled of a well-made Amaretto mousse, and later, the beauty consultant who made Stephanie feel truly feminine again. And finally, the hotel's fashion consultant who came with books of clothing designs and fabric swatches, taking her measurements and promising to scour the boutiques of Zurich to assemble madame's new wardrobe.

Stephanie turned her face into the bright warm sunlight and tilted her head downward toward the lake. Through the window, she saw a lone sailboat beating its way to windward. The sight struck a blow to her heart. Where was Derek? She had called and called, even getting up in the middle of the night, but there had been no answer, only the sound of his voice on the recording. She wished there was a way to remotely listen to the messages others had left on the machine. Perhaps they would provide a clue to Derek's whereabouts. Nat had promised to obtain a device that produced the proper tones, but it wouldn't be here until the people from Mossad arrived, and that was either later tonight or even tomorrow morning.

Her impatience raced through her body and made her insides tingle.

Where was he? she wondered with a lover's longing intensity. What was he doing right now? Had he sailed out to Catalina? It was 2 A.M. there now. Was he sound asleep, the *Valkyrie* bobbing gently at anchor in the secure anchorages at Cherry Cove or maybe Fourth of July Cove?

She saw his sleeping face in her mind and felt tears well up from the tender breakings in her chest. He looked like such a little boy when he slept. Respected professor, tough cop—they were all vanquished by the relaxed face of a man who she knew was still a boy at heart. She remembered how he would smile in his sleep, have little puppy twitches like a dog chasing a rabbit in its dreams, and the way the tough lean former cop with the hard muscles and long leathery scars he didn't like to talk about would cuddle next to her and fall asleep.

Where are you, Derek? Stephanie swiped at her moist eyes before turning back to the table. She looked to see if Nat or Rich had noticed her tears. But if they had seen, they gave no evidence of it.

"The people from the Mossad will want to ask you some questions," Worthington was saying. "But they're good people. You can trust them to treat you well and to protect you for as long as it's necessary."

"When will you be leaving?" Stephanie asked.

Nat had told her his story earlier in the morning. He had told her of his work for the CIA and of how crooked men in the upper ranks had tried to have him killed. He had told her of Tania, his wife, how she had defected from Russia and into his arms, and how Adam Gold had saved their lives. He also told her about Mustafa Salem El-Nouty, and of the farm in New Zealand, and how it was now safe for Tania and him to go back there and rebuild it now that El-Nouty was dead.

She remembered El-Nouty. She remembered how the tall Libyan had looked at her, as if she had been naked to his gaze, and how his eyes had made her shiver. She was glad he was dead, even

294

if it meant saying goodbye to Nat. She told him that she would like to meet Tania some day.

"Probably tomorrow," Worthington replied. "I want to make sure all of the arrangements are solid here before I go back to Tel Aviv and then back to Kiwi land. I want to spend Christmas in Jerusalem with Tania."

"Christmas in the holyland," Stephanie said absently. "I'd love to be there with Derek."

She fell silent again with the mention of his name. Her longing was complete, completely coloring her thoughts and emotions. Where was he? The only thing in the world she wanted more than knowing where he was, was to be there with him.

CHAPTER TWENTY-TWO

The lights along the opposite shore of the Zurichsee painted long shimmering smears of white and yellow on the glassy surface of the water. The wind had died at sunset and had remained still. The air outside seemed so free of pollution that it appeared crystalline.

Steele turned from the window and walked toward the door of his room at the Eden au Lac. He stopped by the door and pulled the Smith & Wesson from his parka pocket. He checked to be sure that every chamber in the revolver's cylinder had a fresh .357 bullet in it, set the safety on, and stuck the weapon back in the pocket. He patted the other pocket to make sure the handful of ammunition was still there. He hesitated, going over Joseph Roten's instructions in his mind. Any deviation and he might be killed.

Sure of his orders, Steele opened the door to his room, stepped across the threshold and pulled the door shut behind him. He walked to the elevator and pressed the down button.

"I still think you should wait until tomorrow," Nat Worthington argued, as Stephanie walked painfully across the room in cushioned running shoes—deliberately purchased three sizes too large to accommodate the bandages on her feet—and a bulky sweater pulled over plain-label Levi's.

"I don't want to wait until tomorrow," Stephanie insisted, as she pushed past him toward the door of the sitting room that led to the corridor. "I want to know if my things are still in the safe deposit box where I left them."

"But the Mossad will be here tomorrow morning," Nat insisted, knowing his arguments were futile in the face of this headstrong woman. "And you could always call the front desk. There's no reason for you to put yourself into pain by walking down there."

"The pain's not all that bad," she insisted, "and I don't want to wait until tomorrow morning. I want to *do* something right now. I'll go crazy if I just sit here. I have to *do* something, don't you understand?"

Nat was standing in front of the door now, facing Stephanie.

"Do you understand?" she asked him. "I have to take some kind of action or I'll go nuts."

Worthington looked at her. He understood. "All right, but both Rich and I go with you."

"All right with me, Nat." Stephanie said. Nat turned to open the door.

"Nat?"

Worthington turned back toward her.

"I don't want to be an impossible bother," she said. "I appreciate what you have done for me more than you will ever—yes, I suppose you *do* know, what with Adam and all. But I hope you understand—I'm not the kind of woman who can just sit around and do nothing."

"I understand," Nat said, then nodded to Seeley. Nat walked out of the room first, his eyes scouring the corridor for signs of danger. Stephanie followed him. Seeley closed the door to the suite and, using his saliva, carefully placed one of his own hairs across the space between the jamb and the door. They'd know whether or not someone had entered.

The trio walked to the elevator and pushed the button. They stood silently and looked at the floor indicator as the car went past them and stopped one floor above.

Steele watched the elevator come to a stop at his floor. The door opened gracefully and Steele was about to step in when he heard a voice calling to him.

"Mein Herr."

The voice sounded foreign yet familiar. Friend or assassin? Steele whirled toward the voice, plunged his hand into his pocket, and found the Magnum. Near the door to his room, he saw a man coming toward him, looking vaguely familiar. Steele tensed. Where had he seen the man? Where had he heard his voice?

"I am glad to have found you before you left," the man said as he continued to walk toward Steele. He was dark, thin, plainly dressed. "The desk telephoned and there was no answer in your room. You are in great danger."

There was no danger in the man's voice or in the way he walked. Confusing signals, a stranger in his hotel corridor. How did the man know he was here? Steele's heart pounded. The man seemed harmless.

And so did an old man who appeared at the companionway of your boat.

Steele snapped the safety off the Magnum as the man stepped into a pool of light spilled into the corridor by a brass sconce.

It was the taxi driver who had brought him from the train station the previous night. Behind him, Steele heard the elevator door close.

Steele flicked the safety back on the Magnum, pulled his right hand from his pocket, and extended it toward the Turkish *Gastarbeiter* who had shared a meal and his dreams of a better life with Steele the night before. The man took Steele's hand and shook it enthusiastically. Then the smile vanished from his face.

"There are men asking questions about you," the cab driver said in his terrible German. "They say they are with the police . . . the government. But something smells with these men. I have seen their type too many times. They are arrogant and they are bad men. They dress like bankers and they offer great sums of money to know where you are. I have told them nothing. You have been too kind to me."

Steele looked at the cabdriver, and for a brief moment felt ashamed that such a small kindness such as he had shown to this man was all it had taken to win his allegiance. And then he felt grateful, thankful that there were still good people in the world, people like this simple immigrant, who were good, honest, decent people.

"How many of them were there?" Steele asked.

"Two . . . three, I think," the cabbie answered. "They arrived at the train station this morning and began showing your picture around."

"My picture!" Steele felt jolted as if by an electric prod. "What kind of picture? What did it look like?"

The cabdriver closed his eyes and screwed up his face as if he were searching files in his head. "A color picture," he said finally. "There was a lady in the picture with you." He opened his eyes. "A very pretty lady. You were sitting at a table, maybe a cafe or a nightclub. I remember there was a name in the background behind you but I don't remember the name."

"I do," Steele said quickly. "It was The Harbor Reef, wasn't it?"

"Yes," the driver said slowly, "that could be it. But it was in English, I believe, and I don't read much of that. German is my only language other than my native tongue."

The Harbor Reef! Steele knew the photograph. It had been taken with a Polaroid camera nearly three years ago, when he and Stephanie had visited the isthmus at Catalina. The Harbor Reef was the only restaurant there, and a damn good one at that. They had been celebrating Stephanie's latest art brokerage, and Doug Bombard, the owner of the restaurant, had taken the picture of the two of them sitting at a table on the patio outside. And for the last three years that picture—the only one of its kind—had resided in Stephanie's wallet! What did it mean? Steele asked himself. Did it make it more likely or less that she was still alive? Or did it merely mean that the men who had kidnapped her had not learned what they wanted from her and had continued the search for him that had begun in Los Angeles?

". . . will be looking for you at hotels soon," the cabdriver was saying. You must leave."

Leave? Yes, Steele thought as he looked at his watch. Both Joseph Rotens—senior and son—would soon be waiting.

"Of course, they'll look for me at the hotels later," Steele said as he started for the stairway. Or maybe right now. Maybe there's a man with a gun waiting at the bottom of the stairs. The thought made his stomach cramp.

"But I have an extremely important meeting I have to go to . . . an urgent one," Steele said to the taxi driver as he began to descend the stairs. "I don't have time to worry about that right now."

"I will take you to your meeting, Mein Herr," the driver insisted. "It would not be safe for you to be seen by other drivers. They would surely turn you in for the money."

Steele glanced sideways at the man as they gained the first landing, walking half a dozen steps, and continued on down the stairs. "How much money are we talking about?"

"More than two thousand Swiss Francs."

Two-thousand francs! About a thousand American dollars. Not exactly a king's ransom, but far more than street cops usually waved around at taxi stands looking for tips. They wanted him badly.

They passed the second floor landing. Steele reached inside his coat and pulled his wallet from his hip pocket. From it he took one of Davidson's thousand dollar bills.

"You passed up a lot of money just to be honest," Steele said, as they reached the landing just above the lobby. Steele put his hand on the cab driver's shoulder and they stopped before descending the final flight. "I want you to have this." He proffered the American thousand dollar bill. The Turkish immigrant looked first at the bill, and then fixed Steele with a hurt, insulted look.

"I can't take that," the man said. "I did not come here to ask you for money, or for a reward. I came because you are obviously a good man and you are in danger."

"But you family . . . your children," Steele stammered in his confusion. "They could—*you*—could use this money, is that not true?"

"That has nothing at all to do with a matter of honor," the cabdriver replied proudly. "I am a man of honor and I must act like one." He pushed the bill away firmly but politely with the palm of his hand, looked up into Steele's eyes, and said: "Come! You have an important meeting to attend. I will drive you."

Astounded, Steele turned to the last flight of stairs and began his descent.

"Are you telling me that without telephoning or any other kind of notification, you simply emptied the safe deposit box and *mailed* the contents to my home?" Stephanie was outraged. She had made her way past two layers of the Eden au Lac's internal bureaucracy and had managed to get to the manager before he left for the

300

evening. She had snared him in the middle of the hotel's main lobby near the frieze by Bernini. Worthington and Seeley hovered about her, trying to look inconspicuous and failing to succeed, due mostly to Seeley's bulk.

"But Madame Steele, I assure you that we had no choice," the hotel manager protested in a desperate whisper. He looked about him after every sentence to see if any of the hotel's other guests were paying attention to the disagreement. "After a guest checks out, we have a policy that all items left behind in our boxes must be returned to them. After all, it wouldn't be fair to deprive other guests of the proper facilities in which to store their valuables."

"Policy!" Stephanie spat. "Policies are for bureaucrats and bankers and anybody else too dimwitted to make intelligent decisions on their own. Not for the management of one of the worlds's finest hotels."

The manager's face brightened momentarily at this unexpected compliment from the angry American woman.

"We assumed that—"

"That painting was among the world's most valuable," Stephanie said. "Priceless! Do you understand? At the very least it merited being handcarried by a courier. Not trusted to the vagaries of the mails!"

As Stephanie said "priceless," most of the color drained from the manager's face. "But the Swiss mails are—"

"I know the *Swiss* mails are reliable," Stephanie interrupted. "But once the package gets to America, it's in the hands of the U.S. Postal Service, and most of the people who work for that outfit are so dense they need a road map to find their way to the bathroom."

Stephanie's vehemence brought color back to the manager's face, but it was a wan, unenthusiastic pink blotched with pale white. He looked about him desperately. The lobby was nearly deserted and the staff were busy straightening out the receipts from the busy afternoon.

"I—Ahem!" The manager cleared his throat nervously. It was time to play his last card, to risk stepping into the middle of what might turn out to be a domestic quarrel. If so, he would either turn this woman's wrath away from him or—he swallowed hard—redouble her wrath. And perhaps incur her husband's as well. She

301

obviously was unaware that her husband had checked in the night before and had put the same painting back into a hotel safe deposit box. The Eden au Lac prided itself on its discretion and respect for its guests' privacy. Confidences were to be respected unless the situation became so desperate that it reflected poorly on the hotel's image.

And things were getting desperate, the manager decided. And desperate situations called for desperate measures. If he was violating a confidence, then so be it. It could hardly be worse than losing a priceless work of art.

"Your husband seemed quite happy with the arrangements we made," the manager said. "I spoke to him last night when he checked in."

He was grateful to see the anger on her face break and scatter like the last dark clouds of a summer thunderstorm.

"In fact, I placed the painting of which you speak back in a safe deposit box. I did it myself, madame."

He watched as Stephanie's face had turned from anger to amazement to relief. Her features softened, and as they did, the hotel manager noticed for the first time how beautiful she was.

Stephanie felt her heart race. Derek was *here!* He was *here!*

"Derek's in this hotel?" She turned to Worthington. "That's why he didn't answer the phone last night or today!" She paused, a puzzled look occupying her features. "But how? How did he know?"

She turned back to the manager and touched his sleeve lightly.

"What room's he in?" she asked eagerly.

The manager looked at her intensely. She didn't look like an angry wife. There was no jealousy or hatred in her eyes, only relief. Still . . . he hesitated.

"Well," he began reluctantly, "normally we don't give out information on our guests but . . ."

"We've both been . . . traveling. My husband and I," she said. "And we've obviously missed connections so—"

"As I said, we normally don't give out such information, but in this case, I think we can accommodate your request."

"Thank you!" Stephanie said breathlessly. And as she followed him over to the front desk, she felt no pain in her feet.

* * *

Steele stepped of the stairs and turned toward the lobby.

"Wait!" The cab driver placed a firm hand on his shoulder. "Not that way." Steele stopped. "There are too many people who might see you. Come with me, out the side. I have parked there just for this reason."

Steele looked out on the lobby. The main doors were straight ahead, the front desk was out of sight to the left, and there was a comfortable seating area to the right near a frieze by Bernini. Save for a very large man walking toward the front desk, the lobby was deserted. As he watched, the large man disappeared to the left. The man looked like a huge walking threat.

"Your're probably right," Steele said quickly. "Lead the way." He followed the Turkish cab driver down a narrow service corridor and finally, through a plain scarred wooden door near the kitchen that led out into the crisp night air.

The day had passed in great jerks and swatches of time. Robert Maxwell sat now in an uncushioned wooden chair across the desk from Cardinal Neils Braun. He couldn't quite bring himself to believe what Braun had revealed to him in the past hour. The cardinal was either insane or . . . Maxwell couldn't think of a credible alternative.

The meeting of the full council had ended earlier in the afternoon, but Braun had asked Maxwell to stay on for Christmas. Maxwell consented. He had no family to spend the holidays with in the States. And Braun had promised him fantastic skiing on the Olympic slopes around Innsbruck.

What Braun had not promised was the astounding tale that had just consumed the better part of sixty minutes.

"Your help will be critical in the transition," Braun said. "You as the 'Great Conciliator,' know that better than almost anyone else. You are respected by every segment of the Christian world—Protestant, Roman Catholic, Orthodox, all. I can also tell that you know the very real value of negotiation, arbitration, conciliation in such a dramatic transformation of the church. Without your help the Church, the Universal Church, could suffer grievously."

Braun was not insane, Maxwell finally decided. He was a genius, an ambitious genius. A virulently anticommunist (and Maxwell had to agree with him on that), hard-line, ambitious genius who wanted to be pope.

Braun's plan had seemed insane, ridiculous. Then the cardinal had begun to explain it, and soon it seemed logical, almost compelling. Maxwell wondered if insanity were infectious.

The only defense against communism, and the eventual conquest of most of the world by the Soviet Union, Braun's argument went, was the Church.

But the Church was fragmented, its attention unfocused, its resources, though formidable, spent by a million hands with often-conflicting goals.

A unified church with a unified goal could go one on one with communism and win, Braun insisted.

His plan was insanely simple.

Once the Shroud of Veronica was recovered, Braun would use it to extort his way past the College of Cardinals to replace the man who presently wore the ring of Saint Peter.

It was logical; Braun argued persuasively. Hitler had used the shroud to blackmail Pope Pius XII for evil reasons. He, Braun, would use it in a similar manner for the good of the Church. He would make sure that an iron hand ruled the Roman Catholic Church.

Gone would be the liberation theologists, priests and nuns who worked hand in hand with guerrillas, who ran guns and weapons for Marxists in Central America, and smuggled guns and explosives to terrorists in parts of Europe. Gone would be appeasement. Gone would be the weak hand at the helm of the Church.

Braun said he already had arrangements with generals in Central and South America to clamp down on dissident priests in their countries. Some had already begun rounding up the offending clergy. Once Braun was pope, he would sanction the most widespread rooting out of evil in history.

"Once we have secured my position in the Vatican," he continued, "once that position is solidified, you will then arrange meetings between me and the top governing officials in the other major religions."

Braun paused and leaned back in his chair. "You know all these people. You have met with them, negotiated with them. That's one primary reason I selected you for the vacancy on the council.''

Maxwell watched as unspoken other reasons seemed to flash behind Braun's eyes. One of the possible reasons made Maxwell grow cold inside.

Braun leaned forward again, resting his elbows on his desk. ''At those meetings, I will use the persuasion of Veronica's Shroud to force concessions of the most historical nature, perhaps a reunification but at the very least a profound realignment, a coming together to marshal the forces of the world's religions under *my* guidance.

Maxwell's head spun. He gripped the armrests of the chair as if it were a rocking ski lift chair suddenly stopped over a yawning crevasse.

It would work. Maxwell was sure of it. He knew the instincts of self-preservation so deeply rooted in the bureaucracies of the world's established churches. He had seen the self-preservation work and knew it was capable of even more compromise with its principles than Braun was suggesting. The shroud would threaten the very structure of the Western world's organized religions. And Maxwell knew that the people who sat atop those structures would do almost anything to preserve their churches and their positions in their hierarchies.

Braun droned on, his words washing around Maxwell's stunned senses like gentle surf.

Death, the elimination of dissent in the churches, both Catholic and Protestant alike, arrangements with military leaders and ambitious politicians eager to use religious support to advance their own ambitions. Onward Christian soldiers! Braun's support would give them the moral authority they needed to move against their own enemies. Enemies of governments and enemies of the Church would all be the same. Political dissent would die with religious dissent.

Christ! Maxwell was unsure if his silent outburst was a plea or a curse. It could happen! It could work even in the United States. The government was riddled with prayer groups and cells of evangelicals. He closed his eyes for a moment and soon the image came to him. It was an article from the *Los Angeles Times* about the prayer groups in the Pentagon. Decisions, important strategic decisions

305

by the Joint Chiefs of Staff, were being made on religious grounds. And television. He remembered the smoldering ruins of the U.S. Marine Corps compound at the Beirut airport in 1983, the screams of agony, and the unheard voices of the 241 Americans who had died there. But most of all, Maxwell heard now the televised voice of Admiral James D. Watkins, the chief of naval operations, as he told a reporter that "I am a moral man and I blame it [the bombing] on the forces of the Antichrist."

Maxwell's head spun like the rides at a crazy carnival. Braun was talking about a return to the old Holy Roman Empire, where emperors and popes appointed each other and where each ruled with the authority of the other, always in the name of God. But more significantly, Braun was talking about a crusade, a modern crusade. God is my sword!

He thought of the Islamic Jihad and the holy warriors of Islam. The time was right, too, in the West. Politicians and military officers and even ordinary citizens were frustrated by their helplessness in the face of terrorism and decay, by the impunity with which Russia could march into Afghanistan or Poland or Czechoslovakia. They were all frustrated and would seize a promising opportunity to rid themselves of their helplessness. It would start with moral authority. Slowly, carefully, Braun would solidify his own moral authority, and from there he would talk with those in the military and government who needed a blanket of further moral authority with which to cloak themselves.

And from there, the awesome public-opinion-molding machines would to go work: vast armies of propagandists with their sophisticated tools to manipulate the facts, and with them, public opinion. And what they couldn't manipulate they would classify as secret. These men knew what they were doing. They knew how to use God and patriotism to lead the people. They would find the right chord to strike, and within the population the sentiments would resonate. And then . . . violence, bloodshed, religious intolerance. My country right or wrong. My God right, never wrong.

The undercurrents were already there, a wild subterranean river coursing just beneath the seemingly solid ground of America and the rest of its allies. One just needed to know where to dig and how deep to tap this wild raging current.

Maxwell's head spun faster. It could work. It would work. It could work. It would work. It could work.

Robert Maxwell fainted.

CHAPTER TWENTY-THREE

The Turkish cabdriver pulled slowly to the curb of the Limmat Quai just north of the Wasserkirche. Late evening traffic swirled around them as the cab came to a halt. Behind them a motorist leaned angrily on his horn. The cabdriver ignored him. Moments later the car, a BMW, pulled around the cab with a screeching of tires and roared on past.

"I will take you all the way to your destination," the cabdriver offered.

"Thank you," Steele replied, "but I have directions to follow."

The cabdriver nodded.

"Can I at least pay you for the fare from the hotel?"

The cabdriver looked at him a long time, his dark brown eyes staring from his nut-brown face.

"Please," Steele said as he pulled several Swiss franc notes from his wallet. "I would have had to pay a taxi anyway."

"If it would make you feel better," the driver said. Steele nodded as he folded the notes into a wad the size of a matchbook and passed them across to the Turkish driver.

"Thank you," said the driver as he stuffed the bills into the pocket of his coat without looking at them. Steele pulled on the door handle and opened the door. "Be careful, my friend," the cabdriver said.

Steele turned to him. "You too." And with that, Steele got out and closed the door. Behind him, he heard the taxi's motor race and then slow as the driver let out the clutch. The horn honked once as the taxi passed him, then disappeared into the bright weavings of traffic, making its way onto and off of the Quai Brücke.

Steele stood there for a moment, smiling to himself. The driver would be home before he discovered the thousand dollar bill wrapped inside the Swiss francs. The man deserved it and it made Steele feel warm inside to be able to imagine what a poor Turkish immigrant could do with that kind of money.

Pushing the thought aside, Steele looked at his watch and noted that according to Joseph Roten's instructions, he still had five minutes to reach the first checkpoint. He walked slowly along the Limmat Quai, pausing in measured turns to look into the display windows of shops along the way.

The night was almost warm and Steele loosened the snaps of his parka to keep from sweating. *Die Föhn* is what they called it, the cabdriver had said. Sometimes during the winter, great high-pressure systems over North Africa would muscle warm masses of Sahara air north toward the polar low-pressure systems that normally dominated Europe in the wintertime. The result was a blast of warm air that melted snow and—in the snow-capped Alps—ski slopes. The avalanche danger always soared during *die Föhn*. It was sort of like the Santa Ana winds that blew through Southern California in the winter, Steele thought as he walked along. Only *die Föhn* didn't spark great grass and range fires and make people crazy. At least not yet.

Steele stopped to look through metal burglar bars into a shop window displaying racks of rings crusted with gems of all colors—red, green, white, blue, yellow. The shops weren't as fancy here as they were across the river on the Bahnhofstrasse. Neither were the prices, he thought.

Then suddenly from behind him and to his left, Steele heard a pair of footsteps scrape along the sidewalk and come to a halt. His next breath solidified in the middle of his chest as he whirled toward the noise, his hand going for the Magnum in his pocket.

Nothing! Steele felt his heart slamming about in his chest like an angry fist as he turned from side to side. He was absolutely alone on the sidewalk for half a block in each direction.

Still cautious, Steele retraced his steps past several doorways. There was no one hiding in a doorway. Puzzled, Steele continued his walk, looking suspiciously in doorway after doorway. He was sure he had heard something.

Nerves, he thought, as he reached the corner of the Torgasse and stepped off the curb to cross the narrow dark alley. His nerves had been so finely sanded down by the past week that his thin veneer of sanity had almost been completely worn away. Straining his eyes to plumb the darkness of the Torgasse, Steele thought he saw movement in the deep shadows. He stepped quickly across the street and back up on the sidewalk as he continued his way north along the Limmat Quai.

His heart was still racing when he reached the Rami Strasse. Looking cautiously about him, he pulled his tourist map of Zurich from his coat pocket and looked at it under the glow of the corner streetlight. Roten had marked a small x on the left side of the Rami Strasse about a block up. Steele looked up from the map and saw a small parklike area just up the hill, right where Roten's x should be located. A bit closer to him, on the same side, was a tobacconist's shop, just where Roten said it was.

Still smiling, Steele stuffed the map back in his pocket and pushed on, up the steep grade of the Rami Strasse.

Joseph Roten, the son, was an odd man, Steele thought, as he made his way toward the tobacconist's shop. A colonel in the Swiss army, bodyguard to his father, a taciturn, physically hard man, angular, muscular, singular of purpose. The adjectives that described the younger Joseph Roten came to mind easily. A small frown passed momentarily across Steele's face. The adjectives described Roten but did not explain him.

He seemed dedicated to his father's safety and well-being, as if he had made a lifetime occupation of it. But why had that been necessary?

And what about Roten's siblings? The two soft, round, almost effeminate men who ran the exclusive gallery off the Augustiner-strasse? Roten's contempt for them was palpable when he spoke of them. How had he turned out to be so different from them?

Questions piled on top of questions. A riddle from the mouth of the Sphinx.

Steele shook his head slowly as he checked his watch. It was precisely 7:30. Just as Roten had said it must be. Steele pushed open the door to the tobacconist's and stepped inside. The air hung warm and redolent of books and tobacco. To his left was a large stand of magazines and books of all descriptions, paperback and hardcover, new and used. To the left were racks of fragrant tobaccos and pipes. Straight ahead, the proprietor was sitting behind his counter reading a paperback book. He looked up as Steele entered.

"Good evening," Steele greeted the man in German.

"Evening," the proprietor replied as he carefully marked his place in the book with an empty pipe tobacco pouch, and stood up. "What can I do for you?" He studied Steele's face carefully.

Steele felt his throat go dry. Had the man with his picture been here with their offers of money? Was there a telephone number for people like this tobacconist to call? Steele swallowed hard against the hard prickly ball of fear in his throat.

"This week's *Time* magazine," Steele replied weakly.

"Over on the wall." The proprietor pointed toward the magazine rack. "At the top, nearly all the way to the left."

Steele searched for the familiar cover as he walked toward the rack. He cast an anxious glance toward the front door of the shop, fearing that at any minute the men who were looking for him would burst in to finish what they had started seven thousand miles west of here. He spotted it from halfway across the store, slotted in between *Der Spiegel* and *International Herald Tribune*.

Moments later, having purchased a small disposable lighter along with the thin international edition of *Time,* Steele stepped back into the almost warm night. He walked a handful of paces and turned to look in the window of the tobacconist's shop. The proprietor was already dialing the telephone.

Was he cooperating with Roten? Was this part of the security arrangements? Roten had been specific about which magazine to purchase and where and when it should be purchased. The man must be a friend.

But as Steele turned away from the shop and continued his climb up the steep hill, he couldn't help but wish that he knew for certain to whom the tobacconist's call had been placed.

It would have been a pleasant night, he thought as he walked along, if there weren't men out there in the darkness looking for him, offering a bounty to the taxi driver or hotel clerk who knew where he was. Steele loosened his coat again as the steep climb wrung perspiration from his body. He passed first one construction site and then another as he approached the next x that Roten had marked on the tourist map.

Steele paused for a moment at one construction site, using the kleig lights to check his map. It was the same here as in the colder regions of the United States, he mused. Construction workers had to labor overtime at night while the weather was good to make up for delays caused by inclement conditions. Turning around in a complete circle, Steele could see at least six new buildings, all decked out in the bright jewelry of electric lights, their skeletons crawling with workers.

Steele now directed his attention back to the map. He found Roten's next x just up ahead and to his left, then pressed on, the noise of the grit under his feet drowning in the animal rumbles of heavy machinery that reverberated from the new building next to him. He quickly covered the next block and crossed the street to the Heim Platz. Half a dozen people milled about in the small concrete square, waiting for the tram that stopped here. Steele milled about with them, scanning the windows of nearby buildings, trying to guess which of them might be spilling light shed by Joseph Roten Senior's apartment lamps.

At precisely 7:40, Steele walked to the trash receptacle at the curb. He lit the disposable lighter and held it near the cover of the magazine as if he were trying to read the date. Then he tossed the virgin copy of *Time* into the rubbish can.

It was a good ploy, Steele thought. From a darkened window, the younger Roten would easily be able to identify Steele in the illumination shed by the lighter's flame. Following Roten's precise instructions, Steele would now linger another five minutes while the Rotens observed him, and—more important—scanned the surrounding area to see if he was being followed. Plans—Roten didn't specify them—would change if there were people following.

Time oozed past. Lifetimes compressed themselves into the seconds that seemed to die slow painful deaths on the face of Steele's watch. Finally his eye was caught by first one, then two candles being lit on the top floor of the building on the southwest corner of Rami Strasse and Zelt Weg.

Steele's pulse quickened as he stepped across the street and made his way toward the building. Two candles! That was Roten's signal that all was well. On the other side of the street, Steele had to wait as a truck carrying a load of ready-mixed concrete backed slowly into an adjoining construction site. As he paused behind the barrier, he watched as a huge hopper, with the dregs of a previous load of concrete slopping down its sides, was gingerly lowered from the tip of a huge cantilevered crane. Steele looked up and saw that the crane's tip nearly touched the wall of Roten's building. From the ground, it looked as if it missed by only inches.

The concrete mixer truck roared with a cloud of diesel exhaust and lumbered its elephantine way through the gates of the construction site to replace a twin that had just pulled out, empty, no doubt.

Finally, the barrier was lifted and Steele and one other pedestrian, a bent old woman with a wire cart full of groceries, were allowed to continue.

Steele approached the address Roten had given him and stepped up to a locked door with a row of numbered buttons, no names beside them. He pressed the button next to 874—once very quickly, then again for a full two seconds.

As soon as his hand had dropped to his side, the foyer door buzzed from its remote release. Steele pushed through quickly and walked toward the elevators. An empty car was waiting for him. He stepped in and pressed the button for the top floor, number eight.

The polished brass doors of the elevator slid shut. Above him the noisy old mechanisms of the conveyance carried him upward gracefully, without the sensation of g forces that characterizes American elevators.

The car stopped as the lighted button for the eighth floor winked out. But the doors did not open. For a moment, Steele thought the elevator was stuck, but then the telephone on the wall began to ring. Steele picked it up.

"Steele?" It was Roten's voice.

"Of course," Steele replied.

"Step into the middle of the car and take off your coat."

"What?" Steele replied. "Why would—"

"Look in the corner of the elevator," Roten replied. "There's a closed circuit video camera. I just want to make sure everything is as it should be."

Steele hadn't noticed it at first, but there it was, a miniature video camera staring down at him. Feeling self-conscious, Steele shed his coat. Moments later, the doors to the elevator slid open and Steele stepped into an elegant paneled entryway with marble floors. Joseph Roten stood in front of him, holding a H&K MP5A machine pistol. Steele froze.

CHAPTER TWENTY-FOUR

Down on the Rami Strasse, a dark sedan glided through the warm night. Inside, four men peered out the windows, watching for danger. Under their expensively tailored business suits, expensively crafted holsters held deadly weapons. Death passed unnoticed when it masqueraded as wealth in a wealthy city.

"There!" said the man next to the driver. He spoke Russian. The others looked as he pointed to a building at the corner of the Rami Strasse and Zelt Weg. The driver slowed the car and pulled it to a stop at the curb just beyond the entrance to a high-rise construction site.

"Up there, on the top," said the man next to the driver. The other men leaned against the windows of the car and craned their necks upward. They saw lights on the top floor of the building, and, next to the building, the lights and noise of laborers working to build while the weather held.

"Turn right here," said the man next to the driver. "We'll park the car just past the building and walk back."

The driver nodded as he stepped on the accelerator and pulled into the thin evening traffic.

"Put that away," Steele said as he stepped from the elevator. He was more annoyed than frightened. "I've had enough of people pointing guns at me."

Roten looked at him, cold calculation flickering behind his eyes. He was a computer comparing his memory with the person standing before him. Roten nodded sharply once, then lowered the muzzle of the H&K until it was pointing at the floor.

"Good evening," Roten said with a smile. "I'm sorry for the inconveniences, but they have proven to be of life-saving importance to my father on more than one occasion."

"I'm beginning to understand why," Steele said. Roten gave him a thin, knowing smile, then turned abruptly and walked down the hall. Steele followed him, gazing as he did at the oils and watercolors on the walls. It was like passing through a very narrow but extremely well-endowed museum. As Steele made his way past the procession of paintings, he recognized several of them as works described by the younger Joseph Roten the night before.

Roten had explained then that the extreme security for his father's apartment had been necessary for more than thirty years now, partly because of the value of the paintings, and partly because of the men he had killed to get the paintings.

After the war was over, Roten said, his father made his way back to Zurich from the Austrian salt mines where Hitler had hidden his stolen art. He had learned much about Nazis and the way they thought. He had also learned to hate them, to hate them with an intensity that only people who are confronted with absolute evil can fully understand.

In the days after the war, he got word to the right people that he was interested in buying the art that many of the SS were using to barter their way to freedom. He also hinted that he had connections that would get former Nazis with the right amount of money to safe places. With two other friends who had been through similar experiences, the senior Roten invited the fugitive Nazis to his shop for the purpose of examining their stolen works of art. While Roten examined the works, the visitors were taken to a room and executed by Roten's two associates. One of the associates, the owner of a butcher shop, then took the body to his shop and placed it in a special grinder, after which it was sold to a company that manufactured canned dog food.

The macabre scheme had worked for nearly a decade. Secrecy had always been on their side. Nazis came to them one by one, by referral and word of mouth. And when a fugitive disappeared and was never seen again by his former associates, they all assumed that Roten had again succeeded in getting one of the *Kameradren* to safety.

The system broke down in July, 1949 when two former SS Oberleutnants showed up at the door of the shop and demanded that they both be processed together. One of them smelled a rat and managed to escape. Since then, the younger Roten had explained, his father had been in danger from men who—though now themselves too old to kill—were wealthy and powerful enough to hire the best of killers.

Roten had returned as many of the works of art as he could to the original owners, but many of them remained unclaimed, their owners dead or untraceable. The orphan works had allowed his father to expand the business from a modest framing shop to an exclusive art gallery.

"These are his favorites," Roten said, stopping at the end of the hall and raising his arms in a motion that took in the art on the walls. "He always kept the best of the orphan pieces for himself."

Steele stopped and opened his mouth to speak, but Roten turned quickly and opened a door at the end of the hallway. "Please step in."

Steele hurried to comply with the request, stepping through the doorway into a book-lined study. The room was illuminated with puddles of yellowish light, and had the constantly-in-use air of a library where most of the occupants have decided to go for a coffee break at the same time.

At the far end of the room, sitting in a wingback chair in front of a welcoming fire that burned in a marble-mantled fireplace, was an old man, his blanket-covered legs propped up on an ottoman. His chair was separated from an identical one to his left by a low piecrust table cluttered with books, papers, and a decanter half filled with amber fluid. The old man was reading a thick hardcover book.

"Father?" Roten called out from the door. The old man in the chair laid the book in his lap and turned toward them.

"Yes, Joseph?"

"Your visitor. Mr. Steele."

The old Joseph Roten adjusted his glasses as he looked up at Steele and blinked several times.

"Well, come and sit down, Mr. Steele," the elder Roten said

impatiently. "I hope you're not planning to linger by the door there until you're as old as I."

The younger Roten nodded his head toward the matching wingbacked chair next to his father. Steele moved forward and stopped next to the old man. He was dressed in a warm-looking wool robe tied at the sash. The bottoms of pajamas protruded from beneath the hem of the robe. His feet were clad in slippers. Steele looked closely at him and found his round fleshy face closer to that of the two sons who managed the gallery than to his eldest son, the lean Swiss army colonel. As Steele leaned over to extend his hand, he heard the old man's son back quietly out of the room and shut the door behind him.

"Mr. Steele." Joseph Roten took Steele's hand and shook it with a surprisingly firm grip. "Welcome to Zurich; welcome to my home. I apologize for not getting up, but the arthritis in my knees has grown savage of late."

Steele expressed his sympathy and sat down in the chair to Roten's left. As he did, he noticed Roten's hand resting on the arm of the chair. It was horribly disfigured and scarred and was lacking a thumb. Steele politely averted his eyes, but not before Roten had seen his look of shock. He smiled wryly at Steele.

"This," he held up his left hand, "is part of my story. But first I want to hear yours." Roten shifted in his chair to be more comfortable as he looked at Steele. "As I understand it, you are looking for your wife, the woman who recovered a painting known as 'The Home of the Lady Our Redeemer'?"

Steele nodded. "She disappeared six months ago, from our room at the Eden au Lac."

"I know," Roten said. "She had called me that afternoon. She said she had read the name of my shop on the back of the picture. She asked me if I remembered it." Roten's eyes seemed to turn inward for a moment, as if he were remembering. In the silence left by his pause, the study became filled with the pops and crackles of the wood fire and with the steady rumble of the crane just outside the window. Steele looked toward the window and through the sheer curtains saw the arm of the crane as it passed by, almost at window level.

Finally Roten pulled himself from his reverie. "I shall never forget the picture," he said. "And I will never forget the men who

318

brought it in to me." He stopped abruptly. "But that, too, is part of my story. And I want to hear yours first, so please, begin."

While Steele related his account of the past six months, Roten pulled a pouch of tobacco from under the pile of papers on the side table. Steele noticed the packet was stamped with the name of the tobacconist just down the Rami Strasse. As Steele spoke, Roten pulled a large briar pipe from the folds of his robe and carefully filled, tamped, and lit it. Fragrant plumes of smoke drifted up from the bowl of the pipe and wafted mostly toward the fireplace.

Steele told him about his search in Zurich, about Davidson, about the killers in Los Angeles, the killers in Amsterdam, and the men who looked for him in Zurich. Before the story was over, Roten had refilled his pipe twice.

"I'm sorry for my outburst in your gallery yesterday," Steele said. "I'll be happy to pay for—"

"Don't be sorry," Roten chuckled. "It's the most exciting thing that has happened to those two spoiled idiots in their entire pampered lives." He laughed again. "Joseph," he tilted his head toward the door of the study, "is the only one of my sons with any brains at all. And *he* takes things too seriously." Roten sighed. It sounded to Steele like Roten had pity for all his sons.

Roten leaned over to knock the dottle of his pipe against an enormous glass ashtray. He scraped and poked at the bowl with a pipe tool and finally sat up to face Steele again.

"Nothing you've told me is surprising," Roten said. "So I suppose I should tell you why I'm not surprised."

He paused while he refilled the bowl of the pipe again.

"It began in 1939, when a man brought the painting into my frame shop. It was summer and I was just out of the university and working for my father. I had taken a degree in art history and had intended to become an expert in restoration."

Roten's visitor, who had conducted himself with the officiousness of a minor functionary employed by important people, stepped from a black limousine and brought the unframed picture into the shop. It was painted on a small piece of wood and the paint smelled fresh to Roten at the time. The man wanted the picture framed by evening. It was an unusual request, but not an impossible one. Roten finished the frame before the 5 P.M. deadline with no trouble.

The man for whom the functionary worked, Roten later found out, was none other than Hermann Goering. The painting was a present for Goering's boss, Adolf Hitler. It was an unexciting sort of scene, painted with skill but no genius.

As the European war intensified, the Rotens followed Goering with interest, fascinated in a black sort of way that they had actually been that close to him. But Goering was of more than academic interest to some of Roten's relatives who had settled in Salzburg, Austria.

Roten's aunt, a sister on his father's side, had married an art dealer there in 1928. Life had deteriorated after Hitler's annexation of Austria. The woman's husband had been drafted and killed in action. In 1943 Joseph Roten was sent to Salzburg by his father to see if he could get his aunt back to Switzerland.

But before Joseph could leave Salzburg with his aunt and what few belongings they could carry, German soldiers arrived. They wee canvassing art galleries, university art departments, and museums, looking, they said, for "patriotic citizens" to help care for priceless works of art that were arriving daily in Munich from all over Europe. They needed experienced and not-so-experienced workers.

Roten and his aunt tried to explain to the pigheaded soldiers that the true art expert, her husband, had been killed as a lowly private in the Wehrmacht. That was all right, the soldiers said; they knew more about scrubbing garbage cans than fine art, certainly Roten's aunt had learned something from her husband that would be useful, and would she and her nephew stop wasting their time and please get into the trucks out front for the short drive back to Munich.

His aunt died of pneumonia in December of 1943, but Roten continued to work in Hitler's central collecting point in Munich, cataloging and caring for paintings that arrived from all over Europe by truck, train, and airplane.

For someone conscripted at gunpoint, Roten considered himself fairly well treated. He was allowed a ration book, given an apartment to share with three other workers from the central collecting point, and even paid a salary. He was told by the Gestapo that they knew about his father, knew where he lived, and if Joseph tried to escape, "something would happen" to his father. Joseph didn't think the Gestapo had enough people to worry about people like him, but he couldn't take the chance.

Whether it was because his work was so good, or perhaps because he had written a letter to Goering to deplore the sorry state in which the art was being stored at the central collecting point, Roten came to the attention of the men around Hitler responsible for the art. Among them was Hans Reger, director of the central collecting point, who singled out Roten for more and more responsibility.

A knock at the door interrupted Roten's story.

"Come in," he called. The door opened moments later and the younger Joseph Roten entered with a tray of sandwiches, beer, and sparkling water. "I thought you might be getting hungry," he said.

Instinctively Steele looked at his watch. It was nearly 9:30. The time had swiftly vanished without a trace.

"Thank you," said the senior Roten. Steele also nodded his appreciation as the son cleared off the table between the two wing-backed chairs and set the tray down on it. He poured the beer from tall brown bottles into heavy lead crystal mugs and then left the room, closing the door behind him.

The room was silent for several moments as the two men surveyed the tray and then began to help themselves. Steele felt his stomach rumble at the sight of food and suddenly realized how hungry he had become.

After they had settled back into their chairs with the evening meal, Roten resumed his story.

"I was gradually given more and more responsibility," he said, washing down a mouthful of liverwurst sandwich with a swallow of beer. "I had, after all, spent my college career—all my life, in fact—learning to care for fine art. But I was lonesome for my family, and constantly afraid of both the SS and the Gestapo. But I threw myself into the work. After all, I wasn't for Hitler as much as I was for the preservation of the art of the ages. I didn't care who had the art. I just knew that I would never forgive myself if I let these works of the masters deteriorate."

He looked vaguely into the fire, as if he saw the works painted with brightly dancing brushes of flame. "They were all there, you know—" His voice took on a dreamy nostalgia. "Titan, Rembrandt, Leonardo, Rubens . . . all of them.'' Roten seemed to mourn for a bittersweet lost memory. "Only the curators at the world's most renowned museums ever have an opportunity to care for so many of the masters.''

The Nazis in charge of the Sonderauftrag Linz—Hitler's art-looting task force—mistook Roten's enthusiasm for the art for enthusiasm for their cause. Roten did nothing to discourage their misapprehension, for it gave him more responsibility, privileges, luxuries, freedom. That freedom allowed him to make contact with Resistance fighters, and through them to get word to the Allies that the world's greatest concentration of art treasures was being housed in warehouse-like conditions in the center of Munich.

As the Allied bombers grew closer and closer to Munich, Roten—now highly respected by the Nazis in command of the Sonderauftrag Linz—lobbied to have the artwork moved from Munich to safer quarters. He suggested the salt mines in nearby Austria.

The idea appealed particularly to the SS, since it fit in with their Wagnerian notions of holding out to the last man in the rugged mountains. For the more realistic among the SS, it appealed even more, since they correctly felt it would be easier for them to loot the works of art to use for barter.

Roten made trip after trip to the Salzammergut region of Austria, and set up his headquarters in Altaussee so as to be convenient to the many salt mines nearby.

"I had a small cottage by the shore of the Altaussersee,'' he said, as he drained the last of the beer from his mug. "It was just off the main road which ran between Altaussee and Bad Aussee. There was a church nearby, a Catholic church whose priest was a man named Werner Meyer.

"Of course, in a small Austrian town,'' Roten continued, "the village priest is an important figure, and I quickly grew to know Meyer well.''

Meyer was initially suspicious of Roten, but as their acquaintance grew into genuine friendship, Meyer began to take him increasingly into his confidence. Not long after, Roten learned that Meyer was a linchpin of the local Resistance movement. Roten, deprived of his Resistance contacts still in Munich, began to pass information through Meyer.

"He was a truly heroic figure,'' Roten said with admiration.

"He risked his life on a daily basis. I was timid, yet he was grace-ful enough to make me feel that my role was important." Roten's eyes reflected a doubt that Meyer had truly been right.

The last days of the war, Roten continued, had been insane. As the sounds of Allied artillery and bombing echoed just over the mountains, many of the Nazis in charge of the caches of art stored in the mines panicked. One of them, a half-mad colonel in charge of a mine in the hills above Bad Aussee, made plans to blow up the priceless contents of the mine rather than "have it fall into the hands of the Jews."

Feverishly, the colonel had his men drag 500-pound bombs into the mine's tunnels and place them next to statuary by Michelan-gelo and paintings by Van Dyck. The bombs were in place when Roten met with Meyer. All the colonel was waiting for was a demolition expert to come and remove the impact fuses from the normally airborne bombs, then replace them with fuses that could be detonated on the ground.

Late one night, a team of men showed up at Roten's cottage with a knapsack full of plastic explosives and fuses. Before dawn could replace the candlelight in the room, Roten had learned how to set the charge and its timer.

"The next day," Roten related, as he tried to make himself more comfortable, "I put the charges in my briefcase and made an excuse to visit the mine. Just before I left, I set the timer and left my briefcase by the entrance of the mine just as the Resistance men had instructed me."

Roten's explosives blew up the entrance of the mine—without harming any of the paintings—and prevented the colonel's dem-olition expert, or anyone else, from reaching the bombs to install detonators.

Days later, Roten received a desperate message from Meyer, delivered by a small boy whose mother ran the inn in the village.

"Meyer had always been so calm," Roten said, "but when I read the message he had left at my cottage, I could read the hys-teria in his writing, the extreme anxiety in the wildness of his penmanship. He had a terrible secret, the note said. Something about a relic stored in a salt mine near Habersam Mountain in the hills above Altaussee.

"I knew nothing about the mine, which naturally aroused my

curiosity. I started making inquiries. The questions I asked nearly killed me and Werner.'' Roten's face had grown long with remembered sorrow, as if the weight of the memory had stretched his face out of shape.

Roten's questions brought him to the attention of the SS commander of the secret mine at Habersam Mountain. An SS Oberleutnant was dispatched to Roten's cottage to question him.

Roten had not yielded to the Oberleutnant's threats and finally found himself handcuffed to the heavy iron bed as they waited for Meyer to come.

Just before dawn there had been the sounds of artillery from the direction of Bad Aussee. The Allies were coming soon; Roten could read the news from the worried way the Oberleutnant paced the floor of the cottage. Then, just after the sky had turned blood red with the dawn, a thunderous explosion rumbled off Habersam Mountain and rattled the windows of Roten's cottage.

''I strained to see what was happening,'' Roten said. ''I must have stood with my face to the window for an hour or more, staring out at the stark flat whiteness of the frozen lake.''

Finally he saw people. At first, they were too far away to recognize. But as they grew closer, Roten could make out a lone figure pursued by soldiers in uniform. And to his horror, he realized the figure being pursued was Meyer.

The SS Oberleutnant walked into the bedroom, his face covered with the first smile he had worn since they had heard the Allied artillery earlier in the still-dim morning. ''We will have some answers soon, no?'' the Oberleutnant jested.

Roten had been sure they had killed Meyer when he heard the crack of a pistol and saw the black-robed priest fall into a snowdrift. The band of killers grew closer to Meyer when he slowly staggered to his feet and turned toward them. Roten stood, his heart wound like a spring, as Meyer raised his head and staggered back toward the killers, who had stopped, momentarily stunned by their quarry's unexpected action.

Then he watched as one of the killers raised his gun and aimed it at Meyer.

''I'll never forget what I saw next,'' Roten told Steele. ''It was a miracle, nothing but a miracle.''

Before the killer could pull the trigger, he was shot dead. From a knoll by the lake, there was gunfire, and finally a huge explosion that blew great slabs of the lake's ice up into the air. When it all settled down, Meyer was alive and his pursuers, to a man, were dead or dying.

"Your friend is lucky," the SS Oberleutnant had said to Roten. "But he won't escape this." He pulled out his 9 mm Luger and brandished it before Roten's face. Then, without commenting further, he walked from the bedroom. Roten heard his boots as he crossed the living room, then the slam of the door as the Nazi walked out onto the cottage's tiny porch.

"I screamed at Meyer to go back," Roten said, "but he couldn't hear me." As Steele listened to Roten's story of what followed, the sandwich he had eaten grew into a greasy knot in his gut.

"I could see Meyer coming closer and closer," Roten said. "He was staggering through the snow toward the cottage with no idea that the Oberleutnant was waiting for him.

"I suppose the Oberleutnant had originally come with the intention of interrogating the two of us, but now . . . with the approach of the Allied troops just over the hill . . . I think he changed his mind and decided to kill us to save time."

Roten grimaced as he shifted his legs on the ottoman. "There was an insanity in those last days. It gripped all of us, caused us to do things that . . . well, I suppose it would be impossible to make you fully understand."

Roten knew that after the SS officer killed Meyer, he would probably come back into the cottage and kill him. So it was as much for his own survival as Meyer's that Roten stretched as far as his handcuffed arms would allow, and managed to smash the mirror fastened to the wall over a small wooden bureau.

"I took the largest shard of the broken mirror," Roten said now as he lifted his mutilated left hand for Steele to see, "and cut away at the flesh and the tendons and the muscles of the thumb on my left hand."

Like a desperate animal chewing off a paw or limb caught in a jaw trap, Roten hacked at his left thumb until it came free and allowed his hand to slip free of the handcuffs. Then, without bothering to bind the wound, Roten charged out of the cottage after the Oberleutnant.

"I don't remember feeling any pain," Roten recalled as he

looked at his scarred and twisted hand with fresh wonder in his eyes. "But I remember the frustration I felt as I ran out the front door. I still held the bloody shard of the mirror in my right hand."

Roten saw the Oberleutnant standing at the end of the porch, his Luger raised; he saw Meyer round the corner toward the door. Roten ran toward the Oberleutnant, the jagged blood shard of glass raised over his head like a dagger; the SS officer aimed his luger carefully at Meyer's head; Meyer froze, his face a mask of weary resignation.

"I heard the shot just instants before the point of glass dug into the Oberleutnant's back." Roten shook his head sadly as he spoke. "Just another second, perhaps half a second and the Oberleutnant would never had been able to fire."

Roten pulled the glass from the Nazi's back and stabbed him again and again. The officer went down, spurting blood from severed arteries shining bright crimson in the snow.

"I don't remember much after that," Roten said, "except that after the Nazi was down, I went to look at Werner." A pained look washed over Roten's face. "He had been horribly wounded in the head. I could see parts of the gray matter through the hole in his skull.

"I must have gone crazy then, because my memory is blacked out. I don't remember anything until an American soldier pulled me off the Oberleutnant's body. He had to slap me and knock the mirror fragment from my hand." Roten looked Steele directly in the eyes. "The American soldier told me later when he'd first seen me, I was straddling the Oberleutnant's chest with my knees and was stabbing at his eyes." Roten's voice grew faint. "He . . . the Oberleutnant . . . was still alive. The American soldier told me he could hear the screams as I continued stabbing."

Roten shook his head. "Insanity. I suppose the only thing a sane person can do in wartime is go insane."

He fell silent for a long moment. Only the sounds of popping knots in the fireplace logs and the rumbles of the crane at the construction site next door broke the silence. They did not hear the whirr of the elevator motor as it leaped to life, carrying the car to its summons in the lobby, where four men in expensively tailored business suits waited.

CHAPTER TWENTY-FIVE

"Carefully," said the man who had been sitting next to the driver in the black sedan. He was clearly the man in charge. All four men were inside the elevator that led to Roten's apartment. The car doors were closed. Two men were attaching shaped explosive charges to the closed door. The ceiling panels of the car littered the floor. One of the men had crawled on top of the elevator car and crouched there, watching the activity below. The disconnected wires of the closed-circuit television camera dangled beside its blind electronic eye.

"Make sure the charges are attached firmly, and then pack the modeling clay around it—just as firmly," said the man in charge. "We want to make sure it explodes outward. Otherwise . . ." His voice trailed off, his meaning clear. The charges could as easily kill them as blow in the doors. Setting shaped charges was an art, not a science.

The man in charge inspected his men's work carefully and finally gave his approval.

"All right, up on top of the car."

With help from the man who had already climbed through the ceiling of the car, the men struggled up and crouched amid the machinery.

"Be careful of the counterweights," the man in charge said, pushing the button for the top floor. As the car started to climb, he unrolled the detonator wires and handed them to one of his men on top of the car. Then, with a helping hand from one of them, he climbed up to join them.

Roten's son had come in to clear away the remains of the sandwiches and to offer refills of beer. Steele declined; his stomach already felt queasy enough.

"After the American slapped me," Roten continued after his son had once more left the room, "I awakened, as if from a dream. I looked at what I had done to the Nazi and suddenly got very faint—probably from the blood I had lost from the amputation of my thumb.

"I also remember another fellow, Polish I believe he was. He limped up after the American had pulled me off the Oberleutnant. This Pole had apparently broken his ankle skiing down from the knoll, hit a rock or something. Anyway, he took one look at the Nazi's face and the slashed remains of his eyes and then he just turned around and got sick in the snow. I'm afraid I followed suit and then lost consciousness."

The American arranged for Roten and Meyer to be cared for by the Allied forces medical staff, and the quick action by American doctors undoubtedly saved both men's lives. They were billeted together in various places, at first in temporary field hospitals and later in a hospital in Salzburg.

Roten recovered quickly from his injuries, but he lingered on, serving as orderly, nurse, and stand-in physical therapist to his war-time comrade Meyer. Finally, when Meyer was well enough to travel to a special Vatican medical facility in Rome, Roten put him on the train with his escorts—two nuns and a lay doctor—and returned to Zurich.

"We stayed in touch over the years," Roten said. "Later, when he had recovered from much of his amnesia, Meyer told me the story of what he had seen in the secret mine at Altaussee. You see, he was afraid he would die, and that the secret of the mine would die with him. So he told me all of the story."

"Which was?" Steele interrupted eagerly.

"I think I'd rather Werner Meyer told you himself." Roten said.

"Meyer? Is he here in Zurich?"

Roten shook his head. "He's in Altaussee. Or he will be by the time you get there."

"But—"

"Listen carefully to me," Roten interrupted. "The picture you have . . . the painting?"

Steele nodded.

"It's the key to everything that's happened to you, to your wife . . . to me, and to Werner, over the past forty years."

"How?" Steele asked. "I don't understand."

"You will soon enough," Roten assured him. "But right now you must pay attention to my instructions carefully. You'll only get one chance. Do you understand?" He looked sternly at Steele, who nodded his acknowledgment.

"You must take the picture to the Thule Gesellschaft Bank. It's on the Bahnhofstrasse, just north of the Paradeplatz. Ask for the officer in charge of the floor. Give him the painting and tell him you wish access to your safe deposit box. He will know what to do."

"But what—"

Roten shook his head. "I don't know. I really wish I could tell you. In the forty years that Werner and I have tracked that painting, we have only been able to learn that it is the key to a safe deposit box and that the contents of that box are of paramount importance to obtaining the Shroud of Veronica."

"The Shroud of Veronica?" Steele asked, more confused than ever.

"Meyer will explain," Roten said.

"Why do I need to wait?" Steele persisted. "Everything I can learn might help me find Stephanie! She's more important to me than anything that's been buried in a mine for four decades."

Roten smiled broadly. "But you don't have to look further," he said. "Your wife is here in Zurich. I spoke with her just an hour or so before you arrived."

Steele jerked forward in his chair as if he had been jolted by high voltage. "Stephanie? In Zurich? How did . . . why—why did she call you? Why didn't you tell me sooner? Where is she?"

Roten raised his hand to silence Steele. "One question at a time, one at a time please." He paused and moistened his dry chapped lips with his tongue.

"She called me for the same reason you did," Roten began. "She saw the back of the picture and called me six months ago.

She has apparently been through a great deal of trauma since then, but she is back on the trail of the painting. In face, she called me in hopes that I had heard from you.'' He smiled.

"But why didn't you tell me about her sooner?'' Steele asked.

"Because I knew that you would hear nothing else of what I said if I had told you that first,'' Roten replied. "And what I have told you is extremely important to me, to your wife, and to the rest of the world.''

Steele stared blankly at Roten through wide, stunned eyes.

"Where?'' Steele's voice was cracked and faint with joy. "Where is she?''

"At your hotel,'' Roten replied. "At the Eden au Lac.''

Abruptly Steele stood up. "All this time,'' Steele's voice was full of wonder. "We've been apart all this time, and we wind up at the same hotel.''

He stood silently for a long moment, his eyes gazing past the depths of the flames in the hearth. Then he snapped out of it.

"Thank you for your time and your hospitality, Mr. Roten. I—''

"Wait.'' Roten's face was suddenly filled with fear. "Promise me you will go to Alt Aussee to meet with Werner. He's put himself in a great deal of danger to meet with you.''

"I—''

Steele was about to say that he would have to ask Stephanie about it when the floor shuddered beneath his feet, followed by the rumbling roar of an explosion.

"Damn construction crews.'' Roten bellowed. "They've hit the side of the building with that crane again!''

But it was not the crane. Suddenly, from beyond the stout oaken doors that led to the study, they heard the short choppy bursts of the younger Roten's H&K MP5A, then the softer coughing responses of silenced automatic weapons.

"Father!'' They heard the young Roten scream. "They're here! They're he—'' And suddenly they knew the son was dead.

"Quick. Close the door, Mr. Steele,'' Roten said. "It is very strong.''

From the hallway Steele heard running feet and the sound of men's hushed and hurried voices.

Steele leaped to his feet and lunged toward the oaken door. Just as the doorknob rattled, his hand found the latch to the deadbolt and turned it swiftly.

Steele heard curses from the other side of the door, followed by the rattle of hinges as someone threw himself against it. The door groaned, but held fast.

Suddenly Steele thought about guns, familiar-sounding guns, guns on a boat on the other side of the world that sounded just like the ones in the hallway. And as his thoughts flashed back, the memory of slugs splintering their way through the decks of the *Valkyrie* caused his adrenalin to surge.

Steele dove away from the doors and threw himself on the floor just as the interior of the door's paneling exploded in a hail of slugs and long jagged oaken splinters.

"Get down." Steele yelled as he rolled across the floor. He came to a stop on his hands and knees and looked toward Roten's chair. The old man had rolled himself out of his chair and was painfully crawling toward a telephone that rested on a small table by the window.

Slugs continued to slam through the door—their velocity mostly spent—and fly through the room at random.

At least one of the slugs maintained its momentum after its collision with the door; or perhaps it passed through an opening left by a preceding slug. As Steele watched Roten crawling across the rich Persian carpet that covered the fine hardwood floors, the slug slapped meanly into the old man's side just below his armpit. The spot turned red almost immediately as the artery began to gush warm and red.

Steele watched Roten's body stiffen and lift under the bullet's impact. At that instant, time seemed distended, stretched to a point of infinite slowness. Then the scene speeded up and Roten's body flew through the air, crashing into the rack of brass andirons, brushes, and other fireplace paraphernalia on the hearth.

Steele scrambled on his hands and knees back to the chair where he had left his coat. He pulled out the Magnum and ducked behind the chair just as the door to the study burst open.

The first man through the door shouted something in a language Steele couldn't understand. Russian? The man took one look at Roten's body lying by the hearth and fired his gun repeatedly into the lifeless form, causing it to jerk backward like a macabre puppet.

"Bastards!" Steele yelled as he raised the Magnum and fired at the lead attacker, a thin man in a well-tailored suit. The slug caught the man in the midsection, doubling him up and lifting him off his feet. The bullet passed through the man's intestines, shattered his spinal column, and exited from the small of his back. He was dead before he hit the floor.

Steele heard other shouts now, these filled with caution and fear. He was sure the language was Russian. How had they found him? How had they traced him despite Roten's precautions?

But there was no time to think, only time to react and survive. He fired a second shot at the men as they moved away from the study's doorway. Their jumbled voices filled the hallway as they sought to regroup.

Anticipating their quick return, Steele scrambled past Roten's lifeless body to the telephone. For just one crazy minute, he wondered how one went about dialing for the police in Zurich. Then it came to him. The operator. Call the operator.

Keeping one eye on the door, Steele reached for the telephone. He picked up the receiver and held it to his ear. It was dead.

He was cut off. Alone. Both Rotens were dead. The telephone line had been cut. No one knew where he was; no one would miss him. He fought the panic that coursed through him like a high-voltage current.

Scrambling back to his coat, Steele pulled out the handful of extra ammunition he had brought along. A dozen more rounds. Four left in the cylinder. Sixteen rounds total. Against? How many men? He had to strike quickly before the men in the hall recovered from their surprise.

But moments later he knew he was too late, as a withering crossfire tore through the room, ripping at the floor, the ceilings, and the walls. Steele shrank back as the slugs' deadly invisible fingers clutched at him. He turned his chair on its side and huddled behind it, but it offered scant protection.

The years of training at the police academy and on the street came back to him. Reflexes, move quickly, survive, survive.

Steel fired twice at the doorway, once toward each side, and then lunged toward the window. He flipped a heavy marble-topped table on its side and scrambled behind it as a train of slugs tracked its way across the room and took chips out of stone.

There were frantic shouts from the hallway and moments later one of the men flashed past the doorway to the other side. Steele shot at him, and then silently cursed at himself. They had suckered him into wasting a bullet. Even if they spoke Russian, they could count rounds too.

For an instant Steele felt smug about the extra slugs he had brought along. *Those* would be a surprise.

But his smugness vanished as he heard a loud thunk and the sound of an object rolling across the floor. Steele scanned the room for the object, and an instant later spotted the smooth round metallic luster of a small hand grenade just inches away from the table.

Desperately, Steele dropped the Magnum and sprang for the grenade. He scooped it up in his hand, felt its heavy malevolent power, and like a small animal paralyzed by the sight of a rattler about to strike, hesitated for what seemed like an eternity. A split second later he lobbed the grenade back toward the open doorway and threw himself face first behind the table.

The concussion lifted the table and slammed it against him, pinning him to the wall. For an instant, he heard nothing but the ringing of bells, then the yawning roar he remembered from the first day of explosives training at the academy, when he had forgotten to wear the protective earmuffs the department issued.

Beyond the veil of thunder, Steele heard voices. He struggled against the heavy marble table that had saved his life and managed to shove it away just as two men burst through the door, their weapons at the ready. One of them saw him move and fired a short burst at him. Steele ducked behind the table and scrambled around for his gun. Where was it?

Frantically he searched the area around him as he heard the footsteps of the men growing closer. Another burst of silenced automatic weapons fire chipped away at the table, sending fragments of marble flying across the room.

There! Next to the wall he spotted the Magnum. Desperately he fumbled for it, then picked it up in his hands. He turned and saw the head of the closest man appear over the top of the pockmarked table top. The man raised his gun. At close range, Steele recognized it as the same type used by the men who had attacked him on his boat.

Steele turned and fired and last round in the cylinder. The left half of the man's face disappeared, exposing his sinuses and the base of his brain. He made a gurgling sound before he hit the floor.

Steele heard the hurried footsteps of the other man exit the room. Quickly, Steele thought, he had to move quickly. They wouldn't make the same mistake with the grenade twice. Next time they'd hold it long enough to prevent Steele from throwing it back.

Desperately he searched the room for an exit. There were only the door and the window. Cold air poured in through the panes of glass broken by the explosion. He had seconds at most before the men in the hallway threw in another grenade.

Steele tucked the Magnum with its spent rounds into his belt at the small of his back and stood up. He brushed the curtain back with a swipe of his hand, and stared out at eight stories of black empty space. Directly ahead of him, twenty-five or thirty yards away, was the lighted operator's compartment of the construction crane he had seen from the street. The arm of the crane was motionless. Steele's eyes followed the arm to its end and then down. The cables from the crane's arms ran down to a metal hopper being filled with concrete from a truck that had backed into the site. The men continued to work. Hadn't they heard the explosion? But as Steele watched, activity seemed normal below. Men guided a hose from the truck to the hopper. Others stood by steadying the hopper. They appeared not to have noticed anything unusual.

With panic threatening to overwhelm him, Steele looked out the window for a ledge, a toehold. But he saw nothing. He looked over his shoulder toward the door. It yawned ominously at him. Any second now he expected to see a gunman step into the room, his silenced weapon firing. Or worse, the thump and explosion of another grenade.

Outside the window, the concrete hopper began to climb as the crane's cables took up slack. Then the arm began to swing—toward Steele. The arm gathered speed, but to Steele, facing imminent death, it moved in slow motion.

What was it Roten had said right after the explosion? The crane.

He had cursed, thinking the crane had hit his building *again*. Steele seized on his only hope. Would the crane's arm reach him in time?

As he watched the arm swing ponderously toward him, Steele thought he heard a familiar clink in the hallway. What was it?

The crane's arm grew closer. Don't let it stop, God. Please don't let it stop.

Steele crouched next to the window sill, waiting for his chance.

Then the clink in the hallway came back to him. He remembered where he had been the first time he'd heard that sound. It was in the desert, at an advanced training and tactics class for SWAT team members. Shit! The clink he had just heard was the sound of a grenade pin hitting the floor.

Steele watched the crane's arm move closer. Twenty feet away, fifteen, ten. Steele crawled up on the window sill. Five feet—

He heard the grenade thud against the floor. He took one look downward at the blackness below him and then leaped at the swinging latticework arm.

He felt the grenade before he heard it. Its shock wave lifted him and pushed him forward, pressing him into the arm's gridwork. Behind him he heard the explosion dimly, its blast muffled by the powerful engines of the crane, of the trucks below, of the hammerings of rivet guns on an adjacent construction site. It was no wonder the workers below had paid scant notice to the first explosion.

He tried to break his fall with his hands, but the extra force of the explosion forced him against the crane's metal arms with an excruciating force. He felt the muscles in his arms and shoulders strain as he reached for a handhold and tried to keep his head safe at the same time. He almost succeeded.

While he reached for a crosspiece on top of the arms's latticework, his head slammed against the metal. Unable to avert his face from the sharp-edged piece of steel, he lost control and fell.

Flailing wildly, the crook of Steele's knee jammed itself into the angle formed by the arm's triangular framework. For what seemed like eons, Steele hung upside down, carried through the night on the arm of the crane eight floors above the ground. He felt the Magnum slide out of his waistband. He did not hear it strike the ground.

Dizzily, he looked down at the darkness eighty feet below. Then a warm thick fluid dripped into his eyes, smearing the vision. It was several moments before he realized it was his own blood draining from his nose. He reached up to wipe the blood away.

He heard shouts from below now, men on the ground who had spotted him hanging there. The crane was slowing.

No. God, please. Don't let them stop it.

With an almost superhuman effort he reached above him and pulled himself up until he was straddling the lower beam of the crane's arm. As he did, two faces appeared at the window to Roten's apartment, less than fifty feet away. They looked down, trying to determine where the body had landed.

The crane moved another thirty feet away from them, dragged by the momentum of the full hopper of concrete, and then stopped. Steele wiped at the blood that flowed freely from his nose and tried to clear his head. The blow to his face had thrown off his sense of balance. He tried to move forward and the world spun. For a moment he thought the crane had started up again. And then things stabilized.

Above him Steele heard someone shout. He looked at the window to Roten's apartment and saw one of the men pointing at him. Simultaneously, both men raised their weapons. Despite his shaky equilibrium, Steele scrambled through the framework of the arm toward the operator's compartment.

The operator must have seen what was happening. The crane's powerful engine roared and the arm began to move again, making Steele a moving target, carrying him into the darkness away from his assailants.

There was more shouting from the window, and moments later the glass enclosure of the crane operator's compartment exploded under a massive assault of gunfire. Steele watched the crane operator jerk and dance and then fell backward out of the compartment.

But the crane did not stop.

Heart pounding, muscles strained to the breaking point, Steele clambered over the girders, aware that he'd be an easy target once he moved again into range of the killers' guns. As he descended, bullets pinged off the steelwork around him.

At the bottom of the crane, brawny arms hustled him to safety as the men asked him what had happened and who the people were who had been shouting at him from above.

Blood from his nose covered his face and neck and matted his hair. Thinking he had been seriously wounded, the construction workers took him to their trailer and made him lie down. They assured him that the ambulance would be there shortly.

Steele lay there, collecting his thoughts. The ambulance, police. Would they believe his story? Foreign nationals involved with crime could find themselves tied up for months, their passports confiscated. There was no due process in this country as there was in America. Would they charge him with a crime?

For a moment he was grateful he had lost the Magnum. Mere possession of a handgun without a license would get him a jail term. Then his hand flew to the pocket of his trousers. Twelve rounds of .357 ammunition rested guiltily there. It wouldn't take much of a search to find a gun. And a paraffin test on his hands would prove he had fired the gun . . . or a gun. Visions of the inside of a cell ran through his head.

The foreman of the construction site was astounded when the man they had thought was seriously injured bolted from the trailer and disappeared into the night, outrunning the workers who were sent in pursuit.

CHAPTER TWENTY-SIX

"It was the strangest art negotiation I had ever been involved with," Stephanie said.

She was seated opposite Nat Worthington in the sitting room of the suite at the Eden au Lac. In the other room, Seeley was watching a Swiss military air show on the television. The announcer's voice was regularly drowned in the roar of jets taking off, landing, or making mock strafing runs.

"How strange?" Worthington asked.

He looked down to make sure the wheels of the cassette recorder were turning, then returned his gaze to Stephanie. She had a remarkable constitution, this woman. The way she had recovered her physical strength and her emotional equilibrium was nothing less than phenomenal. She reminded him of his Tania. The thought of Tania waiting for him back in Tel Aviv made him yearn for home.

"I had been up in northern California, appraising a collection that was about to go into probate," Stephanie replied. "It was a sticky affair—all of the heirs were clawing at each other even before the body was cold. It was worth a lot of money to the gallery, particularly because the will would probably have been contested, which meant additional court fees later on." She looked vaguely out the window at the lights reflected off the lake.

"I went to the airport in San Francisco to pick up Derek, who was flying up for the weekend. And when he walked out of the gate area, he was accompanied by Richard Summers . . . —the owner of the Summers Gallery—'' She looked directly at Worthington. "I told you about him, didn't I?"

Worthington nodded.

"Well, Richard told me that he had an urgent job here for me . . . in Kreuzlingen. Some fellow who had been a sergeant in the SS and had amassed a fortune in art wanted to sell it. Richard selected me because of my fluency in German. He speaks and reads some of it—he was stationed in Austria during World War Two with the Art Looting Investigative Unit of the OSS . . . the Office—"

"The Office of Strategic Services," Worthington finished for her. "The precursor agency to the CIA . . . yes. I know all about it. I used to work for the CIA."

Stephanie looked at him for a moment, and then nodded as if what he had said made sense.

"Well, Summers sent me to contact this man in Kreuzlingen," Stephanie continued. "And he told me to keep my eyes open for a small painting by a man named Frederick Stahl. It was named 'The Home of The Lady Our Redeemer.' I asked Summers why he would be interested in an unknown work by a mediocre fascist painter, and for the first time since I had worked for him, he pulled rank on me. 'Just do it,' he told me. I couldn't figure out whether he was frightened or angry. But since I was to get a thorough look at the collection in Kreuzlingen, I agreed to call him immediately if I saw the Stahl painting."

"I assume you found the painting?"

She acknowledged Worthington's question with a nod.

"I spotted it the first day I was there," she began. "I tried to draw the owner out about it . . . to find out why it was so special to Summers. But the man seemed reluctant to say anything about it. He was extremely agitated, more like a man suffering from guilt than from fear or anger.

"I should have seen how strange things were getting and done something about it," she went on. "But I suppose I was too proud to approach Richard about it. I was hurt that he had treated me as if I were an employee rather than as an equal. It was very uncharacteristic of him. So I said nothing.

"I made an appointment to come back to the estate in Kreuzlingen and do my detailed analyses of all the paintings, and as I was leaving, the estate owner did something extraordinary.'' She paused as if she still could not believe it. "I had said goodbye and was standing in the foyer waiting for his butler to bring me my coat when the owner got a telephone call. He disappeared into an adjacent room, and although I couldn't hear what was said, I could tell by the tone of his voice that he was upset.

"He hung up violently and rushed back into the foyer,'' Stephanie said. "He looked at me for a long time. He would begin a sentence and then change his mind. He was so agitated, I thought he might have a stroke or heart attack right on the spot. Finally he said, 'Don't leave,' and then backed out of the room.

"When he returned a few minutes later, he was holding the painting, the one by Stahl. 'Give it to Father Meyer,' he said. 'Take it now. He will know what to do with it. I owe him this much.' ''

Stephanie paused. "I don't suppose you know who this Father Meyer is?''

Worthington shook his head.

Stephanie looked at him a moment, then continued. "During those months, when I was chained to that bed, I used to think about him—who he might be, where he lived. Maybe . . . maybe if I had gotten the painting to him, all of this could have been avoided.''

Worthington nodded sympathetically.

"Why didn't you ask the man who Father Meyer was?''

"I was afraid to show ignorance,'' Stephanie said. "He might have taken the painting back, and it seemed so important to Summers. Besides, I assumed Summers knew this Father Meyer. So I took the painting and drove back to Zurich that afternoon.

"The first thing I did was place the painting in one of the hotel's safe deposit boxes. Then I went up to the hotel room.'' Her voice started to crack now as she approached the beginning of her ordeal. "I hugged Derek—he was just getting into the shower—and sat down at the telephone to place a call to Richard. That's—''

Her voice faltered. "That's when the men came.'' She cupped her face in her hands and began to sob violently. Worthington got up, fetched a box of facial tissues from the bathroom, and placed it on the table in front of her. Stephanie continued sobbing, unable to talk coherently about the pain she had been forced to endure. Worthington turned then and left Stephanie to her thoughts.

Outside, a red panel ambulance with white crosses on its sides and doors drew up to the entrance of the Eden au Lac. In the vehicle's back seat, KGB Colonel Molotov gingerly touched the bandage on the side of his head with his right index finger, and for the hundredth time, cursed the bad luck that had resulted in his drawing this particular assignment. Not only had his right ear been nearly torn off in the final blast that leveled the warehouse but just this morning he had been put on notice by his superiors at Moscow Center that any further failure would not be tolerated. He was to recapture the woman, at any cost, and make every effort to capture her husband as well. A telephone call intercepted by their agents in Paris had indicated that the woman's husband was in Zurich and that he could lead them to the painting that was the key to the shroud. Molotov knew that his slate would be wiped clean if he could just get his hands on the painting. And that was what he intended to do.

Fortune had smiled on him in at least one respect. It had delivered to him the Jew doctor. The stinking little Jew had given them the girl's hotel room number. Without it they would have had to stake out the hotel, taking the chance that she might slip past. The little Jew had given them the edge they needed. Molotov smiled for a moment as he thought of the Jew, so afraid for the safety of his mother. It was fortunate for Molotov that the Jew did not know that his mother was already dead.

Molotov took another look at his copy of Derek's passport photo, then whispered to the two men in the front seat and the man sitting beside him. "You're ambulance attendants. Remember that. And remember too that we want Mr. and Mrs. Steele alive. Wound them if you must, but don't kill them. They have something that we need."

"I don't understand," Stephanie said as she hung up the telephone. "Where could he be?" She looked at Worthington and Seeley as she walked back to the table in the sitting room. "I've called his room a thousand times. We've left messages on the door, in his mailbox . . . and still nothing.'' She stared disconsolately at her feet. ''Where could he be?''

The remains of a rack of lamb rested on the table. Stephanie sat down and stared morosely out the window. It was ironic, she thought. Here she was again in the real world, the world she had longed for all these months, and still there was something missing, something that made the world real for her. She realized then how much of her existence was defined by her relationship with Derek. Until they were reunited, she would continue to feel that she had not returned to the person she had once been.

Seeley broke into the flow of her thoughts. ''I'm sure he'll call soon. Maybe he's shopping.''

Stephanie tried to force a smile. ''I hope you're right.'' Her voice was so quiet the two men had to lean over to catch her words. ''Of course. It's Christmas.'' She looked at each man in turn and then directed her gaze inward.

At that moment the telephone began to ring. Stephanie picked it up.

''Hello?''

''Stephanie?'' It was Steele. ''Stephanie, is that really you?''

''Derek!'' Stephanie felt her voice crack, her hands begin to tremble. ''Oh, God! It's you. Derek, I'm so happy to hear your voice. Oh, God,'' and she began to weep softly. ''I missed you so much, darling. I missed you so much.''

The tears of agony she had dammed up for so long rushed forward in a flood of relief.

''Steph . . . Steph,'' Steele's voice came urgently over the earpiece. ''Steph, hold on a minute, I need your help.'' Stephanie felt her heart catch. She could hear his heavy breathing.

''Derek? Where are you?'' she asked. ''Are you all right?'' Steele looked around him. He stood in a telephone booth on the Gloriastrasse, just across the street from the entrance to the University Hospital. Groups of students, some of them in medical whites, others obviously undergraduates, walked past the booth in clots of two and three. None of them paid him any attention. But that wouldn't last for long. He was sure there would be alerts out for him in minutes.

In the distance, from the direction of Roten's building, he could hear the wail of sirens. "Yeah, I'm fine . . . right now," he replied. "I'm in Zurich and—"

"I know," Stephanie interrupted. "But *where* in Zurich?"

Steele cocked his head to one side, listening intently as the sounds of a siren grew louder. It climbed the steep hill from the direction he had run just minutes ago.

"Look, do you have a car?" he asked urgently.

Stephanie hesitated. "Yes, I . . . we've got one." Nat Worthington gave her a questioning look. "It's Derek," she said to Worthington.

"What?" Steele replied.

"I was talking to Nat Worthington. He works for the Israelis . . . he saved my life."

"He what?" Steele asked. Just then a police car screamed into view, trailed closely by an ambulance. Together, their blinking lights reminded Steele of an alien spacecraft.

"Never mind," Steele said. "Honey, you have got to get me out of here as soon as you can."

"Get you out of where?" Stephanie asked.

"I'm just across the street from the University Hospital . . . up on the hill above the Old Town on the east bank. I—"

A second police car rounded the corner slowly, with no flashing lights or siren. The officer in the passenger seat was working a spotlight, playing it along the walls and sidewalks. Had someone spotted him? The car was no more than a hundred yards away, the brilliant beam of the spotlight cutting through the night.

"I've got to go," Steele said. "Meet me at the Grossmünster."

"The what?" Stephanie asked.

The cop with the searchlight seemed to look right at Steele.

"Grossmünster. It's a big church. Ask anybody." Without waiting for a reply, Steele hung up the receiver and bolted into the night.

CHAPTER TWENTY-SEVEN

"The Grossmünster," Stephanie said as she finished tying her running shoes and started to pull on her coat. "I think that's a church down near the river."

"I know where it is," Worthington snapped. "And I don't need any help to go collect your husband. I want you to stay here with Rich where you'll be safe." He zipped up his coat and stepped toward the door.

"Damn it." Stephanie cursed as she stepped between Worthington and the door. "I want to see him and you're not going to stop me from that. I'm not a piece of baggage you can just order around as you like."

Worthington glanced at Seeley, who stood waiting for directions, then returned his gaze to Stephanie.

"I could have Rich detain you until I come back," he said. "But I wouldn't want to do that to him. There's no telling what you might do." He turned once again to Seeley. "Get your coat," he said. "I'd rather tangle with the KGB than argue with her any longer."

Worthington motioned Stephanie to one side as he opened the door into the hallway and peered out.

"It's empty," Worthington said, then looked at Stephanie. "This might be dangerous. I want you to promise me you'll follow my orders quickly and without questioning me."

Stephanie nodded her head, knowing her assent was the price she must pay to see Derek. She stepped into the hallway, followed closely by Seeley. She'd make up her own mind when and where

344

to follow Worthington's orders. Seeley had just closed the door to the suite when the telephone began ringing.

"Hurry up!" Stephanie urged Seeley, as he fumbled for his key. "It might be Derek again."

The telephone rang a third time and then a fourth. On the fifth ring, Seeley opened the door and Stephanie rushed toward the phone on the bedside table.

She snatched the receiver from its cradle. "Hello?" There was no answer.

"Hello? Is anyone there?" She slammed down the receiver. "Damn. Damn. Damn," she cursed. "Too late." She stood by the telephone for a moment.

"Let's go," Worthington called from the hall. She and Seeley rushed to join him.

KGB Colonel Molotov smiled broadly as he replaced the receiver of the house phone quietly on it cradle. "She's there," he said to the three men standing at his side. "You." Molotov indicated the driver of the car. "Follow me up the stairway." He turned to the other two. "Take the elevator and wait for us there."

Without waiting for confirmation, Molotov bounded up the thickly carpeted stairs, the pain from his head wounds temporarily forgotten.

Rich Seeley felt the running footsteps through the soles of his feet. "Hold it," he said in a stage whisper as he blocked Stephanie and Nat's advance with one of his massive arms. He pulled up a Mini-Uzi from his shoulder holster and flattened himself against the wall.

"What's wrong?" Worthington asked as he flattened himself against the stairwell wall and motioned to Stephanie to do the same.

"Footsteps," Seeley said. "Running . . . from below."

Worthington paused to listen.

"Maybe it's children playing?" Worthington said. "I don't hear—"

"Children play noisily," Seeley said. "We should hear more than footsteps."

Seeley padded silently down the steps, fanning the barrel of the

Mini-Uzi before him. Worthington was half a step behind, brandishing his automatic. Stephanie brought up the rear.

Molotov pressed himself into the recess of a door to one of the hotel's rooms. Across the hall, the driver likewise tried to force himself out of sight in the narrow recess. Both had their Czech-made machine pistols at the ready, safeties off.

"Hear them?" Molotov whispered.

"How do you know it's them?" the driver whispered back.

"Instinct," Molotov said. "Why else are they whispering? Why haven't they come down the stairs yet? They've been there an awfully long time. They're being cautious. They heard our footsteps. It has to be."

Seeley spotted the two men in the corridor just as his feet had begun to leave the last step of the stairs leading onto the second floor. He was a surprisingly fast man for someone of his size, and would have survived had he not hesitated in midstride to hold back Nat and Stephanie with his arms.

"Get back!" Seeley yelled, as he brought the Mini-Uzi's muzzle to bear on the man standing on the right side of the hallway. He saw the man raise his own weapon, then, out of the corner of his eye, saw another gun in another recessed doorway. Fire and duck; fire and duck. He heard his old drill sergeant screaming at them.

Seeley squeezed the trigger on the Mini-Uzi, firing a burst that caught the man full across the face and hammered his head against the door. From his position a few feet away, Molotov felt the warm wet splatter of blood against the side of his face as he stepped into the hallway and trained his Czech machine pistol on the large man's torso. The huge man stiffened as the slugs slapped into his beefy chest and stomach. But Molotov's look of grim satisfaction faded as the large man continued to turn toward him, seemingly unaffected by the gaping wounds that turned his shirt bright red.

"Die, damn you," Molotov muttered as his clip ran out. The large man faltered; the muzzle of his gun wavered. But still he stood, and shook his head violently, like a bull waiting for the matador to finish off what the picadors had started.

In horror, Molotov watched the muzzle of the man's gun steady on a line of sight that included Molotov's chest. The KGB Colonel dropped the Czech machine pistol and leaped to one side just as slugs filled the air where he had been standing. Molotov whipped out his automatic and squeezed off three quick round at the huge man's head.

Oh, my God. Oh, my God. Rich's been shot. Stephanie stood rooted in horror, her hand closed tightly around the banister. She watched as Worthington moved forward against the wall, trying to reach Seeley. She watched Seeley quiver under the impact of the slugs, waver for a moment, then aim his gun and fire.

The next instant she saw two bullets take out the left side of Seeley's face, leaving a third to rip away the left side of his neck and lay bare flesh and arteries underneath. Bright red blood fountained from his neck as he toppled onto the floor.

Stephanie stifled a scream as excited voices filled the stairway above. The voices were neither in English nor German, but Russian. Worthington turned quickly and scanned the landing above them. He hesitated a moment, then took the steps two at a time. Stephanie watched as Worthington gained the top of the flight and tore around the corner. Instants later she heard gunshots, long sustained jack-hammerings from two or three different-sounding guns—she couldn't tell how many—and the desperate cries of men in mortal pain. Then, suddenly, it was silent.

Fear choked off the words in Stephanie's throat. Who had died up there? If it was Nat, she was again all alone. She felt herself tremble.

Forcing herself to think, she began looking frantically about her for Seeley's gun. Where had he dropped it? She heard footfalls on the landing above. There! In the corner. She spotted Rich's Mini-Uzi against the baseboards in the corner of the corridor.

Stephanie lurched away from the banister, almost tripping on the stairs as she descended. She tried to focus on the gun, tried not to look at Seeley's lifeless body.

"Back in your room or I'll blow your head off too!" Molotov growled at a thin man with even thinner black hair who had opened his door to find out what the commotion was about. The man slammed the door. As he walked down the hallway toward the fallen giant, Molotov could hear the man bolting the door tight. In the distance, he heard excited voices, the sounds of running feet. He had to finish up quickly.

Molotov froze as he saw the shadow play itself across the body of the fallen man. He raised his pistol and stepped into the darkened recess of another door. In a moment he saw the woman step into view. He walked quickly toward her, the pistol in front of him.

"Don't move," he said in English.

A high-pitched cry of surprise escaped from her mouth as Stephanie turned toward the voice. Her heart quickened as, in the dimness of the hallway, she made out the features of one of the men from the warehouse.

"You," she said.

Molotov smiled. "Yes. Me. I've come to collect you."

Inside, he exulted. Just ahead was his chance to redeem himself with Moscow. All he had to do was bring her back alive. He walked quickly toward her, his pistol hanging loosely in his hand.

At the top of the stairs, Stephanie heard more footfalls. Would it be Nat? Or would it be one of this man's associates? The man gained another step while Stephanie still felt rooted on the spot, a nightmare dreamer frozen in an oncoming wake of terror. Another step.

"You will come with us," the man said.

Suddenly, Stephanie lunged for Seeley's Mini-Uzi. She heard the man in the hall laughing. *Laughing* at her.

Angered, she picked up the gun and turned toward him.

"Give me that," he said soothingly as he approached. He was no more than ten feet away now. "Give me that before you hurt yourself." He stretched out his hand.

Would the gun work for her? Stephanie could feel the cold sweat on her fingers making the well-oiled gun slippery to hold. Would it have a safety or something? A bolt? She had read about one of those once in a book. He was almost on her now, his hand only inches away.

She prayed and squeezed the trigger.

The Mini-Uzi seemed to explode in her hands. It bucked and danced and rattled. And in front of her, the man's chest separated into two halves, blood and entrails pouring through the middle. He fell to the floor, dead.

A shadow crawled down the stairwell toward her. Stephanie turned and pointed the gun. Nat Worthington lunged to one side of the stairs.

"Don't," he shouted. "It's me." There was a red stain at the thigh of his trousers. She rushed up the stairs.

"You've been hurt," she said, as she watched him struggle to his feet.

"Nothing serious," he said. "They just nicked me." He stood for a moment and then began to climb the stairs.

"Come on," he said, looking back at her. "We've got to get out of here. No telling if there's reinforcements on the way."

They passed two dead men on the third floor by the stairs. Once in their suite, Stephanie lost no time throwing her newly acquired clothes into a suitcase. She heard Worthington in the next room talking on the telephone in subdued tones. She couldn't understand most of the conversation, but made out Rich's name and the name of the hotel. Worthington hung up the telephone and minutes later they descended to the basement via the service elevator at the end of the hall.

Gerry Anderson stepped out of the taxi in front of the Holiday Inn just outside the Zurich airport. He looked at his watch. It was just before 10 P.M. The aircraft had picked up a strong tailwind over Greenland and had managed to arrive more than an hour early.

The trip had been smooth, but Anderson wore a frown as he paid the taxi and crossed the sidewalk to the lobby. He walked straight to the registration desk, leaving the taxi driver and the bellhop to sort out his bags.

Steele had gone underground. He had eluded the council's people in Amsterdam and simply disappeared. He hadn't been answering his telephone at the Eden au Lac. Braun was angry as hell, and his new acolyte, Maxwell, had come down with a disabling case of cold feet. Braun was having to use drugs for persuasion. It was too warm in Zurich; the weather made him sweat and he hated to sweat unless he was at the gym. The Scotch he had drunk on the flight tasted pasty on his tongue and the boiled sweatsocks American Airlines liked to call an in-flight meal sat like a lump of concrete in his stomach. It had not been an evening to remember.

Anderson handed the desk clerk his American Express card and watched as the man ran it through the embossing machine and gave it back to him.

Ten minutes later, Anderson was standing in a scalding hot shower, letting the water sting away the dirt and smells of travel. The massaging stream of water seemed to work at eroding the jagged edges of his thoughts.

He felt calmer when he stepped out of the shower and toweled himself dry. He had to be calm. It was what had kept him alive all these years. He opened the door to let the fresh, cool air into the bathroom and watched as the condensation cleared from the bathroom mirror.

His reflection stared back at him. Flat belly, long muscular legs, heavily muscled shoulders and arms, and a neck that bordered on unfashionably thick. He smiled. He always saved his best smile for himself.

Still watching himself in the mirror, he touched the scar that ran down his left side, a knife wound he brought back from El Salvador. That was the time he learned that Marxist priests were just as capable of killing as praying. He felt the ragged, puckered edges of the hard scar tissue that ran from just below his left nipple down along the ribs almost to his waist and he thought of the priest.

It hadn't been the first time he had been sent to kill. And it hadn't been the last. But it had been a sort of watershed in his life. It had been the first time he had truly enjoyed the killing. He had enjoyed it so much that it took the priest more than two days to die.

He missed the killing. He lived for it. And as soon as he was finished with Steele, he could go back to it.

But Steele was proving a harder task than he had anticipated. He had slipped away from Anderson's best men. It had taken hours, but Anderson had finally pieced together how Steele could have possibly sneaked away long enough to kill Claude Tewles, though for the life of him Anderson couldn't figure out whey Steele would want to kill his department chairman, from all reports one of his best friends.

Anderson shook his head ruefully as he thought of Steele: a tough man, unpredictable, capable, shrewd—all of which made him nearly impossible to protect. But, Anderson consoled himself, he wouldn't have to protect Steele for much longer if things went as they seemed to be going. Soon Steele would provide them with the information they needed to obtain the shroud, and then he would become expendable.

Steele saw the Volvo pull slowly into Grossmünsterplatz. He was standing in the darkened doorway of a building across the square from the church, pressing himself as deeply as he could into the shadows as the headlights of the car swept slowly past.

His tongue dragged roughly across the bone-dry roof of his mouth. He wanted to swallow, but fear kept his throat dry and constricted. Two police cars had swept past the area twice; both were marked cars with their sirens wailing.

This Volvo, though, was different. Two people inside, cruising slowly. They were looking for someone. Him? He felt his heart beating loudly. The Volvo's brake lights flashed. The car slowed to a stop across the square, too far away to make out the people inside: they were gray shadows behind the window glass.

A moment later Steele watched as the driver's door of the Volvo opened. The man who got out moved like a cop: he bristled with caution, his head moving like a hungry hawk's. Steele could see a weapon in his right hand. He walked slowly ten or twenty yards behind the car, and then an equal distance in front of it. The man—*a cop? Had they found him?*—walked over to the passenger's side and leaned down to say something to the person seated there. He then opened the door and stood back to allow the passenger get out.

Steele felt his heart skip a beat when he spotted Stephanie getting out of the car. The door closed with a solid thunk and she and the man who looked like a cop walked back toward the front of the car and looked around.

Still, Steele did nothing. Was it really Steph? The dim streetlights painted her face with shadows, yet . . . yet he saw how she moved, how she stood, how she moved her head when she talked and waved her hands in the air. Suddenly, he felt as if someone had rolled a great rock from his heart. He stepped from the shadows and took the steps one by one, as if he didn't entirely trust his legs any more. He saw their faces fix on him as he crossed the square. The man who looked like a cop brought his weapon to bear.

"Stephanie," cried Steele, no longer able to control himself. He began to run.

"Derek?" Stephanie said at first, not quite believing it was really he. Then she knew. They met in the middle of the cobbled darkness of Grossmünsterplatz.

"Oh God," Stephanie cried as she wrapped her arms around him. "Oh God, oh God I didn't think I'd ever . . . we'd ever . . . that—" Her voice shattered into sobs of elation.

Steele looked at her, saw the thin face, the faint bruises that looked like shadows in the dim light. She looked to him like a picture-book rendering of a poor orphan. He felt his heart breaking for all she had been through. He pulled her close and held her tight against him.

Her body shocked him. She was thinner, much thinner. Sudden outrage mingled with his joy, as he thought of what she had been through and the people who had put her through it all.

Love abides bizarre partners. Next to the overwhelming love he felt for her sat an abiding desire to kill the men responsible for her suffering.

"Those bastards," he said. "Steph, I'm so glad to see you, I love you so much, so much." And his voice cracked as he felt his own eyes fill with tears of thanks.

Unheard now were the sounds of the city: the mournings of sirens, the crashing surf of automotive traffic down on the Limmat Quai, the distant scratching roar of a jet overhead. They all disappeared along with the Grossmünster and its Platz and the Volvo and all the police and spies and killers and dead old men. They were alone.

Nat Worthington watched them for several minutes, happy in their reunion, jealous of their togetherness. He thought of Tania in the Mossad's safe apartment in Tel Aviv and all at once he felt his own eyes begin to mist over with the tears of happiness, sorrow, longing.

Then the moment was gone. The glare of oncoming headlights made Worthington abruptly aware of their situation. He went to the driver's door of the Volvo and opened it.

"Get in," he yelled. "Hurry." He sat down behind the steering wheel and started the engine. The oncoming headlights grew brighter. Derek and Stephanie ran toward the Volvo hand in hand. Worthington felt a pang of envy as he watched them slide into the back seat. He drove away as Steele shut the door.

The approaching car entered the Grossmünsterplatz just as the Volvo reached the square's other end at the Oberdorfstrasse. Worthington braked briefly at the corner. He glanced in the rear-view mirror, and as he turned right on the Kirche Gasse noted that the car that had entered the square had emblazoned on its side the insignia of the Zurich police.

CHAPTER TWENTY-EIGHT

Steele awoke suddenly. The strange room frightened him until he reached out with his right hand and found Stephanie sleeping next to him. She slept as trustingly as a child, curled up next to him with her head buried in the pillows. He could feel her soft breaths against his bare shoulder.

He relaxed and took in the strange surroundings: the knotty wood on the walls, the open ceiling with its exposed beams, the gray stone fireplace across the room, and the rustic furniture, hand painted in the Alpine country tradition. Bright morning light, still rosy with the dawn, glowed beyond the fir trees he could see through the window.

His mind raced frantically. Where were they? He remembered their drive out of Zurich, Worthington's insistence that they not go near the Eden au Lac for as long as it might be crawling with police.

They had driven south of Zurich. He remembered passing Zug, and turning off the main road before getting to Lucerne. The road had gotten mountainous after that, and he remembered a lot of signs directing people to ski slopes and lodges. There was a lake nearby; he remembered that much, a small lake.

The thoughts came more clearly to him now as he woke up. The Mossad maintained a chalet near one of the ski slopes as a safe house. Steele felt his muscles relax as it all came back to him. The house had a caretaker, an old Jew who had retired from the Mossad a decade before.

Stephanie made a small mewing sound in her sleep and snuggled closer to him. He looked at her face and wondered what she was dreaming about. It didn't matter, he thought, as long as it wasn't a nightmare.

She looked so vulnerable, he thought. So fragile. Yet he knew how tough she had had to be to survive her ordeal. Had it changed her? Of course it had, he told himself. Would it change *them?*

He thought about that one for a long while and finally had to admit that their experiences in the past six months couldn't fail to have changed their relationship. He consoled himself with the thought that changes don't have to be bad.

Gently he touched her; he caressed the outlines of her features, softly ran his hand along her shoulder and up the soft vulnerable curve of her neck where wisps of hair curled in provocative disarray. It was as if by touching her he could retrace the memories and put himself back into the past.

Stephanie awakened slowly.

She drifted upward through layers of sleep like a diver in no hurry to reach the surface. She perceived the world a fragment at a time: first the light gentle touches like kisses on her shoulders and neck, then the bright morning light announcing the new day.

She stirred and threw her leg across Steele's flat male belly, nuzzling closer to him. She felt his hands along her back, caressing, exploring. His touch lingered at the small of her back and then moved lower. She felt herself growing moist. And she felt him growing hard against the back of the leg she had thrown across his belly.

She opened her eyes when he kissed her just behind her left ear. And in her left ear. She quivered.

"Good morning," she said, her voice fuzzy with sleep.

"It sure is," he said.

They kissed, exploring with their tongues like first-time lovers. And then all control vanished.

They made love for a long time. The sun rose in the sky and turned its faint rosy tint into the glaring brilliance of a clear Alpine day. But neither of them noticed the passage of time. They were in a place where time could not touch them. It was a place where

355

people never grew old, never suffered, never died. Only a fool would ever trade this place for heaven.

And finally, they slept again, warmed and exhausted and refreshed. Stephanie slept as she always had, with her head on Steele's right shoulder, her body pressed into the hard angles of his body. He held her with his right arm and fell asleep with his head resting against hers.

When it came, Nat Worthington's knock at the door sounded like thunder. It startled them both, wrenching them from a rest they had missed for more than six months.

"Eight o'clock," Worthington said as he rapped gently at the door. "Banks open in two hours. Water's hot for a shower. Breakfast in half an hour."

Steele stretched as he listened to Worthington's footsteps fade down the hallway.

"Cruel bastard," he muttered in a good-natured way. She mumbled a reply into the pillow. He leaned over to kiss her once more before getting up and stumbling into the shower.

"Interpol has an advisory out on you," Worthington said, as the chalet's caretaker cleared away the remains of the extravagant breakfast he had prepared for them. The Mossad agent seemed somewhat subdued. His face looked pale, and when he walked there was a noticeable limp from the previous night's gunshot wound.

"I checked in with Tel Aviv this morning," Worthington said to Steele. "You're wanted for murder."

Stephanie gasped.

But Steele just nodded slowly. It wasn't surprising. He had been too near too many murders to remain unnoticed. He thought of the murders on his boat, Davidson's chauffeur, Claude Tewles, Amsterdam, the killers at Roten's apartment, and the hapless crane operator. Death had scorched a wide, noticeable path behind him.

"Did they give any details?" Steele asked finally.

"Seems that you were seen near the body of a UCLA professor, Claude Tewles—"

"Oh my God." Stephanie exclaimed. "How did Claude get tied in with all this?"

"It's a long story," Steele began. "I'd better start at the beginning." He took a deep draught from his coffee mug and then began: "I was sleeping on the boat—" He turned to Stephanie. "I couldn't sleep in our house . . . not with you gone. Everything there reminded me of you. It was as if it was haunted." He took a deep breath.

"Anyway," he continued, "it was raining like hell one morning and I get this frantic knocking on the companionway."

He told them about Davidson and the killers and the chauffeur and Gerry Anderson.

"The *Valkyrie*'s gone, then?" Stephanie asked sadly. Steele nodded slowly.

Then he told them about the rest of it: the mysterious motel that was a safe house, the recovery of the painting, and the discovery of Tewles's body. His flight to Amsterdam and the killers who found him there.

"And this priest used the word 'brown?' " Worthington asked. "Are you sure that's what he said?"

Steele nodded. Worthington said he would sure like to know more about this mysterious group of priests in the Vatican.

Except for the occasional interjection or question, Stephanie and Worthington remained silent for nearly two hours as Steele related the story of a string of murders that had begun in Marina del Rey and continued to follow him through the streets of Zurich.

"Everything's tied together by the painting," Worthington said, to enthusiastic nods. "But why?" He pushed slowly away from the table and painfully got to his feet.

"It's getting worse, isn't it?" Stephanie asked.

Worthington nodded. "And the doctor's dead."

"The doctor who took care of me?" Stephanie asked. She looked stunned. "Do you know what—?"

Worthington shook his head. "I called there last night to see about getting some treatment for my leg," he explained. "There was no answer, not even a response to the paper that he carries for the Mossad. This morning I called again. A local Mossad agent went to check on him and found the body."

"But what happened?" Steele repeated Stephanie's question.

"The KGB happened," Worthington said weakly, as he limped away from the table toward the coffeepot. As he returned, his face was drawn and white, and beads of sweat had formed on his forehead and upper lip. A swelling bulged against the fabric of the thighs of his trousers.

"You'd better find someone else to see," Stephanie said in a motherly voice. "You've obviously got a serious infection."

Worthington nodded at her as he sagged painfully into the opposite chair.

"I've made a few calls," he said. "I can't just go into a hospital. You have to report gunshot wounds to the police. And where would all their questions put us? I'm responsible for more than one death in Zurich in the past couple of days. The whole town's buzzing: A Libyan assassin with more hits than Carlos dies at a local hotel; an entire city block in the industrial section goes up in flames; the blood's still wet on the carpets in the Eden au Lac. Gunshot wounds aren't as common in Europe as they are in the States, and it would take a pretty dumb cop to miss connecting me to at least some of the violence that's occurred lately."

He sipped from his mug. "Mossad's Zurich station is supposed to get me the name of another doctor. But they're going crazy right now. They only have six people and all six of them are up to their ears. All hell's breaking loose with a truckload of Russian documents the Swiss police found in front of the warehouse. The head agent is trying to get his hands on the documents without letting the Swiss know that we were behind the explosions." He shook his head slowly.

"If I don't hear from them soon, though, I'm going to get on a plane to Tel Aviv before the infection kills me." He nodded vigorously as if he were agreeing to a statement someone else had made. They sat in silence for a long time, listening to the caretaker rattle dishes and pans in the kitchen, watching the shadows grow shorter as noontime approached.

"There're a number of good reasons you'd better get in touch with your Mr. Anderson," Worthington said finally. "My leg's one of them. The fact that Mossad's people are tied up and likely to be so for the next several weeks is another." He looked directly at Steele. "And I assume that this Father Meyer that Roten told you about isn't likely to remain in Altaussee forever."

Steele nodded.

Worthington leaned back in his chair and closed his eyes for a moment. "I assume you'll be wanting to go to the bank today, then?" He opened his eyes and fixed Steele with a resigned look.

"I think we have to," Steele said. "I'm wanted for murder. There's no way we can turn to the authorities for help. We can't go home, and we can't just stay here. Besides, there are still people out there that want to kill Stephanie and me. The answer seems to be to get whatever's in that damned Swiss bank and get it to Meyer. I don't see any other way. Do you?" He looked from Worthington to Stephanie.

After a time Worthington, too, shook his head. "From your standpoint, there's no other choice. You're in for the long haul. Maybe in a few weeks . . . if you're still alive . . . if I'm still alive . . . the Mossad might be able to help you. I'll give you some numbers, but I'm not sure how much they'll do for you until they solve a few problems they see as a lot more pressing. I really think you should call Anderson."

Steele opened his mouth to say something and then closed it again. Worthington sensed his hesitation.

"Go ahead," Worthington said. "There's a telephone in your bedroom. Call him. The NSA had an effective method of patching phone calls together to reach their people almost anywhere in the world."

Steele tapped his fingers on the table, weighing his choices. Finally he nodded, got up from the table, kissed Stephanie lightly behind her right ear, then walked down the hall to the bedroom to make the call.

"I hope you're feeling better now."

With great effort, Robert Maxwell opened his heavy eyelids. Intense sunlight slashed fiercely at the Venetian blinds, casting glowing slabs of light across the foot of his bed.

Neils Braun, the cardinal archbishop of Vienna, stood by the side of the bed, holding a tray. Maxwell looked up at him, trying to orient himself, to remember what had happened.

"You had a very high fever last night," Braun said. "The doctor came up immediately."

"But . . . what—?"

"He said you were hit by some kind of fast-moving form of influenza." Braun set the tray down on the bedside table. It contained a teapot, silverware set on a linen napkin, small jars of jam and marmalade, and two plates covered with stainless steel domes.

"All I remember," Maxwell said, "is listening to your plans and then . . ." He looked up at Braun. "And then right now. I don't remember anything until now."

Braun nodded indulgently. "You've had a bad night of it all. Just take it easy for the next several days." He turned his attention to the tray and then back to Maxwell. "Are you hungry?"

Maxwell nodded. "I believe so."

"Good," Braun said with a smile as he reached for the tray. "Make yourself comfortable."

Maxwell turned to reach for his pillows and felt a pain in the inner side of his elbow. He stopped and pushed back the cuff of his pajamas. He found a small plastic bandage there. He struggled with one end of the bandage and when he pulled it away, found a small circle of brown dried blood on the bandage and a tiny scab on the large vein in the crook of his elbow.

He pulled the bandage off and rolled it up, then looked questioningly at Braun, a vague sense of unease forming just below the surface of his thoughts.

"The doctor gave you some medication," Braun explained. "Something to help the fever."

Maxwell looked at Braun for a moment and then nodded.

Braun helped Maxwell arrange his pillows to make his sitting position more comfortable, then set the tray down on Maxwell's lap and pulled the domes from the plates of food. There was a hearty American breakfast of eggs, potatoes, sausages, and freshly made bread.

Maxwell looked up at Braun and spoke. "I never imagined I'd find myself being served breakfast in bed by a cardinal." He smiled.

Braun smiled back at him and gave a warm low laugh that seemed to fill the room. "And why not?" he responded, as he pulled the chair from the kneehole of the desk and brought it to the bedside and sat in it to watch Maxwell eat. The American set on the food with a growing appetite. "You are the Great Conciliator, and you are vital to our new church. The church needs you very much and I will make sure you are taken care of." The offer seemed to include more than just breakfast in bed.

Maxwell nodded as he broke off a piece of the warm bread and buttered it.

"The new church," Maxwell said. "I feel more comfortable with your ideas this morning than I have since arriving." Maxwell popped the bread into his mouth and chewed slowly, as if the bread were an idea that had to be digested carefully. Braun could see Maxwell's ideas working in his eyes.

"Your ideas for this . . . new church . . . seem to make a great deal more sense to me now than they did when you first told me about them." Maxwell looked into the distance, as if he could see his thoughts on some distant mental horizon. When he spoke, it was in the tentative tones of a man who has almost forgotten something important. "I remember being upset. Thinking your idea was both insane and—" He paused as he searched for the word. "Necessary. Yes, that's it." He fixed Braun with a clear honest gaze. "I thought it was both insane and necessary."

"And now?" Braun asked.

"Now?" Maxwell's gaze turned inward. "Now it all just seems to make sense."

Braun smiled. "I'm gratified that you feel that way. Very gratified. We have much work to do, you and I. The coming days will take much from us. The coming days and the new church."

There was a sharp rapping at the door. Braun went to it quickly.

"Your grace." It was one of the household workers. "I'm sorry to disturb you, but you have a telephone call. The gentleman says it is urgent."

"Very well," Braun replied. He turned to Maxwell. "I'll be right back. If you need any assistance before then, use the telephone to call the staff."

Braun walked quickly to his study and picked up the telephone.

"Hello?"

"Cardinal Braun?"

"This is he."

"I've found them both. They called me just minutes ago. They have the painting and they're going to the bank early this afternoon."

"Wonderful! Wonderful!" Braun said. "What a lovely gift for the Christmas season! It's almost as if it's a sign."

"We should have everything by tonight."

"Fine, fine. You know what to do?"

"Of course." There was a note of annoyance, as if the question had been a slap at the speaker's professional competence.

"When will I see you?"

"Probably the day after Christmas. It'll take that long to go by the mine. Longer, depending on the location of the mine."

"Go with God," Braun said.

"And you too, your grace. Goodbye."

CHAPTER TWENTY-NINE

"Oh, Derek, I hope he's going to be all right." Stephanie poked at the half-eaten lunch in front of her. "He looked so pale when he boarded the plane. And his leg was swollen so badly."

"They've got good doctors in Tel Aviv," Steele replied. "Besides, he's a hero of sorts. They'll take extra good care of him."

She nodded dubiously and turned her face to the window. Outside, the Bahnhofstrasse was as crowded as ever. The Mercedes were jammed hood to trunk along the street; limos were double parked; crowds of well-dressed Zurichers rushed past the window of the small restaurant, their arms bulging with packages. From a great distance, the sound of carolers reached their ears; they were having trouble staying on key. Across the Bahnhofstrasse a Salvation Army van pulled to the curb and disgorged a quartet of soberly dressed men carrying musical instruments. They were accompanied by a woman who struggled with a tripod, making sure it was stable enough to support the donations pot that hung from it. Her bell slipped from her coat pocket and clanged loudly as it struck the sidewalk, rolling almost into the gutter before a passerby retrieved it. The group arranged itself just to the right of the entrance to the Thule Gesellschaft Bank.

"Make sure you have some spare change," Stephanie said. "Or they'll give us dirty looks when we go into the bank."

"Yes, but they'll probably give us one anyway if it's not large enough," Steele joked. "I—"

A uniformed policeman walked slowly into the restaurant. Quickly, Steele averted his face toward the window.

363

"Derek, what's wrong?"

"Cop," Steele said as he placed his elbow on the table and cupped his chin in his hand, letting his fingers obscure most of his profile. He hoped he looked like a diner engrossed in the Christmas scene on the Bahnhofstrasse. "He just walked into the restaurant."

Stephanie craned her neck slightly.

"He's just talking with the owner," she said when she turned back. "They look like they're friends or something."

Steele relaxed a bit. "Tell me when he's gone."

Stephanie nodded as Steele went back to watching the Salvation Army band unpack its instruments. A young boy of eleven or twelve passed by selling newspapers, and Steele fixed his eyes on the paper's bold headlines. FOUR DEAD IN APARTMENT BOMBING read the biggest headline. Below that was a smaller story: LINK TO WAREHOUSE DISASTER?

Steele held his breath as he quickly scanned the front page. Would he find his own picture there? The paperboy and his papers moved out of his range of vision, making the question moot. Steele looked nervously toward the cash register. He saw the policeman shake the owner's hand, then turn and exit through the front door.

The door to the restaurant was still swinging on its hinges when it opened again. Gerry Anderson entered.

Steele raised his arm and waved it silently, fearful of calling attention to himself. Fortunately, the NSA man spotted Steele immediately and began to thread his way through the tightly packed tables of the crowded restaurant. He looked angry.

"You sure have led us all over hell," Anderson said as he sat down. "What did you think you were doing? Did you really think you could go it all alone?"

He glared at Steele.

"Look," Steele began. "I'm sorry." Anderson's expression softened. "You were right. I should have listened to you from the beginning." Anderson's eyes reflected his surprise. He had come expecting a fight.

"Frankly, I didn't know how much I needed your help," Steele continued. "And now I know I, we"—he looked at Stephanie—"need all the help we can get. And you're it."

Anderson's frown transformed itself into a thin smile.

"Why don't you tell me about it?" He raised his hand to attract the attention of a waiter, who dutifully brought him a menu and a cup of coffee.

"There's two parts," Steele began. "Mine and Stephanie's."

"Well, I know part of yours," Anderson told him, "So why don't you begin with our last meeting and bring me up to speed."

Steele nodded, and as he launched into the retelling of his story, Anderson whipped a microcassette recorder from his inside coat pocket, flicked it on, and set it on the table between them. He didn't ask Steele whether or not he minded being taped.

"That was clever," Anderson remarked when Steele described how he got out of the library to retrieve the painting without Anderson's tail spotting him.

"Yeah," Steele said gloomily. "Clever enough to do myself out of an alibi for Tewles's murder."

"We can take care of that," Anderson said. "We have resources. Continue."

Steele finished his story with only two other interruptions: once when Anderson gave his order to the waiter, the second time while describing the priest in Amsterdam.

"Brown?" Anderson asked. Steele felt it must be his imagination, but it looked as if the NSA man had turned pale at the mention of "brown." "Are you sure? Did he say anything else? Who this 'Brown' was? How he fit in?"

Steele shook his head. "I'm not even sure he was speaking a person's name. It could refer to something else."

The color seemed to return to Anderson's face. "Yes, of course. The man could have been talking about anything. What had he told you before that?"

"He said there was an entire organization . . . in the Curia devoted to . . . ." Steele searched his memory. "Preventing abuses, or something like that. I don't remember exactly. It was all a little heavy, what with people shooting at me."

"Sure," Anderson said. "I understand. Sorry. Go on."

Anderson's lunch arrived just as Steel finished his part of the story. The NSA man had ordered the restaurant's lunch special: an assortment of grilled wursts accompanied by red cabbage and liver dumplings.

"I used to eat here every chance I got when I worked for the consulate," Anderson explained as he dug into the food piled on his plate. He cut a bite from the end of a *Weisswurst* and stuck it into his mouth. Then he looked at Stephanie. "Now, why don't you begin, please?"

She nodded slowly and looked nervously at the cassette recorder. Steele gave her a reassuring wink.

"I was appraising a collection in San Francisco," she began hesitantly. "I—"

"It's all right," Steele told her. "You can trust Gerry. He saved my life, just as Nat Worthington saved yours."

She held his gaze for a long moment, her eyes telling him that she didn't trust Anderson, but that she would continue.

"Richard Summers—the man I worked for—called me away from that job and sent me here to begin the negotiations to purchase the art owned by a man in Kreuzlingen."

"Franz-Dietrich Meister," Anderson said. It was not a question.

"No," Stephanie looked at him. "His name was—"

"His *real* name was Franz-Dietrich Meister," Anderson persisted. "You know him as Erich Bohles von Halbach. But he is really a former sergeant in the SS who managed to escape the hands of the allies just after World War II. He fled to Switzerland with several works of precious art that had been looted by Hitler's organization. He was a shrewd man and managed to parlay those few paintings into a very large fortune."

"But if you knew this—" Steele was angry. "If you knew he was a Nazi, if you knew he had the painting, why—"

"We weren't *sure* it was Meister," Anderson said. "Not until the autopsy was done and he could be identified by the dental records." He paused. "And there was no way to know that he had the particular painting everyone seems to be looking for. There are thousands of former SS members living all over the world with looted art hanging on their walls."

Stephanie nodded slowly, warily.

"Please," Anderson waved his fork. "Continue."

Stephanie resumed her story. Steele listened intently as she described the mysterious message Meister von Halbach had given her concerning Meyer.

"I was going to call Summers while you were in the shower," Stephanie explained. "But then the men came."

"Summers disappeared too," Steele said.

"What?" Stephanie's jaw dropped.

Steele nodded. "I tried to call him that same day. I was going crazy when you left. I called everybody you ever knew. Nobody could locate him. They never have, as far as I know."

Stephanie stared at him for a long time, letting the significance of Steele's words sink in. When she continued, it was in a subdued voice. "I hope he didn't have to go through what I did," she said. Then she told them about the kidnapping, her captivity, the interrogations, drugs, abuse.

Angry tears welled up in Steele's eyes as he listened to Stephanie's account of her captivity, and of her iron-willed desire to survive.

"It got so that all I could remember of you were your eyes," Stephanie said, with the moist hints of tears in her eyes, too. She looked lovingly at Steele, reached out with her right hand, and touched his cheek. "I could never forget your eyes. Some days they were all that kept me going."

For a moment they were the only two people in the world. Steele took her hand in his and kissed it. Then the moment passed. The clinking, murmuring noises of the restaurant crowded in around them once more.

Stephanie sniffed quickly and dabbed at her eyes with her napkin before continuing.

Anderson asked her detailed questions about her kidnappers, their numbers, whether they were all Russian—she told them about Czenek the Pole and El-Nouty and Libyan—their names, what they looked like. She told him about the rescue by Nat Worthington and Adam Gold, and that most of her abductors had been killed at the warehouse. And as far as she knew, those who had not died at the warehouse were killed the night before at the Eden au Lac.

"I killed one of them myself," she said flatly. "The one they called Molotov. He seemed to be the leader."

It was Anderson's turn to be surprised.

"*You* killed Molotov?" He said, sotto voce, "Do you know who he was?"

Stephanie shook her head.

"He was the goddamned head of the goddamned KGB center here in Zurich." Anderson whistled his admiration. "You've done the world one helluva favor."

Stephanie looked at him blandly and continued to tell him about her ordeal.

"So many people died," she said after concluding her recitation. She was staring blankly into the middle distance. "So many people who deserved to live." Steele and Anderson were both silent as a single tear rolled from each of her eyes. Steele took her hand and squeezed it. She returned his gesture with a fierce trembling grip.

"I'm glad Nat survived," she finally said.

"So am I," Steele agreed. "We owe him a great debt . . . your life."

She nodded.

"Nat Worthington will always survive," Anderson said finally.

"You know him?"

Anderson nodded vigorously. "He's something of a legend in the trade."

"The trade?" Stephanie asked.

"Intelligence," Anderson responded. "Depending on who you're talking to, Worthington's either the greatest spy that lived, or a true devil."

"I . . . don't understand," Stephanie said.

"Worthington was a maverick," Anderson began, as he cleaned up the food left on his plate. "He did his job too well, too honestly, and he made a lot of enemies at the CIA who wanted him out of the way before he could embarrass them again. They tried to kill him. He killed them first. There are still those in high places in our government who would like to see him eliminated. That's why he now works for the Mossad."

Stephanie's face betrayed her shock.

"It happens," was all that Anderson would say. The NSA man picked up his recorder and returned it to his pocket. "And now?" He looked at both of them.

Steele reached under the table and retrieved a package wrapped in brown kraft paper and string. "I suppose it's time for this." He untied the string and unfolded the paper. "We drove by the

Eden au Lac this morning before coming here.'' He continued to unwrap the parcel. At its heart was a very small painting that had proved lethal to almost everyone who had gotten close to it.

" 'The Home of the Lady Our Redeemer,' '' Steele said, as he turned it so Anderson could see it. The NSA man picked it up and held it so it was illuminated by the outside light spilling through the windows. He examined it silently, tilting it this way and that, and finally handed it back to Steele.

"So this is what it's all about?'' Anderson said.

Steele nodded as he wrapped it back in the brown paper.

"What are your instructions?'' Anderson asked.

"To present this to the clerk at the Thule Gesellschaft Bank.'' Steele looked across the Bahnhofstrasse at the private bank's discreet entrance.

"And then?''

Steele shrugged his shoulders. "They'll know what to do, I assume. Otherwise I'm back on the street with a mediocre painting.''

"And afterwards?''

"Only Father Meyer knows,'' Steele said. "And he's in Alt Aussee.''

"Makes as much sense as anything else in this whole insane affair,'' Anderson said.

"You ready?'' Steele asked Stephanie. She nodded reluctantly.

Steele slid his chair back and got to his feet. Stephanie followed suit. Anderson remained seated. Steele turned to her and said, "I still think you should wait here while I go over to the bank.''

She looked at Anderson and back to Steele. "We've been apart far too long. It's not going to happen again. Your danger is my danger too.''

Steele smiled. "You're something else,'' he told her lovingly. "Come on.''

They started to walk away from the table when Steele noticed that Anderson was still seated.

"Aren't you coming?'' Steele asked him.

Anderson shook his head. "I've lived in Zurich for too long. I don't want to be recognized. Besides, a man and his wife are about as normal as you can get. Add a second man and the bank may be suspicious.'' He shifted position so he could look at them better.

"Remember, if the painting really is the key to a box at that bank, it's illegal. The only reason they'll give you access is because the arrangements were probably set up before the banking laws outlawed anonymous accounts."

Steele was suddenly worried. "Are you saying they won't honor the painting as proof of access to the box?"

Anderson shook his head. "No. The Swiss are nothing if not reliable. But they won't act if things look suspicious. Just go in there as if you own the place. Act a bit like an arrogant, rich . . . very rich American. They expect that, even prefer it. They won't risk offending you."

"You'll wait here, then?" Steele asked.

"Here, or maybe close by on the sidewalk." Anderson responded.

With that, Steele led Stephanie through the restaurant and out into the street.

The Bahnhofstrasse was filled to overflowing with bright sunshine and crisp biting breezes.

"He makes me nervous," Stephanie said as they waited for traffic to part.

"I know what you mean," Steele said as he looked warily about him. Death had come out of nowhere before. This time he wouldn't let it take him by surprise. "He struck me the same way when I first met him."

The traffic along the Bahnhofstrasse thinned and they stepped off the curb. "I thought he was untrustworthy too, but he's come through every time." They stepped quickly up on the curb in front of the Thule Gesellschaft Bank as a Peugeot squealed around a corner and headed for them. "Don't forget: he saved my life."

"Still . . ." Stephanie's voice trailed off. They passed the Salvation Army band, which was playing a rigid tune that sounded as if it had been written by a Calvinist. Steele dropped a ten franc note in the donation pot as they passed.

"Danke schön," the woman called after them.

Steele stopped and looked up at the building, his heart thudding in his chest. The eye of the former policeman probed deeper than the grillwork and the secure-looking stone and found what he expected: the discreet and neatly invisible metallic glintings that betrayed a variety of modern security devices behind the facade of old elegance. Steele had heard talk of these banks, how they employed scanners built into doorjambs, lobbies, and elevators to check for weapons. Each anteroom, office, and elevator in the buildings was built to be automatically sealed off from the others, to isolate possible thieves, terrorists, or the merely suspicious.

Swiss banks were too discreet to allow publicity concerning their security systems, but it was known in law enforcement circles—and, Steel presumed, in the underworld—that once sealed off, each of the compartments was as secure as the best prison cells ever devised. Soundproof, bulletproof, able to resist substantial explosive charges, they could hold a fugitive for police without his disturbing the daily business conducted by the bank's other, legitimate, customers.

Steele looked at the door. He rubbed his moist palms against each other and then reached for the knob. Would the door be one that led ultimately to their freedom? Or would the people inside see them as the fugitives that they really were and trap them in some impenetrable room to await the arrival of the Swiss police? He had the uncomfortable feeling that this was not a place he wanted to go inside. He swallowed against the fear in his throat and pushed the door open for Stephanie.

"After you," he said. Stephanie smiled bravely and walked in.

The room was not at all like a bank. The room was about the size of a waiting room in a doctor's office. To one side were a sofa and two armchairs separated by a cocktail table. A brass lamp burned on an end table next to the sofa. They were standing on midnight-blue carpeting that seemed ankle deep and was decorated with a pattern composed of the bank's logo. The room was paneled in dark wood hung with hunting prints. A large man with blond hair sat behind a massive wooden desk at the far end of the room. He rose to greet them. It would all have been very corporate or ordinary had it not been for the fact that other than the door through which they had entered, there seemed to be no other way in or out of the room.

"You have business with us, sir?" the man said as he rose. He wore a dark, conservatively cut business suit, and as he came toward them, Steele noted that the suit had been expertly tailored to conceal the weapon the man carried under his left arm. The use of English was explained by the casual dress of the two visitors.

Swiss bankers knew that people dressed like that were usuall[y] American and usually curiosity seekers who wanted to tell thei[r] friends back home they had visited the gnomes in Zurich. But th[e] man's voice was deferential. For Swiss bankers also knew that fo[r] every score of curiosity seekers there was an extremely wealth[y] American who simply dressed inappropriately for the conduct o[f] financial business.

"I have confidential business to discuss," Steele said imperi[-] ously. "And I have very little time. I must see an officer imme[-] diately."

"Of course, sir," the man said as his eyes took in the cheapl[y] wrapped parcel and Stephanie's new—and obviously expensive— running shoes. He returned to his desk, plucked a telephone re[-] ceiver from a hidden access, and spoke into it so softly that hi[s] words were unintelligible.

The man replaced the telephone and turned his attention to th[e] couple. The Americans stood, apparently at ease, in the middle o[f] the reception room.

"The receptionist will see you now," the man said. And as h[e] spoke, a door, camouflaged by the joints in the room's dark pan[-] eling and hidden further by subdued lighting, opened behind th[e] desk. A tall, ascetically thin man with a Lenin beard and nav[y] pinstripes stepped from the door.

"Good afternoon," he said, with a polite but reserved voice. "[I] am Gunter Abels. How may I be of assistance?" He shook firs[t] Stephanie's hand and then Derek's.

"We have an account," Steele said, determined to brazen hi[s] way through. "A box whose access is determined by certain . . . arrangements." Steele looked about him. "I'd prefer to say n[o] more until we're in more . . . private accommodations."

Abels raised his eyebrows. "Of course," he replied obsequi[-] ously. "Pardon me, but . . . but we really have to be careful t[o] screen out those who have no bona-fide business here. Please. Fo[l-] low me."

Abels led them back through the door he had used to enter th[e] reception room. It led to an elevator. Abels entered last, closin[g] the paneled door that faced the reception area, then punched [a] button for the eighth floor. The doors slid smoothly shut and th[e] car moved upward. Steele avoided the receptionist's glance an[d] said nothing during the ride. Rich and powerful people, especially those who maintained accounts and boxes in Swiss banks, didn't usually fraternize with the help. Besides, they had been accepted, at least this far. Anything he might say could not help them, and could possibly raise suspicions. Rich people were quiet people and he decided to see if he could play that part of the role.

Stephanie followed Derek's lead and kept silent.

"To your left, please," Abels said, as the elevator slid open on the eighth floor. He held the elevator door while they exited. They were in another darkly paneled reception area, twin of one on the ground floor. Another heavy-set guard sat behind another massive wooden desk. Only this room had two corridors leading off both sides.

The guard respectfully returned Steele's glance as the trio got off the elevator.

Abels led them to a door at the end of the hall and unlocked it with a key he took from his pocket. The room, which occupied a corner of the building that overlooked the Bahnhofstrasse and the lake, was decorated in a tasteful opulence as if designed to please those who had a great deal of money but didn't want to spend it frivolously.

"Please make yourselves comfortable," Abels said, "while I notify one of our officers that you are here." Then, without waiting for a reply, he turned, executing a perfect military about-face, and left the room. The door slid shut as firmly and solidly as a vault door. Steele tried the knob. It was locked.

Steele and Stephanie looked silently about them. The room was the size of a luxury hotel room and furnished in much the same way. Besides the sofa and chairs, there was a television set, a rack of current magazines, a small computer terminal displaying financial quotes, and a wet bar stocked with liquor. Steele went to the wet bar, set the wrapped painting down on the counter, and filled a tumbler with water from a chilled bottle of Perrier.

"Some bank, huh?" Stephanie said with a false cheerfulness. "Security Pacific could learn a few things from these people."

Steele walked over to the window and looked down at the street. The Salvation Army was playing its heart out, competing for the odd franc here and there. "Maybe," he said tersely, "They're all

373

the same: bankers." He turned to look at her. "Honest people don't ever profit from dealing with bankers."

"My, we're touchy this afternoon," she said, half joking. She walked over to him.

"I'm sorry," he said, putting his hands on her shoulders. "I was just thinking about how this fellow Abels is falling all over himself in a half-swoon. But then he locks us in this room just to make sure. Bank procedure. They all have procedure. Bankers are all like a bunch of Nazis strutting around saying: *Ve haf our orders.* And when they screw you, accidentally or on purpose, it's always because they were just following orders."

He looked at her and saw the depth of patience in her eyes. She said: "It's good to know you haven't changed in the past six months."

Steele looked at her for a long moment, then laughed.

"Sorry," he said. "I'm a little nervous."

"I know," she said.

Just then, they heard a key grumble into the lock. It clicked open and a distinguished man with gray hair and a tightly clipped mustache entered the room. His face was patrician, his suit Savile Row. He spoke English with the terribly proper accent of one who had studied at the best of schools.

"Please forgive the delay," he said as he walked toward them. The door closed behind him. "I am Josef Mutters." He extended his hand. Steele took it and shook its warm firm grip. "I am a vice-president here at the Thule Gesellschaft Bank." He repeated the full name of the bank as if to help his two visitors make sure they were in the right bank. "What may I do for you?"

Steele retrieved the package from the wet bar.

"We wish access to our box," he said as he handed the package to Mutters.

For an instant, the vice-president looked at the roughly wrapped parcel as if it might contain some new American disease. Just as swiftly, though, his professionally obsequious face reassembled itself.

"May we sit for a moment?" he asked. Steele nodded and the three arranged themselves around the sofa. Mutters placed the parcel on the coffee table and began to unwrap it.

He stifled a short gasp of surprise when he saw the painting.

He looked at it silently for a long time. When he looked up again, the obsequious look in his eyes had turned to fear.

"After these many years," Mutters said, as much to himself as to his guests. He nodded to himself, confirming the inevitability of the painting as one confirms death when it finally arrives.

"My father made arrangements for this," Mutters said. "Back when such procedures were still legal. It was unusual, but he saw nothing illegal, and thus accommodated the customer." He looked at them sharply. "But then you must know all about that, don't you? After all, you have the painting."

Steele felt the hand of fear clutching at his intestines. Did the man suspect them? Would he ask them questions they couldn't answer? The police wouldn't be long.

"Of course we know all that," Steele snapped. "We didn't come here for a history lesson. We came to collect the contents of our box."

Mutter's gaze was intense. Steele could see the man's thoughts shifting in his eyes, evaluating, measuring, deciding.

"Of course," Mutters finally said. "Please forgive my lapse of manners. It's just that—" He looked at Steele. This time his eyes had the soft compliant texture of the servant. "This is the last of an era." His voice was nostalgic. "All of the other accounts with . . . unusual arrangement have all been converted to standard procedures. And Swiss law forbids us from re-instituting the practice." Mutters looked like a mourner lamenting the passing of a dear friend. He was silent for a moment. Then, abruptly, he stood.

"By your leave," he said formally. "I must gather a number of items to proceed." Steele nodded and Mutters quickly left the room.

The vaultlike thud the door made each time it closed had begun to play on Steele's nerves. He cracked open a bottle of red Bordeaux and poured glasses for Stephanie and himself. They drank mostly in silence.

Mutters returned just as Steele had filled their glasses the second time. Mutters held the door open as Abels pushed in a small wheeled metal cabinet with a counter-height work surface. In one hand, the vice-president held a sheet of paper and a torn envelope from which the paper had obviously come. He followed Abels into the room and had him position the cart next to the window over-looking the lake.

Abels left and the door made its irritating vault sound again.

Still holding the paper and envelope, Mutters walked over to where Steele and Stephanie still sat. He glanced at the bottle. "An excellent choice," Mutters said. "One of the finest wines available."

"Not bad," Steele replied unimpressed. "Not bad at all."

Mutters picked up the painting from the table. "Shall we proceed with the arrangements," he said.

Steele nodded, placed his glass on the coffee table, then joined Mutters at the cart Abels had brought. Stephanie came up beside him.

They watched as Mutters looked at the paper, placed it and the painting on the work surface of the cart, then unlocked the cabinet doors. He looked at the paper again.

From a shelf in the cabinet he pulled a bottle of turpentine, a rag, and a gray metal safe deposit box. It, too, had a small padlock securing its opening.

Without rolling up his sleeves or even taking off his coat, Mutters opened the bottle of turpentine, drenched the rag with it, and began wiping at the surface of the painting.

Stephanie's breath caught at the back of her throat. Steele's eyes widened, but he gripped her forearm gently to warn her to be silent.

The decades-old paint softened slowly. It had been applied in some places with a spatula and Mutters had to use cloth after cloth to remove the stubborn pigments. The colors ran and smeared to a streaky brown. But finally, after nearly twenty minutes of work, the surface began to change.

"Ah!" Mutters said cryptically, and kept on rubbing.

First one shiny gold spot and then another appeared in the middle of the painting.

Ten minutes later, Mutters was through. He had exposed a gold ingot fixed into a recess of the wood substrate on which the paint had been applied. The ingot was the size of the broad side of a pack of cigarettes. Mutters held it up for them both to see. The ingot was embossed with a series of letters and numbers: the stamp of the foundry certifying the gold as .99999 fine, the weight of the ingot—.25 kg—and the swastika, eagle, and lightning bolts of the SS. Stephanie gasped.

"I believe this is what you were expecting, is it not?" Mutters directed his question at Steele.

"What . . . ah—yes. Yes!" Steele said, trying to hide his surprise. "Exactly what I was expecting."

Mutters held the block of wood out for Steele to hold. "Careful," Mutters said. "It might still have some soft paint around the edges."

Steele took the object from Mutters and held it up to the light. He held his breath, a sharp pain forming in his stomach as he gazed at the swastika pressed into the gold. The tangible symbol of evil brought home to him the awful web that had ensnared them.

He handed the object back to Mutters. The bank vice-president picked up the paper he had carried into the room. As he did, the envelope fell to the carpeting. Steele reached down and picked it up. He noticed then the name on the return address. It was that of Hermann Goering. Below the Berlin address, there was a single word: "Instructions." Steele's hand trembled as he placed the paper back on the table.

Mutters looked at the paper that had come out of the envelope once again, and then, taking a short-bladed knife, pried the ingot from its recess in the wood. Beneath it was a key. He pried the key from its slot and handed it to Steele.

"This is your key to the box," Mutters said. "And this," he handed Steele the gold ingot with the numbers and letter showing, "is your account number. It matches exactly the number as presented in the instructions we were given by the . . ." he cast a searching glance at Steele " . . . gentleman who opened the account and left a trust for its maintenance in perpetuity."

Steele accepted the ingot and the key hesitantly. He could not picture so evil a figure as Hermann Goering holding the very same items.

"Well, let's proceed," Steele said impatiently.

"Of course," Mutters said. "I'm afraid, though, that the access numbers embossed in the gold indicate a Priority One account."

Steele felt his heart wrench. "Which means what?"

"It means that we are not allowed to remove the box from the vault without your presence." Steele relaxed as Mutters continued. "It's highly unusual. Normally, we would bring your box to you here"—he looked around the room—"or in one of the other examination rooms. But with a Priority One account, you must be there to actually witness the unlocking of the box space."

Steele nodded. "Let's not waste any more time."

Mutters grabbed his page of instructions, then led them back to the elevator and pressed an unmarked button.

"This takes us to our deepest vault level. The most secure."

Steele nodded, trying to affect the self-centered disinterest in which the rich usually enshrouded themselves. Somehow it seemed to comfort Mutters.

From the elevator, they walked along a brown marble floor, past corridor after corridor lined with safe deposit boxes of varying sizes.

After descending a flight of stairs, they found themselves facing a bank of large safe deposit boxes, some as large as an office file drawer. Mutters stepped back from the bank of boxes and bent backwards, hands placed in the small of his back as he scanned the numbers from ceiling to floor. He spotted the right number immediately.

"There," he said, pointing with his finger. He indicated a box, about four feet off the floor, whose door looked more than a foot wide and six inches high. Stephanie and Steele stepped closer to examine the box. Both locks were sealed with a thin gold foil.

"Please examine them closely to be assured that no key has ever penetrated the locks since the seal was applied," Mutters said.

The seals were intact.

"Shall we proceed?" Mutters asked. Steele nodded and handed Mutters the key that had been hidden for forty years under the gold ingot. The ingot rested uneasily against his thigh, tugging at the fabric of his trouser pocket.

Steele held his breath as Mutters inserted first the bank's key and then the one from the painting through the foil seals and into the locks. He turned both simultaneously and the lock clicked upen. Mutters opened the door to reveal a standard metal safe deposit box container. He reached in, slid the box from the recess where it had lain undisturbed for more than four decades, then held it out for them to see: The lid was secured with four thick gold seals;

these, like the gold ingot, embossed with the seal of the SS. Mutters looked at the seals and at Steele. His face remained expressionless, the look of a man who has seen everything once and is waiting for a second time.

"Would you like me to take it back to the viewing room for you?"

Steele nodded his assent. As he and Stephanie followed Mutters back out of the vaults, Steele looked at the rows of boxes and wondered what other evils were stored within. Were there people being killed right now for the boxes' contents? The thought made him shiver.

CHAPTER THIRTY

The viewing room had still smelled faintly of turpentine, although the work cart had been removed by the time Mutters had brought them back. He had left immediately afterwards. Impatiently, they had torn at the seals of the box, and found, inside, a metal briefcase of the sort used to protect cameras and electronic instruments. It had an elaborate combination lock that yielded when the numbers were set with the same numbers in the bank account number.

The contents of the briefcase covered the coffee table: papers, many with seals; documents from the Reichschancellery and the Vatican; bound instruction books relating to a fortified installation; the blueprint of that installation identified only as "Habersam Facility"; microfilm labeled "historic testimony, originals at Habersam Facility"; and photographs, scores of photographs.

Steele nervously handed one of the photographs to Stephanie. "No wonder they were willing . . . are still willing to kill for the painting," he said.

Stephanie took the photograph. Printed on expensive sulphur-free paper, a fine-grained image of a face stared back at her. The face was the shadowy image of a young woman or girl in death, the expression a peaceful one of relief as if a great suffering had just ended. Stephanie was struck by the power of the face, the depth of its expression. She felt a kinship with that expression, for it evoked deep within her the same feelings she had felt when Nat Worthington finally placed her in the van and drove her away from the warehouse. Added to the information they had just read about Veronica's Shroud, a shroud containing a female image, the photograph went a long way toward explaining why they were in their present predicament.

"I can't believe it," Stephanie said. "Hitler blackmailed the Pope into silence on the Nazi atrocities."

"Believe it," Steele said. "Here's the document that proves it."

He fished through the mess on the table and pulled out a document, the agreement that guaranteed the Catholic Church's silence, in exchange for which Hitler guaranteed the safety of the Vatican and agreed not to make public any of the evidence relating to Veronica's Shroud. At the bottom, verified by the seals of the Vatican and the Third Reich, were the signatures of Pope Pius XII and Adolf Hitler.

Stephanie laid the photograph back on the table on top of the other images of the shroud.

"What have we got caught up in?" she asked.

Steele shook his head. "Some things make more sense now," he said. "The priest in Amsterdam said his group was trying to prevent abuses . . . of this sort?" He waved his hand over the cluttered table. "But what I don't understand is why the Russians are so hot to get the information. And what's Gerry Anderson's interest?"

"Probably in the Russians," Stephanie said.

They both stared at the material on the table. It seemed overwhelming: the cover-up of a female Messiah by an emperor and a pope, the discovery of the shroud and supporting documents by Hermann Goering, the blackmailing of a pope. People killed by the dozen, by the score, across the centuries from the days of Constantine to the present.

"What do we do now?" Stephanie asked.

"Go to Altaussee, I suppose," Steele said. "We can't stay here for very long. The police would like to nail us. Maybe a little town in Austria is a good place to hide out until we can figure out exactly how to get out of this mess."

"It would also give us a chance to look at this material more closely. We've only scratched the surface."

Steele nodded, bent over the table, and started to sweep the piles of papers into his briefcase.

* * *

The entire business had taken more than two hours. Anderson would be impatient and worried by now. They would collect him from the restaurant, take the Volvo, and drive to Alt Aussee. There, an old priest named Werner Meyer would help them find some answers. And in those answers there had to be solutions: a way to stop the killing that followed the shroud, a way to exonerate Steele of the murder charges. There had to be a way. There had to be.

Steele held Stephanie's hand as he followed Mutters out to the elevator. Out of the corner of his eye Steele saw two men at the end of the hallway walking toward them. He looked at them closely. One of them looked familiar, but Steele couldn't remember from where. Cops and professors—and hunted men—see a lot of faces in their lives.

Mutters nodded at the men and smiled as the elevator doors began to open. He seemed to know the men. The man on the right stuck his hand into his coat, and when it appeared again, it was holding an automatic pistol with a long tubular cylinder attached to its muzzle. Steele felt his insides grow cold; a small gasp of surprise escaped from Stephanie's mouth. The man with the gun stopped suddenly about twenty feet from them and raised the weapon.

"No—" was all Mutters could say before the man shot him. The killer than trained his gun on Steele.

Operating on instinct, Steele shoved Stephanie into the elevator car and frantically punched the button marked *"zumachen."* From the hallway came the sounds of running feet muted by the tasteful plush carpeting. Still the door failed to close.

Steele grabbed Stephanie by the upper arm and pushed her into the corner of the elevator by the control panel. Stephanie watched as Steele gripped the handle of the black metal briefcase with both hands and hefted it like an Olympic hammer thrower. "Don't move," he said. He swung the case tentatively at first, then planted his feet firmly and put his entire weight behind it just as the gunman's head entered.

The metal briefcase was heavy with the papers and documents inside. The apex of one sharp corner caught the killer just above his left ear, the metal edge easily penetrating the thin soft flesh. The next instant, a soggy cracking sound filled the interior of the car as the momentum of the heavy papers packed in the briefcase shattered the man's skull and split the side of his head open like a rotten melon.

The silenced automatic flew out of the killer's hand and clattered against the elevator wall. Steele kept his grip on the briefcase as the man's body sagged, then fell heavily, torso in the car and legs in the corridor. The elevator doors finally began to close, slamming repeatedly against the body.

Steele tossed the bloodied briefcase towards Stephanie as he lunged for the killer's weapon. As the elevator doors slammed into the man's kidneys again, then retracted, Steele saw the second man speaking into a small hand-held radio. There were more of them. But where?

The man saw Steele's gun and quickly stepped close to the wall, out of the line of fire. The elevator closed again against the fallen killer and Steele stooped to get a grip on the body. As he hauled it into the car, the doors slammed against the man's ankles and again retracted.

When the doors opened fully, the second man was standing there, and instead of the radio, he was holding a pistol, the twin of the one Steele now held. For an instant the two men stared at each other, dumb and surprised. Then each raised his weapon and brought it to bear. Steele was a split second faster and a hair more accurate. He felt the pistol recoil firmly in his hand once, twice, and then dived to safety. As the doors closed firmly this time, Steele caught a glimpse of the man as he fell to his knees and then went face first onto the carpet.

As the elevator descended, Steele rolled the dead killer's body over and found two additional clips for the automatic. He stuffed them into his trouser pockets.

"Who . . ." Stephanie's voice cracked. She cleared her throat and tried again. "Who were they?"

Steele shook his head and continued his search of the dead man's body. He pulled out the man's wallet and flipped it open. There was a thick wad of currency: Swiss francs, Austrian shillings, a scattering of German marks. Among the stack of credit cards, Steele found a photo I.D. that identified him as Bernhard Saltzer, an employee of the Thule Gesellschaft Bank.

He held the card up for Stephanie to see. "Herr Mutters wasn't the only person here prepared to service those who came for the contents of that box.''

The elevator began to slow at the ground floor. "Here, keep this," he said handing her the man's wallet. The elevator stopped and the doors slid open. Steele picked up the metal briefcase and pushed at the door that would detach itself from the paneled wall in the reception room. Steele stepped from the elevator. Next to him the guard was slumped over his massive wooden desk, blood streaming from a small round hole in his temple.

Sitting at the sofa was a man dressed in a black uniform with red piping. It took Steele a second to recognize one of the Salvation Army band members. Another stood by the front door to the reception room. Both men looked surprised to see Steele. They froze for an instant.

The Salvation Army band member sitting on the sofa raised an ugly device that Steele recognized as a H&K MP5A. Steele stepped quickly back into the recesses of the elevator, stumbling over Stephanie as he did. They tangled feet and fell to the floor just as slugs from the H&K thudded dully into the paneled walls of the elevator car.

"Schnell! Schnell!"—Quickly! Quickly!—Steele heard his assailant shout. Steele untangled himself from Stephanie and, aiming from his knees, fired a shot at the onrushing killer with the machine pistol. The shot slapped into the man's belly and straightened him up, his face a mask of wide-eyed surprise. Apparently no one had told him he would have to deal with an armed adversary. Steele took advantage of the man's surprise and fired again. most of the man's right eye vanished in a spray of red and pink.

Stephanie climbed to her feet and punched every button on the elevator's control panel. As the elevator doors started to close, Steele fired again and again at the second Salvation Army band member. The automatic ran out of ammunition as the doors closed. Steele sighed as the car began to ascend.

"Where are we headed?" he asked her, as he turned the pistol over in his hand and tried to locate the clip release.

"Up," Stephanie said. Steele slammed a fresh ammunition clip into the grip of the pistol. "Some of the lower floors have to be offices," she explained. "And where there are offices, there have to be fire escapes."

The elevator doors opened into a large cavernous room punctuated by glass-topped dividers. The room was filled with the quiet busy chatter of computers, calculators, printers, and the business of money. Steele quickly concealed the gun in the waistband of his trousers.

Stephanie took in the scene, then stepped past Steele into the room. She walked over to a red fire alarm on the wall and pulled it. A bell began to ring. She screamed: "Fire! Fire! Fire!"

An anxious murmur rumbled across the vast room. People began to rise from their seats. Steele grabbed the briefcase and joined Stephanie. "Fire! We must get out! Fire!" The murmur rose to a loud excited babble. Some of the workers began to gather things from their desks; women went for their purses. A tall man with authority engraved in his face stalked up to them.

"Look here," he said angrily. "What's the meaning of this?"

"Fire on the first floor," Steele said brazenly. "I'm an associate of Josef Mutters." The man stiffened at the name of his superior. "He told me to come and evacuate the floor."

"This is highly irregular," the man replied. "I really must speak with Vice-President Mutters himself." He moved purposefully toward a telephone. The room, however, had erupted into chaos as people pushed and jostled toward an open door in a far corner. An alarm bell, no doubt actuated when the emergency exit had been opened, infected the room with a virulent sense of urgency. Stephanie and Steele joined the masses of people, who were now near panic.

At the bottom of the fire escape stairs, the crowd milled about in a broad courtyard connected by alleys to other streets. The people were confused and hung about, talking in small groups. Many among the group complained loudly that they couldn't see any smoke, some speculated that it must be another fire drill.

Derek and Stephanie detached themselves from the crowd and walked slowly down one of the alleyways leading away from the Bahnhofstrasse. Wailing sirens grew louder—fire trucks no doubt, and perhaps police cars as well, if the bodies had been discovered.

The alley led them to a quiet street in the heart of Zurich's old medieval quarter. They walked silently, each too stunned to talk. A half-hour later they reached the underground parking garage on the Sihlstrasse where they had left the Volvo Worthington had rented.

"What about Anderson?" Stephanie asked, as Steele locked the briefcase in the truck.

"He'll find out what went on," Steele said. "He has his ways." He unlocked the front passenger door and held it open for her. "He's the only person who knows we're going to Altaussee. So we'll go to Altaussee. From what I understand, it's a small enough town. It shouldn't be too hard for Americans to find each other there in the dead of winter. Besides, if we can find this Father Meyer, so can he.

Stephanie climbed into the front seat, turning as she did to look up at Steele. "Derek, I . . . I don't know if I can take much more of this."

Steele put his hand gently on her cheek.

"It's difficult, Steph. I know. But we have to follow this thing through to the end. There's no other way. Anyway, what's important is that we're together again. Right?"

Stephanie's eyes brightened.

"Right."

CHAPTER THIRTY-ONE

"They got away." Gerry Anderson squirmed uncomfortably in a telephone booth at the Zurich airport. At the telephone next to him, a mousy woman with four children was arguing in shrill tones with her husband, something about her mother and his mother. Meanwhile the four children, all under the age of four or five, crawled about like small animals, thoroughly investigating everything from floor level up to three feet. Twice, one of them had tried to shinny up Anderson's leg. The attempts had left chocolate handprints on his gray worsted slacks. He shook his foot gently now, trying to discourage yet a third attempt at scaling his leg.

"How?" asked the voice on the other end of the line.

Anderson explained. The voice on the other end murmured sympathetic sounds. To Anderson's relief, Archbishop Cardinal Neils Braun did not sound upset.

"I'll be able to pick up their trail in Alt Aussee," Anderson said.

"If you get to them before the police do," Braun said. "They may be picked up if their passports are checked at the border."

Anderson was silent.

"I can probably do something about it from the Austrian side," Braun continued. Anderson didn't know what to say. His cheeks burned with embarrassment.

"Yes, your grace," he finally said. "That will help."

"Perhaps," Braun said, letting Anderson stew on purpose. "You had better hope so."

Anderson swallowed hard and jerked his right shoe away as a

small girl of three or four spilled a paper cup of fruit juice. He stretched the telephone cord out to its maximum trying to get away from the harassed mother and her brood.

"So they're going to see Meyer, are they?" Braun asked.

"That's what they said their plans were. Would you like something done with him too?"

"We seem to be dealing with very clever people," Braun said. "Steele and his wife slip away from you and every other professional we assign to them. Meyer eludes those in Munich assigned to watch him." Braun paused. In the silence, Anderson listened to the airport public address system rattling off flights soon to depart. His flight to Salzburg was among those described in three languages.

" . . . perhaps a blessing they fouled up your plans in Zurich," Braun was saying.

"How's that, your grace?" Anderson asked.

"If you had succeeded, Steele and his wife would be dead now, and you would have the copy of the Linz testaments, would you not?"

Anderson murmured his agreement.

"And Meyer is in Altaussee, no doubt along with his foolish cadre of heretics, keeping watch on the mine." Anderson again agreed. "They have proven themselves to be a substantial impediment to our tasks in the past. They might have proven to be such if you and your team showed up alone to retrieve the shroud without Steele and his wife.

"This way, you have the opportunity to retrieve the shroud and the originals of the Linz testaments, *and* to expose and eliminate Steele, his wife, Meyer and all of his followers. Do you see?"

"Clearly," Anderson agreed. "You want me to actually obtain the testaments and shroud before killing them."

"Correct." Braun confirmed. "And you are sure they don't suspect you? That's not why they ran away?"

'No, your grace. You should have heard Derek Steele describing his debt to me to his wife. He apologized for eluding me earlier, promised to let me know everything. In fact, I'll be surprised if he doesn't call in soon on the contact number I gave him."

"Wonderful," Braun said. "Goodbye, Gerry. I trust I will be

seeing you and the testaments soon." He hung up without giving Anderson a chance to reply.

Braun replaced the receiver in its cradle and exited his private quarters. He continued down the hallway to Robert Maxwell's room and rapped faintly on the door. He heard stirring within and in a few moments a distinguished-looking man with a thick shock of gray hair and intelligent blue eyes that stared at the world through gold-rimmed glasses came to the door. The man wore a physician's white coat. The earpieces of his stethoscope protruded from his right pocket. In his left hand he carried a black bag.

The doctor stepped quietly into the hallway and pulled the door shut behind him with only a faint clicking of the latch.

"How's he progressing?" Braun asked as he began walking back toward his study.

"Coming along well," the doctor said in a troubled voice. "Very well, in fact." They walked several paces before the doctor spoke again. "But I don't like this. Not at all."

Braun gave him a bland look and then paused to open the door of his study. The doctor entered first and remained standing while Braun made his way behind his desk and sat down.

"Sit," he told the doctor. The physician sagged obediently into a chair. "Now, what is it that you don't like?"

"All . . . all of this." He waved his hand about in the air. "This business of your involvement with the behavior alteration. It's too dangerous to just inject him and leave him in your hands. I really must be there during the imprinting. He could suffer a severe psychosis if he's not handled right. If he were to find out that his 'flu' were actually drug-induced to lower his resistance, he . . ." The doctor seemed to lose interest in his sentence. He sat there and looked at Braun like a petulant schoolboy complaining to the school headmaster.

"He what, doctor?"

"He might . . . it might induce something like schizophrenia. I've never known this sort of drug-induced schizophrenia to be reversible."

Braun nodded patiently. "But that won't happen. Am I not right that the schizophrenia sometimes sparked by drug-induced persuasion usually occurs in people without strong belief systems to anchor their emotions?''

"Almost always."

"And haven't you been the one to tell me that strong religious beliefs make it easier to imprint information and behavior patterns because individuals who have them are *used* to acting on faith and accustomed to taking direction from a higher authority?''

The doctor nodded.

"Then I submit we have a perfect specimen and are unlikely to run into trouble."

The doctor shrugged. "Still—"

"Still nothing, doctor," Braun snapped. "You know very well I'm right. Don't try to back out on me now. You know that's impossible." The doctor looked at him for a long time, then lowered his gaze and nodded.

"I think we have a meeting of the minds again, doctor," Braun said, his face betraying a certain smugness. "I don't think we'll have to continue the imprinting for much longer. Maxwell's a strong believer."

The doctor got up. "Very well. I'll return tomorrow at the usual time. But I don't think its right."

"Does it really matter?" Braun asked.

Emotions flashed in the doctor's eyes: anger, frustration, hopelessness. He knew there was no point in continuing. Braun would get his way. He always did. Past indiscretions had ensured the doctor's cooperation, no matter what the consequences. "No," he said as Braun led him out of the office. "No, I suppose not."

CHAPTER THIRTY-TWO

Derek and Stephanie arrived in Altaussee on the morning before Christmas Eve. A heavy snow had begun just before dawn and had grown heavier as the day wore on.

The road from Bad Aussee was narrow and followed every twist and turn of a small creek that flowed toward the lake. By the time they reached Altaussee, they had slowed to less than twenty miles per hour. Snow caked on the windshield and turned to ice where the ends of the wipers couldn't reach.

They checked in at the Kohlbacherhof, a small *Gasthaus* at the edge of town adjacent to a small church. Steele used the innkeeper's telephone to call the Washington number that Anderson had given him. The man at the other end informed him that Anderson was not near a telephone, but that he would receive Steele's message as soon as he checked in.

Next, Stephanie called Tel Aviv to check on Nat. They had taken him to surgery. The nurse on the other end took the number at the Kohlbacherhof and promised to give it to Nat. The surgery, she added, was only under a local anesthetic and Nat would be back in his room in a matter of an hour or so. Finally, huddling under an umbrella against the wet snow, they walked the quarter of a mile from the *Gasthaus* to the center of town. Only a tractor pulling a wagon loaded with hay passed them during their walk. The farmer, bundled against the cold, waved at them as he passed.

Otherwise, they saw no one else until they arrived at the center of Altaussee. They passed several small stores: a hardware, clothing, and a shop that sold toys, books, and sundries. All of the

391

stores were housed in individual one-story frame or stone buildings set along the road and separated from one another by narrow alleys or driveways. All of the stores were closed. Christmas had begun for the gentle villagers of Altaussee.

About fifty yards past the book and toy store, they found a combination police station and post office set in a two-story building made of rough gray stone. When Steele tried the door of the building, however, he found it was locked.

"Where now?" Steele wondered aloud.

They stood in front of the building for a moment and turned to look about them. More stores lined the main street on both sides. But, like the three stores they had already passed, most of them looked closed, their windows dark and gloomy. A farm truck, its cab rusted and patched with pieces of metal cut from cans, rattled down the main street past them, etching fresh tire tracks in the snow-covered roadway. Its driver, too, waved at them. They waved back and watched as the truck began to disappear into the thick shroud of snow. But before it vanished, its one working brake light burned brightly as it pulled over to the curb. Steele and Stephanie squinted into the cottony blanket that covered the town and saw, just beyond the truck, light coming from the windows of a building. They watched as the driver got out of his truck and walked into the building.

"Shall we?" Stephanie said, taking a tentative step toward the truck.

"Might as well," Steele agreed, following her. "It looks like the only inhabited place in town." As they got closer, they could discern the outlines of a small cafe and beer hall. They pushed on across the street.

By the time they got to the farmer's truck, the tracks it had left in the snow were already obliterated. Parked in front of the truck at the curb were a battered Mercedes and a brand new Fiat.

They stopped in front of a restaurant. It had a steep peaked roof and windows composed of scores of small diamond-shaped panes set in a dark wood lattice. Snow had gathered in the lower portions of the diamond shapes and left them with the natural decorations that Americans tried so hard to imitate with aerosol cans of fake plastic snow.

Through the window, they watched the farmer greet the people inside. Two uniformed policemen sat at one table nursing cups of coffee and shot glasses filled with a clear liquid, probably schnapps. They accounted for the locked door of the police station across the street. Three more people—rough, heavy types with red faces and the dirndl green clothes of the Alps sat at a large picnic-type table with benches along either side. They drank from nearly empty beer steins.

The innkeeper and a dumpling-shaped woman who had to be his wife stood behind the bar and greeted the new arrival with broad smiles and waves of their hands.

Derek and Stephanie went through the door and traded the crisp cold world of snow for a warm one, redolent with the yeasty aroma of beer, the spicy, slightly sulfurous aroma of cabbage wursts in all their many German permutations, and the humid earthy odors of human beings warming up, drying out after a bout with inclement weather. All heads turned as they walked through the door. The looks they got were not unfriendly, Steele noted. Just curious. Alt Aussee was a place where the roads came to an end before dwindling into footpaths that led into the rugged hills and mountains beyond. Strangers didn't often come to such a place on Christmas Eve.

"*Grüss Gott,*" Steele said, offering them the traditional Austrian greeting.

"*Grüss Gott,*" came a ragged chorus of replies. Derek and Stephanie walked to the bar behind which the proprietor and his wife stood. As Steele crossed the floor, he noticed a wizened old man sitting by himself in the corner of the cafe, nursing a half liter mug of beer.

"May I help you?" the proprietor offered in the soft accents of the Austrian countryside that made German sound almost lyrical.

"Yes, please," Steele replied. "I hope you can help. We're looking . . . looking for a man. Father Meyer." He saw the proprietor's face stiffen almost imperceptibly. "Do you know him?" Steele asked.

"Yes." The proprietor's answer was slow. "I know him . . . I know *of* him." The man said nothing more. Steele felt the eyes of the people behind him boring into his back. When he finally spoke, his voice was shaky. "Have . . . have you seen him?"

The proprietor looked at him seriously for several moments and then laughed cheerlessly.

"Yes, I have seen him." He paused. "I was a small child the last time I saw him. I do not believe I have seen him since then." He paused again. "That would have been in the last weeks of the war."

Steele nodded slowly and turned.

The two policemen sat at their table silently and eyed him with the suspicion that guardians of law and order everywhere have for the unusual.

"Officers," Steele began, his voice even more unsteady. "Have you any idea where I might find Father Meyer?" Both men shook their heads wordlessly. Again Steele nodded.

"But where would he stay if he were to visit here?" Stephanie had turned back to the proprietor and his wife.

They shook their heads in unison before the man answered: "At the Kohlbacherhof perhaps," he replied. "Or perhaps at the old inn." He looked at the wall of his cafe that faced north. "It's a few miles from here. Up the road."

Stephanie waited, but the man was apparently finished talking. "Well," she said tentatively. "Thank you for your . . . information."

They left the cafe and began walking slowly back toward the Kohlbacherhof.

The snow fell finer and heavier now.

"I can't believe it's so hard to find one old man in a place this tiny," Stephanie said.

"They know where he is," Steele said quietly.

"Why do you say that?"

"Didn't you see the looks on their faces?" Steele said. "They were friendly when we walked in and as soon as we said we were looking for Father Meyer, a wall dropped. Their faces turned to stone."

"But why?" Stephanie asked.

"They're protecting him," he said. "That's why."

"Pardon me." The voice came unexpectedly from behind them. Steele and Stephanie whirled to face the old man who had been nursing his beer in the corner of the cafe.

"You were inquiring about Father Meyer?" asked the man.

"Father Werner Meyer? Would that be the priest who had been rector at the village church until the Germans shot him at the end of the war?"

"Yes, it would," Steele replied.

"I know Father Meyer," the old man said. "Perhaps I can help you."

The old man was stooped and bent, but even so, his head was nearly level with Steele's. He had apparently been quite tall in his prime. His unruly shock of gray hair made him resemble Einstein in his Princeton days.

"My name is Gunther," the old man said. He held his bare hand out for Steele. Steele took the hand and shook it.

"I'm Derek Steele. And this is my wife, Stephanie."

The man who called himself Gunther bowed and took Stephanie's hand. For a moment she thought he was going to kiss it, but he merely shook it and then let it drop.

"I can introduce you to Father Meyer," he said. "I will call you." He turned then, and with surprising speed for an old man, walked back toward the cafe.

From his hospital room in Tel Aviv, Nat Worthington could see the Mediterranean. He had to hand it to the Mossad. They had him in surgery with the best of doctors just minutes after getting off the plane from Zurich. The KGB had used "dirty" bullets, the doctors later told him. The slugs had been treated with a virulent form of bacteria calculated to infect a wounded person with a potent form of septicemia—blood poisoning.

A few more hours, the doctors had told him, and he would have been beyond help.

He shifted the telephone receiver from his right hand to his left, struggling to get a better view from the window. His leg throbbed with every tiny movement. But the view of the blue Mediterranean waters was worth the pain. Outside, the setting sun set the water ablaze, rippling fire that danced in the distance. Silhouetted against the day's dying fire was an Israeli frigate patrolling the coast.

* * *

"You're positive?" Nat spoke into the telephone. The Mossad's technical crew had rigged up a scrambler phone and secured him a safe line.

"Absolutely," came the reply, a bit garbled. The distortion was not surprising, considering that the man's voice on the other end had been encoded by a computer, chopped into tiny electronic hash, broadcast into outer space, snared by a satellite, rebroadcast across an ocean, a sea, and the European continent, and reassembled into something resembling human speech at the other end.

Worthington's correspondent worked at a little-known NSA installation just beyond the runway at Baltimore's Friendship Airport. Worthington had known the man years before, when Nat worked for the CIA. The man was honest, outspoken, and brilliant. That was why the NSA brass had exiled him to a crowded little office that shook and vibrated every time a jet took off from Friendship. It was also why Nat trusted him.

"Absolutely sure," the man in Baltimore repeated himself. "Gerry Anderson absolutely did *not* have authority to use the motel safe-house. As far as I can tell, control at Fort Meade thinks he's tracking SIGNINT leaks from NATO bases in West Germany. If he's doing what you say he's doing, the man's a rogue and we'd better stop him."

Worthington agreed with the man, but not for the same reason. His NSA contact saw a rogue agent that had to be reined in. Worthington saw Derek and Stephanie Steele putting their lives in Anderson's hands. As he exchanged parting pleasantries with his NSA source and replaced the telephone on its base, Worthington heaved a heavy sigh and once again cursed the wound that had left him immobilized.

"The Kohlbacherhof?" Gerry Anderson repeated the name into the receiver of the pay telephone. He glanced quickly around him, but saw no one at the autobahn road stop more threatening than two young college students who had just gotten off a motorcycle. He could tell by the way they walked that they were lovers.

"Yes," he told his contact in Washington who had taken Steele's phone call. "Yes, I have that. Would you repeat the telephone

396

number again?'' He nodded to himself as he wrote down the numbers in a small red leather-covered notebook.

"Message?'' Anderson responded to the voice in the earpiece. "Yes. Tell him we will meet in Altaussee.''

He hung up the phone and walked from the booth. Outside, the rented BMW shone like black heat even in the snow. He got into the car and cautiously pulled into westbound traffic. There was no need to hurry. They would be there when he arrived. Still, he felt an urgency in the pit of his stomach. They would be his soon, and with them the bolt of cloth Braun coveted most.

The call came at precisely 7 P.M. Stephanie and Steele were sitting in the basement restaurant and *bierstube* of the Kohlbacherhof talking with the owner's son, a youth of seventeen or eighteen, when the telephone behind the bar rang. The teenager answered the telephone.

"It is for you, Mein Herr,'' he said. Steele walked behind the bar and put the receiver to his ear.

"Yes?''

"Herr Steele? It's me, Gunther. I believe I can help you. That is, some friends of mine may be able to help you meet with Father Meyer.''

"He's here in Altaussee, then?''

Gunther remained silent. "They may be able to help you. Would you be willing to meet them?''

"Of course,'' Steele said.

"Wonderful,'' said Gunther. "Leave the Kohlbacherhof and walk down the main road, toward town. Before you get to town, at the point where the road splits, there is a small shop that sells toys, books—''

"I know the one,'' Steele interrupted. "We passed it earlier today.''

"Good,'' Gunther said. "Meet me outside that store.''

"When?'' Steele asked.

"Now.''

"Now?''

"Have you better ways to spend your evening in Altaussee?'' The man's voice was laced with sarcasm.

"No. No, of course not,'' Steele replied.

"Good," Gunther replied. "My friends are eager to meet with you. Come right away."

He hung up. Steele paid for the beer he and Stephanie had been drinking and then explained the conversation to her as they returned to their room to fetch their coats.

They walked outside. The snow had slacked off to a fine powder sifting down from the sky. The temperature had dropped and the snow squeaked underfoot as they walked.

"Should we take the briefcase?" Stephanie asked, as they walked up the short driveway of the inn to the main road. Steele shook his head. "Let's meet these people first."

They reached the toy/bookstore five minutes later and stood about, stamping their feet as if the cold was an insect that could be tramped to death under the soles of their boots.

A few moments later, something hard jabbed into Steele's ribs from behind. The sound of a car engine starting filled the night.

"Don't make any quick movements, Mr. and Mrs. Steele." He didn't recognize the voice. It was not Gunther's. The battered Mercedes they had seen parked in front of the cafe earlier pulled to the curb. Steele turned his head to catch a glimpse of the license plates, but could see nothing through the glare of the headlights.

"Get into the back seat," said a voice in his ear. The back door swung open. Steele looked as Stephanie opened her mouth as if to scream. Swiftly, a gloved hand clamped itself over her mouth. She began to struggle. Steele moved to help her and a blunt heavy blow slammed into the back of his head.

The blow didn't render him unconscious, but merely cut his legs out from under him.

"That was unwise," a voice said as they were hustled into the back of the car. "There's no need for alarm." There was no threat in the voice. As soon as Steele and Stephanie were inside the car, the doors slammed and it began to move forward.

"I am going to cover your eyes," said a voice. Steele tried to turn his head to the source of the voice but the splitting pain in his head arrested his movement. Moments later, hands pulled what seemed to be a thick black sock over his head. The cloth was opaque, yet thin enough to breathe through without difficulty.

"Please relax," the voice told them. "We don't intend to harm you."

The ache in Steele's head made the words hard to believe. He remembered the killers he had encountered in Zurich, in Amsterdam, in Marina del Rey. He tried to console himself with the thought that, unlike those men, these had merely tried to capture him, not kill him. It didn't offer him much consolation.

The car made its way on paved road for about five minutes, then began to pitch and rattle as it slowed for a rough surface. They were thrown about in the back seat and somehow Steele found Stephanie's hand. He squeezed and she squeezed back. Strength, comfort, hope, love. They communicated all these things wordlessly as the old Mercedes banged its way slowly into the darkness.

After what seemed like half an hour the Mercedes stopped. They were led out of the car and placed, still blindfolded, into another seat, this one hard and cold. Instants later, the sounds of a small engine roared to life in front of them. Steele recognized it as a snowmobile engine.

They started to move and, still holding Stephanie's hand, Steele imagined that they were in some sort of sled being towed by the snowmobile.

They went for another half hour, mostly slowly through brush that plucked at their clothes.

"Duck your heads," they were warned once as they obviously went under some low-hanging objects.

Finally they stopped on a level area and the snowmobile engine died in the night. They were led through the snow. A door opened. Warm air enveloped them as they were led into a room. They heard the door close behind them.

Steele heard a voice say: "Take off their blindfolds," and the sock was pulled off his head. He didn't have to squint to adjust his eyes, for the only light in the room came from a kerosene lantern and a wood fire burning in a crude stone fireplace. Steele looked about him. The room looked like the alpine huts that dotted the countryside throughout the Tyrol. It had a rough bunk and an assortment of rough-hewn furniture. The room smelled of burning wood and coffee.

Stephanie put her arm around Steele's waist. They turned. By the fireplace, each with a tin mug in his hands, were two men. They recognized Gunther. A thinner, more aristocratic man stood beside Gunther. He looked at Stephanie and Derek for a moment and then walked toward them.

"Welcome," he said as he extended his hand. "I am Werner Meyer."

CHAPTER THIRTY-THREE

Meyer didn't look like a priest. In his heavy cable-knit sweater, wool blazer, and wool slacks, he seemed more a professor or research scientist. He did not wear a clerical collar. He shook their hands, Stephanie's first, then Derek's. "I must apologize for the bizarre way you were brought here," Meyer said. "But there are many people who would like to find me now. I had to be sure you were who you said you were."

Steele rubbed the back of his neck. "I am sorry, Mr. Steele," Meyer apologized again, "about your head. But Richard . . ." he glanced at a man by the door. Steele turned to look at him. Richard Stehr had a gently, almost baby-round face with soft blue eyes, set on top of a defensive tackle's body. "Richard is fortunately an expert. You have been done no lasting harm."

"Easy for you to say," Steele replied, but his anger was only skin deep. The words came out as a mild complaint.

"Of course," Meyer said gently. "Would you like to sit down? I have some fresh coffee brewing." He indicated two ladderbacked chairs next to a rough-hewn table on which sat a stack of cups, bottles, hard sausages, and a partially sliced loaf of dark bread.

They seated themselves at the table and watched silently as Meyer used a padded mitt to pluck a battered coffeepot with chipped enamel from a grate in the fireplace. He selected chipped crockery cups for Stephanie and Steele and poured them cups full of the steaming black liquid. He then replenished his own cup and sat down at the table with them. The other men—the two who had brought them to the cabin and Gunther, who had been with

Meyer when they entered—all remained standing. Periodically, they would part the curtains and peer out of the cabin. There were apparently people outside—sentries—for one of the men inside the cabin would periodically motion outside to acknowledge some communication.

"I understand you have gone to some extraordinary lengths to recover the Linz testaments." Stephanie and Steele nodded in unison. "Why don't you tell me how it all came to be?"

"I don't want to be an ungrateful guest," Steele replied. "But since you've brought us here in such a . . . bizarre manner, I'd feel a lot more comfortable if you told us about yourself and"— he looked around the room at the men standing there—"your group."

Meyer's eyes softened. "Of course," he said. "Forgive me for being both too anxious and such a poor host. I understand your reluctance completely." He looked over at Gunther and motioned with his head for the man to join them. Gunther shambled over and took a chair next to Steele.

"Gunther may be able to add the colorful details I leave out," he said by way of explanation.

"I gather my late friend Joseph Roten filled you in on the beginning of all this." He looked around him as if the alpine hut were the symbol of all that had afflicted him for more than four decades.

Steele nodded. "And we've got a pretty good idea what all the killing's about. It's because the Pope was blackmailed by Hitler, isn't it?"

To their surprise, Meyer shook his head. "No," he began. "It's more, much more than that. But let me begin where Roten undoubtedly left off. The past decades have been hard to believe, but they will be more comprehensible if you have some context within which to put them." He took a sip from his coffee mug, made a sour face and leaned back in his chair.

Gerry Anderson squinted over the light snow that fell through his headlights. The snow had nearly stopped. He drive the BMW slowly over the uneven, rocky path that headed steeply up the hillside. Boughs caked with snow reached out from either side and slapped against the side of the car.

The innkeeper's son at the Kohlbacherhof had related exactly what Steele had told him to tell Anderson if the NSA man called or arrived as Steele expected him to: The Steeles left about 7 P.M. and their instructions were to meet a man known only as Gunther outside a book and toy store just up the hill toward town.

Anderson had followed their footsteps, only barely obscured by the slackening snow up to the meeting spot. His practiced eye took in the tire treads, the scuff marks in the snow, and the tire tracks leading away from the store. There were no footprints leading away from the site, so Anderson assumed that Steele and his wife had gone—willingly or unwillingly—with the people in the car.

So he followed the tire tracks, a simple job—thanks to the sparse traffic and the cessation of the heavy snow.

The undercarriage of the BMW scraped hard against a rock now. Anderson stopped and, taking a flashlight with him, continued up the slope on foot.

"The three of us—Summers, Roten and I—kept in close touch after the war. I had told them about what I had seen in the mine and what the sergeant had told me about it. We continued to search for the painting and for the sergeant. He, like many of his comrades, had successfully disappeared."

Meyer slowly got up and went for the coffee pot which he had set back in the fireplace to keep warm. "In addition, I tried as best I could to verify the sergeant's contention that Hitler had blackmailed the Pope. That had two results." He bent over and fetched the pot with the padded mitt. "The first," he said as he walked back to the table, "was a meeting with a small group of people in the Curia who were dedicated to making sure that no other pope ever had to yield to such moral or theological blackmail."

"The priest in the park," Steele said. "In Amsterdam." He looked questioningly up at Meyer.

Meyer nodded sadly. "Father Smith. I had sent him to follow you. To protect you."

"Just before he died, he said something about 'brown.' What could that mean?"

Meyer looked as though he had been slapped.

"He used that name?" Meyer said.

Steele raised his eyebrows. "Then it *is* a name?"

Meyer paused for a moment, as if allowing the impact to sink in. "I suspected," Meyer said, "but I didn't know."

Steele and Stephanie looked at him, waiting for an explanation of his cryptic remarks.

For a moment, Meyer's eyes wore a distant, misty veil. Then the veil suddenly cleared, replaced by a sparkling anger.

"I'll tell you about that in a moment," he said as he sat down. He stared briefly at the thick veins on the backs of his hands, as if he were a public speaker who had lost his place and knew the notes would be inscribed on his hands.

He looked up at them and continued. "The second thing that happened is that I became the object of intense scrutiny by other members of the Curia, people who seemed content to let me go on looking for the painting and the sergeant, but who seemed determined to keep me from ever making use of my information if I succeeded.

"They were . . . are a shadowy group," Meyer said. "I found out who they were at the lower levels . . . fellow priests, the occasional bishop—" He paused. "My abbot in Munich was one of them. I would give a great deal to determine whom he talks to when he relays information about me to Rome."

Meyer was silent for a moment, his eyes distant and vague, as if he were seeing in his mind exactly what he would do if he found the men in Rome. With a little shake of his head, he continued.

"They have left me pretty much alone except for the close surveillance. I assume they are content to let me roam as long as they can somehow benefit from my information, my efforts." He thought about that concept for a moment, as if it were the first time he had ever considered it. "I've been a sort of Judas Goat for them. Sent out into the jungle to attract the tigers while they conceal themselves in the bushes waiting for the tiger with the right pelt to come along. I've been careful, extremely careful over these last years, not to give them any indications that I was aware of their efforts. They make more mistakes that way. Even the most professional, the most fanatical, can be lulled into sloppiness.''

Steele thought of Anderson's man and how he had let Steele leave the UCLA library the night Claude Tewles was murdered.

"So over all these years since the war," Meyer continued, "I made sure to post my important letters to Joseph Roten and make telephone calls to him in secret. Of course, the Vatican knew I was working with him to try and locate lotted works of art. All of our letters and calls regarding the art were done in the normal manner and—I'm certain—were intercepted by whoever in the Curia is having me watched.

"But the situation changed drastically about a year ago. Last—" Meyer closed his eyes for a moment. "Last January, Roten and I managed to recover a semi-famous painting. It was one of the early works of Pissarro, and had been discreetly offered for sale by a former SS colonel living under a new identity in Portugal. We led the police to his villa on the coast near Libson where they took the painting and the colonel into custody. The incident received quite a lot of attention from the journalists.

"As the result of all the publicity, a man I had known forty years before as Erich Bohles von Halbach called me from Kreuzlingen. He was the SS sergeant who came to me that night forty years ago and asked forgiveness for the shooting of the village boy. He was also the one who had shown me the shroud and the Linz testaments in their protective vault in the mine.

"He escaped the explosion and in the confusion that followed, made off with a number of pieces of fine art, including the Stahl painting that everyone has been trying to kill you and your wife to obtain.

"Well, von Halbach was now very wealthy and calling himself Franz-Dietrich Meister," Meyer said, as he pushed his chair back and crossed his legs, trying to get comfortable on the hard wooden seat. "Meister . . . von Halbach, was also dying of cancer, and the moral issues he had managed to ignore or repress for forty years had begun to catch up with him. The guilt-wracked young sergeant had become a remorseful dying old man, afraid for his mortal soul.

"He had grown a bit more sophisticated in the forty years since he had come to my home in Altaussee for confession. He knew the significance of the painting, knew it held the keys to recovering the shroud and the testaments. And so he didn't show up on my doorstep with painting in hand. And a good thing, for the painting would probably now be in the hands of my enemies in the Curia.

"No, realizing that secrecy was important, he decided to act discreetly. He contacted Roten, who immediately called me."

Gunther interrupted to suggest that they eat. The men outside kept watch in shifts, coming in one by one to wolf down cold sausages and bread before continuing their watches. The men were mostly in their forties and fifties and deferred to Meyer.

"They used to be priests," Meyer explained. "They took all they could of treachery and deceit from the Church. But even after leaving the Church, they felt the call to serve God. They live like priests now, but in service to God, not the Church. They help a dwindling number of us within the Church to fight its dishonesty and abuses."

"With the shroud and the Linz testaments, we may even be able to win a few of our battles," Gunther added, then receded in his chair, as if he had added his comment for the night.

Over the simple cold meal, Steele and Stephanie once again recited the tales of their ordeals. The stories had grown shorter with each telling, as they chose an economy of words to rush past the pain and fear.

Meyer, in turn, explained that the nucleus of reformers in the Vatican had steadily dwindled over the years. They were seen as a threat to those who had vested their lives in the power struggles and byzantine bureaucracy. And even those who agreed that Vatican corruption was fundamental and had to be reformed looked upon the reformers as a potential source of embarrassment.

"That is why we were not able to protect either of you so well." Meyer's words were filled with regret.

Steele nodded understandingly before he spoke. "What you've said clears up a lot of things, but it still doesn't explain why the KGB killed your man in the park in Amsterdam. You've been talking about the danger from the Church. But all the danger Stephanie and I have faced has been from the Russians. I don't see where the two—the Church and the KGB—are connected."

"You have really asked several questions," Meyer began. "First of all, the KGB wasn't responsible or the killing in Amsterdam."

He paused as if what he had to say next hurt even to think about. "The Curia killed him."

Steele and Stephanie fixed Meyer with an incredulous look.

"Believe me," he said. "And it wasn't the first time. The Church has money and it has influence. Both of these can be used to hire men, to influence them to kill."

"I thought that went out with the Borgias," Steele said.

Meyer shook his head sadly. "It didn't end with the Borgias and it didn't start with them. They just took it to its greatest extremes. Governments—all governments—have found it necessary to kill people for one reason or another. The killing is sometimes written about in brave and noble terms, but then, history is always rewritten to justify the winners.

"And that's where the KGB and the Church are linked: they are both governments, and as such, act like governments. The Church fears and loathes communism; the KGB fears and hates the Church. And in this joint fear and hatred, there is a brotherhood of violence."

"But what is in the shroud for the KGB?" Steele persisted. "Why do they want it so badly? It can't just be because the Church wants it badly and therefore they should want it too."

"That's partly it," Meyer said. "But mostly, they want it for the same reasons Hitler wanted it."

Steele and Stephanie looked at him with question marks in their eyes.

"The KGB wants to use the shroud and the Linz testaments to blackmail the Church—all churches—into silence on the tyranny of communism. Churches have been a great influence in rallying people against unjust regimes. Poland is just the most recent example. Just look at the connections between the Church and Solidarity. The KGB knows, just as Hitler did, that a government is secure where it is not in conflict with the people's religions. Again, look at Poland, or even at Iran, Central America, or the movements in your own country like the Moral Majority. People everywhere still vote their religious beliefs.

"Hitler, the KGB, the kill-an-abortionist-for-Jesus groups—they're all brothers under the skin," Meyer said. "The differences among them are trivial.

"We must not allow a tyrant—whether he be fascist or communist—to again use the truth to tie the moral hands of the Church." Meyer's words steeled with the strength of his convictions.

"But how can you do that without throwing the Church into turmoil?" Steele said. "The Christian churches, in whatever guise, are all based on a belief in Christ as the Messiah. Aren't you in a position of destroying the Church's unity if you make public the existence of another Messiah? One whose existence could be proven without doubt? Wouldn't some people abandon their own religions to worship this new Messiah? Think of the antagonism between the new believers and the old. I mean, the violence in Ireland is over differences in how to worship the same Messiah. The split would be as bad as . . ." He stopped to collect his thoughts.

"As bad as the differences between Islam and Christianity?" Stephanie offered.

"Exactly," Steele agreed. "Muslims . . . Shiites, Sunnis, others . . . kill each other over which way to worship Muhammed. And they kill people of other faiths just on the general principle that they're infidels. Wouldn't the effect of telling the world about Veronica result in the same thing? And wouldn't that play right into the hands of the KGB? It would cause the same kind of disruption they could exploit, use violence and public arguments as an excuse to crack down on the Church?"

Meyer looked at them quietly with eyes that told them that he had considered their arguments for decades.

"You're talking like the Vatican leadership," he said finally. "That's the same line of reasoning Constantine and his hand picked pope used to kill Veronica and her followers in the first place. The Church has always been in danger—from Romans, Huns and Visigoths, ambitious kings, communists, and Nazis—and it always will be. I firmly believe that."

Meyer leaned forward, his eyes bright with commitment. "But what we have to worry about is the spiritual faith of the people, not the Church. What is important is not the survival of one of the world's oldest surviving bureaucracies and its petty human strivings and failures, but the inner religious faith of those the Church is supposed to serve. Whom the people worship is not nearly so important as that they worship. *Believing* is important whether it's in Buddha, Christ, Muhammed, Vishnu, or the god that carry the sun across the sky every day. People must believe. It's what makes us human and separates us from the animals. Faith in things we do not see is what feeds our creativity, lifts us to feats that cannot be explained by natural phenomena, and enables us to transcend our physical world." He leaned closer now, elbows planted solidly in the middle of the table. "People must believe, and they must believe in the truth. We can be the instrument to bring that truth to them."

Meyer wiped away the beads of perspiration that had broken out on his forehead. "The Church today is founded in great part on a lie. In the long run . . . in the length of time that can only be measured by historians who won't be born for perhaps another century or more . . . in that long view, the truth will make for a stronger Church. But we and those who come after us will suffer for the sins and indiscretions and fears of those men back in 325 A.D. The alternative is to continue to let fascists and dictators and ambitious men use the truth to blackmail the future."

He slumped in his chair, visibly exhausted by his intense, emotional speech.

After a minute or so Steele got up, walked to the fireplace, and used the padded mitts to bring the coffeepot to the table. He asked Meyer, "Would you like some?" Meyer nodded weakly and Steele filled his cup. After filling Stephanie's cup and his own, Steele returned the pot to its warming shelf.

Meyer had rejuvenated his flagging energy enough to sit up to the table, although he leaned on it like a man clinging to the last piece of floating debris from a sunken ship. They listened to the wind whistle, to the wood knots snapping in the fireplace, to the almost impalpable sounds of human beings breathing, moving. No one was willing to break Father Meyer's silence.

Abruptly, they heard shouts from outside the cabin.

"Quick," Meyer said to Gunther. "The testaments." Steele's eyes followed Gunther's bent physique as he shambled to the corner of the hut occupied by a mattressless bunk-bed.

"How did you get that!" Steele exclaimed when he saw Gunther bend low to pick up the black metal briefcase they had taken from the Thule Gesellschaft the previous day.

"Those who work with me are extremely talented," Meyer said.

Steele watched speechlessly as Gunther brought the briefcase to the hearth. The third man in the room, a stocky man in his mid-fifties with a skin-close haircut, joined Meyer and Gunther. Together they lifted one of the rock slabs that comprised the hearth.

As the shouting outside grew louder, the three men put the briefcase in a recess in the hearth, then struggled to replace the stone. Steele shook off his momentary indecision and joined them, his healthy strong back making the chore easier.

They had barely finished when the door burst open with an explosion of sharp biting wind and a flurry of snowflakes. Two of Meyer's men hesitated in the doorway for a moment, holding a semiconscious man by his arms. Meyer nodded to them and they walked forward, half dragging, half carrying the man who was dressed in a warm down parka much like Steele's, thick twill pants, and sturdy lug-soled hiking boots.

"We found him sneaking around outside," one of the men said as they dropped the man at Meyer's feet. The man groaned.

"Turn him over," Meyer ordered.

When they turned him over, Stephanie gasped. The man was Gerry Anderson.

Nat Worthington sighed into the telephone as he listened to the proprietor at the Kohlbacherhof explain that Steele and Stephanie had left more than two hours before to meet someone. Who? He didn't know, but someone else, another American, had arrived shortly afterward and asked the same question. Another American? Nat asked anxiously. Yes, said the proprietor, and described the man. Nat was sure the man was Gerry Anderson.

He thanked the proprietor and rang off. He looked over at Tania, who sat in the visitor's chair, and shook his head.

Slumping into the firm softness of the hospital bed, Nat closed his eyes and cursed himself. He was too late. Anderson was there and they trusted him.

What could he do? Nat tried desperately to think of how he could help them, but the mountains of the Tyrol were a vast and inhospitable place. An army would be unable to find them now, and he didn't have an army. One person or a score would be pointless.

The bed spun a little and Nat knew the fever was still with him.

The infection had regrouped and driven his temperature above 103. The doctors said it was nothing to worry about, but he still felt faint and weak.

He felt Tania's cool hand on his forehead. It caressed him, soothed him, urged him forward into sleep. He tried to fight the drowsiness, but it enveloped him, made him feel as if he were falling into a soft cottony hole. With a reluctant sigh, he drifted off.

CHAPTER THIRTY-FOUR

"The Habersam mine is a large one," explained Gunther. "I should know. I was the superintendent there until the SS arrived." He had taken the plan of the mine and spread it out on the table in the hut. Sitting around the table were Meyer, Steele, Stephanie, two of Meyer's men, and Gerry Anderson, his head patched in half a dozen places with bandages covering the wounds received in his battle with Meyer's three men. His arm was in a sling; the shoulder had been dislocated. Gunther had reduced the dislocation, but it was still sore. All three of the men who had captured Anderson also wore bandages. None was happy about the American joining their effort.

The three men would have killed Anderson had not Stephanie and Steele vouched for him. "He saved my life," Steele told Meyer, and retold in detail the incident in the limousine in Marina del Rey. Reluctantly, Meyer had agreed to let Anderson join the team.

They sat around the table now, planning their assault on the mine. They would go after the shroud and the Linz testaments on Christmas Day. "Our sacrifice shall be our celebration," Meyer had said.

Gunther explained in detail how he and the others—not including Meyer—had labored to cut a passage from an adjoining abandoned mine into the Habersam mine.

"The entrance to the Habersam mine is so thoroughly blocked that it would take a major effort . . . heavy equipment, explosives, to clear it. It was exactly what the Nazis had intended," Gunther said. "For obvious reasons we didn't want to attract the attention that major effort would require."

"Not to mention the expense," Meyer said. "It would be prohibitively expensive."

Gunther nodded his agreement. "I have lived here all my life and have worked at some time or other in just about every mine from her to Bad Ischl. The hills are honeycombed with mines. There are so many of them that a substantial number are not even mapped."

It took less than a year for Gunther to find the right mine. It had to be abandoned so they could work in it without notice, and it had to be close enough for a handful of men working part time to dig a passage from it into the Habersam mine. It took Gunther and his co-workers more than nine years to dig the passage.

"But if you've already cut a passage into the mine, why haven't you hired a safecracker or something to get the shroud out before now?" Steele asked.

Wordlessly, Gunther reached into the black metal briefcase and pulled from it a small bound booklet. He displayed it for all to see.

"The good Sergeant von Halbach told Father Meyer about an extensive system of safeguards, mines, and traps that lined every approach to the vault," Gunther said.

"And in addition," Meyer said. "The vault itself is not only designed to be dangerous to any unauthorized entry, but also von Halbach told me that as an ultimate safeguard, there were mechanisms to destroy the shroud and the testaments to keep them from falling into the wrong hands."

"And this is the key," Gunther said, eagerly thumbing through the book's pages. "Page after page after page on how to avoid, disarm, dismantle the defenses." He paused as he scanned one page in the back. "Including the procedure for entering the vault." He bent the book's binding back to the page and held it up for all to see.

"But surely the explosives or poisons . . . whatever, will have deteriorated over the last forty years," Stephanie said.

Steele shook his head. "People are still being killed by World War Two grenades and bombs that some farmer plows up in his fields or that some gas company worker slams a shovel into."

Gunther looked at her and nodded his agreement. "He's right,

Mrs. Steele. And there are poison gases the Nazis produced, nerve gases like Tabun, anthrax bombs, that are still just as potent today, and probably thousands of times as dangerous now that their metal casings and containers have deteriorated.'' He shook his head. "No, the Nazis made good weapons. We can expect most of them to still pose a danger.''

Stephanie shivered.

"I assume then, that one of you"—Steele looked at Gunther—"is an expert in the sorts of explosives or devices from the World War Two era?''

There was a pregnant pause as Gunther looked to Meyer.

Meyer cleared his throat. "I'm afraid he was killed in Amsterdam,'' Meyer said. "He died in the park next to you.''

"I've learned a bit about explosives,'' Gunther said, "in the course of being a mine superintendent. But an expert? Hardly, Mr. Steele.''

"That's why we'd like you to accompany us into the mine tomorrow,'' Meyer said to Steele. "That, and because you have a young, strong back.''

"No, Derek!'' Stephanie cried. "We've already done enough. Let them handle this part.''

Meyer looked at her with troubled eyes, and then said: "We will help you clear your names, help you deal with the criminal charges that are pending against you, regardless of our success here tomorrow.''

He swallowed, looked briefly at Steele, and then back at Stephanie. "I have no doubt that you will be exonerated if we can offer the proof that sits now inside that mine.'' He paused again, a debater giving the judges time to absorb the information. "However, without the shroud and the Linz testaments, your story—the facts in the matter—will be dismissed as lies, as fantasies. They are too fantastic to believe . . . without some sort of proof. You'll either spend the rest of your lives in a prison or in hiding.''

He got up and walked around the table to where Steele and Stephanie sat. "Your help tomorrow makes our chances of success much greater . . . and improves the chances that you will be cleared of all these charges. On the other hand, should we fail . . .'' He shrugged as if trying to rid his shoulders of the implications. Steele suddenly felt the weight of the decision fall on his own shoulders.

"May I think about it until morning?" he asked.

Meyer nodded. "But you must sit up with us tonight as we study the plans. Preparation is all that will save our lives tomorrow. Preparation, luck, and prayer."

CHAPTER THIRTY-FIVE

They arrived at the mouth of the abandoned mine about noon on Christmas Day. The weather had taken a turn for the worse. The wind whipped up off the valley with a vengeance, driving with it hard, sand-sized grains of snow that stung like cold needles when they found exposed skin. Visibility had dropped to nearly nothing as a whiteout threatened to close in around them. The sun was a vague gray dish against a uniformly gray sky. Steele was grateful for the goggles Gunther had provided.

The snowmobiles crawled through the bright stinging murk as Gunther led them from landmark to landmark, relying on his uncanny knowledge of the area to keep them from getting lost.

Meyer sat behind Gunther on the lead snowmobile, which towed behind it a small tarp-covered sled filled with the tools, explosives, and other items he thought would be necessary. Behind him was a second machine, ridden by Anderson and piloted by one of the three men who had captured him the night before. Anderson still wore his arm in a sling, and had complained so much of the pain that Meyer had suggested that he stay back at the hut. He had declined. Bringing up the rear of the procession was a third snowmobile, driven by Steele. Stephanie sat behind him with her arms around his waist. He had tried to convince her to stay at the hut with Meyer's other men, but she refused. "I told you in Zurich: I've found you and no matter what happens, no matter how dangerous things get, we're not going to be separated again." She could not be persuaded otherwise.

Steele doggedly kept the tail lights of the second snowmobile in

416

sight; he could not see the lead machine, and to lose the second one would mean being instantly lost.

Just as the gray disk that was the sun climbed to the day's zenith, Steele heard the pitch of Gunther's snowmobile drop suddenly. The sound was followed immediately by the brake lights of the second machine. Steele gripped the brakes on his own snowmobile handlebars and squeezed them to a stop.

Wordlessly, they dismounted and helped to pull the supplies sled toward the mouth of the mine. Everyone but Meyer helped. The frail priest had tried to help until Gunther insisted that he stand back. He stood at the mouth of the mine and glowered at the past like a vigorous man who had never accepted his infirmities.

In a matters of minutes they dragged the sled into the shelter of a rock overhang. Ahead of them was an iron gate barring their entrance to the mine. Gunther pulled the tarpaulin from the sled and began to pass around the equipment. To Steele, Stephanie, and Anderson, he handed backpacks that weighed about twenty-five or thirty pounds. He handed all of them flashlights and whistles with a lanyard. "Wear these around your necks at all times," he told them. "If you get separated, stay in one place and blow on the whistle."

He slung a large coil of climbing rope diagonally over one shoulder, then buckled a beltload of carabiners and pitons, as well as a hammer to drive the pitons, around his waist.

"The rock entrance to this mine is very unstable," he told them. "Once we hit the salt, everything will be fine. But the rocks and the shorings that compose the first four hundred feet of the tunnel are in danger of collapse." And as to confirm Gunther's gloomy diagnosis, a scattering of rocks clattered somewhere in the darkness beyond.

"There is a vent hole cut vertically into the upper portion of the salt. If the entrance is blocked, we can work our way out using the climbing gear." Without further words, he walked up to the iron gate, unlocked a remarkably battered padlock, and swung the gate open. They followed him in.

The impoverished light penetrated only the first fifty feet or so of the mine entrance. Everyone had turned on their flashlights by the time they had gone that far. The going was treacherous, with ice underfoot and great stiletto-like stalac-tites of ice suspended from the ceiling.

Steele and Stephanie held hands as they walked. The danger they were walking into weighed heavily on Steele. Life never left you alone to enjoy it, he thought, but in his case, he felt he'd been singled out for more than usual attention.

They walked cautiously along the icy floor, daring to take only small steps as the floor of the mine sloped inexorably downward. Remnants of the pitiful daylight vanished entirely now in the great blackness of the tunnel. To conserve batteries, Gunther ordered everyone but him to turn of their flashlights. His light picked out rotten wooden shorings and the rusty remains of metal ones. It was apparent that the rock faces above and to either side of them hung there against gravity with no support at all. Steele wanted to ask Gunther about that, but didn't. He didn't really want to know the answer.

Suddenly the sounds of rocks filled the tunnel. Somewhere in the darkness, not too far beyond the bright cone Gunther's flash-light carved out of the darkness, came the dull hollow clattering of stone against stone.

"Wait," Gunther said in a hushed voice. He had warned them earlier not to make loud noises. The rocks in this portion of the mine were so poised for a cave-in, he said, that any loud noise might be enough to trigger a collapse. His warning had a chilling effect on any conversation, loud or otherwise. He, after all, was the man who had worked in the mines all his life. The sound of falling rocks continued for several seconds; the tunnel floor vi-brated under their feet, and instants later small rock fragments began to fall around them from the tunnel ceiling.

Stephanie stifled a small cry. Her heart beat rapidly as they listened to the rocks ahead and waited for the thudding and clat-tering to stop. She squeezed Steele's hand and momentarily laid her face against his shoulder.

In a minute the rocks had stopped falling, and once again they were alone in the tunnel with the sounds of their own breathing. Gunther hesitated for several more seconds, then moved forward without talking.

Over and over in his mind, Steele ticked off the things they would have to deal with once they crossed over into the Habersam mine. They had gone over the plans and the instructions from the safe deposit box half a dozen times. The Nazi maps of the mine marked with the locations of the planted explosives and other devices were compared with the mine company maps Gunther had been able to obtain locally.

Not surprisingly, the two maps were not in total agreement. The mining company maps showed tunnels where the Nazi map showed none. Just as cartographers—before the days of aerial and satellite mapping—used to differ on the shapes of the continents, mining engineers of forty years past used comparatively crude methods, a fact that guaranteed that no two mining maps, particularly those of small backwoods mines, would be the same.

In the case of the party now in the mine, though, even minor differences would prove to be dangerous, since it was necessary to know exactly where the Nazi traps were located. A foot the wrong way, or even a few inches, could mean disaster.

"And of course we have no way of knowing if *everything* is properly charted," Gunther had told them the night before. "The commandant of the SS unit could have ordered other protective measures in the last days of the war and not bothered to update the materials in the box.

The ice in the tunnel gradually thawed as they walked deeper into the mine. Filling the tunnel now was the sound of running water.

"The hills are riddled with underground streams and rivers," Gunther had said. "The greatest danger that a miner faces—next to cave-ins, of course—is the disaster that results from blasting through a rock wall only to find an underground stream."

He explained that rain and melting snow seeped into water-retaining layers of rock, which gradually migrated downward. Some of it flowed naturally into fresh-water springs that fed mountain streams. But much of it ran along the cracks and fissures in the rock of the mountains, and eventually into the ubiquitous salt deposits buried underneath. The salt, some of it containing sulphur and other materials, dissolved in the water and was carried down with it toward the warmer layers of rock that lay at the base of the mountains. Eventually, many of these warm, mineral-laden streams of water emerged at the surface again, in the guise of the warm mineral springs around which the great spas of Germany were built.

Steele recalled Gunther's words now as he walked through the tunnel, the walls of rock on either side seeming to press malevolently inward, reaching out for him as if they wanted his life. He had an urge to walk faster, but Gunther was setting the pace. He tried to pass off his anxiety as mild claustrophobia. The real danger lay ahead.

The documents from the black metal briefcase described a series of ingenious killing devices set by the Nazis to protect their prize. There were machine guns whose triggers were set to trip wires—

"Just like the East Germans use in the border zone that separates them from West Germany," Stephanie had said.

Covered pits with stakes at the bottom—

"Just like the North Vietnamese," Steele had added.

Containers of napalm rigged to incinerate those who triggered the mechanism. Those who escaped being immolated would probably die as the flames consumed the oxygen in the tunnel. In the larger chambers of the salt mine, where the formation was stable, antipersonnel mines had been buried beneath the salt.

All of these were marked clearly on the charts, along with procedures to avoid or disarm the devices.

But the presence of booby traps possibly added at the last minute nagged at Steele, as did a single handwritten notation inside the back cover of the booklet.

"What does *'Pfeil'* mean?" Steele had asked Gunther.

"Arrow," the Austrian had replied.

But they found no further reference to arrows. Steele had forgotten it until just now, as he ran down the list of things that squatted in the distant darkness, defying them to enter.

Gunther's light seemed to grow brighter in the tunnel now, and Steele quickly realized it was because the man had walked into an area where the tunnel walls were white. The column quickened its pace, anxious to leave the uncertain stability of the rock-walled tunnel for the more reliable salt formation. Moments later, Gunther's torch seemed to extinguish itself as they entered a giant chamber the size and dimensions of an auditorium.

Gunther stopped. "Switch on your lights for a moment, all o

ou," he said. The gasps of awe came from Derek, Stephanie, and Anderson as they looked about the vast white room.

"Salt formations are considered extremely stable," Gunther said. "In addition to using them to store looted art and treasures, the Nazis actually moved entire factories into mines such as these, where they could continue to operate, safe from the Allied bombings. The hills around us are filled with chambers like this one."

Meyer spoke next: "Some of them had been used by Jews and others as hiding places from the Nazis. On the other side of the valley, there are mine chambers that are sealed off as graves. They contain the bodies of people executed by the Nazis when they surveyed the mines for storehouses and found entire families living in them."

He turned sadly and nodded to Gunther. Then he ordered them once again to extinguish their flashlights. As Steele moved forward, he noticed that there was a faint brown path in the salt, created no doubt by the scuffling of Gunther and his helpers as they cut the entrance into the Habersam mine.

They followed the path around a pile of boards, rusty metal scaffolding, and a conical pile of salt that had collapsed from the ceiling of the great salt chamber.

"Water can do that over time," Gunther explained.

Minutes later they passed out of the huge white chamber and into a spacious corridor. Its white salt walls took the light from Gunther's flashlight and diffused and reflected it so that the passageway seemed to be lit indirectly from within the walls.

About fifty yards into the corridor, it began to narrow, obstructed by piles of salt that stretched most of the way across the floor and halfway to the ceiling.

"These are the tailings we took from the passageway," Gunther remarked. There was pride in his voice, as if these piles of salt were the crowning achievement of his life.

They walked another fifty yards before coming to a rough opening in the corridor walls. The column stopped in single file. A long trail of salt obstructed the corridor in the other direction for as far as the light penetrated.

"This is it," Gunther said with as much pride in his voice as Michelangelo might once have used to announce the completion of his statue of David. They crowded around the opening, Steele climbing the loose talus of salt to get a good look. Stephanie clambered up alongside him.

The opening was about six feet high and a bit less than three feet wide. It reminded Steele of the open face of a coffin. When Gunther shined his light into the opening, the beam revealed a long, straight passageway that continued beyond the ability of the light to illuminate. Steele looked at his watch and noted it was nearly one P.M.

"I'd like to go over a few last-minute things before we enter the tunnel, just so we remember the important items we went over last night," Gunther said. "First of all, remember that there are antipersonnel mines buried in the floors everywhere. The plans indicate a random placement except near the chamber where the vault is. There they are clustered very densely." He looked at the large close-cropped man in his fifties who had helped to capture Anderson the night before. "For this reason, Richard will precede us with a metal detector. I hope the moisture will have rusted the detonators, but we can't be sure.

"Remember," Gunther cautioned, "we have not actually been in the Habersam mine. We wanted to make sure that we didn't take any action that might result in the destruction o the shroud itself. So as soon as we set foot on the other side of this passage, we will be on completely new ground. And because of the discrepancies between the Nazi mining charts and the company charts of this mine, we don't know precisely *where* in the Habersam mine our little passageway leads to."

"That means our prediction on which booby traps we'll face might not be right?" Stephanie asked.

Gunther nodded. "I *think* I know where we'll turn out."

"I pray you are right," Father Meyer said. And then, addressing the group, he said: "Would you like to pray before we enter the passage?"

Heads bowed in unison. Steele was reminded of the old saying that there are no atheists in foxholes.

Meyer began with the Twenty-third Psalm: *"The Lord is my Shepherd; I shall not want. He maketh me to lie down in green pastures; He leadeth me beside the still waters. He restoreth my soul; He leadeth me in the paths of righteousness for His name's sake."*

The priest's voice grew in intensity as he recited the psalm from

422

memory. *"Yea, though I walk through the valley of the shadow of death, I will fear no evil: for Thou art with me; Thy rod and Thy staff they comfort me. Thou preparest a table before me in the presence of mine enemies; Thou anointest my head with oil; my cup runneth over. Surely goodness and mercy shall follow me all the days of my life; and I will dwell in the house of the Lord forever."*

In the dimly lit corridor beneath the mountain, there was a murmuring of silent "amens." Then, taking the rough, dark mountain bread and a canteen of water, Meyer broke bread and said the Eucharist. Afterward they all silently consumed the remaining bread and water. Like paratroopers nearing the drop zone, they wrapped themselves in personal thoughts of their own morality.

Steele and Stephanie stood with their arms around each other.

Finally, without prompting, for they had discussed things many times and to do so again would be to procrastinate, Richard Stehr stepped into the passageway, followed by Gunther, then Steele, Stephanie, Father Meyer, and finally, Gerry Anderson.

"I love you," Stephanie told Steele as he stepped into the passageway.

"I love you too, kid," he said, then kissed her. Reluctantly, he turned and followed Gunther's gnarled but strong body down the narrow corridor.

They had been walking for less than a minute when the sounds of running water filled the passageway.

"What's that?" Steele asked Gunther.

"An underground stream," Gunther replied without breaking stride. "I've listened to it for years now. It used to scare me, but now . . ." he paused as if searching for the words to describe his feelings. "Now, it's like an old friend."

Steele felt less sanguine about the noise and the rumbling beneath his feet, both of which increased as they continued. The tunnel was filled with an air of electricity now, a crackling ozone of emotions, mostly fear, that bound them all and seemed to propel them faster and faster.

They had walked for another ten minutes when finally the light from Richard's light illuminated a white wall at the end of the passageway. There seemed to be a fist-sized hole in the middle of

"That is the very end," Gunther yelled. The roaring of the water was now so loud he had to shout to be heard for more than a few feet. "It's only about six inches thick." As the rest of the party approached, Gunther asked Steele to hand him the shovel that was tied to the back of the Austrian's pack.

Steele was leaning forward to untie the strap that bound the spade-like shovel when Richard screamed.

Steele lifted his gaze. Richard seemed to have shrunk. He had turned to face them, his arms outstretched for help.

"Help me!" Richard screamed desperately. Gunther shed his pack in an instant, fell on his belly and began to crawl toward Richard who had now shrunk to the size of a large stuffed bear that can be won by knocking over all the milk bottles at a carnival.

It took Steele several moments before he realized that Richard had not shrunk at all, but had sunk into the floor of the tunnel. He flailed his arms and shrieked as he sank deeper and deeper. Around him, the hard-packed salt floor had turned dark with water. Condensation from the warm water formed a modest fog in the cool air of the corridor.

Gunther approached him cautiously now, his arms and legs spread to distribute his weight more evenly. There was no telling how far the floor had been undermined. Steele quickly shed his own pack and, crawling on his belly, moved forward to grab Gunther's ankle.

Steele looked up; only Richard's head could be seen now. The man was grasping for Gunther's outstretched hand. Pieces of the tunnel floor broke off around him and disappeared. Steele felt Gunther stretch out and he heard the old Austrian say: "There!" The next instant, Gunther shouted to Steele to "Pull! Pull us both! Now."

Pulling with all his might, Steele edged backwards, tugging against the grasp of the underground currents. Progress was measured in inches.

"Here." He felt strong arms pulling at his belt. Anderson had wedged his way around Meyer and Stephanie to help.

They progressed a foot, a foot and a half, when the tunnel filled with a high-pitched scream. Steele and Anderson fell backward suddenly as the tension was abruptly released. Richard shrieked one last time, then disappeared into the moist hole in the floor.

They sat there, too stunned to move. Stephanie rushed to Steele and held him. Moments later, Gunther's agonized weeping filled the air. Werner Meyer squeezed past to comfort him.

"It was not your fault, Gunther," Meyer said, as he put an arm around his old friend's shoulder.

"But I let him go," Gunther protested. "I had him and I let him go." He began to sob softly.

"You did all you could," Meyer countered.

Steele, Stephanie, and Anderson sat quietly, for perhaps ten minutes, before Anderson motioned them to follow him back toward the auditorium-sized chamber through which they had passed.

Gunther and Meyer were waiting for them when they returned, dragging two long boards the size of a two by twelve. Anderson and Steele jockeyed the boards into the narrow passageway while Stephanie led Meyer and Gunther back to the stack of timbers they had separated from the pile of debris they had skirted on the way in.

It took them more than an hour, but when they finished, the hole in the floor of the passage was bridged with boards.

"We must hurry," Gunther said. "Now that the water has broken through, we do not know how long it will take to eat away at the edges. It could swallow up our little bridge."

Gunther led them across the bridge and made short work of the thin salt wall he had left at the end of the corridor. He worked with the vengence of a man who wants to punish himself. When the hole was large enough, Gunther leaned through it, like a sailor leaning through a porthole, swinging his flashlight through long broad arcs as he surveyed the tunnel beyond. He paused long enough to examine the plan, which had been pulled from the black metal briefcase. He looked at the plan, then stuck his head through the hole, comparing reality to the map. Finally, he turned to the others and spread the map on the floor of the corridor. Steele, Stephanie, Meyer, and Anderson crowded against each other, trying to see.

"We're here." Gunther pointed to a spot on the map near the conjunction of two tunnels. "I thought we'd come out"—he moved a finger grimy with work to another spot less than an inch away—"right here." There was pride in his voice now, leavening his sorrow. "We're about fifty feet off. But that doesn't matter as long as we know exactly where we are at all times."

He folded up the plan and finished widening the hole, so that they could easily gain entrance to the tunnel in the Habersam mine.

On the other side, he insisted that they walk single file, each distanced from the other by at least twenty feet. Only Steele and Stephanie violated the rule.

The metal detector had been lost with Richard. So Gunther used the page-by-page details of the mine to ascertain the placement of the antipersonnel mines. He measured their progress accurately, using a hundred-foot tape measure that he let play out behind him as he walked. He gave the task of holding the other end of the tape to Father Meyer, who protested being given such a relatively safe task. But he yielded to Gunther's insistence. To Stephanie he gave the task of sprinkling small amounts of carbon black on the floor to mark their path, so that it would be easier to find their way out safely.

The carbon black came in containers the size of soft drink cans. Stephanie quickly discovered that Steele's pack contained nothing but can after can of the inky black power.

They all had their flashlights on now, scanning the corridor for signs of booby traps that might not have found their way onto the plans taken from the safe deposit box in Zurich.

They came to the first tripwired machine gun at half past two.

"Wait!" Gunther shouted. They were approaching the intersection with another tunnel when they stopped. Gunther lowered his flashlight. "Look here," he called. There, in the middle of the intersection was a thin wire stretched taut from one side of the corridor to another. Gunther motioned them on slowly. They followed his lead right up to the wire then stopped. Gunther shone his light into the intersecting tunnel to his right. There was nothing but the post to which one end of the wire was attached.

In the other direction, however, was a machine gun on a tripod. It had a square body with a long barrel that ended in a sort of flare. Around the barrel was a perforated metal sleeve, the air cooling jacket. They stared at the gun for a moment, half expecting it to open fire.

Gunther motioned them back to the safety of the tunnel from

which they had come. Steele peered around the corner as Gunther walked up to the machine gun and swiveled it toward the bright white salt wall. Next, he took a pair of wire cutters and clipped the tripwire. It fell slack in the middle of the tunnel intersection.

Gunther started to walk back toward them, then stopped and went back to the machine gun. He bent over the gun and pulled the trigger.

The gun leaped to life, filling the tunnels with fire and noise for perhaps a dozen rounds, and then fell silent as the hammer fell on a dud.

A smell that reeked of cordite and the ghosts of ancient enemies come to life accompanied Gunther back to where the group had gathered.

"That's why we must be careful," he said, then ordered the tape brought up and planted firmly at the edge of the intersecting corridor. He then took the other end and began walking again. As he got to the intervals indicated on the plans, he would turn one way or another to circumvent the mines.

A hundred yards on, he bent to rip the camouflage from a deep pit. A clattering of boards filled the mine, accompanied by a rolling cloud of dust as the materials dropped into the hole. Like the others, Stephanie shone her light into the pit as she walked the narrow ledge between it and the tunnel wall. Barbed metal spikes that looked to be three feet long grinned back up at her.

The mines grew closer together, and the number of booby traps they had to disarm increased as they neared the chamber containing the shroud's vault.

Their first surprise came as they stepped into a huge chamber nearly as large as the auditorium-sized one in the other mine. They had moved inch by inch, skirting a field of mines that had been placed side by side, with barely room for a footprint between the triggers. Gunther took a can of the carbon black from Stephanie and sprinkled it, not in a path, but in the specific places where they should put their feet. Placement had to be precise. To slip or lose one's balance could mean being ripped apart by the explosives and shrapnel buried beneath the salt.

This last minefield was nearly forty feet wide. Gunther had them all wait nearly fifty yards behind as he picked his way through the mines. In the dimly lit distance, he seemed to move to a stop-frame pace.

They all stood silently, holding their breaths. Stephanie looked at Father Meyer and saw his lips moving in a silent prayer.

Finally Gunther straightened to his full height and shouted, "It's all clear. Come one at a time."

Stephanie watched, terrified as Steele picked his way through. Finally he turned around. "Why don't you wait on that side, Steph?"

"No way," she said, with a bravery she didn't feel.

Steele's fingertips tingled as he watched her begin picking her way through. To him, she looked like a ballerina engaged in a lethal solo. The cave seemed to drop away from around him as he watched her step by agonizing step. She seemed to walk forever and not get any closer. Then she was there in his arms. He led her to the side while Father Meyer and Gerry Anderson made their way across.

Finally they were all assembled.

"This is the main vault room," Gunther said, looking first at the plan of the mine and then around him. "The plans show no booby traps here." The chamber was perhaps seventy-five yards square and thirty or forty feet high. The floor was uneven, covered with dimly lit debris, looking like packing crates or irregular piles of rubbish.

"Yes, I know," Father Meyer said dreamily. He looked about him, a sleepwalker suddenly awakened from his trance. "I was here," he said, as if he didn't entirely believe it. "I was here forty years ago." He played his flashlight around the room. "We walked in . . ." He played the light around more. "We walked in there." His flashlight beam fixed on the entrance to a corridor on the other side of the chamber. "And the entrance to the vault is right over . . ." He swung the flashlight beam to the right. "There."

The metal vault door was set into an outcropping of gray rock. It was large, unrusted, and from the distance at which they stood, looked remarkable like the door to the Thule Gesellschaft Bank's safe deposit box vault.

"There wouldn't be booby traps here," Meyer said, still in his dreamy tone of voice, "because there were men here, many of them. Walking about. The sergeant showed me. The main entrance was heavily guarded, and the rest of the approaches booby-trapped and mined to guard against people like us."

Steele led them toward the vault door. He made it halfway across the chamber when he felt a section of the floor move slightly downward. From across the room came the metallic clacking and snicking of a mechanical apparatus.

"Hit the dirt!" Steele yelled as he dived to the ground, pulling Stephanie along with him. A single shot echoed in the room, followed by the dull clanking sound the dud ammunition had made in the other machine gun. Years later, Steele would swear that he had heard the bullet parting the air above him.

"Oh God. Oh God. Oh God." Stephanie was crying hysterically as she sat up and clung to Steele. "It could have killed us. Killed us!" He held her against his chest as she broke into incoherent sobs.

"It's all right," he said soothingly, trying to stop his hands from trembling as he stroked her hair. "We're all right, all right." They rocked back and forth as he tried to comfort her. Her sobs, hysterical at first, gradually lessened in intensity.

"Almost there," he told her. "We're almost there. Just a few more minutes and we can leave."

She lifted her head and sniffed. He wiped at her tears with his fingers.

"I'm sorry," Stephanie said. "It's just that—"

"Sh-h-h-h-h," Steele said. "Shhh. Don't apologize. You've been through a lot."

Suddenly she was aware of the others, huddled together about ten yards away.

"Come on," she said, sniffling once and then getting to her feet. "Let's get this over with so we can breathe easily."

As they approached the vault door, Steele shined his flashlight on one of the piles of debris scattered around the chamber. The piles were the skeletons of men dressed in the uniforms of the SS. There were a score of them scattered about the chamber. But with nerves burned and numbed by the horrors that had already played themselves out that day, neither Steele nor Stephanie nor the others were shocked to see the bony hands and skulls sticking out of olive-drab uniforms.

Instead, they walked like weary gladiators, crossing an arena littered with the bodies of their slain enemies. They crossed to greet the emperor and to receive their reward. It seemed to Steele that they had finally come back to write the ending chapter to a war that had begun in another era and which had waited for them all along. The enemy still fought back at them over time, as if destiny were still waiting to be decided.

The first vault door had two combination dials that had to he turned simultaneously. Stephanie read the numbers aloud as Steele on the right dial and Gunther on the left turned the mechanisms.

"Left dial to the left to twenty-seven," she read from the documents, as Anderson held the light for her, "and right dial to the left to fifty-nine. Get ready. Go." Derek and Gunther moved the dials in unison, then waited for their next instruction.

"That's it," Stephanie said. "That's all the numbers."

Steele and Gunther looked at each other and then, as if a communication had passed between them, turned and gestured to Meyer.

"Father," Gunther said. "Will you do the honor?"

Meyer walked reverently toward the door with the hesitancy of a man approaching the fulfillment of his life's work. He took the handle on the vault door and wrenched it clockwise. Somewhere inside the massive door the mechanism clacked solidly, moving its well-oiled parts for the first time in more than four decades. This sound, too, seemed to solidify this vault's relationship with the one beneath the streets of Zurich, as if they had both been designed by the same man for the same act of destiny.

Meyer strained at the door. It wouldn't move.

Alarmed that they had come so far for nothing, Steele placed his right hand beside the priest's and heaved. Still nothing.

The joy and reverence had fallen into ruins on Meyer's face.

"Derek?" Stephanie asked. "What's the matter?"

"Door won't open," Steele said. "The mechanism moved inside, but it won't swing open." He paused. "Let me see the instructions."

She handed him the papers from which she had been reading. Steele examined the papers with Gunther looking over his shoulder. After a pause he handed them to Gunther.

"We did everything right," Steele said. "It must be the hinges or something."

Meyer's face looked blank, as if his thoughts were focused in another era. "They had some sort of automatic mechanism, I believe." Meyer said finally. "I remember the door almost opening by itself when the sergeant brought me here."

"Perhaps something the camp commandant added?" Gunther suggested.

Steele shrugged, his face dark with thought. Then, a moment later, he said to Gunther, "Take off your rope. Tie one end to the handle of the vault door."

Gunther complied, and when the knot was secure, Steele arranged them along the rope like members of a tug-of-war team. Steele gave himself the anchor position at the tail of the lineup.

"Pull!" he yelled. The rope tightened and swayed as they arranged themselves in a straight line. They took a step back as the nylon climbing rope stretched. But the door remained stationary.

"Harder," Steele urged. "Pull harder."

The sounds of boot soles scrabbling for purchase on the gritty salt floor mixed with puffing and heavy breathing. Finally, a complaint creaked from the vault door, and it swung open.

"All right!" Anderson yelled.

"Thank God," Meyer muttered.

Inside the vault was a room from another age. It was a good twelve or fifteen feet wide and at least twice that in length. It was arranged like an office, with a desk, chair, lamp, and long conference table. The floor was carpeted. The two long walls were covered with wood. The end wall was concrete, and set into it was another safe.

They walked in slowly. Meyer looked like a man exploring an almost forgotten dream.

They played their flashlights around the walls.

"There," Meyer said pointing toward the middle of the right-hand wall. Steele looked, but failed to see what the priest had been pointing at. Meyer walked up to the spot and pointed toward a nail. "This is where the picture hung," Meyer said. "Sergeant von Halbach took it from here. He must have. I saw it that time. I saw it." He turned to them as if he didn't expect them to believe him.

But Gunther and Steele moved quickly past him, anxious to get

431

the last phase of the job done. They reached the end of the vault and spread out the papers on the table.

"The combination is a standard one," Gunther said, as they looked at the papers. "But once the door's open, we have ten seconds to insert the gold ingot from the picture in the slot, here." He pointed first to a drawing of the safe door, then at the slot on the door in the wall beside them. The slot was blocked by a piece of metal. Steele produced the ingot from his pack.

"There must be some sort of counterbalance mechanism inside," Gunther said. "It is probably activated by an object of the correct size and weight." Steele nodded. "Will you hold the light for me?" Gunther asked. Steele nodded as the Austrian turned to the safe and began to twirl the dial.

There were sixteen numbers in all, and Gunther dialed them slowly and precisely. Finally, with the last digit in place, there was a clicking and momentary whir as the slot was suddenly free. The second hand on Steele's watch hit 3:13:26 and kept moving.

"Quickly," Gunther said. "Give me the ingot." The second had moved past 28. Steele handed the ingot to Gunther.

3:13:29.

Gunther turned to face the safe. His hands shook as he brought the ingot to the slot.

3:13:30.

Gunther cursed as he bobbled the ingot.

3:13:31.

The ingot thudded quietly on the carpet.

"Oh God! Quickly!" Gunther and Steele dropped to their knees simultaneously as the mechanism in the safe ground on.

3:13:34.

"Here," Gunther handed the ingot to Steele. "You do it."

Steele stood up.

3:13:37.

Steele rammed the ingot into the slot. It quickly passed out of sight, swallowed in the mechanism of the door. The whirring stopped.

"Did we make it?" Gunther asked.

Steele looked at his watch. "A second or two late," he said, reaching for the handle. "Let's see if it still works."

He started to turn the handle when Stephanie screamed.

"The door! Derek! The door's closing!"

Steele whirled in place and saw the vault door slowly moving on its hinges.

"Gerry!" Steele barked. "You and Stephanie and the father get out and hold on to the rope and see if you can slow it up. I'll help Gunther."

But before any of them could move, Gunther reached up and turned the handle of the safe. There was a hissing sound of springs uncoiling. Instants later, half a dozen harpoon-like arrows shafted through the wood paneling next to the safe and through the air. One impaled Gunther through his right breast and slammed him against the opposite wall. The rest thudded harmlessly into the wall around him.

"Pfeil!" Gunther shouted. The word came back to Steele now with the fullest impact. They had found the arrows.

"Gunther." Meyer started towards him. Steele grabbed Meyer and stopped him.

"Father, get outside," Steele said as he watched the door continue to close. "Take him out of here," he said to Anderson and Stephanie. "I'll help Gunther." Steele physically turned Meyer around and shoved him toward the narrowing gap in the door. "Go on. All of you," he barked. Anderson grabbed Meyer and headed for the door. Stephanie stood her ground.

"Women." Steele turned and ran toward Gunther. He looked dazed, his mouth moving now like a fish out of water. A large quantity of blood had spilled from his wound, staining the carpet under his feet. The end of the arrow protruded about four inches from the upper part of his chest, almost to his shoulder. There was no froth from the wound, which meant the shaft had missed the lung. He might survive if they got him medical care soon.

Steele looked at him, glanced back at the door, which was half closed now, then back at Gunther. He reached out and grabbed the old Austrian by his shoulders.

"This is going to hurt like hell, Gunther."

The old man looked at Steele through eyes hazed with pain and nodded.

Steele took a deep breath and pulled Gunther off the spear that

433

had nailed him to the wall. Gunther shrieked horribly, and then, amazingly, pushed Steele away, staggering toward the safe.

"Gunther, what . . ." Steele couldn't believe the man was still standing.

"Back," Gunther said, in a voice suddenly grown feeble. He backed against the wall and held there for a moment.

Steele cast an anxious glance at the closing door. When he looked back around, Gunther had leaned into the safe and was struggling with its contents. He slid something heavy from the safe and turned.

Steele's mouth dropped open. In his hands, Gunther held a box, a golden box encrusted with jewels that burned green and red and white and seemed to amplify the beam from Steele's flashlight. Suddenly, a horrible remembered sound whispered again in the silence of the vault. Steele felt his body tense as a second volley of spears, undoubtedly triggered by lifting the box off its pedestal in the safe, snaked through the darkness. One of the spears entered Gunther's face just to one side of his nose. The impact lifted him from his feet and slammed him back against the wall. Two more spears slammed dull and wet through his midsection, but his open dead eyes didn't flinch. The bejeweled gold box thudded to the floor, spilling its contents.

"Derek. Hurry. The door."

Steele shot a panicked look at the door, then looked back at the contents of the box spread out on the floor—a bolt of cloth and ancient yellowed pages. If he left now, all of the dying would be for nothing. And the killing would continue.

Fighting the panic that rose in his chest, Steele dropped to his knees and scrambled for the contents of the box. He put them in the box and closed the lid.

"Get out now," he yelled to Stephanie as he lunged toward the door. It was inches wide. Stephanie slipped through easily.

"Here," he shouted as he jammed the box through the opening. She took it. Steele jammed himself in sideways as the gap continued to narrow.

He couldn't fit through! He could feel the steel edges of the door closing on him, pressing his back into the frame. Panic consumed him now. He felt like screaming. Not this close, he wanted to yell. It's not fair. He fought the panic and shoved with all his strength against the edge of the door. He seemed motionless for a moment, then finally slipped through the opening, falling face first onto the salty floor.

CHAPTER THIRTY-SIX

"Hand me the box."

Anderson's voice annoyed the hell out of Stephanie. She ignored his request as she knelt beside Steele on the hard gritty floor of the salt chamber where he had fallen after squeezing through the vault door. Just instants after he handed her the box with the shroud and the Linz testaments, the massive door slammed shut. He had been a split-second away from being crushed like an insect.

He fell panting from the exertion, from the pain, and from the horror of seeing Gunther pinned to the wall, not once, but twice. He would always remember the way the old Austrian's eyes bulged open even after he died, and the way his right arm continued to twitch.

Steele had fallen face down beside the fully uniformed skeleton of an SS trooper. Ignoring the mortal reminder of yesterday's death, Stephanie rushed to Steele and set the jewel-encrusted gold box on the floor next to the skeleton's head. She didn't notice how her hand brushed the jaw of the skull or how it lolled to one side, its deep lifeless eye sockets surveying the dimly lit chamber. She ignored all this as she turned him over and cradled him in her arms. Tears of relief and gratitude shimmered in both their eyes.

"*Give* me the box." Anderson's voice was strident.

Stephanie turned angrily to tell the NSA agent to fuck off, but her angry words died in her throat when she saw the muzzle of his gun pointed at her. In his other hand he held a flashlight, which he pointed into her face. She squinted into the glaring light.

"What—" She could not comprehend what she saw.

"Hand me the box," Anderson repeated himself. "Now!"

In the darkness, they heard a scraping sound, shoes against the salt floor.

"You, father!" Anderson pointed the flashlight at Meyer. "Hold still or I'll shoot her." Meyer stopped.

Steele sat up.

"Hold it!" Anderson commanded. "Don't do anything foolish."

Steele looked up, dazed for a moment, but the new threat rapidly erased the memories of the immediate past.

"Now," Anderson said with the impatience of a man trying to sound patient. "Hand me the box."

Stephanie looked at Steele. He nodded.

As she reached over to grab the box Steele noticed, out of the corner of his eye, a holstered revolver lying on the floor, still attached to the dead SS trooper's belt.

Anderson took the box from Stephanie, who sat down on the floor after handing it to him. It was heavy, at least thirty or forty pounds.

Anderson backed away from them until he was a good twenty feet away: close enough for them to be at point blank range, but far enough so they could not rush him.

"Now turn off your flashlights and throw them over to me. I want to make sure I have enough light to get out of here." They complied. Anderson gathered the lights and put them in a pile at his feet.

"Walk over to them, father," Anderson said, indicating Steele and Stephanie. "And sit down next to them."

Meyer walked over to where Steele and Stephanie sat. He looked at Steele who, with a nod of his head, motioned for the priest to sit down.

"You've given me a great challenge, Steele," Anderson said as he set his flashlight on the floor of the chamber and pointed it at the trio. He unburdened himself of his pack, keeping his gun pointed at them at all times.

He looked down briefly as he set the pack on the floor. Steele moved slightly toward the trooper's gun.

"You too, father . . . and Mrs. Steele." Anderson spoke as he knelt beside the pack and with one hand unbuckled its straps. "I don't think I've ever gotten as much of a challenge from a group of amateurs before." He opened the top flap of the pack, and with his free hand began to unload its contents: first aid supplies, a blanket, canned water, dehydrated food, a small butane stove with a cover that doubled as a pot.

"I almost hate to have to kill you," Anderson continued, his voice growing in pitch as he spoke. "I could leave you in here to die. In forty years or so, you'd look like the rest of these." He paused to swing his arm in a broad arc to take in the skeletons in the chamber.

Steele inched closer to the holster and grabbed it by the narrow end. He began to pull it toward him. He was amazed at how easy it was. He had somehow imagined that the uniform full of bones would be heavy, as if there should be weight in death.

"But I'm not a sadistic man," Anderson told them. "Starving to death is a long and painful way to go." He paused. A smile came to his face, as if a delightful thought had flashed through his mind. "You might even be forced into cannibalizing the one who died first." He saw the horror on their faces and barked a short laugh. "Don't worry," he said as he bent to try and get a grip on the box. It was unwieldy. "I'll give you each two shots at the base of the skull. There won't be any pain."

Steele got his fingers around the snap closure of the holster and gently pried it open. It made the barest of clicks. Anderson was occupied now with trying to maneuver the box into the empty pack. Steele slid the revolver from the holster. He felt the grip firm and cold in his hand.

Anderson had succeeded in getting the box in the pack. On top of the box he had thrown the flashlights. Now he was trying to refasten the straps. Steele nudged first Meyer and then Stephanie with the muzzle of the gun. As they looked at him, he cast his eye down at the revolver. There was no way to tell them, but he hoped they'd scatter in the darkness when the time came.

The time came very soon. Anderson finished with the straps, hoisted the pack and slipped one arm through a strap. He would have to switch his gun to his left hand for just a moment in order to get his right arm through the second strap.

Steele watched, waited. Timing was all. Timing and whether or not the ammunition in the old pistol would fire. Anderson adjusted the left strap, shifted it to make the right one hang open. His hands started to come together. The left hand closed around the gun; for an instant, neither finger was on the trigger.

Now, Steele thought as he brought the revolver up. He nudged Stephanie with his shoulder so that she sprawled on her side out of the light.

Anderson's face changed from one of half-bored annoyance with the petty details of the pack to one of surprise as his hostages began to move. His eyes bulged with fear as he saw the revolver in Steele's hand.

Anderson fired first with his left hand, but the aim was jerky and went wild. Meyer sprang to his feet and joined Stephanie in the darkness. Together they ran toward yet another lump of bones on the floor, hoping to find another weapon.

Steele pulled back the hammer of the revolver, aimed for Anderson's chest and pulled the trigger. The dull thudding mechanical sound made by the hammer falling on a dud round fell like a mortal pain on Steele's ears. He rolled out of the light of Anderson's flashlight as the NSA man switched hands and fired again. The slug plowed a deep trench in the floor at Steele's feet.

Steele fired again on the roll. This time the revolver roared in the darkness. But the shot missed Anderson. Instead, it kicked up the salt at one end of the flashlight and sent it skittering across the chamber, casting wild flashing lights that reminded Steele of a strobe. In the surreal light, Steele caught a glimpse of Anderson running toward the exit from the chamber. The flashlight came to rest with its beam pointing directly into a corridor that led from the chamber. The corridor was illuminated, but the chamber itself was cast into the deep formless darkness of nightmares.

Suddenly from his left, Steele heard the roar of another gun. In the light from the muzzle flash, they saw a white geyser of salt erupt from the chamber wall behind Anderson as he made the safety of the corridor and disappeared into the darkness.

"Derek?" It was Stephanie's voice.

"Over here," he called. Moments later, the three were once again together.

"Steele." This time it was Anderson's voice. It had the hollow echoing tones of sound bouncing through underground distances. "Steele, I have spare ammunition. And it's all live and reliable.

If you come after me, I'll be waiting for you in the darkness. You'll never see me in time. I know where you have to walk to get out.''

"Anderson," Steele called. But there was no reply.

They huddled in the claustrophobic, clinging darkness, fearful of making their position known. Was Anderson waiting for them to go after the flashlight? They squatted for what seemed like hours as the flashlight's beam began to fade toward yellow. Without the light, there was no hope of following their carbon-black trail out of the mine.

Finally, Steele stood up in the darkness, revolver in one hand, the other trembling with indecision. Was the flashlight bait? Was the starved rat finally forced to have a go at the cheese in the trap? Finally, he tucked the revolver into his pants, sprinted toward the light, grabbed it, and dived away from the spot, trying to turn off the switch as he waited for the roar of bullets and the impact of slugs.

But the roar never came. The only sounds in the darkness came from his own heavy breathing. Had Anderson left? They might die if he was there waiting for them to try and make their way out of the mine. But they'd surely die if they didn't try. To conserve the flashlight's flagging batteries, he flashed it once to determine where Stephanie and Father Meyer were, then turned it off and walked slowly toward them.

Darkness was their friend; it would hide them. Darkness was their enemy; it could lead them into booby traps left by an old foe.

They gathered up the water, gas stove, Gunther's climbing rope which was still attached to the vault room door, and one of the blankets that Anderson had dumped from his pack. The blanket was made of an aluminized plastic, and reinforced with some sort of fibers. It was of the sort motorists and campers carry for emergencies. This was definitely an emergency.

Steele lit the small gas stove, and in the gently blue light it cast they made their way along the trail of carbon black that Stephanie had so carefully laid down on the way in.

The anemic light of the gas stove took them as far as the massive minefield that guarded the immediate entrance to the chamber

440

Steele pulled out the flashlight then and used its remaining minutes to guide them through the minefield step by step.

The rest of the going was made easy by the dark trail that snaked around mines and booby traps. In several places they could see where Anderson had tried to obliterate the carbon black. But his efforts only smudged the trail.

Anderson had also tried to isolate them by pulling the bridge boards from the roiling underground stream in Gunther's tunnel. But after only a dozen or so tosses, Steele was able to entangle the far end of one of the boards with the climbing rope and pull it to them. With the rope tied around his waist, he crossed the single shaky board while Stephanie and Meyer hung tight onto the rope's other end.

Once on the other side, he replaced all of the boards so the others could cross.

It was dark by the time they reached the entrance to the abandoned mine. The snowstorm had cleared completely, leaving a dark moonless sky filled with stars. A sharp wind keened up from the valley.

One of the snowmobiles was gone and Anderson had removed the distributor wires from the other two. He had either taken the wires with him or thrown them into the snow where they would remain hidden until the spring thaw.

Steele looked first at one of the snowmobiles and then the other. He removed a sparkplug wire from one, and—taking it over to the other vehicle—fastened it first to the distributor and then to the high-voltage coil. The engine roared with the try of the starter.

The three of them mounted the snowmobile with Steele at the controls.

"He has gone to Innsbruck," Meyer said, breaking out of a nearly catatonic silence. "Anderson has gone to Innsbruck."

"How do you know?" Steele asked, raising his voice above the roar of the snowmobile engine.

"Brown," Meyer said.

"What?" Steele asked, "I don't understand."

"I told you I would tell you what that meant, didn't I?" Meyer said.

Steele nodded slowly, afraid that the events of the day had unhinged the old priest's mind.

"It was not brown, the color," Meyer said quietly. Steele turned off the snowmobile engine to hear him better. "No, it was Braun." He paused, looking off into a place where neither Steele nor Stephanie could go. "Braun. He mentioned the name just before he died, as if Braun were to blame. I prayed it would not be him. But it must be."

Meyer fixed Steele with pain-filled eyes.

"Braun lives in Innsbruck," Meyer said. "Anderson has taken the shroud to him. We must go there."

Steele waited for more information, but Meyer had fallen silent. Steele started the snowmobile engine once again and steered the machine down the mountain.

CHAPTER THIRTY-SEVEN

Dawn had barely begun to sculpt the shadows in Bernini's colonnade around Saint Peter's square when police began setting up the crowd-control barriers in preparation for the Pope's weekly audience.

For a very long time, Wednesday had been the day when the Pope granted audiences to people "without rank or name" from anywhere in the world. Even though this Wednesday fell on the day after Christmas, the Pope saw no reason to postpone the weekly audience.

The Pope walked thoughtfully from his private chapel, fortified by more than ninety minutes of matins, lauds, and the prime of his daily audience.

He paused at a window of his apartment in the Apostolic Palace, and looked out at the activity below. At the very periphery he saw the beginnings of the crowd that later would parade through the auditorium that Paul VI had built solely for the convenience of the public audience. He particularly enjoyed the public audiences. These were real people, the flock that God had chosen him to administer to. No one cold take that away from him, not even Braun.

The Pope fought the rage rising within him. He had trusted Braun with the most sensitive issues of the Church, had defended him from those who felt the cardinal from Vienna was too combative, too lacking in charity and forgiveness. Standing there, looking down at people who had gotten up in the middle of the night to get here before the sun rose, the Pope felt tears of frustration, anger, and sadness welling up in his eyes. If Braun had his way—and the young cardinal has almost always succeeded—these public audiences would very soon pass into the ambitious Austrian's hands.

The Pope took a long shuddering breath, held it, and let it out in a sigh that could have encompassed the universal sorrow of the world, but which this morning only included the unearthing of the shroud and the Linz testaments.

Braun had awakened him late last night with the news, and the demand that the College of Cardinals be convened immediately. Braun emphasized that he wanted an orderly transition.

Orderly transition. The Pope snorted as he turned away from the window with his uncharitable thoughts. He walked toward the dining room. Despite the crisis, he was hungry.

Immediately after Braun's telephone call, the Pope had sent his secretary of state, Richard Borden, and a team of Vatican archivists to Innsbruck to authenticate Braun's claim. The Pope looked at the old clock with the wooden cogs hanging on the wall. When would Borden call? It had been a sleepless night for all of them. When would he call?

He walked into the dining room and greeted his staff. They bade him good mornings with sad, searching eyes. Did they know? How?

The call the Pope had been waiting for came as he scanned the front page of the *Rome Daily American*.

In his private study, he took the call.

"Yes, Richard?" The Pope said trying to sound cheerful. "What have you found?"

The Pope's face crumpled like paper. The young, vigorous former resistance fighter seemed to age decades in a matter of seconds. His erect carriage sagged, and his strong shoulders slumped. He searched jerkily for several moments before he found a chair to sit in.

"Yes," the Pope said in the voice of an old man. "I understand." He listened for perhaps half a minute. "Is there anything . . . anything at all we can do?"

Shaking his head as if his secretary of state were in the room with him, the Pope's voice was emphatic when he spoke. "No!

You mustn't. That would make us as morally bankrupt as he. Leave there as soon as you can. I need you here."

Slowly the Pope replaced the telephone on its receiver and even more slowly got to his feet. He passed by the window again on his way back to the chapel. Dawn had colored the square a rosy pink. The crowd had thickened. He looked on them now with the bitter fondness of someone saying goodbye to a loved one.

And then he went to his private chapel to pray for a miracle.

"It's magnificent, Gerry, simply magnificent." Braun walked around the conference table in the ecumenical council meeting-room once again. On the table, the Shroud of Veronica lay stretched flat, covering most of the massive wooden table. The bejeweled gold box and the Linz testaments rested on a small table brought in from the reception foyer.

The shroud was nearly twelve feet long, woven of linen, and bore two head-to-head images—one anterior, one posterior—of a young girl entering puberty. The faint straw-colored outlines of her wounds were visible in the bright light of early morning.

Beyond the closed door to the council room came the muted voices of the men the Pope had sent from the Vatican to authenticate the shroud. Braun had enjoyed watching them work. As professionals they had been excited to examine such an obviously genuine part of history, but as people loyal to the current pope and his doctrines, they went about their task with heavy frowns, knowing what their authentication would mean.

The most troubled of all was Richard Borden. It didn't really matter, Braun thought. Like Constantine's scribe who had inter-viewed all of Veronica's townspeople, Borden and the others had all outlived their usefulness to him. And like the scribe, their days and their lives were finite.

A knock sounded on the door.

"Get that, please, Gerry," Braun said as he leaned over the table to stare into the face of the image.

Anderson's shoes thudded dully on the bare wooden floor as he walked to the door and opened it. Richard Borden, soon-to-be-come-ex-secretary of state, was standing on the other side.

445

"Please tell the cardinal that we will be going now," Borden said.

Braun lifted his head. "How is the Pope this morning, Borden?"

The secretary of state struggled to control his temper. "He's quite well, your grace, and has agreed to your . . . request. When may we expect you in Rome?"

Braun looked at him for several moments as if carefully considering the question. "When I'm ready," Braun said, then turned his attention back to the shroud.

Just then, a mild vibration shook the floor. The gondola had arrived to collect the Vatican party. Anderson closed the door on Richard Borden's face and returned to Braun's side.

"Would you like to be head of my personal security detail?" Braun asked, still gazing down at the shroud.

"Yes sir," Anderson said eagerly. "Of course, your grace."

Braun smiled up at him. "Then you must work well with our Mr. Maxwell. You'll be responsible for his safety as well as mine. He's an enormous asset to us. He will be able to go places, say things, accomplish great tasks that are unachievable by any other. Can you work with him?"

Anderson nodded. "How . . . how is his therapy coming?"

"Without a hitch," Braun said. "But you'll have to make arrangements for the doctor once it's all over."

Anderson nodded.

"And in your new position, you will have to refrain from doing it yourself." He noticed the momentary look of disappointment on Anderson's face. "You simply will not have the time nor the privacy to . . . indulge your—"

"Interests?" Anderson offered.

Braun smiled and nodded. "Yes. Your interests."

Anderson stood protectively beside Braun for several moments. "Ah, your grace?"

Braun looked up at him and raised his eyebrows.

"What about Rolf? He's been your personal bodyguard for so many years now."

"Rolf is getting old," Braun said quickly. "And he lacks a certain . . . a certain finesse that the new job requires."

"Will you tell him? Soon?"

"Just as soon as he returns." Braun stood up straight. "Meanwhile, repack all this." He waved his hand over the conference table. "I have to pack. We've got a charter flight to Rome at noon. I'd like to be out of here by eleven." He turned and walked toward the door. "Would you inform Maxwell and have the staff pack for him?"

"Of course, your grace," Anderson replied eagerly.

Steele came out of the doorway of the Hotel Central just before 10 A.M. He held the door open for Stephanie and for Father Meyer. The brightness of the day made them all squint as they walked down the Gilmstrasse toward the parking lot where they had left the Volvo. Steele carried bags for them all.

"It's way up there," Meyer pointed toward the north, his long thin finger describing a group of jagged peaks. "I was there once, nearly thirty years ago, before Braun was made a cardinal."

They had reached the corner of the Erlerstrasse and turned right, toward the university.

They found the car five minutes later. Steele first unlocked the doors, then started the engine to warm it up. While Stephanie settled herself in the passenger seat and Meyer arranged himself in back, Steele threw the bags in the trunk and brushed away the light dusting of snow that the wind had deposited during the night.

Finally he slipped back behind the wheel, put the transmission into gear, and drove out of the parking structure.

The roads in Innsbruck were slushy with snow and patchy with ice where the extreme cold had overcome the ability of the road salt to melt. The roads cleared, however, once they reached the autobahn and headed for the airport where Steele had booked a helicopter flight from a company that offered sightseeing tours of the ski slopes.

"The helipads's on the roof, toward the rear of the chalet," Meyer said. "According to Braun's housekeeper—who has been working with us for nearly twenty years now—the entrance to the house from the helipad is never locked. It connects with an elevator . . . and a staircase that leads down the center of the main chalet. The guards are stationed at the perimeter of the grounds and have their own quarters separate from the main chalet. Braun doesn't like to be reminded of his need for security, so the main chalet is off limits to the guards except in an emergency. The only security man allowed in the chalet under normal conditions is Braun's chief bodyguard, Rolf Engels. He's a big man and loyal. You will have to kill him if he confronts you. He may be getting on in years—he's nearly as old as I am—but he's still formidable.

"Terrific," Steele mumbled. "The best we can expect is for half the rounds in these old revolvers to work." He thought of the revolvers and the extra ammunition they had taken from the skeletons of the SS troopers in the Habersam mine.

"With any luck, we can use the revolvers to bluff our way out," Stephanie said hopefully. Neither Meyer nor Steele made any reply.

They arrived at the airport less than thirty minutes later and were directed to the proper terminal. Steele introduced them to the helicopter pilot, who expressed surprise when Steele told him where they wanted to go.

"It's a busy day for the Nochspitze," the pilot said.

Steele asked him what he meant.

"I have a request to pick up the cardinal at eleven and bring him back here. He's chartered a jet to Rome. Some emergency, I guess." He paused and added, "The cardinal doesn't like to be visited unexpectedly. I'll have to give him a call first, if you don't mind."

Steele looked at Meyer who quickly unzipped his down parka to reveal his clerical collar. The effect on the pilot was immediate.

"I'm carrying important information to the cardinal," Meyer said, which was not entirely a lie. "He is expecting me and will be angry if I'm delayed. You may call him, but I assure you that he is expecting us."

The pilot looked at Meyer with respect in his eyes. "Of course, father," he said. "Just follow me." He reached for a wool knit hat, pulled it on over his bald head, and headed for the door.

They fastened their seatbelts as the Jet Rangers's turbine engines whined to their idling pitch. After running through his preflight checklist, the pilot turned to them and nodded. With a sudden start, the engine's pitch increased and suddenly the ground fell away from them as they drifted forward nose down.

"Oh-h-h-h!" Stephanie gasped, as the pilot leaned the stick sharply over, forcing her against the window. The copter banked steeply now and climbed rapidly enough into the sky to leave butterflies in their stomachs.

CHAPTER THIRTY-EIGHT

Neils Braun had just finished packing his bags when he heard the thwack-thwack-thwack of the helicopter blades in the distance. He glanced at the elegant Piaget watch on his wrist to make sure that he was not late. The helicopter was early. That was fine, he thought. The sooner he could get to Rome, the sooner he could assume control.

Reassured that he was not running late, Braun took a last look around his quarters and smiled. It would be the last time he would view it through the eyes of a cardinal. In seventy-two hours, give or take a handful, he would be pope. He looked forward to the abdication ceremonies.

He used the telephone by his bed to call his manservant and told him to take the packed bags to the helipad and wait for the helicopter. Then Braun walked briskly down the stairs to the conference meeting room.

The chalet on the Nochspitze was situated at the very top of the peak on a ragged, uneven, roughly square plateau about a quarter of a mile from sheer cliff to sheer cliff. The Cardinal's Nest perched on one cliff overlooking the Inn Valley and the Olympic ski slopes of the Axamer Lizum.

About a hundred yards from the Cardinal's Nest, and connected to it by a covered, heated passage, was a small cottage designed to house a dozen men, the men who, in shifts of four, patrolled the area around the Cardinal's Nest twenty-four hours a day.

Like their counterparts who maintained security at the Palace of the Archbishops in Vienna, they were all seasoned men, veterans chosen from the ranks of the world's best military and antiterrorist units: SAS, GSG-9, Delta Force, and some units so secret that even their names were classified. That Braun was able to find and recruit these men was a testament to his extensive alliances within those groups, and to the generous salaries he paid them.

The twelve men were under the direction of Rolf Engels, a former member of Hitler's elite Mountain Corps. He had been recommended early on by a member of the ecumenical council as a suitable bodyguard for the then-up-and-coming bishop who spoke so eloquently against communism and who had very quickly become a target for its agents of violence.

Rolf Engels was at the gondola house drinking hot tea with the gondola operator and his security men when he heard the blades of the helicopter. Quickly, he glanced at his watch. His eyebrows rose slightly when he noted the time.

"Bernhard," Engels said to his soldier. "Step outside and tell me what you see."

Bernhard, a ruggedly built man in a white alpine camouflage suit, stepped outside. He was back in a moment.

"A yellow helicopter," Bernhard reported. "With black writing. It's too far off to make out the words on the side, but it looks like the same one the cardinal usually flies."

Engels nodded. "Thank you, sergeant." He took another sip from his tea, looked in his cup to see how much was left, and sighed.

"Better crank up the gondola," Engels said to the lift operator.

"Would you like me to come with you?" Bernhard asked.

Engels shook his head. "Strictly routine," he said, draining the rest of the by now lukewarm liquid from the plastic cup. He tossed the cup into a trash can, followed the gondola operator into the motor shed, and watched while he started up the smoothly oiled mechanism that carried the gondola car up the almost sheer cliff to the Cardinal's Nest.

* * *

The helicopter's skids had barely touched the snow on the chalet's helipad when the door opened. Steele jumped out first and helped both Stephanie and Meyer out. A set of stairs led down from the pad to a railed catwalk that led across the roof to a door set into an outhouse-sized structure.

"I'll wait here," the pilot spoke to Meyer. "No need for me to go back to the airport and then return for the cardinal's trip. Tell him to take his time. I'll be here."

Meyer nodded and joined Steele and Stephanie, who waited for him on the catwalk.

As Meyer had promised, the door was not locked. Steele pulled out the heavy old SS revolver as he stepped through the door. There was nothing but a set of stairs leading downward.

"Come on," he whispered, and began padding softly down the steps. The stairs were made of welded metal and covered with a rubbery nonskid material. They descended in silence.

At the first landing, they heard a door into the stairway open, followed by what sounded like the grunts and thuds of a man struggling with a heavy object. His sounds grew louder.

Steele went to the landing door and turned the knob. The door was locked. Below them, in the stairwell, the noises grew closer. Steele reached into his rear pocket and pulled a credit card from his wallet. Then, tucking the revolver in his belt, he knelt before the doorknob and inserted the card between the door and its jamb. Moments later, he was rewarded with a satisfying click. The door came open when he pulled on it.

Beyond the door was a stretch of attic, its flooring covered with a scattering of cardboard boxes and wooden crates.

Steele motioned Stephanie and Meyer to get inside. They complied as the noises from below grew louder. As Steele closed the door, they could hear clearly the breathless efforts of the man making the noises.

Steele pressed his eye to the narrow crack between the door and jamb, and moments later watched as a thin man staggered up the stairs with two massive hard-sided valises. The man paused on the landing long enough to wipe the perspiration from his face, and then continued on up the final flight. A few seconds later the stairwell was flooded with brilliant white light.

When the stairwell had once again fallen into the yellow dimness made by the low-wattage light bulbs, Steele opened the door and led the two others downward.

The whumping of the helicopter woke Maxwell. He awakened in time to feel the building shiver slightly under the aircraft's landing, although he didn't know that was what had caused the noise and the vibration.

He felt awful as he sat up in his bed. His usually clear, orderly thoughts swirled in his head like the lights from the mirrored ball he had once seen suspended above a dance floor.

He sat on the edge of his bed. He was hungry, that thought was clear. And thirsty too. Oh, Jesus. Thirsty as he had never been before. Thirsty like a hangover, only a thousand times worse. Somehow the thirst seemed connected with the disorganization of his thoughts.

But he put it all down to the flu. Braun said it was the flu. The doctor said it was a severe case of the flu. Maxwell shook his head and tried to remember the doctor. The memory wouldn't come.

Shakily, he got to his feet and shuffled into the bathroom. He filled the glass by the sink with water from the tap and drank it. He was still thirsty. He drank another glass.

Unsatisfied, Maxwell put the glass back by the sink, made his way back into the bedroom and sat on the side of the bed with his head almost between his knees. After several moments, he knew what he wanted, what he *had* to have: orange juice. Just the thought of it made him frantic.

Slowly, he got to his feet and, stumbling to his closet, pulled out his robe. It took him three tries to get his right arm in and five or his left. He fumbled with the sash around his waist and finally left it untied.

In the kitchen. He remembered having orange juice for breakfast once, in those little cardboard boxes. They must have them in the kitchen, he thought as he walked to the door of his room.

He passed the telephone and momentarily considered calling the kitchen and having them send up the orange juice. But they were such nice people and worked so hard, and besides, he figured it was time for him to get out of bed and get going again. He couldn't remember which number to dial anyway.

He opened the door to his room and stepped into the hallway. He stood there a very long time before remembering that the stairs were to the right.

Anderson was replacing the shroud and the last of its documentation in the jeweled gold box when Braun walked in. They felt a slight creak run throughout the structure as the helicopter settled down onto the reinforced landing area above.

"The helicopter's early," Braun said as he walked to Anderson's side and inspected his work. "I want you to remain here and wait for the side effect of the drugs to wear off of Maxwell. Then bring him to Rome."

Anderson nodded.

"Pack the box up in a suitcase or something and bring it up to me at the helicopter."

Anderson nodded again, picked up the lid of the box, and began to replace it. Braun turned to leave.

But before Braun could take half a dozen steps, the door to the council meeting room flew open and slammed back against the wall with a bang.

Braun stopped so quickly he almost stumbled; Anderson dropped the lid to the box as he whirled to confront the noise. The lid clattered dully on the wood of the table.

"Steele." Anderson spoke with the incredulity of a man confronted by a ghost.

Pressing his advantage of surprise, Steele stepped quickly forward and motioned Stephanie into the room.

"Cover him," Steele pointed at Braun. Stephanie stepped forward and leveled the old revolver at him. She pulled back the hammer.

At the sound of the revolver's mechanism, something flickered in Braun's eyes. But his steely self-control kept his face hard and straight.

"What is the meaning of this outrage," Braun blustered. "How dare you invade my privacy like this."

"Shut up." Stephanie said with authority. Braun tried to back away. "Stay still."

Braun mustered a dignified pose, but behind his composed exterior his mind whirred. He had talked his way out of worse situations in his life. He looked the angry but attractive woman approaching him and recognized, from a photograph he had once seen, the woman who worked for Richard Summers.

Anderson had backed away from Steele, trying to put the table between him and the old revolver that might or might not be capable of tearing a terrible hole through him.

"Don't be fooled, your grace," Anderson said. "Those guns are relics. The ammunition's forty years old."

"Hold it, Anderson!" Steele ordered. "Stop right where you are." Steele smiled. "Just look over here, your *disgrace,*" he said harshly. Braun's head turned. "Your stooge here has stopped because he knows that the gun just might blow his head off." Steele grinned at Anderson. He paused. "Are you willing to chance the odds that the gun *might* not fire?"

"No," Braun said trying to restrain his anger. "No, of course not. You've obviously got us at a disadvantage." As he faced Stephanie's gun, Braun tried to figure out where Rolf would be. The old soldier was a man of routine and he made his inspections of the guards on a schedule that kept better time than most watches. His mind raced, trying to remember. Then the floor beneath his feet rumbled faintly. The gondola lift motor had started. Of course. Rolf always visited the gondola shed in the mornings. He liked to go over its mechanism with the operator to make sure it was safe.

Inwardly, Braun smiled. It took the gondola about three minutes to climb the precipitous slope. Three minutes. He had to keep them talking long enough for Rolf to finish making his rounds.

Steele stepped back until both Anderson and Braun were in his field of vision. "Put your gun on the table," Steele told Anderson. The NSA man hesitated as if he was calculating the chances that Steele's revolver wouldn't fire. Steele stepped toward him. "On the table, *friend.*" Anderson reached inside his coat. "Easy," Steele said. "Bring it out by the grip with thumb and forefinger. If I see a finger near the trigger you're a dead man."

Anderson nodded and pulled his gun out from under his armpit and laid it on the conference table. It was a heavy U.S. Army Colt .45 automatic.

"You were clever, Anderson," Steele said. "And convincing. You certainly made a fool out of me."

"Now don't be angry, Mr. Steele," Braun said, his confidence rising with the knowledge that Rolf would be along shortly. "We're reasonable men. Why don't we talk—"

"Reasonable?" Steele thundered. "You call killing people reasonable? You self-righteous, hypocritical bastard. We ought to kill you right now. You've got the nerve to try and call yourself reasonable? You've betrayed everyone and everything you've come in contact with. You and the other slime like you, all your buddies in the Vatican who want to destroy the truth." He looked toward the box. "Or lock it up so no one will know what it really is. You want to hide Hitler's blackmail, hide the shame." Steele paused. "Or maybe you want to blackmail somebody yourself." Steele looked at the flicker of recognition in the cardinal's eyes.

"Who do you want to blackmail, Mr. Cardinal Archbishop? What are you going to do with the shroud?"

"You misunderstand me, Mr. Steele," Braun said.

"Yeah," said Steele. "Hitler and Eichmann and Goering and Mengele were misunderstood too."

Braun raised his hand slowly. "Please let me say something, if you will?" Steele nodded. "What I want to do with the shroud is nothing more than save the Christian world from communism."

Steele looked at him in shocked silence for a moment. "You're joking," Steele said, then coughed a small cynical laugh. "I know people like you, Braun. You're out for yourself. You don't give a good goddamn for saving anything or doing anything that doesn't benefit yourself. You and all the other little pious frauds like you just want power. You don't care how you get the power or which side you have to be on to get it. You could just as easily be the fucking premier of Russia. You're interchangeable, people like you. Just unplug you from one side and plug you in on the other. The rest of us can't tell the players without a program. Well, whatever you've got in mind for the shroud isn't going to come through for you."

Steele walked toward the box on the long conference table. "We're taking the box with us." He glanced up at the ceiling. "We've got transportation waiting. So I want you and Anderson here to lie down on the floor." Steele waved the muzzle of the gun at both men. "Down here in the middle of the floor. Face down, legs spread."

Neither Braun nor Anderson complied. "Now." Stephanie

rodded Braun with the muzzle of her gun. He jumped as if shocked by an electric wire, then glared at her.

"Go on," Stephanie said. "You heard him."

"We can kill you now," Steele said. "Just like you had people killed. Or you can lie down on the floor and let us take the box peacefully."

"You must let me explain," Braun wheedled. "You just don't understand."

"Perhaps not, but I do." Meyer's voice boomed through the room, stronger, louder than either Steele or Stephanie had thought possible. "Perhaps Mr. Steele and his wife don't understand, but I certainly do. I should. I've spent enough years studying you."

"Damn you, you foolish old man," Braun cursed as Meyer approached.

"Yes," Meyer said blandly. "I probably am damned. But what does that make you?"

The two men stared silently at each other for several moments.

"Why have you done it?" Braun said "There was no good reason. Why have you done these things, you meddlesome, senile old man?"

"I've had two things that kept me alive all these years," Meyer said. "After that day in Altaussee. One of them was to recover the shroud. The other was my pride in you."

"What are you saying?" Braun said. "You're talking nonsense, riddles."

"They tried to tell me," Meyer said, his eyes focused on a memory. "They tried to tell you were the man at the top, but I wouldn't believe them. I couldn't believe them."

Braun turned to Steele. "Would you try to get this old fool to stop talking nonsense?"

Meyer fished about in the deep pocket of his parka and pulled from it a wrinkled and much-folded envelope. His hands shook as he unfolded the flap of the envelope and pulled out a crinkled piece of paper. He walked up to Braun and held the paper out in his hand.

"Look at this," Meyer said.

Braun stared at Meyer as one looks at an asylum inmate. He hesitated for a moment, then snatched the paper from the priest's hands. The cardinal's eyes scanned the page quickly; then he handed it back to Meyer.

"So?" Braun said.

Without answering, Meyer pulled another piece of paper from the envelope and offered that. Braun rolled his eyes, but took the piece of paper. Moments later, he handed that back to Meyer. The performance was repeated for yet a third piece of paper.

"My patience has its limits, old man," Braun said. "And your riddle here has just about reached that limit."

"What do those pieces of paper mean to you?" Meyer asked

Braun gave Meyer an exasperated look. "They mean nothing, not together at least," he said. "You gave me a copy of a letter from my father to my mother, a copy of my birth certificate, and a copy of the Wehrmacht's notification of my father's death on the Polish front."

Meyer nodded slowly without taking his steady, sad gaze from Braun's face. Meyer handed the papers back to Braun. "Look at them again. Look at the dates."

Braun looked toward Steele. "Why must I—"

"Take the papers," Steele ordered.

Scowling, Braun snatched the papers from Meyer's hand and examined them again.

"Look at the dates," Meyer said.

Steele watched the interplay of the two men with increasing fascination. There was tension between them, that was for sure. But it wasn't the tension of two old enemies. It was something more . . . personal than that.

Anderson, too, watched the drama played out between the two clergymen, but not with any regard to the issues between the two men. Rather, Anderson was waiting for Steele's attention to be completely directed to Braun and Meyer.

The scowl on Braun's face gradually gave way to a look of astonishment as he examined the papers Meyer had given him.

Meyer read Braun's face: "So the dates do mean something?" Meyer said.

"I . . . I don't understand," Braun said, looking first at Meyer and then with confusion at the papers.

"It's quite simple, actually," Meyer said. "The letter to your mother from her husband was written by a brave Oberleutnant

458

from Radom, about sixty miles south of Warsaw, on September 7, 1939. That same brave Oberleutnant—

"My father," Braun interrupted.

Meyer ignored him as he continued. "That brave Oberleutnant died in battle on September 9 in the German assault on Warsaw." The old priest paused, licked his lips, then resumed. "You were born August 2, 1940, nearly eleven months after this brave Oberleutnant died."

"I still don't understand," Braun said softly, genuinely confused. "You've gone to great lengths to prove that I'm illegitimate. So, I'm illegitimate? That hardly justifies your behavior for the past forty years."

"No, ordinarily you'd be right," Meyer said. "But you're not just any bastard. You're *my* bastard."

Braun's face drained of color as if a plug had been pulled. His mouth flew open. "You . . . you're my *father?*"

Meyer nodded.

Attention was riveted on Meyer and Braun. Anderson lunged for his pistol.

"Derek!" Stephanie's scream dragged Steele's attention away from Meyer and Braun.

Steele leveled the revolver at Anderson and pulled the trigger. The hammer made an important click as it fell on a dud round. Steele felt his stomach drop through the floor. Anderson's hand was inches away from the Colt. Steele followed him with the muzzle of the revolver, brought the hammer back and pulled the trigger again. And again the revolver's hammer fell on a dud round.

Anderson grabbed the Colt and let his lunge carry him in a roll off the other side of the table and on to the floor.

"Get back," Steele yelled to Stephanie, but she stood her ground and aimed her revolver toward where Anderson had disappeared behind the table.

In an instant Anderson jumped up, firing wildly with the Colt. The first slug slammed into Werner Meyer's larnyx, pulverizing his spinal column and tearing most of his neck away.

As Meyer's lifeless body began to fall to the floor, Anderson trained his gun on Steele. Steele fired at him again, but for the third time, the revolver failed to fire. Anderson tugged smoothly on the Colt's trigger. Stephanie fixed her sights on Anderson and pulled the trigger of her revolver.

Stephanie's revolver kicked in her hands. The slug struck Anderson in the shoulder just as he fired the Colt, causing his shot at Steele to go wild. He dropped the Colt on the floor as the bullet's impact spun him around. Stephanie fired again. Her second shot struck Anderson in the back with enough force to slam him against the broad expanse of glass that overlooked the Inn Valley.

As they looked on in stunned silence, the window buckled under the impact of Anderson's body. The shattering glass sounded like crackling thunder, but its intensity paled under Anderson's screams as he teetered against the sill for a second, then toppled from the window in a hail of glass fragments. They heard his steady wailing scream for several seconds.

CHAPTER THIRTY-NINE

When he got out of the gondola car at the top of the cliff, Rolf looked up at the helipad, puzzled that the cardinal hadn't already taken off. He was usually out like a flash. Never liked to wait. Rolf shook his head slowly and started up the steps to the chalet, listening to the lazy shwoop-shwoop of the idling helicopter blades.

The next thing Rolf Engels heard was the crashing of glass and the screams. As sturdy as the chalet was, with its stone walls and thick wood, it was not surprising that he failed to hear the shots fired in the council meeting room.

But the screams and the glass. Something was definitely amiss. As he stealthily let himself into the chalet, he checked off the available men he could summon. Three men were taking their shift off by going into Innsbruck. One was by the gondola shed. That left him with two men on duty up here plus three more sleeping in the barracks.

It would be enough, he thought, as he slipped quietly into the grand foyer that had once been the lobby back in the days when the chalet had been a resort. From within the building, Rolf heard the excited murmurings of the domestic staff. The housekeeper came running down the hall.

"Oh, Herr Engels," she cried. "I am so glad you're here. Something has happened in the council meeting room. I heard breaking glass, and a loud noise. It could have been a gunshot or perhaps an explosion of some kind."

Explosion? That surprised him. He had heard no explosion. Immediately, he thought of the new natural gas logs the cardinal

461

archbishop had recently installed in the huge fireplace in the council meeting room. Rolf had been against it from the start. It was unsafe, he had argued unsuccessfully. Hadn't the cardinal read of all the stories about homes and office buildings—sometimes entire blocks of buildings—that had been destroyed because some undetected gas leak had been allowed to build up and then had exploded from a harmless spark? Rolf had lost that battle.

But now, the fact that he might have been right was uppermost in his mind as he raced up the stairs toward the council meeting room.

Robert Maxwell failed to find the kitchen in his ramblings. In his drugged haze, he kept descending the stairs until there were no more stairs to descend.

He shuffled his dazed way along the corridors of the chalet's subbasement, which contained the heating and utility units, the auxilliary electrical generators, and a former coal bin with stone walls and a secure thick oaken door.

Maxwell had reached the end of the corridor next to the coal bin, and was about to turn around and return to the stairs when he was surprised to see light shining from under the coal bin door. He was even more surprised to hear soft classical music coming from behind the door. Maxwell thought he recognized the strains of Bach's Second Brandenburg Concerto.

He stood there for several moments, not believing his ears. But in a moment he realized he was listening to a radio as an announcer came on to tell the listening audience that they had been listening to Bach's Second Brandenburg.

Maxwell was feeling proud, in a drug-dazed sort of way, about recognizing the work, when he heard the station being changed. Then he realized that there was someone behind the door. His muddled thoughts didn't extend to asking why someone would be living in an old coal bin; he only recognized that someone who lived here could tell him where to find the kitchen and the orange juice he so desperately wanted. He knocked on the door. "Hello?" he called. "Hello, I'm lost. Can you help me?"

Inside the former coal bin, which had been cleaned up and equipped as a Spartan jail cell, Richard Summers started so violently when he heard the knocks that he almost knocked the radio off the table.

"Rolf?" he said, knowing the voice on the other side of the door was not that of his jailor.

"No," came the muffled reply. "I'm Robert Maxwell." There was a pause. "I'm a guest of Cardinal Braun's, but I've gotten lost. Can you show me how to get to the kitchen?"

The glimmerings of hope flared in Summer's mind. Would this person let him out? Would he be able to escape once he got out? Optimism took hold of him as he jumped to his feet. He had to try. Braun would keep him alive only for as long as he continued to be a good source of information. And there was no guarantee of how long that might last. Under the influence of Rolf's crude coercion or the inducement of drugs, Summers had told them nearly everything he knew about Stephanie and Derek Steele and the mysterious customer in Kreuzlingen. He had to escape now. He wouldn't get another chance.

"Yes," Summers lied. "I can show you the kitchen." He paused. "But first you must help me get out of here. The door is locked."

Summer's words triggered a tiny alarm in Maxwell's clouded thoughts. "Why is the door locked?" he asked. Then he added, "I really want some orange juice. I'm very thirsty."

The man sounded off, Summers thought. Although the voice was adult, its tones and word choice were almost childlike. Was he talking with an imbecile? He decided to risk it.

"I made a mistake," Summers said. "I left my keys outside. See if you can find them and let me out and I'll help you get your orange juice."

"I really want some orange juice," Maxwell said and then looked around in the corridor. There at the end was a red lanyard. When he got close to it, he saw there were two keys tied at the end. He walked back toward the door behind which he had heard the Brandenburg.

"You really know where the kitchen is?" Maxwell asked.

"Of course," Summers said. "I live here, don't I?"

The answer sounded logical to Maxwell. He fitted one key in the first lock and turned it, then directed his attention to the second.

* * *

463

"Stop him," Steele shouted to Stephanie. In the confusion, Braun had grabbed the box with the shroud and the Linz testament. He was halfway to the door when Stephanie turned and fired her revolver. It was her turn to be rewarded with a dull click.

Braun bolted through the door with the box under his arm and ran left down the corridor toward the stairwell. He passed the entrance to the dining room and rushed past the doors to the kitchen. Near the end of the hallway, he stumbled momentarily on the carpeting and resumed his headlong rush toward the stairwell door at the end of the hall.

Stephanie fired again. This time the revolver jumped in her hand, but she missed. Steele rushed past her, sprinting down the hall.

"It's through here," Summers told Maxwell. They were standing on the stairwell landing that led to the third floor.

"Why won't you come with me all the way?" Maxwell's voice was almost a whine. "I might get lost again."

"Just walk through that door and across the hall. The first door you come to will lead to the kitchen."

Maxwell opened his mouth to protest, but Summers had already left him.

Steele was halfway down the hall when Braun jerked open the door to the stairwell. But instead of rushing in as Steele expected him to, Braun seemed to hesitate.

Braun was shocked into hesitation by the sight of Robert Maxwell standing in front of him in the doorway.

"Maxwell!" Braun exclaimed, momentarily forgetting Steele. "What are you doing here?"

If Maxwell had not been administered his morning dosage of the mind-altering drug that Braun was using to facilitate the persuasion process, or if Maxwell had stayed in his room as he had been instructed to do, he would have responded calmly to Braun's question. But Maxwell was not a rational man. The drug-assisted

464

persuasion used by Braun had caused the subject, Maxwell in this case, to develop an almost father-son relationship with the persuader, Braun. And in the childlike state induced by the drug, Maxwell's insatiable thirst had become an overpowering motivation, one in which he felt betrayed by Braun. He grabbed Braun's shoulders.

"Why did you leave me?" Maxwell asked. "You were there and you walked out. Why?"

Braun looked at him wildly, the sounds of Steele's running footfalls pounding in his ear. For an insane instant, Braun considered trying to explain that he had suddenly left their session because Gerry Anderson had arrived with the shroud and the Linz testaments. But Braun knew Maxwell wouldn't understand him until the drug wore off.

"Let me go," Braun said and tried to push his way past Maxwell. But the younger man was stronger. Steele's footsteps grew louder.

"Why did you leave?" Maxwell's voice had grown petulant. Braun tried again to push past the younger man, but he only succeeded in almost losing his grip on the box. Finally, in desperation, he twisted away from Maxwell, freeing himself from the grasping fingers and fled in the opposite direction.

Braun heard another shot echo in the hallway as he pushed his way through the kitchen doors, heading for the service stairway built as a way to separate the guests from the daily household chores of a hotel staff.

Most of the vast kitchen was unused except when the Cardinal's Nest hosted large dinner parties. It was a huge room, perhaps forty feet square, with a gleaming stove, freezers, and food processing machines lining the stainless steel counters. Pots hung from racks dangling from the ceiling. It was a kitchen that could handle a state dinner for any president or dictator in the world. But on this morning it was deserted except for the cook, who was preparing a large pot of stew for the guard staff.

Steele raced through the doors of the kitchen, followed closely by Stephanie. Behind him, he heard a childlike cry of delight: *"There's* the kitchen!"

"Stop!" Steele shouted at Braun, who was only a few paces in front of him. "Stop or I'll shoot."

From the corner of his eye, Steele saw the cook drop to the floor. Braun ran, heedless of Steele's threat.

On the run, Steele aimed the revolver and pulled the trigger. The gun roared, striking a thick skillet next to Braun's head just as he turned the corner of a counter. The intense gonglike sound startled Braun and he lost his balance, crashing to the floor, still holding on to the jeweled box. Steele was on top of him in an instant.

"Give me that," Steele said. When the cardinal refused to relinquish the box, Steele tucked the revolver in his belt, bent over, and tried to wrest it from Braun's hands.

"Call Rolf!" Braun screamed at his terrified cook. "Call him now."

Stephanie rushed over to the cook and covered him with her pistol.

Rolf padded quietly down the carpeted hallway, his .44 Magnum drawn and ready. As he approached the door to the kitchen, he heard the shot and the sounds of a scuffle.

Steele grappled with Braun for the box, trying to loosen the man's almost deathlike grip on it. Suddenly Braun lashed out with his free fist, catching Steele on his forehead and stunning him for an instant. Braun was nearly standing when Steele recovered. Carrying the box under one arm, Braun tried to stagger to the stairwell. Steele stepped quickly over to him and leaned into a right hook that caught Braun on the left side of his head and knocked his feet out from under him.

The jeweled box and its contents flew out of Braun's hands and scattered on the kitchen floor as the cardinal landed heavily and lay very still on the black-and-white tiled floor.

It was silent for an instant save for Steele's heavy breathing and the vigorous bubbling of a stew that needed to be stirred.

Then Rolf Engels burst into the kitchen. He raised the Magnum to shoot when, suddenly, out of the corner of his eye, he saw another person, this one with a gun leveled at the cook. Years of military and bodyguard experience had equipped Rolf to make instant assessments. He decided quickly that the woman with the gun was a secondary target to the man who stood over the cardinal. It didn't much matter to him if she shot the cook. Engels was hired to protect the cardinal at all costs.

So Engels returned the Magnum's aim toward the man, centered the sights so the slug would hit him in the small of the back. Rolf had seen the power of the .44 Magnum. He had once fired one at the rear of a fleeing car. The slug had passed through the trunk, through the person in the back seat, through the driver, though the dashboard, and into the engine compartment, with enough force to stall the engine. At the very least, this man's spinal cord would be shattered, his heart pulverized, and the entire front of his chest ripped away with the insides exposed. He squeezed the trigger.

Steele bent over to gather the box and its contents when the .44 Magnum's slug passed through the space his chest had occupied just seconds before.

"Get down, Steph!" Steele yelled when he heard the Magnum's cannonlike report. He dropped to his knees next to Braun as a second shot boomed through the kitchen. Somewhere behind him Steele heard a hiss, and movements later smelled natural gas.

"Turn off the stove, Heinrich!" Steele heard a shout. Rolf cursed at himself. His second shot had smashed into the pastry ovens and had undoubtedly shattered a gas valve or pipe. He looked over and saw that Heinrich was still huddled on the floor next to the woman. The former mountain trooper hurdled over the counter and turned off the gas under the stew pot, almost ripping the cowling from the stove and throwing the hot stew on the floor. Swiftly he blew out the stove's pilot lights.

Stephanie saw the huge man vault over the counter and as she crouched on the floor, pointed her revolver at him and pulled the trigger. When nothing happened, she felt like crying.

Braun began to stir. Steele pulled the revolver from his waistband and knelt beside the fallen cardinal.

"You're taking orders from me, understand?" Steele growled as he stuck the muzzle of the revolver under Braun's chin. Braun nodded.

"Good," Steele said grimly. "Now tell your man to hold his fire. If he shoots the woman, you're dead."

Steele waited a moment and then jammed the revolver muzzle harshly into the cardinal's throat. "Tell him or I'll blow your fucking head off!"

"Rolf?" Braun said weakly. "Rolf, is that you?"

Engels turned from the stove and trained the .44 Magnum on the woman. He had begun to pull the trigger when Braun called out to him.

"Yes, your grace," Rolf said, relaxing the tension on the trigger.

"Rolf, hold your fire," Braun said. "I'll be killed if you don't. Do you understand?"

Rolf looked down at Stephanie with hatred in his eyes. He hated above all being kept from doing his job properly. "Yes, your grace," Rolf replied.

"And above all," Braun said. "Don't harm the girl."

The smell of gas grew intense in the kitchen, but it was hardly noticed by the troupe of actors playing out their life-or-death performances.

"Stand up," Rolf said, looking at the woman on the floor. Stephanie complied. Rolf stood behind her, holding the muzzle of the Magnum to her head.

"I want to see the cardinal," Rolf announced. "Have him stand up so I know he's all right or I'll shoot the girl."

Holding the revolver steady under Braun's throat, Steele got to his feet, pulling his hostage up with him. Derek's heart skipped when he saw Stephanie across the kitchen standing in front of one of the largest men he had ever seen.

Rolf and Steele stared at each other for several seconds. "We are either going to gas ourselves or blow this place up if we don't act soon, Amerikaner," Rolf said.

"It's up to you," Steele replied. "Let her go and I let your precious cardinal go."

Rolf smiled a broad evil grin. "You think I am dumb? You are wrong."

Suddenly there was a clattering at the far corner of the kitchen. Rolf Engels was lightning fast. He looked over, saw a man he didn't recognize, and in an instant, fired the Magnum.

"Where's the orange juice?" was the last thing Robert Maxwell said before the .44 Magnum slug made a nickel-sized hole in his right cheek. The bullet passed through his skull and out the other side, coating the white enamel freezer, just to the rear of where Maxwell had been standing, with most of Maxwell's head.

Richard Summers heard the shots, and he heard someone yell

"Derek." It sounded like Stephanie Steele's voice. He froze on the stairwell in a long moment of indecision. He heard other shots, other voices. Then he heard a voice warn: "Get down, Steph." It had to be Stephanie. She must still be alive.

Summers rushed back up the stairs toward the voices.

CHAPTER FORTY

Richard Summers felt the blood drain from his face when he stepped into the council meeting room and saw Werner Meyer's body on the floor. He knelt beside the body with tears welling up in his eyes, and for an instant, saw himself forty years earlier, kneeling beside the same man in another Austrian town.

He felt for a pulse as he had done then, but this time found none. Through a curtain of tears, his eyes recognized the damage that no team of doctors could ever repair.

"I'm sorry, old friend," Summers said. He placed a hand on the rapidly cooling shoulder of the old priest and gave it a gentle pat. "Goodbye."

He stood up and looked around the room. The golden lid encrusted with jewels caught his eye first. He went to it, lifted it up, and for a moment gazed at its opulent colors in the brilliant morning sunlight.

Then he saw the gun, an American Colt .45 automatic. It lay on the floor near a gaping hole in the windows. He went to it, picked it up.

He stood up with the gun and suddenly he was a young soldier again, marching through Altaussee. And he remembered how frustrated he had been when Meyer had been shot, and how happy he had been when the army doctors nursed him back to health.

He walked back to where Meyer lay still in death.

But it had all gone wrong. Czenek, who had helped save Meyer's life back then, joined the wrong side. The shroud that started it all never really let go of him—of him or any of the others. He

470

looked down into Meyer's face. The shroud had risen from its grave in the Austrian salt mine and had come back to kill, again and again.

He had had six months in his cell to grieve over how he had stupidly involved Stephanie in it all. He should never have sent her. Her troubles were his fault.

He turned away from Meyer and walked toward the hall.

He stopped by the door, trying to breathe resolve into his thoughts. After a moment, he squared his shoulders and walked purposefully into the hallway. This time he would not be frustrated; this time he would not fail. He walked into the hallway looking for Stephanie. He knew he had heard her voice. He looked into a small sitting room. Empty. At the end of the hall, he began to smell gas. Cautiously, he padded up to a door at the end of the corridor and looked through a thin crack. What he saw made his hands tremble for a moment. There was a standoff between Steele and Rolf; each held a hostage against the other.

Braun was coughing and choking violently from the gas now. Steele was giddy from the lack of air.

"Look, Ralph, or whatever your name is, you're going to kill your beloved cardinal if we don't get out of here soon. Why don't we continue our Mexican standoff outside and maybe get someone to switch off the gas at the main valve?"

"A Mexican what, you say?" Rolf asked.

"Never mind," Steele shook his head. "We have to get out of here before we're all killed." Rolf shook his head. The American woman had already reached a state of near unconsciousness and Rolf felt the American man would not be far behind. The former mountain trooper breathed shallowly through his nose, hoping to outlast them all. He told himself he had to: the cardinal's life depended on it.

"Okay," Steele said, then coughed. "*You* stay here. We're leaving."

Dragging Braun with him, Steele began to move toward a swinging set of double doors with a small glass window in the top half of each. Through the small window, Steele recognized the large formal dining room he had seen from the hallway.

"Stay there." Rolf's voice rose in pitch. Steele could see the

471

beginning of panic in the man's eyes. "Stay there or I will shoot her."

Steele continued to move slowly toward the door, his eyes flickering from the big man's face to his trigger finger and back. If there was any movement from the man's trigger finger, Steele would stop immediately. He tried not to look at Stephanie's face; he knew it would unnerve him. But he looked anyway and his heart caught as he watched her semiconscious head lolling on her shoulders. Frustration and anger welled up in him; for an insane moment he wanted to drop Braun and rush to her aid.

Stay calm. He told himself. Stay calm. You're playing a dangerous game with all the lives here.

As Steele and Braun neared the door, there was no tensing of the big man's trigger finger. Instead, he started to move toward them. The loyal bodyguard was not about to let his charge out of his sight. Steele pushed open the door with his back. Rolf moved quickly to close the distance between them. Steele waited for him to arrive at the door, and then they went though simultaneously.

All Steele notice when they stepped into the hallway was how sweet the air was. He did not notice that the cook was no longer in the kitchen.

Summers pushed his way into the kitchen through the service entrance as Steele, Rolf, and their hostages moved out. Keeping close to the floor to avoid as much gas as possible, he began to move towards the doors into the dining room when his eye caught the glimmer of more gold, more jewels. He crawled toward the box. Beside it was a bolt of cloth, partly unfolded. Next to it were the scattered leaves of the Linz testaments.

He recognized the treasure at once, and almost without thinking sat down next to it. He ignored the tingling in his fingers and the pounding in his heart. As he took the shroud in his hands and began to unfold it, he suddenly knew the exultation of discovery. For a brief burning moment, he was Armstrong stepping on the moon, Michelangelo finishing the Sistine Chapel; man discovering fire. The thing that had haunted his entire adult life lay in his hands. He gazed into the image, entranced.

As soon as Steele backed through the doors into the dining room, he knew something was wrong, terribly wrong.

Rolf began to smile. Then he dumped Stephanie on the floor

and stood there grinning. Instants later, steely muscled hands and arms clamped themselves around Steele's neck and arms and twisted the revolver from his hand. He was pushed face first onto the floor. The last glimpse he had before hitting the floor was that of the cook, staring timidly around the doorway into the hall.

Suddenly he felt old and used up. He had lost . . . they had lost. He thought of his last look at Stephanie, her head so beautiful, so . . . so not ready to die. Summoning all his strength, he lashed out at his captors, but they were very young and very strong. He felt the toe of a boot slamming into the side of his head, and for a long moment, the world turned fuzzy.

"Good shot, David." Steele heard Rolf's victorious laughter through the fuzz. After a short while, he heard Rolf's voice again, this time in a more respectful tone.

"How are you feeling, your grace?"

Braun's comment was unintelligible. Then Steele heard Stephanie's gentle weak voice. "Derek?" she said.

"Over here," Steele said. Someone, maybe the man called David, kicked Steele in the head again.

"Shut up, swine," the man said.

"Are you all right, your grace?" Steele heard Rolf say.

This time, the cardinal replied, "Yes, a bit shaken." There was a pause. "I see you've proved yourself once again."

"Thank you, sir," Rolf said proudly.

"Take me up to the helicopter now," Braun said. "Help me up."

Steele heard the rustling and grunts.

"What shall we do with them?" Rolf asked.

The tone of Braun's reply made Steele's blood run cold. "Whatever you wish, Rolf. Whatever you wish." There was a pause, then Steele heard Braun's voice again, this time closer. "Turn him over."

The three men pinning Steele to the floor complied. Steele blinked and looked up. Braun spun dizzily above him. Steele had barely focused his eyes when he saw the cardinal lean over him and spit. Steele tried to turn his head, but the strong hands held it. He closed his eyes as the spittle struck him on his forehead.

"Go gather the box and its contents," Braun said to Rolf," and then let's leave. I have an appointment to keep in Rome."

The loud voices dragged Summer's attention away from the shroud. For an instant, he considered taking the box and trying to escape with it. It was one of the most valuable artifacts the world had ever known.

But when he heard the evil laughter from the dining room, he knew he had no choice. Holding Gerry Anderson's Colt .45 in his right hand, Summers duck-walked toward the dining room door, staying out of sight behind the counters.

He reached the swinging doors in time to see Braun spit on Steele's face.

Enraged, Summers stood up and burst through the swinging doors. Rolf had turned toward the kitchen to fetch the shroud and the Linz testaments.

Summers took in the scene instantly. In front of him was Rolf, his jailor and tormentor for the past six months. The rest of them were to his left, near the door that led into the corridor. Steele was pinned to the floor by three men, Braun still standing over him; Stephanie struggled with two other men nearby.

Summers stood there in the open door, a tide of stinking gas pouring past him, Rolf bringing a gun to bear on him. His eyes locked with Stephanie's for just a moment.

Then Summers raised the .45. He felt the automatic recoil in his hands, and in the same instant felt the terrible crushing blow of Rolf's slug tearing through his intestines. He was thrown back for a second and then . . . whomp!—he was picked up by the force of a great explosion and thrown forward again into the dining room.

Rolf saw the muzzle blast from Summer's gun and steeled himself against the impact. He had been wounded before and it didn't concern him overly. He was a big man and his body could take a lot.

But what it couldn't take was what followed his own shot. Rolf Engels's last view of this world was how the fire from his gun seemed to continue on back and behind Summers. As the kitchen ignited, Rolf knew they should have never installed gas anywhere in the chalet.

The fireball rocked through the dining room, setting it aflame in a thousand places. Steele felt the weight on him vanish. He sat up and viewed the scene from the *Inferno*. Rolf and someone else were burning like torches. Their mouths were open as if they were screaming, but Steele heard nothing over the roar of the flames. The dried wood and furnishings of the old, old building burned eagerly.

Steele got to his feet and rushed to Stephanie. Braun stood nearby, frozen like marble. Barely seconds had passed when the security men rushed back into the room. Steele was prepared for a struggle, but the men were dragging a fire hose from a corridor box and paid no attention to anything but the fire.

"Steph, get up." He slipped his hands under her armpits. "We've got to get out." She stood up shakily.

Suddenly, like a statue coming to life, Braun was all over them.

"The shroud, you must help me get the shroud." His eyes glinted from fires that burned within. He pulled and tugged at Steele, nearly causing him to lose his balance. Steele lashed out and caught the cardinal with the back of his fist. Braun fell to his knees.

"Get your own fucking shroud." Steele screamed over the roar of the flames.

As he and Stephanie left the room, Steele looked back at a scene he would never forget. Four of the uniformed security men were playing the hose around, trying to extinguish the worst of the flames. A fifth was wrestling with Cardinal Braun, who was trying his best to walk into the flames.

"No, let me go," Steele could hear Braun crying. "Let me go. Let me go."

Suddenly, Braun loosed an inhuman scream as he turned on the security man who was trying to restrain him. Braun continued flailing at the man until, finally, with the superhuman strength people are capable of only when all they hold dear is at stake, he broke the beefy man's grasp and lunged into the flames. The security man tried to follow the cardinal, but the flames beat him back.

They all stood transfixed—Steele, Stephanie and the security guards—staring at the wall of flames, not believing what they had just witnessed. Then, instants late, they heard Braun's shrieks rising above the roar of the flames. The shrieks began low and rose through the full range of the human voice into a range that seemed to border on the edge of hearing. The sound continued for what seemed like a very long time, but which was probably only a few seconds. The shrieks seemed too loud, too powerful to come from a human being. But the thing that would chill Derek and Stephanie for the rest of their lives was the tone of the shriek. It didn't sound like pain; it sounded like a man in ecstasy.

As the shriek ended, Derek and Stephanie raced for the stairwell, and to the helicopter they prayed would still be waiting on the roof.

EPILOGUE

The first of the cardinals had begun to arrive at the Vatican in response to his summons. He had begun chatting with them when he was interrupted by Richard Borden, the Vatican's secretary of state.

As he walked into the room, Borden wore an expression on his face the Pope could not decipher.

"I apologize for disturbing you, your holiness, but I felt you would want to receive this as soon as possible." Borden handed him a yellow telex, then left the room.

The Pope read the message three times. It took him that long for the true import to sink in. The telex was from the bishop of Innsbruck.

He read the telex a fourth time, and then turned to his visitors who by now were consumed with curiosity.

Filtering the joy from his voice, the Pope announced solemnly that: "Cardinal Archbishop Neils Braun has died."

Gasps filled the room.

"How?" said the archbishop from Paris.

"Where?" asked the archbishop from Milan.

The Pope proffered the telex and tried again to keep his inner joy from seeping through to his face and voice. For the first time since he was a small boy, he truly believed in miracles.

"Shall we say a word of prayer for our departed brother?"

The Pope delivered a prayer of condolence and intercession. And in his heart he sang a prayer of thanksgiving.

* * *

During his rebellion against King Saul, David escaped the King's soldiers by hiding in a jungle-like refuge called En-gedi.

Ein Gedi, as it is called today, is an oasis on the shores of the Dead Sea. Replete with streams and waterfalls and lush with vegetation, it has been, over the centuries, a place of refuge for those seeking asylum. It is a site of small resorts and vacation cottages where visitors can come to lie on the beach, or float in the saline waters of the Dead Sea, or take bus trips to nearby Masada, symbol of Jewish resistance against oppression.

The symbolism of Masada and Ein Gedi are not wasted on the Israelis. Soldiers in the Israeli Army are brought to Masada to be sworn in. And agents of the Mossad are brought to Ein Gedi to succor their wounds and hide from the enemies who pursue them as Saul once pursued David. The Mossad safe houses are scattered through the area and look, to all appearance, just like other rental condos or cottages. It is only by observing the gardeners and housekeepers who staff the cottages that one senses their uniqueness. The staffers are, in fact, commando-trained Mossad agents charged with protecting those who have done their service for Israel.

"It's over," Stephanie said. She was sitting on a narrow railed balcony overlooking the Dead Sea. She handed the copy of the *International Herald Tribune* to Steele who sat next to her. The front page carried the story of the burning of a Vatican-owned retreat outside Innsbruck. There was an aerial photograph of the structure in flames that the helicopter pilot has taken with a small pocket camera just after lifting off. Next to the aerial shot was an official Vatican photograph of Braun with the caption: KILLED IN FIRE.

Steele read the story closely.

"Here," he said finally, pointing to a paragraph toward the end of the article.

"Police are still searching for two survivors of the fire who were rescued by a helicopter waiting to take the Cardinal to the Innsbruck Airport."

"That's us," Stephanie said. "They must know our names. wonder why they didn't say more."

Before Steele could answer, the door behind them opened.

478

"How about a cold one?" Nat Worthington asked. He stepped out on the porch carrying a tray of bottled beer. Tania followed him with another small tray of glasses.

"Sure," Steele said as he got up to help serve the beer. Nat shook his head. "I'm fine," he said. "The doctor says you have to stop humoring me. I might get used to all this pampering." He walked now with only a slight limp, which the doctors said would probably vanish in time. They had caught the infection before it could do extensive damage. Nat walked over to a small round table and set the tray of beers down on it.

"Have you seen the paper?" Steele asked.

Nat picked up a beer, poured it into a glass, and handed it to Stephanie. "Of course not," Nat replied. "You guys never let me get to it first." He poured another glass of beer for Tania, who had walked up behind Steele and peered over his shoulder at the paper.

"It's quite a story," Tania said finally.

Nat finally handed Steele a beer and a glass and then settled back in a chair with his own. Steele handed him the paper. Nat looked at it for a moment, then whistled softly.

"Quite a story," he said.

"Why aren't we named?" Derek asked Nat. "Aren't we being hunted? Isn't Interpol still scouring the earth for us?"

Nat laughed and took a long draught of beer. He then sat the glass on the table in front of him. "I told you Mossad had friends. It may take a while, but there'll come a time when you can prove Tom Wolfe wrong." He paused. "You'll be able to go home someday . . . without being arrested by your former buddies."

Tania took the paper and began thumbing through it. She walked to a chair beside Nat and sat down.

The four of them sat there in silence for a long time, looking out at the Dead Sea, and through the shimmering haze, at the massive bulk of the Masada in the distance.

"Oh," Tania said. Heads turned to her. "Listen to this . . ." Her voice was low and awed. "You'll never believe this." Then she read from a story on an inside page of the paper.

" 'Villagers See Religious Link in Ruins' is the headline . . . 's a sidebar to Braun's obituary."

She read the story aloud. Workers who arrived at the scene after

479

the fire, the story reported, said the entire structure had been completely burned except for a patch of linoleum that had been identified as having covered the kitchen floor. The linoleum, some said, was in the shape of a woman.

"It had eyes, hands," one worker was reported to have declared. "I swear I could see it. It's a miracle, a sign from God."

The Innsbruck fire chief was quoted by the paper as saying: "Fires can do some strange things. We've seen many instances where burned structures seem to have pictures of faces in them. But it's like finding ships in the clouds or a face on the moon. It's just a matter of human imagination."

The bishop of Innsbruck issued a statement agreeing with the Innsbruck fire chief.

In later years, another pope would have to contend with a small but zealous cadre of Innsbruck churchgoers demanding that the Vatican declare the site of the image a holy shrine. That pope would make the same reply that had been given by the man who was pope when the Cardinal's Nest burned down: "Faith in the unseen is stronger than faith in things we can touch or see. The truest test of our faith in a supreme being is the willingness to believe without seeing. And in the long run, the Christian churches—all churches, for that matter—are better off without such visible signs. Because there will always be those who will see and never believe."

The Pope never directly told anyone whether or not he believed in the sign.